HONORABLE

INTENTIONS

BY

JUDITH KOLKIN

PublishAmerica
Baltimore

First printing

ISBN: 1-4137-6071-6
PUBLISHED BY PUBLISHAMERICA, LLLP
www.publishamerica.com
Baltimore

Printed in the United States of America

DEDICATION

Dedicated to all those who made it back from the conflict in Vietnam—and all those who didn't.

PART I

~ Chapter 1 ~

June, 1970
Parris Island, South Carolina

The chilled five a.m. air made my sweat turn cold. Billy propelled his lean body off the ground as fast as it touched. It took all my strength to keep up with him, despite the past ten weeks of training. This extra five-mile jog as punishment for last night's incident made each breath want to come out as a desperate gasp. But if I let that show, it would seem he had won, again.

I forced myself to maintain even breaths as I spoke. "The sarge can force me to run, but nothing in this blasted military can force me to kill."

Billy turned to me, his teeth gleaming orange from the first streaks of dawn. "Proves my point, Belkin. You're nothing but a damn fairy."

My foot slammed hard, the pain almost making me stop, but the fear of lagging behind forced me on. "Go to hell."

Billy's head angled towards me. "You Jews couldn't even kill Nazis yourselves. Waited for real men like my father to do it for you."

My back stiffened, feeling like it did Friday nights when Grandma lit candles for her slaughtered family. "Jews did fight back, but Vietnam's different!"

Billy gave a quick one-two punch into the air. "Communists are bad as Nazis."

My ankle twisted on a mound of sand, piercing into my calf. "That's government propaganda!"

Billy spit at the ground. "You one of those pinkos want the commies to win?"

Sweat streamed down my face. "No, but the Vietnamese can think for themselves!"

Billy swiped at his chin then wiped it on his chest. "The *Columbus Herald* said communism's practicing on Vietnam, then going for the rest of Asia!"

Thick liquid clogged my throat, but I shouted through it. "Those are military industrial complex lies!"

Billy sprinted ahead, then turned to face me while jogging backwards. "Choking on your own words?"

My chest tightened as much as it had last night when the announcement came in that our leaves were cut back from two weeks to one, and we had to report back to Parris Island on July 1st. The rumor I had feared was confirmed. They needed huge reinforcements to replace last year's 200,000 sent in after Tet. Billy had stood up and hollered, "Why wait? Let's nuke those friggin' gooks now!"

A shout came from down the line of thirty bunks. "I'll drop it myself, dead center on Hanoi!"

I had been writing a letter for Leon, the black guy in the bunk next to me, to his girlfriend, though this was not one of the usual letters. This was a proposal of marriage. We were at the part where he promised to hold her in his arms through good times and bad when I stood, fighting Leon's sudden grasp of my wrist and yelled back, "Nuclear war is death to the whole planet. You're both crazy!"

That's when Billy stormed over and swung his fist at my face. Leon jumped up and blocked it, but I jabbed back and next thing I knew, Billy had hold of my shoulders and was shaking me, while my hands were on his face, pushing him away. Leon pulled me back and someone else grabbed Billy, but not before the sergeant saw us and we were ordered on this extra run. That was bad enough, but when the sergeant left, Billy raised his arms in victory, like he'd won a boxing match, and all but Leon applauded. I was the loser. And now, barely able to breathe, I felt a loser all over again.

I inhaled deeply, feeling the salt air burn my raw throat and tried to sprint faster, same as Billy had. I made three strides when I began to cough and couldn't stop. I had to stop running while my chest wracked for needed air. Billy laughed, then dashed on. I forced myself to begin a fast walk, unable to bear the vision of him entering the mess with his arms raised and me conspicuously far behind. I tried to increase my stride, but it was impossible.

Five minutes later when I did arrive, I remained outside for a minute to return to normal breaths, then walked in with my hands on my hips. Billy was carrying a full tray of food towards the table with the other gung-hos, when he glanced at me and grinned. "Look who's here, thought you'd passed out by now."

8

I took one step towards him and spoke louder than necessary. "Swallowed spit down the wrong pipe."

Billy's smile broadened. "Coughs like that end up in a gook's crosshairs." There were a few chuckles from the gung-ho table as I found myself staring into Billy's back. Almost every eye in the room was on me as I yelled to his sparse stubs of blond hair, "I'm not afraid. It's that I know the difference between right and wrong."

Billy's shoulders shrugged while he kept walking and the gung-hos snickered more. I turned away and saw Leon sitting with Wesley, who was waving his fork in the air as he spoke. I went to the food line, getting scrambled eggs, toast, oatmeal and coffee, then headed for their table. They were from the same neighborhood in South Cincinnati. I envied that, wishing I had someone else from home, the Bath Beach section of Brooklyn.

Leon's round face was wrinkled at the forehead as Wesley said, "It's who you know, man, not what you know."

I placed my tray next to Leon. "Can I join you?"

Wesley looked up, revealing his perfectly aligned teeth. "We do accept whites and fools, my man, and you prove to be both."

I nodded, taking a seat next to Leon. "White is from birth parents. The fool part is all mine. Hadn't flunked out of college, I'd be home in a warm bed, never setting foot in this hellhole."

Leon spread butter on his toast. "Not me, didn't think of college, not once."

Wesley sipped his coffee then waved his cup towards me. "Folks ain't got the means for draft dodging in our neighborhood. Unless your number was over two-hundred, it was just a matter of what day the notice would come."

I scooped oatmeal in my spoon, watching the excess drip over the sides. "Not where I live. Anyone who could get into college, went. I was 2F, student deferment, and blew it for too many nights in the back seat with Naomi."

Leon grinned, his cheeks mounded shiny and smooth. "Maybe it was worth it."

My head tilted back towards Billy's table. "Not for this. Besides, she's gone. Ditched me for Charles and I was too depressed to study and flunked out the first term."

Wesley looked me in the eye as if unconcerned with what he saw. "Don't sweat it. You'll have it easy."

I swallowed some oatmeal and pointed the spoon towards him. "What's that mean?"

Wesley leaned back and rubbed at a scab on his hand. "The whites get the desk jobs. That's how it's set up."

Laughter from Billy's table made me shift uncomfortably in my seat as I kept my eyes on Wesley. "Where'd you hear that?"

Wesley looked back at me, the crease at the top of his nose pulled on his eyebrows. "My cousin told me, he came back two months ago."

I speared my fork into the eggs and shook my head. "That doesn't sound right."

Wesley shrugged. "He told it like it is, my man." His look shifted directly to Leon, as if this was just between them. "He said to get on garbage detail or volunteer for mine sweeping, but to keep my ass out of the jungle if I have a choice, and never ever go in a hole, no matter what the man promises."

I swallowed the tasteless eggs like medicine, then tapped the table to get Wesley's attention. "Did your cousin go along with the killing?"

Wesley's head jolted back. "What kind of question is that?"

"An important one." My eyes shifted between Leon and him. "Or else we're the same as savage beasts."

Wesley turned to Leon, his eyes wincing into slits. "You know any blacks who get a choice what they go along with?"

Leon shook his head. "No, sir, not that I ever heard."

I wanted to ask Wesley if his cousin mentioned the crazies who collect dead people's ears, but Billy's voice stopped me. "Nuke the gooks, nuke the gooks." I turned to see him standing on a chair waving a hand in the air like a conductor's baton as his whole table picked up the chant.

It was almost time to leave, and I bit off a piece of toast, chewing like it was hardened gum. "He disgusts me."

Leon turned his back on Billy, then pushed his plate aside. "I dropped that letter in the mail. Not your fancy words, but had to make sure she sees it 'fore I gets home."

Lights out had been ordered five minutes after the fight, and I recalled Leon's tightened jaw when it was announced. "Sorry I never got to finish, but she'll read what's in your heart and say yes, or at least wait till you get back."

Leon tapped his empty plate with his fork. "I wouldn't trust her without no ring."

Wesley slapped the table. "Man, there's a whole line of brothers looking at her behind. You'd best forget Dolores. There'll be a hundred wining and dining her."

Leon's shoulders hunched around his neck. "She said she loves me."

"While you're next to her, man." Wesley leaned closer to Leon. "Not while you're gone. I give my ladies memories they can never forget so they'll be there when I get back. But I know they're not going to stay put while I'm away, ring or no ring."

Leon had described Dolores to me as a girl who helped him with his math after school and then went home to make dinner for her family. "That's not fair. This Dolores sounds…"

Wesley's finger pointed straight at me. "Ladies don't want a man that's nine thousand miles away. The trick is to leave them guessing. Let them hope you'll go back to them when you return."

Leon's hands clasped and began rapping on the table. "Dolores is different. I knows it."

"None of them's different." Wesley grasped Leon's wrist. "I'm telling you 'cause I'm your friend and don't want to see you played no fool."

Leon shifted in his seat and I banged an elbow on the table. "Leon can figure out Dolores for himself."

Wesley pushed back his chair and raised his hands. "If that's what he wants, it's okay by me. Now if you two fools will excuse me, I have business in the can."

~ Chapter 2 ~

Bath Beach, Brooklyn

The same apartment buildings, two-family houses and trees lined the sidewalk, but I didn't have the sense of belonging I'd had before. It was more the cigarette butts and candy wrappers in the street that seemed to pull me in.

I'd been Lenny Belkin, the kid who preached about needed programs for the poor, listened to the topical folk music of Bob Dylan and Phil Ochs, attended anti-war and pro-civil rights rallies at Brooklyn College, and thought I was going to change the world. But this time as I walked down the street, my mind was only a half step away from boot camp. My feet marched to the sergeant's tempo, ready to blurt out, *yes, Sergeant* at a moment's notice. I purposely tried to switch my walk to the more carefree one I had before, but it felt awkward, out of rhythm, and I even tripped on my own feet. *Damn that Naomi, she screwed me but good.*

I entered my apartment house off Cropsey Avenue. The lobby was empty and the elevator up arrow was lit in green. I was too anxious to wait and ran for the steps, slamming my soles on the hard treads like I used to as a kid. But the resounding echo of my return felt childish, and I continued the rest of the four flights up tapping the steps quietly.

I reached our door and turned the handle, surprised that it opened, then entered to the conflicting sounds of soap opera from the living room and muffled strums of a guitar from farther away.

My mother rushed towards me from the couch. "Lenny, darling, ach, look at you, so skinny! Come give your mama a hug."

I enclosed her in my arms and her ear pressed into my chest. It had been four years that I was taller than her, and it still felt wrong. Though last year when I reached five feet ten and became taller than my father, that somehow felt good.

She grabbed both my arms and stepped back, staring at my buzzed-off brown hair, blue tee-shirt, jeans with the hole by the pocket, and finally my spit-shined black boots. Her head shook like she couldn't believe I was real. "You're a good boy, Lenny, coming home to your mother."

I bent to kiss the top of her head, but the sprayed stiff layer of hair kept me out of range. I had forgotten about that. The same thing had happened when I tried to kiss her at my high school graduation. "Of course I'm back, Mom. It was only boot camp."

She pulled my arm and rushed for the kitchen, stopping in front of the table graced with the special occasion glass-covered dish. She lifted the lid then cut a thick hunk of her marble cake with the silver cake server, whose shine sent a small rainbow onto the glossy white wall. I wondered why I'd never noticed that before when she handed me the cake on a napkin. "Here, eat. Such skin and bones could make a mother cry. When Grandma sees you, she'll make you eat her whole noodle kugel yourself."

I took a huge bite of the cake and mumbled through my mouthful, "Delicious, Mom."

She watched me chew and slapped a hand on her cheek. "You look so different, Lenny. Another ten weeks and I wouldn't recognize you."

I puffed out my cheeks. "Look better?"

There was no smile and no shove on my arm like she sometimes did when I told a joke. All she did was shake her head. "It's not that, Lenny. It's your lips. They're so tight, not like before when they were always opened and showed your nice big teeth."

I swallowed the thick wad of cake and opened my mouth just wide enough to speak. "The sergeant wanted tight lips so I got used to it."

She clucked her tongue. "Sergeants, a little power and they get carried away." She grabbed the back of a chair, glanced through the window, then turned back to me. "You know I don't like this Vietnam War, but I do believe boys have a responsibility to serve their country."

"I know. We discussed this before I went in." I felt her stare at my thinned face and took another big bite of cake, chewing it into a sweet paste.

She went for the refrigerator and pulled out a bottle of milk, shifting her gaze between it and me. "If there was a way out, I would be for it, but going to Canada means you can never come home again, and that's impossible."

The cake suddenly tasted sour and I swallowed fast. "I know, Mom. We don't have to go over it again. I'll do what I have to do. Don't worry."

She placed the milk on the table, her back staying towards me. "Ach, who can't worry? The world is so crazy." She lowered herself into a chair and

13

focused out of the window, seeming to gaze at the park two streets down. I expected her to say, *No peace, even in America,* like she did most nights when listening to the television news. But she just clasped her hands to the sides of her face and kept quiet.

I felt as uncomfortable as the night before I left when she wouldn't take her eyes off me except for the moments she covered her face with her hands to cry. Only now it was like she couldn't stand the sight of me, this person who was too skinny and had tight lips.

I watched her stare over the lower rooftops on our street, remembering how being higher than the two-story houses used to make me feel powerful, like I was Superman soaring above the Metropolis. But now I saw the small patches of backyards below as targets from a helicopter jump, with the roofs, telephone poles, and spiked fences as hazards if I missed the mark.

My mother raised her arm and pointed two streets away to Grandma's building, its red bricks and windows reflecting in the sun. It had always looked more inviting to me than our own house of dingy brown. "Your father left work early to set up the extra table. Aunt Eve's coming, and so is Steve. They'll be there soon. We shouldn't keep them waiting."

She hadn't mentioned Anna and my arms tightened, though I didn't know why. Weren't we waiting for her to get out of the shower, like we so often did? But then the silence from the bathroom screamed in my ears and the music drifting from her room forced me to realize she'd been in there all this time. I peered out of the kitchen at her door. "Isn't Anna coming with us?"

My mother's bottom lip trembled like she was cold, only it was June, and the day warm. She pointed towards Anna's room. "Go ask her yourself. She doesn't talk to me anymore."

Anna had never not talked, the trouble was to get her to shut up, especially when she was mad. I stepped into the hallway and stared at her shut door. "When did that start?"

My mother's gaze lowered to the floor. "The day you left."

The music from Anna's room grew louder and her voice began ranting along with it, "Where have all the flowers gone? Long time passing…"

I went to her door and turned the knob, though I'd stopped doing that on her eleventh birthday when she'd demanded privacy. The door was halted by a latch that had never been there before. I shook the door trying to open it. "Anna, it's me, Lenny. Can I come in?"

She stopped singing and paused before she spoke. "Not now. I'm busy."

I pushed the door so it opened a thin crack. "Unlock this. I want to talk to you."

There was a movement from the floor, though I couldn't see her clearly. "No, I have to finish. Go away."

We had fought before I left and she hadn't sent me any letters, but I didn't expect this. "Come on, Anna, I just got back, and we're going to Grandma's."

I saw what could have been her arm wave in the air. "I'm not going!"

I pushed on the door, widening the crack a bit more, and saw her leaned over a large piece of oak tag with a magic marker in her hand. "Why not? What are you writing?"

She glared at me through the thin opening. "What does it look like? I have to finish these and get them to Scott's house by three. I don't have much time. Now, leave me alone!"

"No!" I felt like I did at fourteen, with Anna twelve, arguing about whose turn it was to do the dishes, and I slammed my shoulder into the door.

It lurched opened and Anna leaped to her feet. "What's the matter, Lenny? They destroyed all your common decency already?"

I stepped back, feeling like a snake's tongue lashed in my face. "That's not why…"

Her eyes shifted to the floor and I glanced down at the large red words. *Baby Killers Belong In Jail.*

My toe pushed towards the sign. "What's that for?"

Anna's hands slapped on her hips. "An anti-war rally at the student commons this afternoon. Jane Fonda's speaking."

A bit of chewed cake backed up my throat, burning the sensitive skin. "And I can't see that?"

She grasped her elbows. "You're one of them now."

My back stiffened. "I'll never be one of them."

Her face turned as red as the magic marker. "They trained you and you're going. You're one of them!"

I gripped my waistband, squeezing it within my fists. "I'm not getting caught up in their war. It's do my time and come home. I told you before I left!"

She stepped back and leaned on her left hip. "You're still part of it. The politicians won't listen, so it's up to the soldiers to stop it!"

I heard crying in the background and purposely lowered my voice. "You know I can't do that to Mom."

Anna's arms flew out from her sides, and she began to yell louder. "You're just like the rest of them!" She grabbed the posters from the floor, grasped her jacket and purse from the bed and stormed past me. "I can't stand even being close to you!"

15

I grabbed her arm. "Wait a minute!"

She yanked herself from my hold, rushed for the front door, and screamed the moment before the door slammed. "Don't wait up for me!" The floor shook where I stood and I listened to the sudden quiet, realizing even the wails had stopped, replaced by an eerie stillness where my every breath became a siren and every thought an alarm. I stayed paralyzed for a few minutes, listening to my inner desperate cries, then headed for the kitchen to comfort my mother, if I could.

* * * * *

The smells of pungent onions and sweet cinnamon through Grandma's door brought on a hunger greater than I had expected, though I doubted even all that good food could get rid of the foul taste I still had from Anna.

My mother rang the bell, and we heard Grandma's shuffling steps on the linoleum. "Sylvia, Lenny, that you?"

My father's voice called in the background. "Don't, Mama, let me get it."

There was a hushed argument, like there always was, then a moment later the door opened and it was Grandma, her hands slapping on her cheeks. "Lennichka, oy gevalt! I wouldn't recognize you, come," her fingers grasped my arm and began to pull, "I made luckshen kugel special for you."

My father patted me on the back as I passed. "Welcome home, son."

I glanced over my shoulder. "Thanks, Dad."

Sylvia's whisper was just barely audible. "Sol, she's getting worse."

I was glad to be pulled away from that conversation into Grandma's glossy white kitchen. She pointed to the yellow wooden step stool against the wall and I sat on it, feeling like I did as a kid, placed on a throne.

Grandma stood, making us very close to the same height. "Lennichka, some people are sour grapes, no?"

I knew who she meant, though I would have used poisonous snake instead. "You mean Anna?"

She nodded, her breath coming out slowly. "Anna, her tongue is all thorns, no honey left in her mouth. To you, too?"

I surrounded one set of knuckles with the other. "More like barbed wire."

She shook her head and turned away, then pointed to her kugel cooling on the stove. "Smell good, Lennichka?"

"Delicious, Grandma. Better than anything I've had in a long time."

Her cheeks began to spread, then stopped midway and tensed. "Tell me, Lenny, what is said in the Army where you are?"

I scrunched my face. "In the Marines I can tell you the food is terrible."

The already thick lines across her forehead deepened. "Not food, what do they tell of the war?"

"The war?" I felt her eyes probe mine with a gentle stare. "They tell us, Grandma, that we have to work as a team, follow exact orders, stick to assigned positions, keep our boots and packs dry, and," I hesitated, but her raised eyebrows made me go on, "clean our weapon daily so it doesn't jam."

Her head leaned slightly back. "That all? No reasons?"

My foot slipped off its step and banged into the stool's leg. "Reasons? The reason, Grandma, is to stay alive in the face of an attacking enemy. That's the reason. It's the same in any war."

She winced at my angry tone and I felt bad. "That's not only reason, Lennichka. When I was child in Russia, soldiers come for my father to join, and all night talk why they must fight, never how, only why."

I'd heard that before and didn't want to go over it again. I gripped the stool under my hips and leaned forward. "There are no good reasons for war, Grandma. Leaders of countries should have other ways to solve conflicts."

Her hand went over her mouth, then slid down as her head shook ever so slightly. "That is so, but some leaders know only hate."

I didn't want a lecture on the Cossacks or the Nazis and hoped that wouldn't come. "Grandma, none of the reasons for Vietnam are necessary."

Her hand dropped from her chin to her chest. "Leonard, one thing you should remember. In war, it's not who you have to hurt, it's who you have to help."

"I know that, Grandma," though I feared from her use of Leonard that she no longer felt I deserved the throne.

There were three fast thumps on the front door and Grandma turned, grasping the pockets of her apron as my mother shrieked, "Eve, I thought you'd broken down on the road you were so late. It's not like you!"

"Now, Sis," Eve's prominent voice boomed as strong as ever, "just takes longer to put on my makeup these days, more to cover you know."

I followed Grandma out of the kitchen. Eve gave a quick kiss on Grandma's cheek then threw her arms around me, pressing her chest into my stomach. "Lenny, my boy, you had me so worried. Why didn't you call the second you got in?"

But without waiting for an answer, she pushed me out at arms' length and curled her lips so all her teeth showed. "Where's my uniform? You know I've waited nineteen years for this, and I'll never get it from my own son. The least you could do is wear a medal."

Her grip began to pinch as I remembered her telling my mother that boot camp would make a real man out of me. "I don't have any medals, Aunt Eve, and I don't wear the uniform when I don't have to. I'm not proud of it."

She dropped her hand on her heart. "Ach, it's a good thing my Morty didn't hear that, may he rest in peace. It's a disgrace how kids today don't honor their country."

Steve, my favorite cousin, entered behind her carrying several bakery boxes wrapped in string. "Mom, turn it off. Lenny already knows your Sara Bernhardt routine." He extended his hand to me which I grasped. "Nice of the hawks to let you out of their clutches for a week." Our hands dropped and he pointed back to the door. "Come to the car with me. I have a new vacuum for Grandma."

I was happy to escape Aunt Eve's story about how her husband was so brave in World War II people wrote him letters extolling his courage and heroism. Ten years ago when he died, she began carrying them with her and read them to whomever she could.

We raced out of the apartment like when we were kids anxious to play super heroes and used to jump from high steps pretending we could fly. We reached the elevator then looked at each other and ran for the steps. Steven reached them first, scrambled down to the eighth one and jumped. He grinned up at me and tapped his chest. "I'm still better than you."

It had always been my dream to beat him, but it had never happened. I stopped on the eleventh then leaped like I had done at Parris Island off the thirty-foot wall into the pile of sandbags.

Steven screamed, "Watch out!"

The explosive reverberations from my landing made my calves twinge with pain, but I felt more like Superman than I ever had as a kid. I sat back on the steps and began to rub my legs.

Steven stared at me. "Damn, they made you crazy."

At first I was annoyed he saw me as crazy when I wanted him to see that I was finally stronger. But it was true. I never would have done that jump before. I nodded and felt the throbbing in my soles. "The Marines are run by maniacs, but they're not the only ones making me crazy."

His Adam's apple shifted in his neck. "Anna?"

I rubbed my ankles, which was the closest I could get to the bottom of my feet. "You know?"

He nodded. "She's right, you know."

I was furious and slammed the side of my fist into the banister. "Doesn't anyone understand I'm not like that?"

He jumped back and raised his hands. "Don't be so touchy. I wish you the best of luck."

It didn't feel good that he thought I'd hit him, then I realized how good it could feel if I did. I shook my head and looked back into his retreated stance. "Thanks for the luck, man, I'm going to need it."

~ Chapter 3 ~

July, 1970
Camp LeJeune, North Carolina

Sergeant Tibbs burst into the far end of the barracks and held a stack of papers high in the air. "Your assignments are here in my hot, itchy hand!"

The eight-track tape of Bob Dylan I'd been ready to pop into the player, dropped on my bunk. I knew this was coming, especially after last night's film of faceless enemies, showing faceless seductive ladies with razors taped on their thighs, faceless children with grenades in their hands, and even a faceless dog with dynamite strapped to its stomach.

I snapped to attention, my stomach feeling like it did when the dog's body exploded next to two GIs that had crouched down to pet its fur.

"If you hear your name in this group," shouted the sergeant above our heads, "it means you're being shipped out this Friday."

I glanced at Leon knowing Dolores was going to Myrtle Beach with her girlfriends on Friday and he had planned to hitch there if he could get a pass. She still hadn't agreed to wear his ring and he was anxious to try again.

"Bates, Wesley," boomed the sergeant.

Wesley shouted back, "Yes, Sergeant, I's coming," and went to be handed his orders.

I watched him strut like he didn't care, when the next name made my knees cave in.

"Belkin, Lenny."

I forced myself straight and tall, counted each step as if it were my last, felt the orders slapped in my hand and shouted back, "Thank you, drill Sergeant!"

I began back towards my bunk, listening to the next names. "Creeden, Jack, Ferrara, Tony, Langdon, Billy."

My ankle caved in at Billy's name, but then I turned fast and watched him jog to the sergeant with a grin that showed all his teeth.

"Very grateful to serve, Sarge!" Billy held his orders high like a trophy as others applauded.

Sergeant Tibbs continued. "James, Robert, Sears, Richard, Turner, Leon. That's the full list for Friday. Saturday, listen for your name…"

His voice droned in the background while I skimmed my orders. I was leaving tomorrow at 0700 for Camp Pendleton in California. The rest I guessed from the rumors. There would be a twenty-four hour layover, a stop on Guam, then a final flight to an airstrip in Vietnam.

"Moment of truth, hey fairy man?"

I looked up into Billy's eyes, feeling a gush of sweat down my back. "Your moment of truth. I already know mine."

Jack Creeden swatted his papers on Billy's arm. "It's countdown, man, time to kill those gooks."

Billy rolled up his papers and held them to his eye like a scope. "There it is, moment of truth, dead center in the cross hairs." He turned till it was pointed straight at me, and yelled, "Bang."

The sergeant boomed louder over the buzz in the room. "You all have your orders. Pack your gear and make your calls. Your time has come, good luck."

The air exploded with thirty voices at once. I looked back at Billy and whispered under my breath, "Bang yourself."

Billy had already turned away, his arms waving like a conductor as he led his group, "Nuke the gooks, nuke the gooks!"

Leon came next to me, his papers squeezed in his hand. "Lenny, can we write another letter?"

I nodded, wishing I had Naomi to write to, but knew anything from me would be ripped up and thrown away unread, especially now that I was going to Vietnam. My family popped into my mind, including Steven, but there was nothing more to say to any of them. I nodded to Leon, envious he had Dolores who wanted him the way he was, even though she hadn't agreed to be engaged. I began to write, seeing words appear, *Thinking of you will get me through the next 365 days till I can see you and hold you again.* Damn, Leon was lucky. I had no one to think about like that.

* * * * *

Our transport jet lifted off the ground at 0800 hours. The neat rows of barracks became smaller and smaller until they seemed not to exist at all. The events of the past four months vanished with them, replaced totally by fear of what lay ahead. The plane flew into a thick fog. I strained to see through it, but it was useless. I closed my eyes hoping to think of something happy, picturing myself bike riding as a kid. I began down my block.

"You feel that shake?" Richard poked his elbow into my arm. "What's wrong with this pilot, is his license to fly or to kill?"

I sat up straighter and glanced through the window at the haze. "Complain to the stewardess."

Richard crossed his leg and shifted in his seat. "Sure do wish I could, but this here Marine Corp's got something against hiring good looking chicks."

Naomi's stunning smile flashed in my mind. "Ain't that the truth."

I shut my eyes, trying to remember what her lips felt like when I seemed to fall through a dark tunnel and the next thing I knew, there was a hard shove on my shoulder. "Lenny, wake up, this tin can's ready for touch down."

* * * * *

Our time at Pendleton was one long ordeal of being moved from room to room, waiting in the canteen, then lined up by a desk, handed bunches of papers to sign that were placed in a thick folder, then given papers we were told not to lose. Richard, Wesley, Leon and I kept occupied playing Hearts. And ours wasn't the only card game going among the thirty-five guys in our transport. The rest of the guys talked while a few wrote letters or read magazines. But the overall mood was very somber. Even Billy seemed unusually quiet as he sat in a corner playing Rummy with Jack.

The lift off from Pendleton was a relief. But after fifteen minutes of only vast ocean in every direction, continual shifts of movement began on the benches that lined both sides of the plane.

Richard, sitting on my left, pointed to the window behind him as he scanned the seventeen guys on the opposite bench. "How long you think we'll be in Guam?"

Billy slid his legs out straight and leaned further back. "Probably like at Pendleton. I hope we don't get stuck there too long."

Richard grabbed his knees and leaned forward. "I do. I hear there's Philippine women who get naked faster'n a jack rabbit at the sight of a uniform."

Wesley's arms went behind his head like a pillow. "Not faster than my ladies."

Billy pointed a finger at him. "Your ladies are the kind that walk the streets."

Wesley smiled as if Billy's remark didn't matter in the least. "Not my luscious love toys. They line up to give me S-E-X, as much as I can take, which on your average night happens to be a whole lot of sweet delight."

Billy shook his head and gave a half laugh. "Wesley, we know you're all talk."

Wesley's grin stretched even wider. "I understand your jealous nature. Not everyone has such fine ladies as mine to think on when times go lean. Maybe we can find you one in Guam."

Billy gripped his knees and leaned towards Wesley. "I can find my own without your help."

Richard waved his arm. "I'll take one. I hear they're sexy and willing, right on base. Like picking an apple from a tree."

Billy's foot kicked in Richard's direction. "You can have one of Wesley's easy apples. I go for cherries that are only mine."

Naomi's breasts flashed in my mind, as they had glowed in the moonlight on that first night we parked by Plum Beach. They had shimmered with a tender warmth that sent shivers through my then virgin body. I had believed they were the only breasts I'd ever need to see. It was losing those breasts that hurt most when she said Charles was her new man. All I had wanted to do was reach out and touch them one more time.

Billy's voice jolted my thoughts back to the plane. "I'll bet you can't!"

Wesley's chuckle made me sit up straighter. "Oh, a fool is so easily parted from his money. I swear to you William Langdon from my beloved state of Ohio, whether you believe it or not, I can get it on Guam."

Billy pulled a bill out of his pocket and waved it in the air. "Ten bucks says you can't!"

Wesley glanced around the plane, then back to Billy. "You're on, man, ten bucks it is, from your pocket to mine."

Leon nudged my shoulder. "You in, man?"

"What do you mean?"

"I say he does it. What do you say?"

I looked at Wesley on the other side of Leon. He was leaning back and smiling at the eight guys who had pulled ten-dollar bills from their pockets and were holding them out towards him.

Wesley quickly scanned the two rows of faces. "No problem, I'll take you all on."

I looked back at Leon. "I don't see how he can."

Leon's head tilted towards Wesley. "You never seen him in action."

"On Guam? I don't believe it."

Richard leaned forward to peer past me to Wesley. "This mean you ain't picking me no apple?"

Wesley laughed. "Son, you on your own. I'm going to be busy."

Billy's hands gripped his knees. "How will we know?"

I was curious about that, too, then realized I had sided with Billy against Wesley and shifted uncomfortably in my seat.

Wesley tapped his chest. "You'll know 'cause I'll tell you. I'm a man of my word."

Billy's left fist punched into his right palm. "That's not good enough. I need proof. Someone has to watch."

Wesley's cheeks flattened. "I'm not going to tell some lady she has to be watched. What you think I am?"

Jack Creedon, sitting on Billy's left, extended his leg in Wesley's direction. "Thought you could talk a lady into anything?"

Wesley shook his head. "You guys are nasty. I'll bring her underwear for proof, but no watching."

Billy's jaw jutted forward. "Not good enough, you can buy underwear at the PX."

"Hold on, here." Wesley's arms raised in the air. "Underwear's all you get. You can smell them to know they're not bought."

The thought of Naomi's satiny smooth bikinis made my fingers rub together, wishing I was touching them now.

"Smelling underwear's sick!" Most gazes stayed on Wesley, despite Billy's shout. "We watch or pay up."

Wesley spread his arms out to his sides and glanced both ways. "Let's take a vote. Who accepts the underwear, say aye."

Several ayes came calling back.

Wesley nodded, glancing up and down the plane again. "And who says nay?"

A few nays were called out from Billy, Jack, and Tony. I realized I hadn't voted for either, being too immersed in the thought of Naomi's soft skin within my hands. I closed my eyes and could almost feel her for real. My head leaned back on the plane's window and I pretended I was with her again on that wonderful moonlit night on Plum Beach. Their voices became waves in the background and the only words I heard were Naomi's soft whisperings of *never let me go, Lenny, hold me forever.* I knew there was arguing going on around me, but it was of no concern as long as I had Naomi in my arms. We lay on the beach for a long time, feeling like it was all night, though I knew I had to get her home by three.

Next thing I knew Richard's voice yelled, "Rise and shine, Marines. We have arrived in the land of ladies and sunshine."

I opened my eyes, losing the feel of Naomi faster than she'd vanished from my life once she met Charles. I shuddered within the stark light that glared in through the window. Leon had his hands cupped over his eyes, looking down at the base that seemed to rush up at us. There was a sudden jolt and I gripped tight to my seat, though immediately eased my hold as the plane rolled down the runway. Several guys grabbed their duffels and began forming a line at the door. I joined them, standing behind Leon and Wesley, flexing my feet to uncramp my legs. It felt good to finally move, except at the first step out of the plane, the sudden blast of the sun's heat made me stop.

It felt almost like walking straight into flames when Richard pushed from behind. "You think this is hot, the next stop is Vietnam!"

I shook some of the sweat from my forehead and followed the others towards a long building in the distance. Jack Creeden rushed up to Wesley's side. "We'll need some proof, like listening at the door. Don't forget that."

Wesley's fist pressed softly into Jack's arm as we trudged forward. "I said I'll get you proof, but it's my terms or nothing. Seducing a lady is delicate business."

We continued towards the green structure, then entered to find rows of folding chairs set up within a wide open space. One by one we were called to a desk at the front where our papers were taken, signed, stamped and piled in a folder. New papers were issued that were then also signed and stamped.

I sat waiting for forty-five minutes while a large fan pushed the stifling air around. But even with the fan, the heat made it hard to breathe. Sweat drenched my shirt and I wished I could pull it off. I had never been that sweaty before, except with Naomi. I closed my eyes and remembered the time our bodies were so wet it had seemed we were in a hot bath. A long gasp of air gushed from my mouth. It was those sorts of thoughts that cost me my 2F and got me drafted.

A trickling from my forehead slipped into my eye and burned. I squeezed it tight, feeling tears begin to form. I swiped at them with the back of my hand then slumped in my chair. If only all this would go away and I could fall once more into Naomi's arms.

"There's one for you." Billy's voice made me sit up and turn around. His hand hit Wesley's arm, then pointed to a Filipino woman in a white pleated skirt and yellow blouse, carrying a stack of folders to the officer behind the desk.

Wesley leaned back and crossed his arms in front of his chest. "Too tight assed."

I watched her pick up another stack of folders and walk back towards the door, taking short, stiff steps, as Wesley continued, "I'm finding me a sweet brown face with long hair to flow like a waterfall on my chest."

I closed my eyes and thought of Naomi's silky hair on my cheek. It was wonderful for a moment, then my name was called. I jumped up with my papers in my hand and rushed forward.

* * * * *

Forty-five minutes later, with all papers dispensed, we were informed that cold Cokes could be purchased at the canteen on the other side of the base. We were also told to report back in three hours at 1600, and not be one minute late.

I ambled to the canteen, the heat keeping my and everyone else's pace slow. Trickling in a few at a time, we each ordered two Cokes to start.

I swallowed both mine fast and went back for a third, noticing the postcards next to the cash register. I picked up three and stayed at the counter to write.

Dear Grandma,

I'm in the middle of the great Pacific Ocean on a hot sunny island that would be ideal for lying on the beach and getting a suntan like we do at Coney Island. Only they could use a Nathan's hot dog stand and a boardwalk with lots of arcades and frozen custard. I'm fine.

Love, Lenny

I turned that one over and began another.

26

Dear Mom and Dad,

 It's beautiful here in the middle of the Pacific Ocean, but I recommend a big beach umbrella, a cold can of Fresca for mom and a chaise lounge with a large bottle of Coppertone for dad. This sun is even more blazing than our heat waves in Brooklyn.

          Love, Lenny

 I was deciding whether or not to add, 'P.S. Say hi to Anna,' when Wesley's voice boomed, "I'll go to the ocean if I damn well please. I'm not under your military command."

 I looked up to see Wesley seated at a small round table with Billy leaning over him. "But what about the bet?"

 Wesley shoved his chair out from the table and stood, facing Billy dead on. "I'm too hot to care about your damn bet."

 "But the guys..." Billy's arm shot out to his side.

 Wesley saluted Billy. "On leave, sir, thank you, sir." He abruptly turned on his heels, approached the counter where I stood, and rapped one hand on its glossy wood surface. "Two Cokes and two bags of pretzels, please." It was placed in front of him and he reached deep in his pocket, paid, then turned to me. "You coming?"

 I swallowed the stream I had just poured in my mouth, feeling as hot and dry as I had before. "Sure, I could sure use a dunk in the ocean."

 Wesley held up one of his bottles to me and tipped it in my direction. "Amen to that." He swallowed its contents in one long chug, slammed it down and rushed through the door, holding the other bottle to his head. Jack and Billy charged after him, followed by Richard and Leon.

 I caught up to Leon's side and tapped him on the arm. "This heat is brutal."

 Leon slid the back of his hand across his forehead. "We get hot in Cincinnati but the only time I felt heat like this was a time a building down the street was on fire. Man that was hot, almost burnt my skin standing half a block away."

 Richard shook his head, drops of sweat scattering from his chin. "I can't figure how this whole island doesn't go up in flames."

 We reached the beach seeing Wesley with his pants halfway down and his khaki boxers loose around his long thighs. He tossed his pants over his boots and his shirt on top of that, then yelled as he ran towards the blue swells of waves, "Pacific Ocean, this here's Wesley Bates, city boy and the best damned lover ever was." He ran in to his hips then stopped to splash water on his chest. "Oh, baby, you feel so good!"

I couldn't help but stare beyond him into the turquoise water, its stunning color holding me still. I had always thought the ocean a murky green, the way it looked at Coney Island. The only turquoise water I'd ever seen was in the swimming pools at the Brighton Beach Club, where it sparkled cleaner than a bath and was icy cold on hot days. I had loved that turquoise water as a kid, though they were mere pools. This was much broader than I could ever have imagined. I ran to the beach and stripped down to my underwear, anxious for the water's cold shock to my skin. But as I ran in, its warmth felt like a cruel joke.

I pushed against the incoming water towards Wesley, shouting, "I've never been in ocean this warm before."

Wesley turned to me, swirling the water with his arms. "Damn, this is my virgin voyage. It feels mighty good to me!"

I began towards him when he thrust a mass of water in my face. I raised my arms to resist, and was about to splash him back when a huge wave crashed on top of me. I tumbled under water and was thrown into the bottom sand till I was able to kick and get back above the surface where Leon, Richard and Wesley were splashing each other. I gulped at the air, then joined them feeling like a kid in the Brighton pool.

Billy and Jack suddenly appeared on either side of Wesley. It seemed they wanted in on the fun, but then in a synchronized move they both jumped on Wesley and forced his head under. Wesley's arms flailed wildly out of the water, but they didn't let him up. I thrust my shoulder into Billy, knocking us both backwards under the water, then surfaced to see Richard and Leon struggling with Jack.

Wesley was coughing off to their side, then yelled, "Damn fools, you near drowned me!" Billy and Jack started for him but Wesley rushed for the beach, grabbed his clothes before they could catch him, and sprinted, his long legs moving fast.

Billy gasped for a few breaths, then grabbed Jack's arm and shook. "Follow him!"

Leon, Richard and I immediately surrounded Jack when a huge wave knocked us all under. I tumbled to the side, surfacing to hear Jack call to Billy, "I don't know where he went!"

Billy scanned the beach, then pointed west. "Try that way, we can't let him out of our sights!"

* * * * *

The sweat on my lip felt like it was boiling out of my skin as I watched Billy glare across the plane at Wesley. We were in our same places as before, only this time, there was a battle line between the two sides that no one dared cross, not even to stretch their legs.

Billy's foot slammed into the floor and shook us in our seats. "You lying son of a bitch! You owe me and everyone else that bet against you on this friggin' plane. Now pay up!"

Wesley slapped his hand over his heart. "It's not a lie. I told you I had myself the sweetest tasting honey ever set foot on that base. You all the ones need to pay me."

Billy's finger thrust forward, pointing straight at Wesley's face. "That's crap. No one saw you so don't go spouting your stories like the stud of the year. Proof is proof and you don't have any."

Wesley placed a second hand over his heart and sat up straighter. "I don't need no evidence for an asshole who near drowns me. I'm a man of honor. You, William Langdon, are an attempted murderer."

Billy kicked into the air. "And you're nothing but a damn liar and we all know it. It's how you people are."

Wesley gripped the sides of his seat and jerked forward. "What do you mean my people? You calling me a liar 'cause I'm black?"

Billy shrugged his shoulders. "It's in your blood, inbred from the days of lying to the master. You can't help it."

Wesley's arms locked absolutely straight. "Don't give me no master talk. I ain't never been a damn slave and no one's 'bout to treat me like one. And don't be mouthing off my mama taught me to lie 'cause my mama took me to church every Sunday and made me an upstanding citizen. My word's honest as God's."

Billy smiled. "You're about as honest as a skunk. What beautiful lady is going to take you to bed five minutes after she meets you?"

Wesley spread his hands out in front of him. "The nurse, like I told you. And it was all your doing, can you beat that?"

Billy shoved himself back in his seat. "Baloney! Don't drag me into your lie!"

Wesley's finger crossed his heart. "For real. It was 'cause you near drowned me and I couldn't stop coughing that I went to the infirmary. And there she was, sitting behind her desk, looking so fine in her crisp, white uniform. She had me sit on the cot and listened with her stethoscope like so." He paused to touch different parts of his chest. "Then she had me lie face down on my stomach while she pressed into my back with hands soft as black velvet and told me, *'Don't worry, dear, exhale from deep inside and all the water will come right out.'*"

Billy scuffed his feet into the floor. "You mean she poked you like a pig is more how it went."

Wesley smiled, spreading it extra wide. "She was gentle as a lamb, and it was then I knew that she was an angel of mercy come to give me a beautiful send off before going to Nam."

I checked my watch at the reminder; three hours and twenty minutes to go. I shuddered, then looked back at Wesley as he continued.

"First she pushed hard on my back and all that nasty ocean water streamed out of my mouth like beer foam slipping down the side of a glass. Then her velvety fingers rubbed gently on my skin and I thought I had already died and gone to heaven."

Billy slapped his thigh. "Last person going to heaven is you."

Wesley swayed his shoulders like he was snuggling closer into the woman's arms. "I already been to heaven and it definitely didn't push me out. No, that sweet angel's hands slid under my chest and then, Lord have mercy, she spread herself out right on top of me, her breasts pressed soft against my back and her lips like warmed syrup on my neck."

I ached for Naomi's breasts and shifted in my seat like it was suddenly unbearable.

Wesley went on, "She worked some island magic on me, man, I was under a spell deeper than no woman ever done before. And next thing I knew, she reached into my pants and wrapped those delicate fingers around my pole. Man, it swelled so big I thought it would explode right through her hand."

I felt myself harden and covered it with my arm, wishing it was Naomi's arm pressing down instead of mine.

Wesley's voice went on. "She turned me over and opened my pants like opening a jar of honey ready for her first taste of my sweet nectar." Wesley's head leaned back into the side of the plane and his voice trailed off into a series of tender ooohhhs and mmms.

Billy slammed his feet on the floor. "Then what?"

Wesley jolted upright, his eyes bulging wide and steady. "Then what you think? I don't give away a lady's secrets. The act of love is private, man, sacred like an act of God."

Billy's fists pushed into his knees. "It's all lies, all of it. Never happened, not even close!"

Wesley leaned back and tapped his hands on his stomach. "That right?"

"That's right." Billy squeezed his hands together. "Now pay up. We all know you lost."

Wesley looked from face to face at the others sitting on Billy's side. "That so?"

Jack's boot slammed back into the bar under his seat. "That's so. No one believes anything you say."

"I do!" Leon's unfamiliar shout drew all eyes. "I know him since we's kids. If he says it, he did it."

Wesley turned to Leon and rapped him on the arm. "Just for that, brother, you can be the first to see this." He reached deep in his pants pocket and pulled out a white bra, swinging it by its strap.

Billy's jaw lowered as he pointed to the swaying white cotton. "You bought that, it doesn't count!"

Wesley stretched his arm towards Billy. "Does this smell like it came from a store?"

Billy crossed his arms in front of his chest, glanced at Jack, then back to Wesley. "It probably stinks from being in your pocket."

Wesley brought the bra to his own face and took a long breath in. "Man, this smell ain't never come from me." He leaned forward, dangling the bra in his hand. "Anyone want to check this out?"

Richard's arm extended and Wesley reached it past Leon and me, right into his hand. Richard then raised it to his face, took a long inhale, and smiled. "Man, this is way too sweet for your stinking body." He held the bra out in front of Leon. "Turner, you know this joker the longest. He ever smell like that?"

Leon turned his head away, but at Wesley's poke, grasped it with two fingers and took a quick sniff. "That ain't Wesley, not that I ever knowed."

He passed it quickly back to Richard, who placed it in front of my face. But what I hoped would be the fresh lemony scent Naomi wore, hit me like the thick overpowering heat we just left on the ground. "Coconut, yuck."

I passed it back to Richard who flipped it across the aisle to Billy. It landed on his leg and Billy grabbed it, crushing one of its cups within his grip, then gave it a quick pass under his nose. His head shook and he slapped the bra back down on his leg. "That's easy. He bought coconut oil and the bra and rubbed it in himself."

Richard pointed to the white cotton that seemed to glow in our gray light. "Look closer. It's stained under the arms and the elastic's stretched. That bra's not new."

Billy scrutinized the underarm panel, then held it out to Wesley. "This filthy piece of crap doesn't prove a thing. You stole it from someone's laundry and told that ridiculous fairy tale you expect us to believe. We're not all stupid enough to fall for your lies. Pay up what you owe and get this over with."

Wesley hunched his shoulders around his neck. "I ain't paying crap. I told you what happened and it's the truth. I'm not so low I go scrounging in a lady's laundry to make up a story for you. You have all the proof you need right there in your hand, even if you're too dumb to know it. Why don't you ask the others and let them decide?"

Billy threw the bra on the floor and stomped his boot on top of it. "No one has to tell me what to think. You're the one owes me, that much I know."

Wesley's eyes stared at the bra, then slowly shifted up to Billy. "I ain't giving you a dime."

There was silence as their eyes locked on each other, when Billy's boot began smearing the bra into the floor.

Wesley jumped up from his seat. "Stop that!"

Billy jumped up, too, his body colliding right into Wesley. They fell on the floor, Wesley ending up on top. He clutched Billy's shoulders as if ready to give him a hard shake, but then Billy's hands grasped Wesley's throat and squeezed. Wesley's teeth gritted as he pried at Billy's hold.

My focus was on Wesley's face when I heard Jack's shout, "Get that bastard, Billy, don't let go!"

Wesley was pulling at Billy's grip when Leon's voice piped in, "Wes, hit him in the nose!"

The shouts started coming from everywhere but Billy's voice rang above the rest, "Ready to pay, you lying bastard?"

Wesley's teeth separated and his eyes opened wider.

I wished Wesley would punch Billy's jaw and break it so it would have to be wired shut, except Wesley's eyes closed and his tongue pushed out from his mouth.

I was terrified he was almost dead and screamed, "He's choking!" But no one seemed to hear and Billy's hands didn't budge. Next thing I knew I was

32

diving on top of Billy, aiming for his arms. Wesley's body crashed down on my back, then I felt other thuds, like more bodies piling up. I wanted to reach around to Wesley's neck to see if it was free, but couldn't move.

I was about to yell, *Wesley, are you alive?* when another voice shouted, "Up, all of you, before the captain comes back here!"

The weight above me lightened, then someone gripped my arms and lifted. I realized it was Richard and was about to say, *thanks,* when he shoved me back into my seat and stared straight into my eyes. "Don't start no riots, Belkin, there's enough battles where we're headed."

The thought of Vietnam made my throat clog. I swallowed hard, then saw Leon lift Wesley and place him in his seat. Wesley's eyes gazed unfocused and Leon slapped his face. "Talk to me, man, tell me you's all right."

Wesley's head arched backwards and his hands went to his neck. A faint whisper came out. "I'm all right."

Leon began massaging Wesley's upper arms and muttered, "That bastard needs a dark alley education."

Wesley's eyes stared at the ceiling as he faintly gasped, "I'll be the teacher."

I reached across Richard and Wesley and tapped Leon's knee. "He need medical attention?"

Leon glanced at me but went right back to attending Wesley. "He's tough as bricks, Wes is, I seen him beat worse than this."

Richard's hand appeared with a piece from a Hershey's bar and held it in front of Wesley's mouth. "Suck this, best healer I know next to my mama's herbs."

Wesley's lips parted and Richard slipped the brown square inside. Wesley's jaw twitched back and forth as I remembered my grandmother's remedies like coke syrup for stomachaches and chicken soup for colds, but chocolate was never one of them. I was about to ask Richard about it when he pushed up Wesley's eyelids with his thumbs and peered in. "No popped vessels, you held up good."

Wesley put a hand on Richard's arm. "Thanks."

Richard patted Wesley's shoulder. "You're sound as a church bell."

I wondered where Richard learned his medical knowledge when he turned and pointed at me. "But you, your brain must have leaked into the ocean. You near started a stampede inside this here can!"

My face flushed hot. "He was choking. What was I supposed to do?"

Richard's arm popped out to his side. "Not get everyone killed."

33

I turned to scan the opposite side of the plane, then back to Richard. "You see anyone dead?"

Richard poked a finger in my chest. "Lucky I don't. A charmed stampede if ever was one. I ain't never seen one before where no one got crushed."

I wanted to argue when Wesley stood and looked at Billy, while gripping Leon's shoulder. "I still have to get my ten bucks before we land."

Leon clasped his hand over Wesley's. "Want me to beat it out of him?"

Richard jumped in front of them both and spread his arms out like barricades. "You ready to be court martialed, 'cause I ain't, not for ten bucks."

Wesley pointed over Richard's shoulder towards Billy. "My honor's at stake."

"Honor or a cage," Richard put his face right in front of Wesley's. "That's the choice a rattler makes seeing easy pickin' mice set in a trap."

There was a sudden roar behind Richard and we all looked. Billy had slipped the bra on over his shirt and said in a high pitched voice, "Wesley, darling, I know we just met but you can take my bra to show your friends while you tell them all about how I begged you to take me."

Billy strutted down the center of the plane to the sounds of laughter and whistles, swishing his ass from one side to the other. Wesley started for him but Leon grabbed him from behind and kept him back.

It was Richard who went up to Billy, then glanced at everyone watching. "You all can poke fun if you want, but truth is, Wesley won that bet and the proof is right here on Billy's chest. And lord almighty if you think this ugly hulk has turned into a sex pot, there's special deferments for your kind."

Jack jumped up behind Billy amidst a few catcalls. "Only proof that bra can be is if we saw it on the girl."

Richard raised his arms high in the air. "Hush up, y'all. If Perry Mason was here he would take the scent on that there brassiere and sniff for the same smell of coconut on Wesley. We got any bloodhounds in here can do that?"

A buzz erupted then Tony's arm shot up. "My mama always said I could smell a new lady in town from ten miles away." There was laughter and applause and Tony took a bow.

Richard pulled Tony to a standing position. "How 'bout that, our very own coon dog. Here, take a good whiff of this." Richard turned him towards Billy. Tony wrinkled his nose, and quickly leaned in and out, then shook his head like he was trying to shake off the smell. Richard then turned him towards Wesley. "Go ahead, Romeo, there's your next victim."

Leon's hands started on Wesley's buttons then spread the shirt apart.

The air hushed to complete silence as Tony walked to Wesley and leaned into his chest, staying for the count of four before straightening up.

Richard rapped him on the back. "Okay Deputy Dog, what's your verdict for these sorry assed Marines?"

Tony put one hand on his hip and pointed the other at Wesley. There's a lot of stinking sweat on Wesley's body, so much I almost missed it, but it's there all right, the same smell that's on Billy's bra."

There was a roar like a freight train had just clamored onto the plane. Richard raised his hands and yelled above the noise, "Shut your traps. This trial is still in session."

The air quieted and Richard loudly cleared his throat before speaking. "This here conclusion is that Wesley and the bra both rubbed against the same woman to get the same scent. All you belly crawling creatures of the night can feast on that. And as my pardner, Perry Mason would say, this case is closed."

There was a moment of silence, then Billy pulled the bra out from his chest, letting it snap back into place. "He rubbed it on his skin, just like he rubbed it on this bra."

Richard turned back to Billy, letting both hands slap against the sides of his thighs. "Guess your head can't see through your tail. The court has ruled, over and out."

Billy stomped the floor. "I don't pay losers!"

Wesley's arm punched into the air. "It ain't right, I won the bet, he should pay."

Leon threw his arms around Wesley. "You stay put. Ain't worth no jail cell, can't tell me it is."

Wesley glared at Billy through narrow slits. "Not for jail, you right. But I sure know one life ain't worth saving."

The hum in the air felt like vibrations shaking the plane apart, as I shuddered at the reminder of what lay ahead.

Jack pointed to the bra on Billy. "Tony's nose couldn't find a cattle ranch."

"That's right." Billy's fists shot straight up in the air. "Justice prevails!"

Wesley's fist slammed into the bench, almost jolting me out of my seat. I wished it had gone straight into Billy's face as I turned back to the window. All I could see was solid gray, no moon, no stars, no sky. I didn't know what was worse, not knowing what was out there, or knowing what was in here. I slid forward, closed my eyes, and tried to see Naomi's breasts shining in the moonlight. But all I saw was Billy with the bra on, his arms up in victory. It wasn't right. None of this was right.

~ CHAPTER 4 ~

August, 1970
Long Binh, Vietnam

It was too hot to breathe, hotter than Guam. I ran off the opening bottom ramp of the plane we'd boarded in Saigon onto the landing strip at Long Binh. Ten of us went straight for a transport vehicle twenty feet away. I climbed inside, sitting third from the end on the bench.

Richard sat next to me. "Sun's gonna burn me to a heap of ash."

Leon was opposite us, pulling at his moist shirt. "Not me, more like I'll drown."

Wesley sat next to Leon and stared at the floor. There had been no chatter from him for the past three hours, not even thanks to me for jumping Billy and saving his life. Instead I felt like he blamed me for Billy's claim to win.

I shifted forward, fighting against the sweat that made me stick to the seat. "I hope there's cold showers where we're headed."

Billy entered and looked at Wesley. "You mean it's too hot for the lover boy?"

Jack chuckled as he followed Billy to the other end of the bench.

Richard swatted a mosquito on his arm and flicked it at Billy. "Shut it, man, too much hot air in here already."

Billy's shoulder twitched towards Wesley. "I ain't the one blowing smoke."

An officer in pressed camouflage with a radiophone in one hand and a clipboard in the other appeared in the opening. "I'm Lieutenant Hutchison. Your deployment area is ten miles south of the DMZ. Without resistance, you should be there in thirty minutes. Keep your M-16s on safety, but be ready to deploy. Reports show recent Viet Cong mobilization near this location."

He left as fast as he came and a moment later our truck jolted into first gear.

No one said a word. The only sounds besides the engine's rumble were restrained coughs from the road dust. Billy pointed his M-16 at the scrub and hills, looking through the scope. From what I could see, no magnification was needed.

Billy's gun jerked to the left. "Something's out there, I saw it!"

The truck suddenly came to a halt. My fingers gripped tighter on my M-16 as I stared outside, not moving anything but my eyes. A shot fired, then several more. The bench trembled and I couldn't help but think it would explode any moment.

The truck jolted forward and accelerated. I glanced to the back, seeing Wesley's gun raised to his shoulder, he and Billy both looking through their scopes. I considered doing the same, but my arms didn't rise.

Ruts on the road shook the whole truck and blew up dust so thick it blocked all outside vision. Gunfire blasted from the front of the truck, then an elbow jabbed into my side. I had slumped into Richard and straightened up fast, listening to the engine rumble loud, then realized there was no more gunfire behind it. I sat stiff in my seat, trying to hear through anxious ears. Each clatter of the truck ended with an imagined explosion.

The truck finally stopped, though I didn't dare move. A soldier appeared looking in at us, his blonde clumped hair seeming as hard as the M-16 he pressed against his chest. "Hi. I'm Corporal Joseph McCormack. Welcome to the 16th parallel. You're the new replacements for the 44th and 45th squads. You're going to follow me out of that hellhole truck into this bug infested hellhole jungle. Don't worry, you'll deal with it as it comes, everyone does."

He grabbed a clipboard that had been hanging on a nail in the truck. "First off are those that come with me to the 44th, Wesley Bates, Lenny Belkin, Jack Creedon, Billy Langdon, and Leon Turner. The rest of you go to Corporal Smith over there." He pointed to his left and we began jumping from the back of the truck.

The drop onto hardened earth was a relief after the hour of unsettling shakes. I stared into the lush green to the left and began following our corporal in that direction. He pointed straight ahead. "We've been right here, ten miles out of Long Binh, 'bout a month. That is, Diego, Moustafa and me. Sergeant Marshall, he's been here eight months. Everyone else is gone."

I was two people back in our single file march. "Gone where?"

McCormack's shoulder twitched from under the strap of his M-16, but he never turned around. "Finished their stints, dead or wounded. We've been waiting a week for replacements, told to hold our location and sit tight, but the sarge don't like sitting tight."

The makeshift base came into view, six tarps set up like tents in two rows of three, facing each other like opposite sides of a street.

Joe pointed in their direction. "This is your new home sweet home; red ants, poisonous snakes and razor edged leaves for your ass."

I shuddered in the heat, when a dark-haired man, dog tags flapping against his bare chest, rushed towards us. "Jose, Sarge has orders to recon the east base of hill 37. HQ suspects tunnels and wants a report by 1100. That only gives thirty minutes to put together a unit. Sarge says four, two on point and two on rear "

Joe then turned back to look at us. "Which one of you asked about the rest?"

The strap of my pack suddenly slid off my shoulder. I hunched it back on as I half raised my arm.

Joe pointed to my face and smiled. "You, curiosity is half the battle, come with me and Diego. The rest of you, pitch tents. The sergeant will get to you later."

My mouth filled with spit as I approached him, feeling his eyes quickly size my height and weight. "What's your name?"

I swallowed the spit, feeling it cling to my throat. "Lenny, Lenny Belkin."

He had me follow him to the first tarp on the left. "Belkin, drop your pack right here. It's time to gear up, man, you don't want to get caught short."

I slapped at a creeping feeling on my legs, nervous it was snakes or ants. "Caught short on what?"

Joe pulled his own pack upright. "Watch Diego, he's the one never forgets his comb or c-rats."

Diego was already making a small pile on the ground. "Look to the future, man, never knows when you could get trapped."

The creeping on my legs shot right up my thighs. I began scratching, looking at Diego to see if he felt it, too. But he showed no notice of his legs as he dropped an ammo clip in his left cargo pocket and tucked a knife in his belt. I scrounged for those items and did the same, then also took his lead, finding a water tablet, three Band-Aids, and a pain capsule. He put them in his sock, as did I, and placed a c-ration can in his right cargo pocket. I was deciding which can to take when a large black man came and looked down at us. "Joe, Diego, and you, kid, the sarge wants your asses, now."

Diego didn't bother to look up. "Moustafa, you tell the sarge two more minutes."

Moustafa's head jerked backwards. "You tell him. I take his orders, not yours."

Joe shoved the unwanted items from his pack under the tarp and stood. "I'll tell him." He turned to Diego. "Make sure he has water." He tilted his head towards me then left with Moustafa towards the sarge.

Diego slipped a snare in his chest pocket and buttoned it closed.

I copied that, and also the tying of a camouflage bandana around my head, like he did. He then pointed to a twenty-gallon tank resting on a stump. "Pure H-2-O, courtesy of Uncle Sam, incorporated." We filled both our canteens then went straight for the sarge, who was crouched over a map.

The sergeant pointed at the brown curvy lines on the right. "HQ wants that hill and needs to know what they're up against by 1600. They suspect a tunnel head right here." His finger moved two inches down to a thick red dot in the middle of several green lines.

I knew green meant sea level, but I couldn't get my bearings. "Where's our location now, Sergeant?"

He looked up for a moment, going from my face to the name stenciled on my shirt, then focused back to the map, his finger sliding left to a penciled circle within an area of dark brown lines. "This is our base right here." The terrain we were on was higher than where we were headed.

He glanced up at me again, as if wanting another look, then turned to Joe. "You have only six hours to get a fix on that hole and recon whatever else is on that hill. The lieutenant doesn't like to be kept waiting."

"Neither do I." Moustafa's arms flew up from his sides, coming down with slaps on each side. "And you know what I'm talking about. I'd better have that desk job when I get back 'cause I ain't humping no more after this, not for the racist pigs running this war."

"Damn it, Moustafa!" The sergeant's hand slammed on the map. "That's between you and HQ. And until I get a change of orders, you better move your ass wherever I send you!"

Moustafa kicked at the dirt next to the map. "If you and the lieutenant wasn't trying to kill off all us darkies, I'd have that job. You tell him that, and tell him if he don't want a revolution on his hands, he better give it to me. You tell him that before you give him the report."

The sergeant sprang to his feet, his lanky five-foot-ten looking frail next to Moustafa's bulky frame, and poked a finger into the bigger man's chest. "You listen here, Moustafa. For the last time, I got nothing to do with desk jobs, get that through that thick skull of yours. And the best you gonna get outta me is, if you find the tunnel locations, I'll put you in for a commendation. Now get the hell out of here and find what's on that hill."

Joe's hand snapped up to his forehead. "Right away, Sarge."

Diego and I did the same.

Moustafa mumbled as we followed Joe away from the sarge, "Same oppression wherever white men's in charge."

A hundred yards outside of our camp Joe turned and looked at both Moustafa and me. "Diego and I will do point, you two take rear, stay thirty feet back."

I watched Joe and Diego slip ahead into the darkening forest, not knowing what to do. I turned behind me to Moustafa, who was standing three steps back. "Don't worry, kid," he whispered. "I'll watch your ass."

I whispered back, like he had done, watching his eyes shift left and right, though never at me. "My name's Lenny."

Moustafa shook his head, continuing to avoid eye contact. "You're too new to have a name."

He came up behind me and pushed me forward with his arm. I began walking, turning my head halfway back. "What the hell does that mean?"

Moustafa's gaze shifted up a tree. "There's no sense starting with names in case you don't last. Easier that way."

Sweat slid from my forehead into my eye and burned. I squeezed it shut as I scanned the ground ahead with my other eye. "I'll tell you anyway. I'm Lenny Belkin, drafted 'cause I flunked out of college, but no way I agree with interfering in another country's civil war. I think our position here is illegal, immoral and unjust. So that's who you got with you today in case I don't last."

Moustafa's gun poked into a bush on our right. "No one cares and no one wants to be here. Your only concern now is keep me alive or you'll find yourself alone face to face with Charlie and he don't question if your morals want you here or not. You got that, kid?"

A branch snapped under my foot and I froze. Moustafa grabbed hold of my pack and kept a tight hold. "What's the matter with you?"

I mouthed the word, "Sorry," too scared to let it have sound. He then pushed on my back but my legs stayed put. Another push and I forced my leg to raise but every leaf, rock, root, and twig now seemed a threat.

Moustafa rapped me on the arm. "Come on. We're falling behind."

I stepped with my toe, keeping my eyes fixed on the ground, hardly touching down before lifting my foot again. My pace quickened from not letting my feet land for long. Leaves brushed against my face and I hoped they didn't hide snakes or red ants or spiders, but I couldn't watch them and my feet at the same time. I began praying to the God my grandmother said she used to believe in before World War II. *Please, keep me away from them, the bugs, snakes, bullets, traps, bombs, snares, and the razor-like bamboo shards guys talked about.*

I heard a rustling sound ahead and stopped in mid step. There it was again, someone or something up ahead. Sweat gushed from every part of my body as Moustafa's exhales on my neck made me even hotter. Leaves scratched ahead and I caught a glimpse of Marine khaki. It was Joe and Diego looking up in opposite directions. I approached, looking towards the same spot Joe did.

"You hear that?" His voice was so low I wasn't sure if it had been him or a mere wisp of wind, when his arm stretched tighter.

I pointed up also, but didn't see anything unusual. "The leaves?"

His elbow flexed slightly as he looked towards me. "The birds, they're restless, they feel something."

My raised arm twitched. "Maybe they feel us?"

"No, listen." His head tilted to the left. "There's an alarm in their chirps. Hear it?"

I tried to distinguish the rustlings, buzzes and rattles from the chirps, hearing a shrill screech. "Is that what it is?"

His head gave a short nod when his gaze stopped on a leaf a foot above his head and his gun pointed to a drop of white ooze. "It's fresh, they're very close." He suddenly scanned a full circle around us and started for a clump of thick shrubs. Diego and I followed when a series of three shots burst from above. Joe flattened on his stomach and I feared he was hit. Diego went down next to him and I dropped to the ground, rolling under a broad fern.

Moustafa fell next to me, and pointed his gun in the air. "It's up there."

I peered through the spaces in the fern, seeing only lush green. It all looked in proper place when a clump of leaves began to quiver. In that split second I raised my M-16 and started firing. The frenzy of blasts reverberated in my head as leaves erupted in fragments, then a body in black fell from the air. I stopped shooting, feeling my shoulder throb like someone was pounding it with a hammer.

"You got him."

I turned to Moustafa, whose gun was pointed at the same spot as mine. "There more?"

His eyebrows arched as he reached for a rock and threw it twelve feet from where we lay. The air remained quiet, even the birds were silent. Another rock hit the ground and I noticed Joe's head slightly elevated, looking around. I was relieved he was still alive as he inched over to the fallen body and pushed it over with his hand. It flopped backwards, sending a heavy gush of air from my mouth as if it had been me. I desperately needed a deep breath, when Joe's M-16 blasted higher into the same tree. The noise shattered through my head and I almost shut my eyes when I noticed bursts of light from an adjacent tree. There were more blasts, then a horrifying shriek, and a second body hit the ground. After that it was silent, vacantly silent, as if there were no more air left to carry the merest sound. Moustafa turned slowly with his M-16 pointing into the branches of each tree. I did the same, though the muscles in my arms felt so tight I feared my fingers wouldn't be able to pull the trigger.

Joe threw a rock at a tree and we watched it bounce off and roll along the ground. It remained quiet after that, till five minutes later Joe sat up and waved his arm in the air. "Coast is clear."

I crawled towards him, having to pass the first body, the one I had shot. The thickened blood on its shirt made my neck veins suddenly pulse. I was about to gag and put my hand on my throat, when the throbbing suddenly made me excited that my own blood was still inside my skin.

I turned away from the body and got to my feet, walking past it, then glancing only momentarily at the other body on my way to Joe.

His head tilted back towards the first body when I arrived. "I owe you."

I turned to it again, feeling my whole body throb, even my feet, thinking it would make the whole jungle floor tremble.

There was a hand on my arm and I realized my eyes had closed. "You all right, kid?"

The sudden scene around me brought me back to the jungle. I nodded, feeling a quaking under my feet. "Just realized what I did."

Moustafa slapped me on the back. "First kill, kid, broke your cherry."

A gush of sweat slid down my sides.

Joe talked, but it was to Moustafa, not me. "Kid's got the third eye."

A shudder shook some of my sweat loose. "Third eye?"

Joe pointed his M-16 towards the trees. "You blasted that snipin' bastard before you ever saw him."

One of my heels caved into the soft earth under it. "Pure luck, I didn't know what I was doing."

Joe stroked the trigger on his gun. "Your brain knew where he was before your eyes did. I'll take you over most humps six months in."

I was suddenly cold and my whole body trembled.

Joe took a step towards me. "You got the shakes, kid?"

My throat clogged but I managed to swallow it mostly clear. "I'm not a killer."

Joe pressed his M-16 tighter across his chest. "No one here's a killer. We save each other's lives, that's it. You think Moustafa's a killer?"

I watched Joe point at the second body, knowing I was taking too long to answer. "No."

"Damned straight, no." Moustafa kicked at a tree root sticking up from the ground. "White folks think they's so high and mighty."

Joe raised his hand. "Shut it or we'll pull in more Charlie's. Let's go, we've got a mission to do." He turned, pushed a branch out of his way, and began moving at a faster pace than before.

I followed behind Diego and Moustafa, feeling an acidy saliva burn in my throat.

After five minutes, Joe stopped and turned back to us. "No evidence of any more, those two were alone. We'll go back to positions, only this time I want the kid with me, he should learn the sights."

Moustafa shifted his shoulders under his pack. "You mean I have to watch Diego's ass?"

Diego made a kissing noise. "Hey, man, the girls dig it."

Joe raised his elbow towards Moustafa. "You want point?"

"Not that," Moustafa stepped one foot out to the side. "You're the best lead. It's Diego, man, he's a jinx."

Diego's upper lip curled out. "You talkin' that time I tripped a wire?"

Moustafa poked his finger at Diego's chest. "Sure am, and that rear got blasted."

Diego leaned into Moustafa's face. "You think you could have…"

Joe shoved his arm in between them and pushed Moustafa back. "Stop this. All we got is each other, remember?"

Moustafa hunched his shoulders, looking only at Joe. "I'm cool, but I walk in front of Diego."

Diego pulled on Joe's pack. "Fine by me, I'll keep his precious ass so well covered it'll sleep like a newborn babe."

Joe clapped his hand on his M-16. "Good. Keep it tight, only twenty paces behind the kid." He began walking and I followed a close two steps behind, staring at his feet, afraid of tripping a wire like Diego had done.

Joe's pace quickened and I kept up, telling myself that the faster we moved the harder it would be to get hit. Thick sweat oozed from my body, feeling like steam from a hot burning engine. But hot as I was, that engine kept me right behind Joe. That was the only sense of safety there was. Otherwise, each jagged mound and soft recess of earth was unnerving.

Joe came to an abrupt halt and I stopped behind him, troubled by its cause. He pointed his gun to a leaf with a jagged rip and I stared at it, though was unable to determine its meaning. "A signal?"

"Gun snag, and see the angle of its crease?" He pointed behind us. "They were moving that way. You see any sign of drying?"

I looked at the solid green color and shook my head.

"Right, no brown or yellow. Happened sometime in the last twelve hours. Probably the ones we already hit, but could be others."

I looked warily into the thickly woven branches behind us. "What do you think?"

Joe rubbed the leaf between his fingers. "I'd say it was the same ones."

I felt a tingling sensation on my arms, like the hairs suddenly went straight up trying to detect what was out there. "How do you know?"

Joe pointed to the center of his chest. "Sweat gushes right here when someone's got their eye on me. Happened even in school when the teacher was about to call my name. Can feel those eyes every time, comes right out of this spot like someone opened a spout."

The thick film of sweat on my body suddenly felt thicker. "You're not sweating now?"

Joe patted his chest. "Same old sweat, that's it."

Diego appeared at that moment. "What you see, boss, tracks?"

Joe looked at Diego then at Moustafa. "A leaf, showing it to the kid."

Diego scratched his arm. "He read it?"

"Can now." Joe dropped the leaf then pulled a compass from his pocket and pointed thirty degrees to the right. "We'll descend this way and approach the tunnels from the west."

I thought back to the map. "But shouldn't we keep going straight? Sarge said they were due north."

Joe looked at me with only one eye. "That would put us upwind. You want them to smell you coming?"

"No, but…"

Diego cut me off. "Deodorant don't work so good out here."

"Especially yours." Moustafa mumbled at Diego.

Joe shoved the compass back in his pocket. "I hope you clowns are done, we got ground to cover." He turned and began heading west.

I followed, only this time, instead of just watching his steps, I expanded my vision, anxious to catch any signs that could help. The sweat from under my arms increased. It was too heavy for my already drenched shirt and streamed into my pants, dripping down my legs.

A piercing sound from above made me stop and stare at a swaying branch.

Joe noticed I'd stopped and came back. "It's one of them Langur monkeys that looks like an old Vietnamese man with a white beard. Ever see one?"

I was unable to see anything through the leaves. "No, but how can you tell?"

"Listen." His head looked upward but his eyes closed. "Ears can tell more than eyes. Chatter means they're feeling safe, but one sharp cry by itself, that's an alarm."

There was a singular shrill call again. "Alarm? For what?"

Joe opened his eyes. "Us, four ugly Marines with M-16s. We're too close for comfort, don't you think?"

I stared into the tangle of branches for signs of snipers hidden behind leaves. "Only us?"

Joe's fingertips tapped on his chest. "Don't feel anyone else."

There was another alarm from above, then Moustafa arrived. "What y'all waiting on?"

"Langur, doesn't appreciate our presence." Joe pointed up then turned west and began moving. "Let's leave the poor monkeys in peace."

I followed him, hearing Moustafa say to Diego, "Hold up, the new kid never heard monkeys before."

I stared around me hearing constant sirens in my head. Each rustling, click, snap, crack, chatter, and buzz put me on alert. I tried to decipher each one, but it was impossible without knowing every animal, insect and tree in the jungle. Instead, I tried to hear each sound's intent. Was it fear or anger, or merely busy and routine? A few felt tense but Joe didn't stop so I assumed their alarm was from our presence as it had been with the monkeys.

We continued on, the brush and vines thickening the further in we went. My sight became more and more limited till I couldn't see past five feet in any direction. The air became hotter, thicker and steamier, and the foliage was so dense it could hide a platoon. My breathing became shorter and faster and I longed to be out in an open field with unobstructed views.

I continued to stare at every inch, suspicious of what it might conceal when some brush looked higher than the others as if the earth had been pushed up in that spot. Joe was only two steps away from where a bit of bright green showed from under a thick mass of decayed vines.

I charged towards him. "Stop!" I threw myself into his side and pulled him with me into a thorny brush that stabbed into my shirt.

"What the hell...?"

"Don't move!" I pushed down on him with my elbow while I jabbed into the dead vines with my gun. We both found ourselves staring at a deep pit.

"Damn," Joe's head strained to see into the hole, "I was good as down there!"

My throat tightened, making me unable to respond as I raised off of him and inched closer to the pit. Joe peered down with me. Two snakes hissed at us from eight feet down, their tongues lashing like M-16 tracers headed right for our faces. They slithered part way up the wall and my whole being shook.

I aimed my gun at one and had its head in my sight when Joe pushed it off target. "They hear that and they know the trap is disarmed. Use your knife, I'll show you."

I lowered my gun and watched Joe wave his knife in the hole above the snakes, daring them to go for it. One of them lunged and Joe swung straight across, slashing its neck. Its two parts writhed as they fell.

Joe looked up over his shoulder. "You want the other one?"

I leaned back. "No."

"I'll take it." Diego's leg brushed against my side, his knife pointing forward. "Come here you slimy bastard."

The second snake lunged and Diego raised his knife out of reach. "Fooled you, you lousy VC pawn. First you're gonna sweat."

"It's cold blooded, you idiot." Moustafa knelt on one knee next to him. "The sweating one is you."

The snake lunged again. This time Diego sliced at its head, hitting its jaw and cut halfway in. The snake jerked wildly as it fell then thrashed into the body of the other snake on the ground.

Diego slapped his knife against his leg. "Gotcha, you slithering rat."

Moustafa kicked dirt in the hole. "Don't go patting yourself on the back. Was your breath killed it, the knife missed."

Diego stuck the point of the knife in the ground. "That was no miss. I cut the sucker's spine and saved the skin."

Joe's head tilted in my direction. "The kid saved my skin." He turned to me and studied my face like he was looking for puzzle parts that fit. "Tell me, kid, how'd you catch that hole?"

The snake suddenly flapped in the air and my jaw tightened shut. All I could do was point to the shred of green still stuck to the vine.

Joe looked then brought it close to his face. "How did I miss that?" He turned back to me. "For fresh off the plane you have the damnedest senses of a scout. You grow up in the woods?"

I smiled, feeling a soreness where my jaw released. "Brooklyn's mostly concrete 'cept for some trees on the side streets."

"Brooklyn, damn." Joe's eyes widened. "Must have some signs you read.

I pictured what I saw walking down the street. "One way, no parking, and stop, that's about it. Signs worth seeing are in Manhattan, Broadway, there's hundreds of them flashing all night."

Joe's knife angled in my direction. "One day you get me there, kid, think you can do that? 'Cause from now on, you're my man on point."

Moustafa pushed halfway in front of me, facing Joe. "No way, man, it's your eyes saved me, a few times. The kid just got lucky."

Joe held up the leaf in his hand. "Yeah, lucky for me." He then faced the three of us, focusing on Moustafa. "I'll stay point, but the kid stays on my heels the rest of the mission."

Moustafa's shoulder twitched. "He's new, remember that, don't get sloppy."

Joe slipped his knife back in its sheath on his belt. "Quit complaining, there's four sharp eyes in front of you. Your job is to worry about the rear."

Moustafa turned to Diego. "Bad luck behind me and beginner's luck in front. Worse odds than my chances at a desk job."

Diego pointed the tip of his knife at Moustafa's chest. "You're no great comfort yourself."

I wiped my sweaty palm on my pants, afraid Moustafa was right, when Joe jumped down into the pit. I turned to see him holding the first snake body high in the air. "Scout, this is for you."

I expected Diego or Moustafa to go towards him, but they didn't. Joe's hand with the snake pointed directly at me. "You, kid scout, come here."

Both Moustafa and Diego looked at me, though the last thing I wanted was to touch that snake. But Joe's eyes stayed on me and not wanting to ignore him, I extended my arm into the pit. "Here, I'll help you up."

He placed the snake on my hand and I immediately pulled back. "You crazy?"

Diego laughed and reached into the pit. "Come on, boss, he don't know."

Joe grasped Diego's hand and climbed out of the hole, both snake bodies hanging from his other hand. I stepped back when he ordered, "Attention, private!"

47

I snapped my legs together and stood still as he tucked a snake in Diego's pack pocket, then walked behind me. I wanted to turn and see what he was doing with that long piece of the first snake when he leaned his head over my shoulder. "Kid, you may have good eyes, but there's something you don't understand."

I squeezed my hands together, fearing he'd touch the snake to me again.

Joe walked around to my other shoulder, nothing touching me yet, as he continued. "Out here in the jungle, where luck is all that keeps us breathing another day, you take luck very seriously. When something's out to kill you and you manage to stay alive, that's luck you want to keep with you. You kept us alive from these snakes and you earned wearing that luck."

My hands squeezed tighter and I expected Diego and Moustafa to laugh at this joke, but instead they remained quiet. Joe came around to my front, pulled out a compass and faced west. I realized he no longer had the snake in his hand and I immediately looked over my shoulder, not seeing it.

I assumed he put it in a pocket, like he did Diego's, but still, a terrible creeping feeling went up my legs as Joe motioned twenty-five degrees to our left. "Okay you two, thirty feet back, don't get lost."

Diego tapped his M-16. "Not to worry, boss. You is glued to my sights."

Joe wiped his eyes with his sleeve and turned to me. "Let's go, stay sharp."

The creeping up my legs increased and I desperately wanted to feel for the snake when Joe started right into a fast pace. I stayed close behind him, trying to convince myself that the snake was dead and not on my legs. I kept my focus shifting from the ground to the trees, to Joe, when he stunned me by pushing his sleeve up and licking his arm.

I rushed right up to his heels. "You get bit by the snake?"

Joe raised his exposed arm. "Salt. My vision's blurred, need salt."

I felt the sweat on my upper lip and licked it.

Joe shook his head. "Not exposed skin, germs."

I spit on the ground hoping all the germs flew out with it while keeping a four step distance. It seemed impossible that I would make it back alive from this mission, but there was nothing else to do but keep going.

~ CHAPTER 5 ~

Highlands, Vietnam

The sarge jabbed his finger into the upper brown area on the map. "Intelligence reported movement in that area. That activity had to come from somewhere."

Joe's finger made a circle an inch below the sarge's spot. "We searched the whole eastern base and I'm telling you, Sarge, there was no sign of holes."

The sarge's eyes squinted and scanned across the rest of us before looking back at Joe. "You sure you went to the right hill?"

Joe's body shot up straight. "Yes, that's where we were, Hill 37. You want us to go back?"

I stopped breathing, petrified the answer would be yes.

The sarge shoved his hand into his sweated hair. "Damn it HQ will be pissed. They had intelligence it was there."

Moustafa dropped his pack next to his feet with a thud. "Nothing's gonna please them 'cept we dig it ourselves so their intelligence can pretend they's smart."

I scratched at my leg. "Shouldn't they be happy there is no tunnel?"

Diego leaned close to my ear. "It's a game, kid. HQ wants to look like they know what they're doing. Truth don't matter."

I felt a wriggling up my spine and shed my pack off fast, touching for a snake I couldn't find.

The sarge slammed his hand down on the map. "Lieutenant's going to be mad! He already put out the order to blow the holes."

Moustafa stepped in closer, bumping his toe into the sarge's boot. "He can take it back, same as he took back giving me the desk job."

The sarge kept his eyes on Joe. "Get him away from me before I volunteer him to the thirteenth valley.

"No need for that." Moustafa flexed his shoulders toward his back. "You want me gone, I can make myself scarce, no problem.'

The sarge snapped his gaze to Moustafa. "Then leave, now!"

Moustafa grabbed his pack and began dragging it, muttering, "No one in this damned Corps wants to see the racist truth."

The sarge wiped his forehead then tapped his finger on Hill 37. "No question he's going to ask about the other side."

Joe's knee came down hard on the map. "Couldn't. Time was up after that one side. Tell him we found human shit, small piles of rocks and blackened leaves, but no entrances or air holes for tunnels."

Diego edged his elbow in my side. "No point standing here, kid, they could be at it a while." He began heading towards our tent. The thought of a place to lie down seemed just what I needed. I lifted my pack and was halfway there when someone pulled it from my hand.

"Looky here."

I turned to see Richard examining the back of my pack. "Where'd you get that critter?"

I followed his gaze to the snake tail protruding from my side pouch. Richard already had the pocket opened and was pulling it out.

"From the bottom of a pit."

Richard draped it over his hand and stroked the underside. "Damn, brown with yellow belly, same colors as a timber rattler, without the pattern. These here are beauties."

I noticed the criss-crossed skin for the first time. "Joe gave it to me for good luck."

Richard stroked the etched pattern. "Looks to me like king cobra. Don't get these in Texas, but I seen pictures."

The memory of its lunge from the pit made acid churn in my stomach. "I'm just glad it's dead."

Richard held it by its tail. "Can understand that. Four feet, at least, and thick, too. Bet it's some tasty meat. You eatin' it?

"Eat it?" Acid rushed up from my stomach and I spit it out to my side. "You crazy? This thing's poisonous!"

Richard raised the snake, looking it up and down. "Only part poisonous is the head, the rest's prime number one grub."

The moisture on my tongue soured. "You eat this?"

Richard slid his finger down its skin. "You kidding? We fight over it back home. Sprinkle with mama's hot sauce and hold over a hoppin' fire. No sir, nothing better. You never tried it?"

50

The rancid taste of rotten scallops I had as a kid suddenly recurred. "No, and I never want to. You take it, I don't ever want to see this snake again.

Richard's head shook. "This snake's your good luck, I can't take it. Why my mama says snake is God's creature with the most magic. She tacks them to the door, claiming venom repels vermin."

Looking at that snake only made me feel it creeping up my leg. "Then send it to your mother."

Richard raised it closer to his face. "That's mighty thoughtful of you, 'cept its luck can only go to you. But the meat," he flashed a smile, "that's for us Marines. Power of the enemy to give us the upper hand."

I lifted my pack and glanced towards Diego next to the draped tarp. "It's all yours, bon appetite."

I began for Diego when Richard stepped to my side. "Why'd you chop its head off?"

I kept my gaze straight ahead, not letting myself turn to look at it. "I didn't, Joe did. But I was the one spotted the pit the snakes were in."

"Sharp peepers." Richard paused to whistle. "You said snakes?"

We reached Diego and I dropped my pack. "He has the other one."

Richard held up his snake to Diego. "You took one of these?"

Diego pulled his snake from his pack. "This here's the baby."

Richard's hand reached for it but stopped one foot away. "Lord almighty, head and all. Why I know a man in Amarillo could stuff that skin so it looks ready to leap."

I'd been pulling my camou blanket from my pack when the thought of the snake's open jaw made me grip my knife.

"Want me to skin it?" Richard had said it, and I turned to see him slide his finger down the side of Diego's snake. "No need to waste fresh meat."

I spread the camou on the ground, lay back and tried to imagine anything but the snakes when Diego said, "Never thought I'd eat snake, man, never in a million years. But this place changes everything you believe about yourself, that's the truth."

I suddenly felt snakes creeping all over me and sat up, pushing them off when Richard spoke. "We had fist fights over snake in my house. Winner got the thickest piece and the rattler tail to sell to the store, if'n Mr. Henderson was in a fit mood to give up a dollar."

I pulled my knees up to my chest and shut my eyes, hoping Richard and Diego would take the snakes and leave. In my head I saw the snakes alive and hissing and headed right for me, when Joe's voice startled me. "What's he want me to do? Dig a tunnel myself?"

I opened my eyes to see Diego slap the snake against his leg. "Sarge must've bet the lieutenant we'd find an underground arsenal like that other squad did. Now he's pissed he lost."

"Pissed isn't the word." Joe dropped his pack and kicked it on its side. "I never saw him this mad. Something's eating at him and if it keeps up, it's going to come down bad on us."

Diego flapped his snake into his stomach. "Maybe his wife really is having an affair with the neighbor. Remember how he threw her letter in the fire then wouldn't talk for eight hours?"

Joe's eyes widened as he slid his thumb and forefinger along his eyebrows. "Could be, or else this means he won't get the promotion he wanted. But I can tell you one thing for sure. It was time to get the report back and that's what I did."

Joe sat on his pack and turned to me. "About today, kid, I owe you big time. Anything you want?"

I glanced at Diego and Richard, then back at Joe. "I want those snakes as far away from me as possible."

Joe reached over and ran his fingers up my arm. "You got the creeps, kid?"

I rubbed at the spots he'd touched. "I got the creeps and I'm tired and hungry."

"Hungry?" Joe suddenly stood and began rummaging in his pack. "You, kid, are going to be treated to Joe's thanksgiving feast."

He had a foil package in his hand when Moustafa's shouts made me turn to the sarge's spot. "I did the mission, man. It ain't my fault there were no tunnels. You said you'd recommend me to the desk job!"

The sarge's arms flew up in the air. "I never promised you nothing. Now get the hell away from me so I can tell the bad news to HQ."

Moustafa's arms raised and I feared he was going to strike the sarge. But then he flexed his hands flat to the sky and looked straight up between them. "Lord have mercy, oppression never ends."

The sarge turned his back on Moustafa, lifted the radio phone, and walked away from him.

Moustafa focused on Joe, then scuffed his feet in the ground and arrived amidst a cloud of dirt. "You got to talk to him, man. You heard him promise to give me a desk job."

"He didn't promise." Joe ripped at the top of the foil bag. "But I'll talk to him when he calms down, which may not be till tomorrow as riled as you got him now."

Moustafa flexed and unflexed his fists. "He promised."

Joe added a thin stream of water to the foil bag and held it up to Moustafa. "Join us, I owe you, too."

Moustafa dropped his pack and lowered himself on it. "It ain't right the desk jobs go to whites only."

Joe placed a blue cube on the ground and lit it with his Bic. A blue flame burst upward, grazing the bottom of the foil bag.

My eyes glanced away to Moustafa. "Where's the desk job you want?"

Moustafa didn't bother to look back at me. "Long Binh. People there left, there's openings."

Joe switched hands on the foil bag, shook it a few times over the flame, then brought it to his face and sniffed at the rising steam. "Mmmm, get a load of this, genuine beef stew."

My stomach cramped as he stirred it with a spoon, then held it out to me. "First taste goes to the scout."

Diego rushed to my side standing directly in front of the bag. "Wait up, what about me?"

Joe's arm pulled back. "Only one would feed you is your mother." He placed the foil bag back in front of me.

I grasped the bag and lifted a spoonful to my mouth. The broth burned my tongue but I swallowed it anyway, feeling tiny chunks slide down my throat. Moustafa's hand reached for the bag and I let him take it. He ate a spoonful, passed it to Diego who did the same, and passed it to Joe who immediately gave it back to me. I made sure the spoon was full this time, wishing I could eat the whole thing and not pass it along, but Moustafa's grip was already on the bag.

It made the rounds again when Richard crouched next to Joe. "Reckon there's enough flame left to cook this here snake?"

Joe pointed to the burning blue cube. "A few more minutes, that's it."

The snake in Richard's hand was now pink and shiny. "Hell, five minutes can hardly sear a frog. Take at least twenty to crisp all this meat."

Diego took his snake and held it up to the flickering light. "Don't forget there's two. Need enough igniter for both."

Joe slid his arm into his pack. "Let me see what I have."

Richard walked to my side. "I do 'preciate your looking, Corporal, while I honor this skin to its rightful owner."

The cold, wet skin suddenly draped around my neck with a thick drop making its way down my back. I jumped to my feet and threw it to the ground.

"Hot damn." Richard crouched by my feet, carefully lifting the skin. "The head's done sliced off. Can't bite you no more, remember?"

I wiped at my neck with both hands. "Head or no head, I told you I don't want it!"

Joe pulled out three cubes, placed them on the ground and began to cut them in smaller pieces.

Richard held up the skin and stepped back from me. "Once it's dry the skin turns smooth as silk. You'll like it then."

"More like smooth as a woman's ass." Diego made his snake swing in front of my face. "Here, touch it, you'll see."

My hand ached for the feel of Naomi's skin as I batted the snake back to Diego. "Get this slimy thing away from me."

"Afraid of a dead snake?" Billy's voice nearly made me fall on my ass as he appeared behind Joe with Jack at his side.

"No, I'm not afraid." The words lashed out of my mouth, like they had come off the tongue of the snake. "It's just not my favorite thing to hang around my neck."

"Not my favorite thing, neither, especially when they's alive." Wesley's voice was unmistakable. I turned behind me to see him approach with Leon. "But let my uncle put one of them suckers in a smoker, and mmmm, mmmm, tastes good as sausage smothered in roasted peppers and sweet onions."

Richard jabbed Wesley on the arm. "Another man knows the goodness of slithering meat."

"Not as good as ribs, mind you," Wesley looked to the flame, which was down to half the size it was before. "Saw the campfire and was hoping for a down home barbecue."

Diego's snake's tail grazed through the flame. "Don't get that real charcoal taste from plastic explosives, but fire's fire. Can you cook?"

Wesley's lips spread wide into his cheeks. "I can cook the grease off a flea. Anyone got some hot sauce?"

Diego's hand gripped his stomach. "Stop it, man, you're making me hungry for my mama's chili."

Wesley rubbed his hands together, then squeezed them into a tight ball. "Man, you ain't had real cooking till you tasted mine. When we go back stateside you're all invited to my restaurant for the biggest, baddest barbecue ribs you ever saw."

A rock hit the ground and everyone looked to Billy who was throwing a stone in the air and catching it with the same hand. "Wesley, we all know you don't have a restaurant, any more than you had that girl in Guam."

Wesley crossed his arms in front of him. "Bet I do. I'm the premiere chef at Roscoe's of South Cincinnati. The line's out the door every morning for my five alarm eggs and sausage on a steaming hot buttermilk biscuit."

Billy's finger shoved into the air towards Wesley. "All bets with you are off before they start."

Wesley spread his hand over his heart. "I kept my end of the deal. You the one didn't pay a penny of what you owed. Seems I'm the one got the shaft."

Billy's lips curled out like he was going to speak, but the next words came from Richard. "Hot damn, Wesley, I'd say I got my money's worth from that story you told."

Wesley gave Richard a sideways glance. "Don't forget you got it for free, probably do the same with the movies."

Richard slapped his hip. "How'd you know? Most every Saturday my brother swept the place for Mr. Thackett, then he'd let me in the side door once the lights went out."

Wesley's glare flashed on Billy. "Seems everyone wants free entertainment these days." He then turned to the rest of us and spread out his arms. "Well, you fine folks here in this land of rice and c-rats, I'm going to give you one more free show. Master chef Wesley is going to demonstrate how cooking snake is done right."

Billy threw his stone towards Wesley then leaped right in front of him to catch it. "It's not hard for one snake to know how to cook another."

Sweat gushed down my sides as the two of them stood face to face when Richard dangled the skinned snake between them. "Fellers, that's a jinx we can't have. My mother always said, sour words make rancid meat, and I'm too hungry for this here snake to be spoilt."

Wesley turned away from Billy and shrugged. "No need to fret on that. I got a tin of spice so hot it can burn the foulest taste out of anything, even worms if you had to eat them."

Diego draped his snake over his shoulder. "Might have to take you up on that the way things go around here."

Wesley pulled a small can from his pocket and held it up for all to see. "My own special culinary secret, cayenne pepper. Improves the flavor of all your foods while it also cures most what ails you."

Billy coughed like he was clearing his throat then looked across the eyes that suddenly turned to him. "With all that promise, does it improve your honesty, too?"

Wesley held the can close to Billy's face and grinned like he was doing a

TV commercial. "At first taste, my man, one can only speak the truth, and nothing but the truth."

Billy shoved the can away from his face and looked directly in Wesley's eyes. "I thought you said you ate that stuff."

Richard pushed himself between them. "You Marines is acting like two starved rats in a bag while my stomach's begging for some of this here snake. Time to cook this slippery reptile before it goes stiff."

Wesley immediately turned to Richard's skinned snake and carefully touched its shimmering meat. "Too bad we don't have no Worcestershire and lemon to marinate this baby, have to make do with what we got."

Richard grasped his stomach. "Amen. I'll cut hunks and put them on sticks, like I do back home."

Wesley stared at the snake and scratched the side of his face. "Shame to cook it without something sweet under the cayenne. Sweet and hot, that's how I like my food and my ladies."

Richard held his snake out to the rest of the group. "Hear that? Anyone have something sweet for this feast?"

Diego pointed to his pack. "I gots c-rat peaches."

Wesley's arms shot straight up in the air. "Hallelujah! A touch of Georgia sunshine in this rat-hole jungle."

Joe's eyes scanned the group. "You heard him, everyone hand over a can."

Wesley glanced around the circle of faces. "Don't fret, only need the juice, you get to eat the fruit."

Each person scattered to their gear. I dug in my pack noticing the snake skin on the ground. It lay deflated, looking like it could have been part of the vines that covered its pit. I picked it up and stroked my thumb along its outer side. Its textured leather reminded me of sliding my fingers along the vinyl lace tablecloth in our kitchen at home and my jaw trembled.

I rushed over to Richard who was placing chunks of meat on sticks and dropped the skin in front of him. "Here, send this to your mother. Tell her the good luck is transferred to her."

Richard's eyes widened. "You sure, man?"

Wesley dropped a stack of sticks next to Richard's rock. I nodded and began walking away, hearing Wesley's voice in the background. "Man, I could see that baby as a belt and hat band with enough left over for a double wide tie."

Diego was slitting his snake straight down the belly while Leon sat next to him whittling points on his stack of sticks. Jack placed rocks in a circle, flat side up. Joe followed him, setting a blue cube on every other one. Moustafa dripped peach juice from cans into a camouflage cup. I began for my pack to get my can and noticed Billy stood behind it, his arms crossed in front of his chest.

I was about to say, *You waiting for orders to launch a nuclear warhead?* when Joe looked up at him and said, "Man, invite the sarge. He needs something to gnaw on besides that damned radio."

Diego raised his knife, thin streaks of meat stuck to its surface. "Yes, get his ear away from that cursed Lieutenant Hutchison."

I had four cans in my hand and was checking labels when I turned to Joe. "Cursed?"

Joe was cutting another blue cube into smaller pieces. "Made a bad decision, sent a platoon into an ambush."

Moustafa slammed his cup on a rock. "Bad decision nothing. Pure racism is what it was. Wiped out two whole squads of Negroes demanding fair treatment. Conducts business the white country club way, you can't control 'em, execute 'em."

Wesley whistled long and slow. "Sounds like a man in need of a lesson. Is he tight white, sticks to his own 'cause he don't know no better, or fright white, scared out of his mind of dark skin?"

Moustafa scratched the side of his face. "Ole Hutch? He's the I'm the man and you can't touch me type, won't even look at you when he tells you not to make no waves or he'll assign you to the thirteenth valley."

Wesley's head tilted to the side. "What's that?"

Moustafa's back straightened, like he was suddenly called to attention. "It's known as the valley of no return. Word is there's only two ways out, first as a POW, or second if you're luckier, in a body bag."

A cold rush ran down my back, making the sweat feel like ice.

"Damn." Wesley snapped all three sticks in his hand at once. "Sounds like old Hutch is a hanging judge and lynch mob in one."

Moustafa poured juice from another can in his cup. "That's right, and not about to change his ways. But one thing I'm gonna do is get him to assign me, a black man, to a desk job."

Wesley tapped his broken sticks onto his palm. "You don't think you should stay away from that man?"

Moustafa's chin jerked up like it was struck from underneath. "Can't no more than I can avoid the VC. Either one would kill me if they had the chance. What I want is my ass behind a desk, then I've won the war."

"That's a lot to want." Wesley reached forward to pick up another stick. "For me, I just want to go home on two legs."

Moustafa opened another can and shook his head. "My father always told me to climb to higher ground. I'm just putting one foot up the mountain."

I wanted to ask how many desk jobs there were when the sarge's voice boomed into our group. "Better fill up those bellies fast 'cause Hutchison didn't take kindly to the news. He says there's tunnels and he's sending us back. He's calling in thirty minutes to say when."

Diego stood, his skinned snake hanging by his side and pointed his smeared knife towards the sarge. "We already looked, didn't you tell him that?"

The sarge folded his arms in front of his chest and leaned towards Diego. "Oh, I told him all right, you bet your sweet ass I told him. But he claims you didn't go far enough, says there's a village beyond that hill and the tunnels should be close to that, maybe even a direct site."

Diego's knife slid against his leg. "No one told us to go to no village."

"That was then!" The sarge's arms broke apart and both pointed to the ground at once. "This is now."

Diego's hand with the knife jerked upward. "And what are we supposed to do? Ask the villagers to escort us to the entrance?"

The sarge's chest swelled and his eyes shifted across each of us in a quick sweep. "Listen, men, HQ got word the VC are planning an attack on Long Binh. Now I don't have to tell you what that means. Half our supplies and ammunitions are on Long Binh and I don't think any of you want to do without those."

My throat tightened as I stared at the snake skin draped over Diego's shoulder, afraid that my luck was now gone.

The sarge continued. "Destroying all tunnels within fifty miles of Long Binh is top priority. And there have been helicopters shot at with automatic weapons from near that village, so there's no question it's a hot site."

Billy threw a rock in the air and stepped forward to catch it. "Why don't they just bomb the whole friggin' area?"

The sarge turned to look at him, shifting his weight from one foot to the other. "It's not that simple. Above ground bombs don't destroy tunnels. You have to get in them to blow them up. And we can't get in them until we know where they are."

Wesley placed his free hand on his hip. "One thing I'm saying up front is I ain't going down one of those holes, just so we's clear on that."

The sarge's head snapped to Wesley's direction. "Didn't know I had a new lieutenant in my ranks today. Should I salute you, sir?"

Wesley grinned and shook his head. "No, man, it ain't like that, I just know my rights, and no enlisted men can be forced down no tunnels."

The sarge squinted at Wesley with only one eye. "No one said you would be forced, Private uh…" He pointed his arm towards Wesley and snapped his fingers.

"Bates," said Wesley, straightening his back to stand taller. "Wesley Bates."

"Private Bates," began the sarge, pausing to brush his hand through his hair, "for your information, and everyone else who stepped on Vietnam soil for the first time today, the U.S. armed forces gets KKKs to go in the tunnels for us."

Wesley's eyes glared back at the sarge. "What's this about KKKs here in Vietnam?"

I gripped my knee and squeezed, feeling my fingers pulse hard into its sides.

The sarge shook his head and stared at the ground. "For you newbies to this country, KKK in Vietnam stands for Khmer Kampuchea Kron. They are Cambodian nationals who live in Vietnam, but sympathize with Cambodia and see the North Vietnamese as the enemy who has already taken two of their provinces. They hate the VC even more than we do."

Wesley broke another stick in his hand with a loud crack. "I never said I hate anybody. If I kill it's only to go home alive. But that don't mean I'm going to fight alongside anyone called KKK!"

The sarge's right cheek twitched to the side in a momentary half smile before returning to its previous flat. "No need to get worked up, Bates. I told you, it has nothing to do with the KKK back home."

Moustafa pointed a stick with snake meat on it towards Wesley. "Don't let them fool you, man, KKK here is the same as it is at home. They're vigilantes made legitimate by the American government. The KKK is used here same as it is at home, to kill people just 'cause they're not white."

The sarge stamped his foot, sending a dark cloud of dust up to his knees. "Don't start that crap! The whole world is unfair. But we've got a job to do here and your own ass depends on how well you do it!"

Moustafa's arms raised towards both Leon and Wesley. "You darkies believe that?"

The sarge stared at the side of Moustafa's head, but didn't say a word. My hands squeezed in and out of fists while the murmurs of the jungle screamed in my ears.

"Sarge!" Richard's voice was like a gun blast in the silence. "If that village hides a tunnel we're good as mice in a snake hole. They won't tell us where it is!"

"'We'll beat it out of them!" Billy jumped in the center of the circle with his fists in fighting position.

The sarge smiled before turning back to Richard. "That's right, we're U.S. Marines. No one's tougher than us."

Jack punched his arm straight up in the air. "Marines, the kick ass brigade!"

Billy shot his fist in the air next to Jack's. "Marines, top of the food chain, kings of the world!"

Diego hoisted his skinned snake and shouted, "Top of the food chain or not, I'm hungry! If we have to hump I want to eat while the eatin's good. Are we ready to barbecue?"

Joe flicked his lighter, holding the flame next to a blue cube and turned to the sarge. "All right with you, boss?"

The sarge nodded. "Fire it up. Just be ready when the lieutenant's call comes."

Joe lit each piece, making a circle of flares that looked like candles on a birthday cake. I made a wish that the lieutenant's orders would never come, but blowing out the flames was not possible.

Moustafa dripped sauce on each stick of meat as Wesley sprinkled them with cayenne and distributed them to each man. I took mine, holding them over a flame, not believing I'd ever eat it as I watched the ivory-pink colored flesh sear into brown. I turned the meat, holding it above the flame like the others did, till I saw Joe put his into the middle and let it catch fire like kids do with marshmallows. After a minute he removed them and blew out the flames. What showed were thick masses of black on the outside no longer bearing any resemblance to snake. It looked better that way and I stuck both my pieces in my flame, too, watching them catch fire and burn. They could have been pieces of coal or wood or burnt hot dogs like we had in summer camp. I pulled mine from the fire and brought them near my face for a whiff. The smoke rushed up my nose and I bit into a chunk, feeling it sizzle on my tongue. I huffed on it for a minute as my stomach grumbled and then began to chew. It was like the burned ends of toast and I bit off a bigger piece next, listening to my own noisy chews along with everyone else's.

I was about to take another bite when Joe held up his empty stick, and announced, "When we're all back in the world, every one of you is invited for a real barbecue at my house."

Wesley stopped chewing for a moment and raised his half eaten meat. "I'll bring the hot sauce and a hot date."

There was laughter and mumbling, but mostly more chomping on the chewy meat. I began my second piece, imagining myself back in my apartment, Joe's call ringing in the background, but then a real ring sounded. It was the sarge's radio phone. I swallowed the chunk in my mouth whole and began to cough.

* * * * *

Joe lay down on his camou blanket to catch some sleep. I did the same, glad the mission would not begin till daybreak. Diego was assigned to the first watch from eight to midnight.

I used my pack for a pillow feeling a hard edge from my ammo stick into the back of my head. I repositioned the pack, but then it was a c-ration can. I decided to leave it and close my eyes, tired enough to sleep through anything that protruded into my head.

Joe shifted to his side, his back turned to me. I watched his back move up and down with his breaths, then closed my eyes seeing a blackness that swirled itself into a funnel that went back into a point. I found myself next to the VC soldier I'd killed that afternoon. His stomach was blasted wide open and lumps of gray intestines mixed with red clots floated on top. I stared at them, afraid I'd throw up when two large diamonds appeared in their midst. Their sparkling brilliance mesmerized me and I became excited that if I sent one to Naomi it would win back her love. I reached towards the one on the left and they both leaped straight up in the air, no longer diamonds, but suddenly the eyes of a snake. It lunged for my face as I sat frozen in place, screaming, "Help!"

I felt myself being shaken and screamed, "No!"

The shaking got harder and I knew I had to grab the snake before it destroyed me. I opened my eyes and there was Joe, shaking me by the shoulders. "Wake up Scout, it's only a dream."

I felt a tightening around my chest. "No, it's the snake!"

He flicked his lighter next to my body. "Look, man, no snakes."

I looked down, seeing only my legs when Diego leaned over us. "What's going on?"

Joe held the lighter up to his face. "The scout had a nightmare. Vietnam special."

I sat up on my knees. "It seemed so real, the snake coming for my eyes."

Diego crouched and looked at me straight on. "The snakes are dead. We ate them. Their only revenge will be the runs."

I slid my hand down my face. "It jumped out of the dead body."

Joe's lighter flicked on and off. "That's all tricks in your head. It's a nightmare, nothing more."

Diego pointed his M-16 back over his shoulder. "Listen to Joe. He had to tell me the same thing when I was new."

I shifted back out of Diego's shadow noticing Moustafa sitting on a log cleaning his gun, the bright moon shining on his spot. I pointed in his direction. "Don't he sleep?"

Joe leaned back on his heels. "Not much, most of us don't. You get used to it."

I grasped my own arms and squeezed. "I'll never get used to it. It's wrong, all of it, so wrong."

Joe's finger drew a circle in the dirt. "You feel guilt about that kill?"

My breaths stopped and my body froze. They both stared at me and I forced myself to swallow to release my jaw. "Yes. It's his war, not mine. I had no reason to take his life."

Joe's hand blotted out the circle. "You'd rather he killed you or me or Diego or maybe Moustafa?"

"No, not that." I stared back into the dark streaks on his face. "We don't belong here. It's wrong."

"Sure it's wrong." Joe slid directly in front of me. "But he was shooting at us. And don't kid yourself. The South Vietnamese don't want to be communist any more than we do. They need us."

Spots moved across Joe's face from shifting leaves above. "We're military pawns, doesn't that bother you?"

One of Joe's shoulders shrugged. "It's the kids that get to me. The fear I see in their eyes because the north wants to take over their land and torture their parents. Man, if someone did that to my kids, I'd want other people to come help me."

My hands dropped to my knees. "You got kids?"

His lips spread, showing glistening teeth. "Not yet, but Marie and I want a whole mess of them. Kids and a house and a yard big enough for a baseball game with a barbecue on the side. We're getting married soon as I get back."

I wondered why Naomi and I never considered all that when Diego slapped his hand on his M-16. "Got it all worked out, don't you?"

Joe's eyebrows twitched. "Sure, why not?"

Diego scanned behind him before looking back. "'Cause things don't work out like Ozzie and Harriet, that's why. Take my sister. She's got three kids, no husband, she's stuck on welfare and there's drug dealers in front of her house. Who protects them?"

Joe poked Diego's firearm. "You do."

Diego's eyes squinted. "Lot of good I can do from here."

Joe gave his M-16 a shove. "You'll make it back, we'll all make it back. You'll see."

~ Chapter 6 ~

Highlands Village

This was the second day the mission was delayed. I sat on the rock stained with the snake's blood, unable to stop thinking about Naomi. If only I hadn't left her picture at home.

Moustafa had been lecturing non-stop to Leon and Wesley since yesterday. They sat on stumps while he preached about Allah and Islam and how it was the only true religion of blacks no matter where in the world they were born. I watched from thirty feet away as Leon jolted his gaze to the trees beyond Moustafa, reacting to a noise. It was the break I had been waiting for and I began to get up, but then he looked back at Moustafa. I shifted on the rock, feeling like a door had slammed in my face. I was anxious to talk to him about whether or not I should write to Naomi, tell her how much I missed her and ask for a photo. Leon's feelings for Dolores made me sure he would understand, but it had to be to Leon alone. Wesley would give me an earful on how I should forget any woman that would dump me. And Moustafa still called me kid.

Moustafa began to cough and turned away from his disciples. I walked towards them, hoping that after a day and a half, Moustafa would take my intrusion as a chance to rest his voice. I certainly didn't want a repeat of yesterday when he pointed to me and proclaimed as if speaking to a large congregation, *The white devils don't want us to speak. They purposely stop our solidarity to keep us slaves.*

I had shouted back, *I'm no white devil. I just want to speak to Leon.*

But Moustafa had turned away from me and spoke to Leon and Wesley only, *Allah commands you to resist the temptation of white friendship. Their sole intention is to destroy you.*

You don't know my intention, I had shouted back, *you don't even know my name!*

Moustafa had brushed his hands down his arms, like whisking away dirt, then went on. *Temptations are all around us, disguised in innocent forms...* Leon had glanced at me and shrugged, as if to say another time. But another time hadn't come and my conflicts over whether or not to write to Naomi, and what I should or shouldn't say, had become increasingly desperate.

Moustafa continued coughing and I went directly to Leon, seeing this as my only chance. Leon turned to me and was about to speak when Moustafa loomed before me, his finger pointed between my head and the sky, his voice resonating into the air, "Allah's word is too sacred to disturb. Unless your skin turns black, don't interrupt us again. Kindly leave this holy ground and let us serve Allah in peace."

Wesley grinned at my dismissal but Leon raised his eyebrows and tilted his head in my direction, giving me hope he would talk to me later, though I still wished it could be now.

Moustafa spread his arms out just wide enough to include Leon and Wesley, then proceeded on. "Allah loves all his black children, but in that love he commands them to rise above the oppression that's cast upon them by Satan's white race, to cast aside the names that Satan's white race has forced on them, to cast aside the menial jobs Satan's white race has forced them to take, to cast aside the slums Satan's white race has forced them to live in..."

I went back to the blood stained rock, angry at being linked to Satan and hurt that Leon chose Moustafa over me. I picked up my pad from the ground and began to draw what I hoped would look like Naomi's face. Her lips curved up on one side, but then as the line went across, it took a downward slant, turning it into a sneer. I drew over it, but it only made the sneer more pronounced. It seemed she was mocking me, or worse, scorning me. No, it couldn't be, she hadn't read my letter yet. I drew her hand with my envelope in its grip. If only I could draw her ripping it open like she was anxious to see what I wrote. My pencil touched the paper, but in my head I pictured her ripping it into a hundred pieces and throwing them in the trash. I squeezed my eyes, feeling them assaulted by a knife that stabbed all the way to my heart, when Joe and Diego returned from the sarge.

"Going back is bad luck, Amigo, don't forget that." Diego sat on the rock next to mine.

Joe crouched in front of him and drew lines in the dirt with a stick. "Stop with the grandmother crap. We made it once, we'll make it again."

Diego shoved his foot over the fresh lines. "You're wrong, man, luck is a one time gift, after that it tempts fate and God don't like that."

My mind pictured Naomi slamming the cover down on the trash.

Joe hit his stick on a rock. "Orders are orders whether God likes them or not."

My hand squeezed the pencil, anxious to begin the unwritten letter, Leon's help or not. "What are the orders?"

Joe's mouth twitched on one side while the other stayed flat. "He's sending us ahead on recon, you and me."

My chest pounded as if I'd been shoved, though no one had touched me. "Why me?"

Joe stuck his stick in the ground between us and leaned into it. "He says we already know the lay of the land and he likes your instincts. Says the two of us alone can get close enough to report on the activities in the village without the squad walking into a trap."

I pressed the pencil point into the paper, feeling it snap like that twig I stepped on my first hour out in the jungle. "But what about us?"

Joe drew a zigzag with the stick. "We'll keep our distance."

Diego whistled a low, single note. "You lucky devils…"

The center of the pencil snapped, slamming my hand into the pad. "I'm not a devil and nothing in this is lucky!"

Diego stepped back putting his hands up in the air. "Take it easy, man, didn't know you had grenades for stones."

Joe chuckled and tapped Diego on the thigh with his stick. "Maybe that's how the scout gets his radar?"

Diego shoved the stick off his leg. "Don't alter my precious rocks, amigo. Do what you want with yours but mine are going home as original equipment."

"You two dressing for the prom? Get a move on!" We looked up to see the sarge scowling down at us.

Joe stood and looked at me. "Ready?"

I grasped tight to the pad on my lap. "Don't I get time to prepare?"

Diego slapped his knee. "Three seconds to write goodbye letters, fill up on ammo, and pack the Mickey Mouse compass that points home to mommy."

I watched Joe grab his pack and turned to Diego. "I'll take that compass."

"Amen, brother." Diego began staring into the air beyond me. "Cuccifritos, panellas, empenadas, my mama can cook!"

My mouth began to water even though I'd never heard of those foods before. I wanted to ask Diego what they were, when Joe pushed my pack into my stomach. "Time to push on. Anything you need to know I'll explain on the move."

I followed Joe, listening to Diego in the background. "And flan, man, cut me a double hunk with caramel dripping down the sides."

I swallowed hard, disappointed that the thin spit in my mouth wasn't thick and sweet.

The sarge walked next to Joe holding up the map in his hand. "Go west northwest marking the trail to here. We'll leave when the interpreter arrives, supposed to be in thirty minutes." He then turned to me. "Joe tells me you said the ground felt too quiet for tunnels at 37."

I tripped on a tree root and took a quick step to catch my balance. "Only a hunch, Sarge, I had no way to know."

His hand went up in a stop motion. "And at the hill you said you didn't smell any VC in the wind."

My ankle began to turn but I managed to set it straight. "A joke, that's all."

The sarge turned and blocked my path, forcing me to stand still. "I don't take any observations as a joke, private. I take them as a sixth sense, something we desperately need around here where the only help we get are intelligence reports not worth squat. We rely on Joe to spot traps, but now he says you saw one he missed and you felt a sniper's position before he did. Between the two of you I expect the entire squad to arrive at this village intact to carry out our mission. Do I make myself clear?"

My back stiffened taller like I was back in boot camp. "Very clear, Sarge. But with all due respect, I'm new and I'm sure there are others with more experience that will see more than me."

He met my gaze head on. "I don't need a private telling me whose talents I want. That's my call, understood?"

I nodded. "Understood."

Joe rapped on the radio transmitter hanging from his pack. "I'll check in when we get there."

The sarge stepped aside. "Good, and teach the scout kid here how to use that thing."

"Right away, Sarge." Joe began towards the trail we took yesterday and I followed, relieved at moving away from the sarge, but more worried about where we were headed." Joe's fingers pointed behind him to the transmitter. "Crank it then press the button to speak. Think you can do that?"

It looked like a phone from old movies and I pictured Naomi waiting nervously near one for my call. "Guess so, how far is the range?"

"Depending on land obstructions, anywhere up to fifty miles." Joe's body leaned forward as the foliage thickened and grazed the top of his head.

I looked to the sides, trying to grasp my surroundings, when Joe pointed to a fallen log. "Wires can be hidden in the vines."

I stared down at the interwoven, browned vines as I raised my foot to step over them. My toe scraped their top and I heard explosions in my ears, but then realized there was only silence. Joe was moving ahead and I quickened my pace, trying to catch up. I feared my clumsiness was more typical of me than what Joe expected, when I arrived right on his heels. "Why did you tell those things to the sarge? I can't really feel tunnels or smell VC."

His head moved in a deliberate arch while he forged ahead. "Maybe you can. All I know is you saved me twice. That makes you my good luck."

I stared up ahead at a clump of dead leaves hanging from a branch, wondering if that was their natural position or if they had been altered. "What if my luck has run out?"

"Then we're both in trouble." Joe's head shifted in broader sweeps than before.

I kept quiet after that, following his footsteps, afraid he and the sarge had made a fatal mistake about me.

Joe crouched lower as he continued on, his shoulders the same height as his waist. I crouched as low as I could, to about chest height, feeling branches scrape the back of my shirt while I wished for the first time in my life to be shorter. Taller no longer seemed more powerful. Closer to the ground felt much less a target, and distinct brackish smells suddenly became extremely important, as did the differing textures under my feet and sounds from any distance.

A sudden burst of flight by several birds straight above made my breath stop till I heard the chatter of monkeys follow it. I pictured the old man monkey faces gritting their teeth, wishing they had reached the birds in time, though maybe some of them did. And there was the unsettling buzz of insects that abruptly invaded my hearing, but faded as we kept moving.

Joe cut branches every twenty yards, indicating our trail to the squad. He had explained that a branch straight down is for straight ahead, cut from the front shows a turn to the right, and cut from the back means left. But so far all his signs were for straight ahead. I wondered if the VC were reading our trail and if they used the same system, when Joe stopped right next to the snake pit we'd nearly fallen in two days ago. It was uncovered, left that way by us with no sign that it had been touched. I hoped it meant the VC hadn't been in these woods since and with any luck, they no longer cared about this section of land.

Joe pulled out his compass with one hand and swiped at his forehead with the other.

My glance flickered momentarily on his chest. "Feel anything?"

Joe looked up from his compass towards his left. "Time to shift twenty degrees northwest."

His arm pointed and then he began in that direction. I followed, realizing that the terrain was changing. We were suddenly in an area of tall grass, the elephant grass Joe had warned me about the day before, when he was talking of his previous missions.

He'd told me, *You can't believe how sharp it is, seven-foot razors waiting to cut every inch of your flesh. Never have your sleeves rolled up in that stuff no matter how hot it is.*

I protected my face with my arm, feeling the blades scrape the outside of my sleeve. My breaths turned to shallow pants and my heartbeat resonated hard in my ears. I peered under my elbow, trying to see how much more of this there was, but vision was impossible beyond a few feet. The VC could be a mere three arm lengths away and I'd never know. Sweat streamed down my sides and I wondered if Joe was oozing sweat from the center of his chest. But the sounds of Joe pushing through the massive leaves weren't slowing down. It took all my focused strength to keep from getting cut while moving fast and not losing him from my sight.

Another ten minutes of the grass, then it abruptly ended. I stood inside its edge, seeing a clearing that dipped down to a valley. My breaths went from barely reaching the back of my mouth to sifting down my throat as I scanned the patchwork of small fields below. The seven huts set against the edge of the next hill were similar to a peaceful painting in my grandmother's house.

I began to step towards it when Joe grabbed my arm and held me back. "Don't be a fool, they have constant surveillance."

I glared at the imprisoning shoots I had to stay within while Joe raised his M-16 and began peering through the scope. "Damn, there's chickens running around."

I peered through my own scope, noticing a narrow stream running through fields. "Farms have chickens, so what?"

Joe shifted his gaze to the left. "Stateside farms have chickens, but here if they're lucky it's rice and a few rows of corn or soybeans. Luxuries like chicken are long gone. This place must supply the VC."

I scanned the fields, finally seeing the chickens. "That should make the lieutenant happy."

Joe gave a quick chuckle. "You met him yet?"

I lowered my scope and turned to Joe. "Only real quick. When we touched down in Long Binh he got us on the trucks. He didn't say much then but hearing him scream through the radio at the sarge don't make me want to meet him again."

"That's him at his best, you ain't seen his bad side yet." Joe paused then exhaled a long, low whistle. "Damn, look at that."

"What?" I raised my scope in the direction he had his. There were two kids, a boy wearing only shorts, probably around eleven or twelve, and a girl his same size wearing a straight tan dress with long hair tied behind her back. She had what looked like a doll in her arms, until its head moved. "A baby," I gasped, watching the girl's gentle sways keeping it calm. The sight of them held me captive when I realized my gun was pointing at them, only I couldn't take my eyes away. Something about the girl's protective arms making the baby feel safe. If she only knew what was coming, or was it better she didn't know?

"The kid just snagged one of the chickens, the sarge has to know right away." Joe draped his gun over his shoulder and reached towards his back for the transmitter.

I pulled it from his pack and handed it to him. "What's the big deal if a kid plays with chickens?"

Joe turned the crank without answering and I looked back through my scope, seeing the boy hold the chicken on the ground and stomp on its neck.

"Sarge, you there?" Joe's voice was crisp and tight.

"Ten-four."

"It's a VC supply post, all right. There's damned chickens running around and they're getting ready to prepare one right now."

I watched the boy leave the first one on the ground and start chasing another. "He's going for a second one."

Joe glanced at me while talking into the transmitter. "You hear that? At least two chickens. Looks like they're planning a big barbecue for the VC. Tell that cook from Cincinnati to bring the hot sauce."

The sarge's voice crackled from the box. "What's your estimated window?"

"My guess?" Joe scanned the next hill like it had a clock. "There's one chicken's already killed. Two hours if they begin cleaning it soon."

"Roger." There was popping static from the radio, then the voice again. "We'll increase our pace, meet you in twenty minutes and go right in. Over and out."

I watched Joe coil the cord. "At least the VC are smart enough to want chicken instead of snake. I wish that's what we had."

Joe stuffed the phone back in his pack. "Believe me, they'd rather make it for you than the VC."

I leaned into a blade's shadow so I didn't have to squint. "Aren't the villagers VC?"

Joe wiped his upper sleeve across his forehead. "They're tortured if they don't cooperate. They're only VC out of fear."

I looked in the direction of the girl and the baby, but couldn't see them without the scope. "And we're going to save them?"

Joe leaned forward, shading his eyes with his hand. "Destroying the tunnels will slow their invasion into the south. It helps."

I sat down from my crouch, shifting slowly to make sure the blades didn't cut into my pants, then raised the scope to my eye. The kids were no longer in the same spot. I scanned to the left finding them by the center hut, the boy entering with a dead chicken in each hand. The girl waited outside with the baby, rocking it in her arms till he returned. He was carrying two buckets and they headed for the field. "They're going for water. I guess it's cooking time."

Joe nodded and pointed to the edge of the field. "Must be, 'cause there's an old man that keeps staring into the woods, like he's expecting company."

I pushed away a blade blocking my view of him. "And we crash the party with guns and grenades?"

"You got a Betty Crocker cake?" Joe turned his scope towards the woods. "Besides, man, we're hoping to miss the party. With luck we're in and out before they arrive."

I watched the girl shift the baby to her other arm, feeling like one of those raw chickens was being shoved down my throat. I leaned back and pulled the shirt from the sweat on my chest, taking a deep breath before I could speak. "Like you said, Joe, they didn't choose to be VC, and there's kids and a baby, so what makes them the enemy?"

Joe put his gun down and looked directly at me. "Look, Scout, I don't like this any more than you do. But it's no joke, those VC up north are vicious and the people in the south are terrified. They need us, we have to help."

A raw chicken taste welled up in my mouth and made me spit on the ground. "Marines against peasants, that's how we help the people?"

"Ain't saying it don't stink." Joe slapped his gun against his chest. "But to help the right people, yes, that's how we help. You haven't been here long enough to know there's no innocents in this country, not a peasant and not a kid."

71

Joe picked up his scope again. I raised mine, looking for those kids, finding them at the stream. The girl bent low, dipped her hand in the water, and used it to wash the baby's face. The boy sat in the stream's center, splashing his own chest, then switched to thrusting water at the girl. She immediately put a protective arm around the baby, but instead of turning away, she kicked water on the boy, her mouth spread wide as if laughing. I was surprised they could do this in spite of the war. The rancid chicken taste returned to my mouth and I spit it onto the grass next to me, watching it slide down a blade. It probably was better the kids didn't know what was coming in an hour's time, or less.

I looked back towards them but they had moved. The boy was running with a bucket in each hand while the girl held onto the baby, keeping up with his strides. They reached the center hut at the same time as the old man who had been in the field. His natural stooping posture leaned further forward towards them and pointed to the left. Both kids looked and listened, then bowed, allowing him to enter the hut before them.

I switched my focus to where the old man had pointed. "You think that's where the tunnel is?"

Joe was focused beyond that spot. "Maybe."

I began scanning the ground for a hole. "You think they'll bring the food to the tunnel so Charley don't have to come out?"

Joe lowered his gun and turned to me. "Would help us. We could add a few grenades for seasoning."

I looked at the radiophone wedged into Joe's pack. "If we find the hole we can forget the village, right?"

Joe turned back to the woods and began scanning. "I don't see the tunnel, do you?"

I glanced back to the middle hut, though there was no smoke to indicate that the cooking had started. "We can follow the food when it's ready."

Joe laughed while continuing to look through his scope. "And you want a pizza delivered to us while you're at it?"

"Wisecrack all you want. This could work and we wouldn't have to storm the village." I tapped Joe's leg and pointed up to the radio transmitter. "Ask the sarge."

Joe shrugged and dropped his pack. "Hell, it's not up to me." He pulled the phone and turned the crank. "Sarge."

"Roger, ten four."

"The scout boy here thinks the chicken's going to be delivered to the tunnel and we should hold off and follow it."

"What?" There was a crackling pause and my sweaty palm slid its way down my M-16. "Tell him those tunnels are better protected than Fort Knox and the plan stays as is. The villagers tell us the location and the two Cambodians HQ sent go in and blow them up. Are we clear on that?"

"Roger." Joe turned to me and raised his eyebrows. "Clear as a bell."

The radio squawked. "Good. Sit tight and watch for changes."

"Sitting tight, roger and out." Joe pressed the off button and placed the receiver back in his pack.

I surveyed the edge of the woods, still desperate to find the opening. Maybe it was just inside of that line. And why did the woods stop at that point? Was it naturally like that, or had it been done by these villagers, or maybe their ancestors? And did that line hold any significance for the tunnel? The darkness of the woods beyond it made me uncomfortable. I shifted my position, feeling a blade scrape on my pants.

Joe tapped on his watch. "The squad should be here in five minutes."

A shudder ran down my body and I suddenly envisioned a whole load of Viet Cong rushing through the field.

Joe lifted his pack and slipped it on. "No stopping this now, time to get ready."

I stood, glancing across the valley, wishing I could stay within this elephant grass forever when there was a crunching on thick blades behind me and Moustafa appeared.

"Tell me, Scouts, is this going to be easy?"

Neither Joe nor I answered and Moustafa's foot stamped next to mine. "Son of a bitch, I better be behind a desk after this."

The rest of the squad came up behind him and formed a loose huddle around us. The sergeant had a colonel on one side and the two Cambodians on the other, before stepping into the center and looking at Joe and me. "Which hut has the chickens?"

I pointed in its direction. "The middle one."

The sergeant turned to look straight at it, took a sweep of its surroundings, then scanned all of us. "This is how it plays. Joe, you go in with Billy, Jack, Diego, and Richard from the left. Moustafa, you take the scout boy, Wesley, and Leon around from the right. I'll go straight to the center with Colonel Mitchell and the Cambodians to set up interrogation. Operational plan is one of you watches the outside while the rest clears everyone out of their huts, hands tied behind their backs, even old people and kids, and bring them to the center hut. That's where we'll get the information we need, understood?"

The raw chicken taste returned to my mouth, but I was afraid to spit in case he took it as an insult.

The sarge gripped his M-16 with both hands and pulled it out from his chest. "And do not discharge your weapons unless absolutely necessary. Alerting the VC is the last thing we want. Use your knives if there's a choice. Now let's get in there fast and quiet, and take these gooks by surprise."

I swallowed the rancid taste in my mouth and rushed behind Moustafa, Wesley and Leon, who moved out faster than I expected. I followed them down the hill to the edge of the field, straight to the hut on the right. Starting from the first hut we removed an old woman and younger woman with a baby, then four women and an old man, and in the third, an old couple, and brought them all to the center hut. The others were already there with Richard and Diego stationed at the door, each setting up grenade launchers. The Cambodians were patrolling the outside far ends of the village.

Inside, the hut smelled dank from the earthen floor and was dark from only one window and no electric lights. The villagers were bunched together on the right side of the room, all partially stooped forward from their hands tied behind their backs. The boy and girl I had seen in the field were next to each other in the front of the group.

Wesley, Moustafa, Joe, Leon, Jack, Billy and I surrounded the group with our M-16s pointed directly at them. The sergeant and the Colonel were on the left side of the room, facing the crowd. The raw chickens were on a table in the corner behind the sergeant. Their taste filled my mouth making me want to puke. I turned back to the crowd, trying to swallow it away.

The sarge pointed to the boy and girl I had been watching before. "Billy, bring those kids over here."

Billy grabbed onto the ropes that held their hands and pulled them up higher than necessary as he pushed them forward, straining their shoulders behind them. I wanted to yell out to them that it would be over soon and they could go back to splashing in the river, but aside from not knowing their language, I couldn't break ranks and undermine the sarge's authority. Sticking together would get it over with faster.

I watched, feeling that as long as I had my eyes on them, they would be safe, and waited for a moment when they would look towards me and I could give them a nod of reassurance. The boy's features tightened and never shifted as he made his way towards the sergeant. The girl had two thin streams of tears on each side of her nose, her eyes continually glancing behind her at Billy's gun.

A woman from the right side of the room screamed and threw herself forward on the floor towards the kids. The girl shrieked and started for her, but Billy yanked hard on her rope, not letting her more than one step in that direction. The woman started inching forward, but the sergeant yelled for her to be stopped and Jack put his gun two inches from her head. She lay there, trembling, staring at the kids, her mouth opened but silent.

Billy grinned like he did when he chanted *Nuke the Gooks* back in boot camp, and continued to push the kids towards the sarge. I wanted to grab their ropes away from him and lower the kids' arms from their painful angle, then punch Billy in his lousy grin. I hoped to get all those chances later, after the sergeant found out the location of the tunnel.

A toddler on the right side of the room began to cry and then several voices erupted at once.

The sergeant shouted above them all, "If you cooperate with me, no one gets hurt!" Colonel Mitchell immediately followed with a translation in Vietnamese. Some of the noise stopped but most continued.

The sergeant yelled again, louder this time, "Everybody shut up or we'll shoot your children right where they stand." He pointed to the boy and girl now directly to his right. I felt sweat surge down my face while Colonel Mitchell imitated him in the same angry tone. I turned from the group to watch the kids, though I knew that was not proper procedure. The room quieted and I returned one eye on the villagers while I wiped the other side of my face on my shoulder.

There was a long, silent pause as the sergeant scanned the mass of villagers. Most of their gazes were down on the floor instead of at him. The sergeant slammed on a table causing everyone to look up. "Who's in charge here?" Colonel Mitchell translated, adding a stamp of his foot, but all they received in response were silent stares.

The sarge's eyes narrowed, then he began to scream, "I want the person who talks to the Viet Cong!" Colonel Mitchell screamed in the same tone. All sounds of breathing stopped and most villagers bent lower to the ground.

"If that's how you want it," the sergeant raised his M-16 in the air. "Billy, bring those kids right here." Billy pushed them in front of the sarge, continuing to hold the ropes unnecessarily high. I turned to the kids, desperate to be between them and Billy.

"Whose kids are these?" The sergeant glared into the crowd. Colonel Mitchell translated, but again, no one answered.

The sergeant pulled out his survival knife and pressed its point to the boy's temple. The boy winced and the woman lying on the floor shrieked.

The sarge pounded on the table with his other hand. "Bring her here!"

Jack brought the mother forward and Billy gave the boy's rope to Jack also, keeping the boy next to the sarge. Billy then wrapped his arm around the girl, pulled out his own knife and pressed its blade against her throat. The mother quickly glanced at the girl, her cheeks drenched with tears, but then her face was grabbed by the sarge and forced to look at him.

I had hoped the sarge would tell Billy to put away his knife, but he began yelling at the woman. "We know you're preparing food for the Viet Cong. Where is their tunnel?" Colonel Mitchell yelled the translation.

The mother wildly shook her head while crying words in Vietnamese. Colonel Mitchell yelled back as if admonishing her for lying.

The woman cried out again and Colonel Mitchell returned with furious words. The woman sobbed a desperate sounding plea when Colonel Mitchell turned to the sergeant with his finger pointed at the woman. "She refuses to tell!"

The sergeant pressed his knife harder on the boy's head, sending a line of blood trickling down. The mother started shrieking and Colonel Mitchell yelled back at her in a flurry of words. The boy then said some angered words to his mother, and Jack jerked him back with the rope. Some of the boy's blood dripped down to the ground and the mother suddenly became completely silent.

The sergeant moved his knife to the boy's chest, angling it to his heart. "Tell us the location of the tunnel!"

The woman spoke in desperate cries, though Colonel Mitchell shouted to the sarge she was still telling lies. The sergeant raised his knife, and in a sudden shock, stabbed the boy in the shoulder. My arms tensed and my finger tightened on my trigger, though my gun was still pointed at the crowd, not the sarge. Blood oozed down the boy's arm in two distinct streams, but his face remained stoic. I was desperate to see him playing in the stream again and became furious at the mother for not stopping this.

The sergeant moved his knife back to the boy's heart, screaming, "Next time's for real!"

The mother struggled against her own rope as her whole jaw trembled.

But it was Billy who broke the horrifying silence. "You want me to do this, Sarge?"

Billy's knife was on the girl's neck. A surge of vomit pushed up from my stomach. I was desperate to spit it out, but feared any distraction in this already too tense hut. I breathed in deep through my nose and swallowed the vomit back down, keeping my eyes on the girl.

The sergeant's arm waved sideways towards Billy. "Wait for orders, you hear me?"

Billy nodded and I swallowed once more against the horrid taste.

Angry words came from an old man in the corner and Colonel Mitchell yelled back at him, then turned to the whole crowd and screamed some more, his arms flailing out to his sides. He sounded like he was scolding, lecturing, and blaming them for their situation. He paused and stood with his hands on his hips as if waiting for a response.

No one spoke and he yelled more. Still no one spoke.

I stopped breathing, afraid that even that slightest shift in the air would spark an explosion.

Colonel Mitchell then threw his arms up in the air and turned to the sergeant. "These stubborn sons of a bitches refuse to tell!"

"Oh, they'll tell all right." The sergeant raised his knife with its fresh streaks of red, high in the air for everyone to see. The temperature in the room seemed to raise ten degrees and sweat gushed under my shirt. The sarge slid the knife down the boy's face and stopped at his chin. "Last chance for someone to tell where the tunnels are before this boy gets it." Colonel Mitchell translated in a cold, deliberate voice, his hands still on his hips.

Sobs from the boy's mother were the only sounds in the room.

The sarge pointed the knife to the villagers. "This is your fault!" He moved the knife back to the boy's face, then in a sudden motion, threw the knife straight down into the boy's foot.

The mother screamed and threw herself onto the floor next to her son's foot. The girl, too, had begun to scream, but abruptly stopped. I feared her throat had been slit, and turned to see her eyes and teeth both clamped shut and a thin line of blood running down her neck. She was alive, but Billy had pressed in too hard purposely to shut her up. Sweat gushed down my own neck, and I wished it was somehow possible to trade places with the girl and make this between Billy and me instead of him and her. But circumstances as they were, my hands were as tied as the villagers.

The boy remained silent, though his lips quivered and tears streamed from both his eyes. I felt if this didn't stop in the next minute, I would snap and start shooting, starting with Billy, then the boy's mother for letting this happen, then maybe even the sarge and the colonel. I glanced down at the boy's foot, seeing the bloody mass on the top, but also the stream from underneath. What was wrong with these people? Why didn't they end this?

Colonel Mitchell was yelling into the crowd. The old man yelled back and the colonel turned to the sarge, "Nothing. They'll tell you nothing and they don't give a shit about the boy."

"They'll talk!" The sergeant pulled his knife out of the boy's foot and raised it above his shoulder. "This time, they'll talk!"

"We'll make them talk!" It was Billy, followed by a loud howl, like an Indian war cry from an old western movie. I turned in time to see a quick flash of his knife, then it was covered with blood. The girl's eyes and mouth opened fully, her head slumped forward, staying there, limp and lifeless.

The mother wailed, her hands and face rubbing into the dirt on the ground.

Billy looked smug, pointing his bloody knife towards the crowd. "They'll talk now, Sarge. Ask them anything you want."

The girl's eyes flickered, and for a moment I thought she was still alive. But her eyes stopped and the next thing I knew the crosshairs in my scope were pointed dead center on the top of Billy's nose.

"Scout, no!" Joe's voice pierced through my brain and stopped my finger. A split second later would have been too late as I lowered my gun and ran out of the hut, gasping for air.

Diego turned to me from behind a grenade launcher. "You all right?"

"The kids." The words stuck in my throat and I couldn't go on.

Diego looked closer into my face as if checking for fresh wounds. "What happened?"

The stoic, tortured face of the boy flashed in my mind, followed by the girl's flickering eyes. "It's friggin' crazy in there, man. The sarge stabs the boy's foot and that wacko Billy slits the girl's throat, all for the God damned tunnel. Why don't they just tell us where it is, and we'll go? It could be so simple."

"Nothing's simple in this war." Diego put his hand on my shoulder. "To them it's about honor. To us it's about the next stinking place to blow up. The two ways of thinking don't mix."

I dropped myself into a sitting position on the ground and looked up at Diego, having to shelter my eyes from the glare behind him with my hand. "What kind of honor is that? If the mother had just told us, the girl would still be alive. Nothing else can make sense."

"Put like that, no honor at all," Diego extended a hand down to me.

I shook my head and grasped my legs, staring out across the stretches of farmed and scraggly earth towards the edge of the woods. The mist in the field made it seem like cellophane curtains hung in the air with shadowy dots behind them, like flies or bees. I looked through my scope to get a better view and saw the dots weren't insects at all. They were people setting up artillery on the edge of the forest!

Suddenly I grasped what was going on. The villagers knew the VC were out there and they'd kill them if they told. They hoped the Viet Cong would kill us first, before we hurt them. What they didn't know was that the weapons being set up across the field were aimed to kill them as much as us.

I jumped up. "Diego, they're out there, man. Look through your scope. I gotta tell the sarge. We're going to be shelled!"

I stormed inside. "Sarge, Charley's at the edge of the forest. They're setting up mortars and launchers. Could start firing any second."

But as soon as the words had blurted from my mouth, I saw the boy, blood oozing from his chest, being dropped from Billy's arms, right onto the girl where she lay on the ground. The mother fell on top of them with a wail that pierced my chest sharper than any knife could. I watched her, hands still tied behind her back, caressing both kids' motionless bodies with her face. I began for her to untie her hands so she could at least touch her dead children, but the sergeant stepped in front of her and announced to the squad, "Leave the villagers in this hut. Colonel, you get them tied together so they can't escape. The rest of you, outside, to fight for your flag and freedom."

Billy stepped closer to the sarge. "We still need the location. Give me another kid. They'll talk."

I wanted to kill him and raised my gun when a blast made the ground shake with such force, I almost fell. I caught my balance and ran outside to see a thick cloud of dirt over the field not more than a hundred feet away and Diego aiming a grenade towards the far edge of trees. Richard handed him another grenade, which he immediately launched right behind the other. The two landed about a hundred feet short of the forest.

Diego began loading another grenade. "Did any get hit?"

I raised my scope, but there was so much smoke and dirt I couldn't see through it. A mortar plunged down a hundred feet from us creating dense fountains of dirt.

Diego yelled through the thunderous noise. "What's their location? I can't see!"

I lay down trying to position my scope under the thick clouds and was able to see vague movements in the far distance. I took my best guess. "Four hundred feet."

An explosion landed ten feet closer to us than the last. I stayed in my low position waiting for another moment of clearing to scope more. "They're advancing. There's a few halfway across the field!"

Joe took over behind the other launcher, and I began handing him grenades. The sergeant came out of the hut with the villagers tied together like a chain gang and lined them up in front of us as a shield. He ordered Leon, Moustafa, Wesley, Billy, and Jack into positions behind them, ready to fire their M-16s once the VC came within a hundred feet. Billy carried out the two dead kids and placed them on the ground, lying down on his stomach behind them and resting his weapon on the boy's back. I wished I had shot him, but I couldn't now. At the moment he was needed to kill VC, though it shocked me to even think that.

The M-16s started discharging and the sparks from ours and incoming fire flickered within the thick haze. Some of the villagers fell, though it was impossible to say which side shot them. I saw Billy aim at a running toddler who got away from his mother and dove to Billy's side, slamming the butt of my M-16 on his shoulder.

He grasped his arm and glared up at me. "Shit, Belkin, you one of them VC?"

I wanted to smash in his head when Richard came and pointed to our left. "Sarge ordered a napalm hit. Wants everyone by that side field for a chopper lift, now!"

The Cambodians rushed by carrying a body, its head covered by a shirt. I grabbed Richard's arm before he left. "Who's that?"

"Jack. Hit in the face. Didn't make it." Richard rushed after the Cambodians, shooting into the field as he ran.

I returned to Joe and helped him dismantle the grenade launcher. I grabbed the tube while he took the rest, and we ran. We were almost all the way to the edge of the huts when some shots came at us and we threw ourselves on the ground.

I stayed down, feeling every blast in the air as if it were a hit, waiting for the one that would rip me apart. But then it quieted for ten seconds and I looked up. Several feet to my right was a body. No, it couldn't be. My throat choked, but I had to tell Joe. I pointed to it. "Joe, it's Diego."

Joe rushed to his side and grasped his head. "Talk to me, man, say something." Joe slapped at his cheeks, then began breathing in his mouth. I crept my way to them as Joe began lifting him within his arms. "He's not breathing. We have to get him to the chopper."

The sarge came up behind Joe. "No, you and Scout get the other launcher. Wesley and Leon will take him." I looked at Diego, his chest blown apart, and his eyes opened wide, looking merely stunned. Maybe it happened so fast he was gone before the horror could hit home.

I watched Leon and Wesley lift him and followed Joe back to the other launcher. He began dismantling it, throwing the tube on the ground. "I hate them, man. Diego was too good for that!"

I grabbed the other parts and began running with him, hearing the chopper in the distance and knowing it could only stay in position for thirty seconds before the risk of being blown up increased to eighty-five percent.

We passed Billy who was running backwards, shooting his M-16 while yelling, "Commie bastards, wish I could stay to watch you fry!"

Blasts of gunfire and mortar landed near us, but we kept running. We were twenty feet from the chopper landing when I heard Billy yell, "I'm hit. Help. I can't move!"

Two Cobra gun ships appeared overhead, their clattering blades and staccatos of rapid fire obscuring the rest of the gunfire. The deeper whir of the Huey behind them began lowering to fly us out.

Joe dropped the launcher and grabbed my arm. "Let's go back."

I pulled against him, towards the chopper. "No. It's Billy. Leave him."

Joe gripped harder on my arm, screaming above the explosive noise. "He's alive. We can't leave him. I need your help."

The Huey angled down and all I knew was I wanted to get on it and get the hell out of there. "Forget him. He deserves to get shot. I'm getting on that chopper."

Joe's huge strength wrestled its power over mine and pulled me with him. "We're going back. You don't leave a man who's hit."

The wind of the Huey almost knocked me down as I followed in Joe's grip. "What if they can't wait for us?"

Joe pulled harder, and we were only five steps from Billy. "They'll wait."

Billy's arm rose towards us. "I'm hit bad. Help me."

Joe went for his legs and motioned me to his head. "We'll take care of you, just don't pass out on us, you hear?"

Billy nodded and Joe began lifting. I noticed the Huey hovering just above the ground and men jumping on. I began to stand without grabbing Billy's head. "Let's go. We'll miss it."

Joe shrieked. "Lift his head!"

I followed his orders, though I feared it meant certain death. We began running when I saw the last man jump on board and a blast hit the ground about ten feet from the chopper.

We were running as fast as we could, both of us screaming, "Wait!"

I doubted they could hear us with all the noise when the sarge's head peered out of the opening, yelling straight at us.

The cobras did a high circle, which was their location signal to the Chinook with the napalm. "Please," I prayed out loud, "wait for us."

We arrived at the moment it started to lift. The sergeant reached out of the opening with both arms, as did some others. Billy was lifted and I grabbed onto Wesley's and Leon's wrists who pulled me halfway up. The Huey tilted on an angle which slid me in the rest of the way. I rolled, stopping on my back, and gripped the floor with my fingertips.

Joe crouched next to me, his cheeks and mouth spread so wide I could count his teeth. "We did it!" He raised his hand, waited for mine, then gripped his hand around my wrist in the military handshake reserved for those earning special respect.

I grasped his other forearm and squeezed. "I can't believe we did it!" I felt exhilarated but also not worthy. He knew and Billy knew I would have left Billy to die.

I sat up, then noticed behind Joe the two bodies in the corner, Jack and Diego. It had just happened, maybe ten minutes ago at the most. I felt real bad for Jack, but it was losing Diego that hurt most. I thought of his sister's kids who had needed his help and the ladies he said were waiting for him and wondered if anyone really wanted or needed me to come back the way they did him.

Joe turned to them, too, and touched his hand to his head in a salute. "You were a good friend, amigo. I'll miss you." He wiped his hand across his face then looked at me. "Damn, Scout. Diego and I have been together here for four months. Under these conditions that's like a lifetime, only your real lifetime is supposed to be stateside. His life shouldn't have ended here. He didn't deserve that."

I turned away from the body, wishing it had been Billy instead. "No, Diego didn't deserve it. That's for sure."

The roar of jet engines blared above the chopper's clatter. We slid forward to see two jets soar past us unloading their napalm strike on the valley we just left. Fiery orange flames flashed under the black smoke billowing up like chambers of hell. Who could possibly deserve that, the villagers who only an hour ago were living peaceably on ancient, cleared land? I thought of the kids, the hot flaming gasoline on their skin, and was thankful they were already dead. At least Billy had saved them from this ghastly torture. Only too bad Billy wasn't down there with them, getting his dose of burning flesh, too.

I glanced towards him. He was lying on his back with the sergeant pressing broad white bandages on both of his mutilated thighs. "It's all right, kid. You're being taken to the closest field hospital. They're pros at these kinds of hits."

Billy clutched at the sergeant's arm. "I'm dying. I know it. Don't let me die!"

The sergeant shook his head and smiled. "It's not that bad, son. They sew up these wounds all the time."

My gaze shifted to Diego and, without warning, I threw up. I was still by the open door so at least it went outside of the chopper. I then lay flat on my back and closed my eyes, willing myself to relax and make it back to base without having to throw up again.

The chopper began its descent, putting my stomach and its contents on tilt, but I pressed on them, trying to keep my insides intact, and a few minutes later we touched down at the field hospital.

Four medics came up to the chopper, hauling away the two dead bodies. I lifted my head enough to nod my good-byes.

Two other medics slid a stretcher under Billy while he raised his hands a mere inch off his chest. "Promise me you'll save my legs. Promise me!"

A medic pressed his wrists back down. "Don't worry, man. Our docs are the best. They'll patch you up good to go."

Joe leaned over him as they carted him off the chopper. "You'll be back on the line in no time."

Richard shoved Joe's shoulder. "Don't listen to him, man. You've got your one-way ticket home."

The sergeant gave him a stern look as he was being carried off the Huey. "You do what the doctors tell you, and don't give them any lip."

Billy saluted, though his fingers were loose and bent. "Yes, Sarge."

The medics turned the stretcher and his eyes caught mine. I smiled, not able to think of anything to say, when Billy winked at me.

I stayed silent, feeling too uncomfortable to speak, not even able to wish him good luck.

The Huey lifted off and I stared down at the sight of Billy being rushed towards the white building with the large Red Cross on its tin roof. He became smaller and smaller but the image of his wink kept looming larger in my mind. Had he been smiling when he winked, or was it a grin, or a leer like he was going to come back for me? He had reason to. I almost shot him in the hut. I smashed my gun in his shoulder, and I didn't want to save him. But I did actually save him. That had to count for something.

I found myself wishing he had been struck through the heart, then there'd be no worries of him and maybe it would even help me forget what he did to those kids. Oh, those kids! How could he have killed them like that, and why hadn't I stopped him? Though he did save them from the napalm, which is worse. So maybe I could forget it. Or could I?

My stomach felt sick again. I leaned back into the side of the chopper thinking Billy's wound might still kill him when the sergeant appeared and crouched down between Joe and me. "Going back for Billy was extremely brave. I'm putting you both in for medals of commendation."

"Medals?" I pressed on my stomach, hoping to keep it settled.

Joe shook his head. "Wasn't brave. It's code, never leave your own man."

I gripped my shirt, feeling uneasy. "Joe's the one for the medal, not me. He forced me into it."

Sarge looked from Joe to me. "Medals are for bravery under fire. That's what you did, and I'm sure Billy will tell his folks about you."

I wanted to ask if he'd tell his folks he killed two kids right in front of their mother when Joe leaned in closer to me and the sarge. "He can tell his folks whatever he likes. I just hope he makes it."

The sergeant tapped his fingertips together in front of him. "So do we all."

I nodded, feeling awful that I didn't mean it, with the idea of a medal only making it worse.

"In any case," the sarge gripped his knees and began to push himself up, "that was a brave piece of work you did. Be proud of yourselves." He turned and headed for the lieutenant who was sitting where Diego had been lying a few minutes ago.

Joe rapped me on the arm. "You're a hero, Scout. Those chicks in Brooklyn will dig you for that."

I shook my head knowing Naomi who would only hate me worse for going along with what happened back there. "Not with the chicks I know. Besides, you know I wasn't a hero."

"You did the hero thing." Joe's fingers slid into his hair, stopping halfway. "And when the chips are down, that's what counts."

I was about to confess that I hoped Billy died when Joe's elbow poked into my side. "Don't put yourself down. You're a hero and don't you forget it."

I leaned my head back into the metal, shocked he could say that when he knew all that I almost did back there. It was only because he stopped me that I wasn't headed to Long Binh's stockade for Billy's murder, or at the least, reprimanded for desertion of a fellow Marine. I stared into the corner where Diego's body had been, remembering how he called the Long Binh jail, LBJ, courtesy of Lyndon Baines Johnson, our President who sentenced us each to a year of hell.

I turned towards Joe's ear. "I'd be locked up if it wasn't for you."

"You came through as a hero." Joe gripped his knees and pushed himself back into the wall. "You killed the enemy, and you saved your own men. That's hero. All other thoughts are leftover from stateside, and don't apply here."

It felt like he was talking about the sniper I had killed a couple of days ago in addition to what happened in the village, making the two situations merge. I had no doubt I was here to keep my own men alive and that doing so meant they would be there for me. But I still wished I had killed Billy and not saved him in the end.

The boy and girl lying dead in a heap flashed in my mind and I feared another bout of throwing up. I pressed my forearms into my stomach to settle it down. The chopper descended and the pressure in my stomach increased as the outline of what had to be our base camp grew larger. The neat rows of rectangular buildings encircled by six cannon-sized guns looked well secured and protected.

I noticed Joe also looking towards the opening and pointed. "At least it will be safe in there."

"Looks are deceiving." Joe's arms pushed his knees flat on the floor. "It's safer than the jungle, but the perimeter gets bombed every night."

I looked at the fortified circle, feeling the increased vibrations of the slowing chopper as if they were aftershocks from those bombs. The hoped for safety shattered with the hovering engine's screaming roar.

~ CHAPTER 7 ~

Base Camp

The touchdown felt abrupt, like it happened too soon. For a moment I thought the ground had slammed into us, instead of us landing on it, but I knew that didn't make sense. My fingers pressed into the floor while I let out a long breath, then I joined the line at the opening. I jumped, falling on one knee before gaining a full footing and running through the rotor's swirling wind. The thrusting air fought me till I reached the opened space of the field where most of the squad already stood. The clatter of the blade increased and the helicopter lifted off, sending a thick cloud of dust into our faces. I covered my eyes till the wind subsided, then looked around.

The lieutenant was whispering in the sarge's ear who looked at each of us in turn, then raised one arm. "I want to congratulate every one of you on a job well done. You conducted yourselves with integrity and kept the importance of this mission in mind at all times. I'll file the appropriate reports, and you'll go down in history as the brave men you are."

A new wave of nausea hit my stomach as I imagined him writing that we interrogated the villagers, elicited the location of the advancing VC, attacked them, and ordered a napalm strike on them and their base of operations, which turned out to be the village. I would prefer to write that report myself—that we killed two kids, never found out where the tunnels were, the VC found us before we found them, but thanks to napalm we burned them all, enemy soldiers, old men, women, babies, huts, crops, chickens and all. I looked back at the sarge, whose nod and grin seemed to acknowledge us as heroes. There was a general mumbling and I peered at the ground instead of his eyes.

The sarge and the lieutenant turned and began walking. I followed along with everyone else when Joe's voice intruded upon my unsettling thoughts, "At least we get to shower, put on clean fatigues and get the kids to do our laundry."

My nausea eased with the walking and I realized how dirty I felt. "Where's the showers?"

Joe pointed to a lower field straight ahead. "Over beyond the tents. I'll show you. We can get clean, then," he leaned in close and whispered, "go for a sweet smoke."

I didn't know why it was a secret, but he was still close and I whispered back, "They sell cigars?"

One eye winked and his voice became even lower. "Weed, you know, never did it at home, but here, hell, it helps you forget."

My thoughts went to Naomi and that time we shared a joint and I kept talking into her breasts like they were microphones. I saw them shimmering in my mind and I wanted nothing more than to take them in my hands.

Joe's arm bumped into mine. "You there, Scout?"

The breasts jolted away and I stared at the squad in front of me, their heads quivering in an illusion from the thick, steamy air. My own head was suddenly overly hot when a vision of the dead kids floated in front of me. I grasped my stomach, trying to hold its contents down as I turned to Joe. "They allow it?"

Sweat dripped from Joe's face onto his shirt, but he did nothing to stop it. "There's times and places they don't see."

The dead kids reappeared, only this time pointing their fingers in angry accusations at me. I snapped the back of my hand against Joe's arm. "How soon?"

Joe swiped at the sweat on his cheek. "Not when you're coming in. Everyone's watching you, trying to get a fix on how bad it will be for the next squad sent out. Have to wait a few hours."

I saw the girl's eyes bulge from the knife pressed against her throat, when an officer in a clean uniform came up to my side and began walking next to me. "I'm Major Smith, reporter for *Stars and Stripes*. There are a few questions I have for you."

My breaths quickened, fearing he'd heard my conversation with Joe.

He pulled a pencil from his pocket and flipped his pad to a fresh page. "I understand you were just under attack. Tell me what you saw in the way of heroic acts."

The knife went into the girl's throat and blood dripped down her neck. I winced, then turned away from him, hearing myself say, "Sorry, no heroes to talk about."

The major turned to Joe and raised his pencil in his direction. "And you?"

Joe pointed back to me. "You had the right person. Go ahead. Ask him what he did."

Major Smith turned back to me and I pictured Billy lying on the ground, wishing we'd never saved him. I glared at the pencil, anxious for it to disappear. "Not me. He's the one did it."

The major flipped his gaze back to Joe. "And what is your name and rank?"

Joe slapped his hand on his M-16. "Corporal Joseph McCormack Jr., sir."

The sergeant stopped in front of a tent surrounded three layers high with sandbags. We were only twenty-five feet behind him.

Joe grabbed my arm and raised it. "And this here's Private Lenny Belkin, best damned scout ever come out of Brooklyn. He's getting the same medal I am so get that in there, and make sure his parents get a copy."

I saw Naomi and Steven holding up the paper, both furious, and yanked my arm out of his grip. "Leave me out of this!"

The major leaned closer to Joe. "What heroic act did you perform?"

"We went back for a wounded Marine, is all." Joe tilted his head towards me. "The two of us. And we were damn lucky to make it back to the chopper in time."

My mind pictured Billy using the dead kids for a shield, and it was all I could do not to scream that to the major.

He stopped writing for a moment. "And what statement would you like to make for our readers on your heroic save?"

Joe scratched his head and squinted like sun was glaring in his eyes, only it wasn't. "All I can say is I'm glad Billy made it out alive. It wasn't anything heroic. It's what we do for each other."

The major jabbed his pencil into the pad. "Don't underestimate yourself. This war is full of brave acts that do us proud. The world would be more respectful of our great country if they recognized how many brave acts our young men commit each day."

He turned to me and I felt the sweat on my face raise twenty degrees. "And your statement for the folks at home, Private Belkin, is it?"

He pointed his pencil at my face, only it felt to me like the pin of a grenade he had already pulled. "Leave me out of this and make sure you don't use my name in anything you print!"

The major smiled, seeming amused by my outburst. "Surely you want your folks at home to know what's on their brave son's mind."

I pictured Billy's sneer as he held the knife to the girl's throat, the terror in her eyes pulsating from my chest to my head. "You want a statement?"

The major's curving lips unnerved me even more.

"My statement is I don't see what's heroic about saving a maggot who killed innocent kids, then used their bodies as a shield!" I was about to add that Billy acted without orders from the sarge when I noticed the major's pen was still. "Write that down! You asked what happened and I'm telling you!"

He tapped the eraser on the pad before pointing it at me. "Think of your parents, son. What you want me to write will only serve to upset them worse than they already are. Imagine what they go through each time they see bombings on TV and hear the body counts. They're worried it's you, every day. But here's your chance to replace some of that fear with a sense of pride. What do you say?"

I pictured my parents in the living room watching television, except it wasn't the news, it was *Mission Impossible*, and their only thought of me was pride that their son hadn't run to Canada. I became even angrier and yelled, "They can't be more upset than I am!"

The major waved his pencil in the air. "It's clear you're very tired and under great duress. I'll simply write that you're very proud to be serving your country. It must be true or you wouldn't be doing such a fine job."

I was about to scream, *That's not what I said!* when a firm hand grasped my shoulder and the sergeant's voice boomed in my ear. "Yes, sir, this soldier is one of my best. You can quote me on that in your article."

The major looked at the sergeant and nodded. "I can tell quality when I see it."

I was furious they were using me to distort the truth and pulled out from under the sarge's grip with my finger pointing at him. "Why did you let him do it, Sarge?"

The sarge grabbed my arm and pulled me into the tent. The flap dropped behind us as he held me firmly in place on the wood planked floor with twenty lined up cots that felt like soldiers standing guard. "Listen, kid, don't you ever pull that crap in front of a reporter again. You hear me?"

"But you let…"

His grip squeezed into my arms. "I don't care how good you are at what you see in the jungle. What you see on a mission stays within the squad. Is that understood?"

I blinked, unable to sustain my gaze against his piercing stare.

His grip tightened. "This is war, them against us. They would have done worse to you if they had the chance. Cut out your guts, stuck nails in your eyes, splintered bamboo up your ass, stuff so bad you can't even imagine it.

My goal out there is to carry out the mission and keep my men alive. If it takes something ugly, then that's what it takes."

Streams of sweat poured down the sides of my face. "But he didn't have to kill the kids!"

The sergeant shook his head without moving his eyes from mine. "You're wrong. It's better they're dead. Torture a kid and the rest of their life they're out for revenge. Those kids would have killed you first chance they got. Believe me, Billy saved American lives."

The flap opened and the rest of the squad began pushing in. A thick hand slammed across my mouth and I was dragged away from the sarge when I heard Wesley's voice. "Don't worry. We'll take care of him. You go finish out there with the major. Make us sound good."

I was shoved onto a cot where I was held down, Richard at my shoulders, Moustafa on my feet. Leon stood like a guard ready to pounce, then Joe came in, shaking his head at me. I began to squirm frantically when Wesley leaned directly over my chest, pressing with a strength that nearly stopped my breath. "What's the matter with you? Brass is going to come down on all of us with talk like that."

I gasped what I wanted to yell. "What if she was your sister?"

"She's not!" Wesley's teeth revealed their crooked bottoms. "Your sister and my sister and everyone's sister is safe and sound in the good old U. S. of A. That girl out there don't mean nothing to you, me or anyone else in this room. You got that, man? She's nothing to you but some gook bitch."

I began to cough and Wesley eased his arm. I inhaled desperately, then gasped, "Doesn't anyone care?"

Joe's massive hand pressed over my mouth as he leaned over me in front of Wesley. "Scout, listen to this cook here. You have to keep your mouth shut. It's for your own good. Can you do that?" I struggled to free my head from under his grasp, but couldn't. "It's for your own good. You could end up court martialed on trumped up charges. You want that?" I grasped Joe's hand and shook my head under its hold.

Wesley peered over Joe's shoulder. "It's over, man. Billy's gone. Damn, if anyone's mad at Billy, it's me. He still owes me that ten bucks."

Leon began to laugh. "Guy took the cheap way out."

Joe laughed and I felt my mouth spread in a smile. He raised his hand off of me. "You okay now?"

I nodded and sat up, coughing from not enough air.

Wesley pounded me on the back. "You not going to flip out on us again, are you?"

I shook my head then saw Joe put his hand on Wesley's shoulder. "Thanks."

Wesley returned with a soft jab to Joe's arm. "No problem, man. We got to keep each other alive out here. That we got to do." Wesley then raised both hands high and turned in a semi circle, holding our gazes with his. "Folks, it's time you all got some friendly advice from me, best cook and giver of information you ever hope to meet. As you have all witnessed by now, the leaders of our fine country and armed forces, otherwise known as the man, want us to fight for his piece of land, his piece of the pie, and his precious right to play with a piece that shoots an automatic clip. But," he paused to glance across all of us before going on, "old Wesley here sees the piece he's fighting for a little different from what the man wants. I'm keeping myself alive for the only piece worth fighting for, and that's a good piece of ass!"

We all laughed, but Wesley moved his arms forward with his palms straight out and we quieted down. "And I's recommending to all'a you to keep that in mind while here in the Nam. You is to get yourself out of here alive so you can go home and get yourself all the hot U. S. of A. pussy you can. Is there anyone here who disagrees?"

I put up a hand like I was in school then realized it wasn't called for. "You figure that one out all by yourself?"

Wesley pointed at me. "You the one needs to know it most. And me, oh yes, I'm a Wesley original."

I rubbed my chest where it was still sore. "You're one of a kind, all right, and next time you try to choke me, I'll shoot your ass off."

"Man." Wesley shook his head and began unbuttoning his shirt. "What's the point in shooting my ass? I'm not keeping you from some sweet babe with burning thighs and breasts bursting from a black satin bra." Wesley's eyes shut and his lips pursed into a small circle, then a soft whisper, "Oooh, baby, that's sooo good."

His eyes opened and he scanned us gawking at him. "Man, what you watching for. Go get your own babes." He laughed, then grabbed his pack and pulled it four cots down. He reached in for a towel, then begin unzipping his pants. "I don't know about the rest of you, but I sure could use a shower." He dropped his pants, threw the towel over his shoulder and began singing Marvin Gaye's song, *"Let's get it on, let's get it on..."*

I began muttering a song by The Animals that stuck in my head since hearing it three times on Guam. *"We gotta get out of this place, if it's the last thing we ever do. . ."* I took a deep breath, then the next line, *"We gotta get out of this place, 'cause girl there's a better life for me and you..."*

Wesley sauntered out of the tent, singing louder than before, *"And if you feel like I feel baby, come on oh come on, let's get it on…"*

When the flap opened, I glimpsed the major and the sarge still out there. I stopped singing and listened through the sudden quiet of the tent. "That's very interesting, Sergeant. What would you estimate the body count?"

I swallowed into my dry throat waiting for the answer. "You mean Viet Cong or villagers?"

The major's smooth voice answered. "Both, they're considered the same."

A hesitation and I pictured the sarge scratching his face. "Could be as low as thirty-five or as high as a hundred, hard to tell."

"I'll write a hundred. It's usually higher than we think. And the wounded's full name?"

A pause, then, "Billy. Billy Langdon, private."

There was a slight rustling of the flap from a breeze. "Any medals for the private?"

"I expect a Purple Heart and a commendation for bravery under fire."

I heard myself begin to yell, "No!" when Joe's hand slapped across my mouth. "Damn if you aren't a one track son of a bitch. Calm down, I'll get you some smoke."

I heard the major ask about the deceased as Joe let go of my mouth and gripped my arm hard enough to bruise. "Can I trust you to stay quiet?"

I nodded and he led me through the flap as the sarge was spelling, D-I-E-G-O.

I kept my head turned away from them and remained quiet, following Joe's lead down a path to a corner of a field with boulders and a few trees. We stopped five yards before the first tree and Joe crouched by three rocks arranged in a triangle. He moved them to the side and began scooping at the dirt with his hands. I watched him dig, nervous that a snake would lunge up from the hole when a thin gray line appeared and Joe pulled out a dingy plastic bag. It was rolled and held together by a rubber band. Joe removed a joint twice as thick as a cigarette and stuck it between his teeth.

I reached towards his mouth but he pushed my hand away. "Listen, Scout, only reason we're here in daylight is 'cause you saved my life. But that don't mean I'll let you put me in the brig."

He kept the joint in his mouth and reburied the bag, putting the rocks back in their original triangle. He then looked a full 360 degrees around before pulling his Bic from his pocket and lighting the joint's tip.

A thin stream of smoke drifted up in front of me, its musty smell much more tempting than a cake fresh out of the oven had been at home. I grasped it out of Joe's mouth and placed it a bit too deeply in mine, inhaling so hard the flame felt like it directly touched my throat. I felt scorched, but still held the smoke in my lungs till I was desperate for air. I gave a hasty exhale, then another inhale. This one was deeper and I swallowed the smoke, holding it till I became dizzy and had to crouch low with one hand touching the ground to keep my balance. Joe's hand extended towards the joint, but I wanted one more hit and sucked in another stream of smoke before handing it to him. I watched Joe puff, but beyond him saw Billy with his knife on the girl's throat. I punched at the air, thinking I could reach him, but fell forward, my face landing in the dirt. My head was too heavy to lift and I stayed down, turning my cheek to the ground. There, lying next to me, was the boy and girl dead in their heap, their blood streaming towards my face. I gripped the earth, pulling away, when the blood turned into a snake. Its tongue lashed at my eyes and I shot up to a sitting position.

I felt a grasp on my knee, then Joe's voice. "You had enough?"

He stared into my face, the joint in his hand burning a stream of smoke that was split like the cobra's tongue. At first I pulled back, but then the ash fell and it went back to one stream. I took it from his hand and sucked in as much smoke as my mouth would hold, wanting a thick screen in my head to stop seeing those kids. My head felt uncomfortably faint, and I lay back on the grass, letting the smoke drift upward in a slow dance. I felt myself float with the rising smoke then giggles spilled from my mouth like when girls hear a dirty joke.

"You're high as a kite, man." Joe took the joint and pointed what was left of it down at me. "You'd probably laugh at an oncoming tank."

"Man, a damned launcher couldn't put a dent in me." I reached up for more, but Joe raised it out of reach.

"Any higher and you'll have to crawl back to the tent."

I watched the thin thread of smoke waft up from his hand, feeling like I was caught in its swirl.

Joe slid his other hand in his pocket. "Just make sure no brass notices you can't walk straight."

I looked up at Joe sure I had the answer to that problem. "I don't need to walk. I'll fly!"

Joe laughed and I suddenly felt stupid, wanting to hit him if only I could reach, when he began singing, *"Puff the magic dragon, lived by the sea…"*

I found myself joining him in the next part. *"And frolicked in the autumn mist in a land called Honalee…"*

We sang the next few lines together while I envisioned people on my street in Brooklyn running towards me, but never getting any closer. They were still far away when Joe stopped singing, and I looked up at him, relieved that I wasn't alone.

* * * * *

Joe and I entered the tent twenty minutes later. Wesley stood shaving in front of a bamboo edged mirror on the wall. He turned to us and crinkled his nose. "Man, that weed is stuck to you thicker than grits. I wouldn't let the sarge get a whiff of that if I was you, not the way he looked just before. Especially you, scout boy, he came in here like a mad dog asking where the hell you'd gone."

His serious glare amused me and my cheeks widened. "Tell the sarge I'm just fine and he doesn't have to worry about me anymore."

Wesley shook his head then pointed his razor directly at me. "You don't get it, Scout. He wasn't worried, it was like I said, he was mad, m - a - d, foaming at the mouth kind of mad."

Joe took a step in front of me. "Where's the sarge now?"

Wesley pointed the razor up in the air. "He, my man, was called in by the brass."

Joe's thumbs hooked into his waist. "For what?"

Wesley tapped the side of his razor on his palm. "If I was placing bets, I'd put money on the crap that came out of your buddy's mouth."

I stepped out to the side of Joe. "What's the problem? I needed time to calm down, but now I'm okay."

Wesley's chest leaned in my direction. "Boy, you are far from okay. And you better get your ass straightened out before you get us assigned to some hump that blows us away just to stop you from talking."

He glared into my face and I tried to stare back but it looked like his head was twirling in circles. I knew I had to sit down or risk falling, and started for my cot.

I flopped on my back hearing Wesley's taut whisper. "You better do something about him or me and my boys will have to do it ourselves."

I bolted upright, gripping the bed to hold steady. "What you talking about?"

Wesley's razor lurched forward. "We're not going down 'cause you want to act like you is better than us. You got that?"

I tried to keep a steady sight on him. "Better than who?"

"Us." Wesley tapped his chest. "Us blacks, Afro-Americans, you know, the ones white folks like you want to keep down."

I pushed myself up straighter, feeling the metal edge dig into my fingers. "How do I act better than you?"

Wesley's hands went to his hips. "By making it sound like you're the only one that don't want to kill and the rest of us do it for fun."

"What? I never said that!"

Wesley pointed the razor right at my nose. "What you didn't say don't mean squat. The brass will see what they always see, us blacks are savages and the sweet, upset white boy is innocent. Fact is, shit always comes down on us and this ain't no different. You good as drop a bomb on our black asses yourself if you don't take back what you said."

I stared at Wesley, confused by what he said, and upset that his face kept vibrating. If only the joint would wear off I could think and see clearer. I tried to piece together what he said about how the brass would react. I gripped the cot tighter and stared at him straight on. "Billy was white so there's no way his actions should come down on you. And the sarge shouldn't have let him kill those kids! Doesn't that matter?"

Wesley stormed over to my cot and rapped the back of his hand into my chest. "I care as much as you do, but right now I care more about getting me out of here alive than I do about those kids. And I don't want no friggin' crusader getting me pushed into a VC trap 'cause the brass wants bad shit kept quiet. You got that, mister high and mighty?"

"Don't blame me," I began, when Joe's arm shoved between us and he said to Wesley, "Thanks for the warning. Got your message loud and clear."

Wesley backed off a couple of steps then looked Joe directly in the eye. "You straighten him out, man, or else we all go down, you along with us."

Joe gave a quick nod. "I won't let that happen. Trust me."

Wesley's shoulders rolled backward. "All right, Corporal, do what you have to do." He flipped his razor on his bed, turned to the door, then left the tent without another glance in my direction.

The overly hot sweat on my chest suddenly chilled and I shook from the unexpected cold. Joe grabbed my arms and pushed me towards the footlockers that had somehow appeared in the tent. "Time to get cleaned up. Let's go, on the double, take off your boots and get a towel."

I retrieved the thin olive drab terry that was supposed to dry fast and threw it over my shoulder. Joe began to steer me towards the front flap when a young Vietnamese boy, not more than twelve, appeared in the opening. I was alarmed at the similarity to the village boy when Joe went straight to him.

"Well, look who's here, my boy Tuan." Joe placed his hand on the boy's back and pushed him inside. "I have a tall stack for you today."

Tuan's lips spread across his entire thin face. "Thank you, please."

Joe handed his full laundry bag to the boy. "You bring it back tomorrow."

Richard entered the tent, a towel wrapped around his waist and his hair in shiny clumps. "Did the others say if there's mail? They were going to check when I left."

I glanced at my cot hoping a letter from Naomi had somehow appeared, but there were no envelopes in sight. "Wesley was the only one we saw, and he didn't say anything about mail."

"The mail in country can take a month to find you." Joe's hand rested on Tuan's shoulder. "Not like Tuan here. He knows who's on base better than the generals and can pick up and deliver in twenty-four hours. Now there's a service the U. S. Military should model their mail after."

I found my laundry and stuffed my jungle encrusted uniform into the bag. Tuan took it from my hand and I looked up at Richard. "You got laundry for the kid?"

Richard opened his pack and began putting things in. "No time for clean clothes. I'm shipping out."

Tuan's eyes opened wider like he understood and was interested to know more, but then I thought it was because he felt bad about being rejected. I held up my finger for him to wait while I found the two chocolate bars I had in my footlocker and placed them in his hand.

His eyes fixed on the brown Hershey's wrappers. "Thank you, please, clean laundry, tomorrow be back, promise." He waved goodbye with the chocolate bars in his hand and made his way out of the door in a hurry.

I smiled to myself when I heard Joe ask, "Where you going?"

Richard tightened the strap on his pack. "Volunteered for one of them assignments they have at HQ, parachuting into the highlands. I always did love to jump from high places. Used to jump off the roof of my house just for fun."

I watched Richard check the ammo clips in his pack. "When you leaving?"

Richard stuffed the ammo in their pockets of his pack. "Catching a chopper out in thirty minutes."

I wondered if his leaving was because of what happened in the village, or worse, because he wanted to get away from me and what I did. "Why you going so soon?"

He bent forward to tie his boot. "I reckon all that snake I ate is making me want to lunge and strike." He finished tying his boot and looked up at both of us. "But tell you what, you get any more of them good eating cobras, send up some smoke signals and I'll be right back to skin 'em for you."

Joe laughed. "Won't eat snake without you."

The thought of the coming chopper reverberated in my head, mixing up my fears that Wesley had said something to him about me to make him want to leave with thoughts that maybe this was something I should do, volunteer for a mission and get the hell away. But I didn't want to go anywhere, I was tired, and scared, and I had no intention of parachuting into the highlands. There was a reason that mission was volunteer and it made me shudder without even thinking about it.

Richard stood and lifted his pack. "Maybe see you again sometime."

Joe's hand went out to him. "Good luck and see you next time we nab some snakes."

Richard grabbed Joe's hand military style, with knuckles pointed up. "Send up a flare and I'll follow it in. I can land on a dime."

I held out my hand which he grasped. "I'll keep a dime handy, though I never want to see another snake again in my life, not even in the zoo."

Richard squeezed my hand tighter and laughed, then made his way out of the tent. I watched him leave, feeling the tent unsettlingly empty. We had kept each other alive in battle. Now this breakup seemed to leave a vulnerable hole.

"Let's go." Joe was holding the flap opened and I followed him outside and onto the path towards the showers. We saw Wesley standing in front of another tent talking to three blacks. Their conversation stopped as we neared and he looked at me from the side of his eye. I felt accused and wanted to shout, *You don't have to worry, all the heat will come down on me, and me alone,* but before I could, he turned back to his group and Joe pushed his hand on my back to keep me moving. I did keep on walking but was sorry I hadn't spoken my piece. What was wrong with what I did? His worries seemed too far-fetched.

We arrived at the edge of the open-air platform of six shower heads. I felt the spray bounce off the two naked bodies that were holding one body part at a time under the low pressure flow. They were two white guys, one with a thick hairy chest that hardly indented at the waist and the other one thin, almost frail, and blond.

The hairy one was rubbing soap in his hair as he talked. "It was like ants on sap when the sugar maple's flowing. I never did see people heap onto garbage like that 'afore, even the trashy po' folks back home didn't do that. I seen mangy dogs that alls folks shoo from they yards in the dumps, but that's it."

The blond had one arm up lathering his side. "It's sho' enough welfare come to Vietnam."

"But, Lordy Gosh," the hairy one turned his back into the water, "how can they eat it after coming off those filthy trucks?"

The lean one stood still under the water like he was thinking hard. "It's 'cause they like primitives, like those tribes in Africa. They live like animals, don't know no better, eat off the ground then crap in the open as if they ain't no shame to it. Like you see in the zoo."

The hairy one shook his head while the water ran down the back of his neck. "In all my days back in the hills, I ain't never seen folks that ignorant."

I wanted to yell that we had just destroyed a civilized village of huts, crops and families, and had we left any survivors they would be forced to live like mangy dogs, when Joe grabbed my arm. "No arguments."

I understood he was keeping me out of trouble and with worrying about Wesley and the sarge, I had enough on my mind already. I nodded to him. This was a shower, that's it.

We stepped up on the platform and I pulled the string for the water to start, then put my face directly in the flow. I let it stream onto my closed eyelids, hoping it would clear out the haze from the weed so I could try to figure out what Wesley had meant. It didn't make sense that only the blacks would get sent on a mission to keep what happened back there quiet. If anything, it would be all of us, and if that was the case, it was up to me to make sure that didn't happen. A second surge of water on my face seemed to make that even clearer. And it was up to me to do whatever was necessary to keep us all alive. That much I could see.

I began rubbing at the sweat and grime on my chest, but then felt something crusted on my stomach. I rubbed at it, trying to loosen its hold except it held fast like glue. I used my fingernails, scraping bits of dark brown particles off my skin then watching them drop to the floor, dissolving into a red liquid before trickling down the drain.

I turned to Joe who was working off the same thing from his skin. "What is this stuff?"

"Billy's blood, man." Joe scraped at his stomach. "That boy is made of some tough crap."

I began trying to pull it from the hairs that led into my belly button. "Tough isn't the word. It's like damned cement."

Joe began scraping at the hair on his thigh. "With blood this tough he'll definitely make it home alive."

The raw soreness where I had scraped began to throb. It wasn't fair that he got to go home when I had to stay. But at least he couldn't come after me for wanting to leave him on that field to die.

Joe picked up a brown bar of soap from the platform floor and handed it to me. "Here, use this."

I rubbed it onto my stomach, feeling it lather thicker than my own soap, when the dark haired guy came up behind us. "Pardon my interruptin', but did your buddy just get shot?"

Joe reached behind himself to scrub his back. "Yes, Billy, mortar hit on both legs."

The guy stamped his foot on the platform. "Pigs in crap, don't that beat all. My buddy's arm was clear blowed off. Made me puke when I's supposed to be helping him. And us only been in the Nam for eight days."

Joe shook his head while reaching higher on his back. "Tough break."

"Tougher 'n dried rawhide." The hairy guy took a step closer. "His nickname's Horse 'cause he could ride 'fore he could walk. We met in boot camp, sentenced by the same judge, do the Nam or go to jail. And ain't it something, armed robbery both of us, and our towns is just eighty-five miles apart, right down route 136 in Caton County, Tennessee. We's like brothers, cut from the same mold, and we's promised to keep each other alive. You think they can fix him up?"

Joe scrubbed at a patch on his forearm. "Probably, they got doctors drafted right out of medical school up on the latest techniques."

The hairy guy gripped the back of his neck. "I hope that's so 'cause I feel useless as a donkey done stepped in a beaver trap, that I didn't do nothing to save him."

Joe scraped at his wrist. "Nothing you could have done. You can't stop those things."

"Truth is," the hairy guy put his hand next to his mouth like he was telling a secret. "I was tying my boots with my head down and never saw no leaves rustling up ahead or nothing."

I watched my last bit of scraped off blood drift towards the big holes in the center of the platform then looked up at the deep crease down the guy's forehead. "Don't blame yourself. It's not your fault. You didn't start this stinking war."

His crease eased into a faint line. "Still feel worthless as a muskrat's been skinned. Anyway, I sho' is sorry 'bout your buddy. Hey, I'm Rascal and this here's Spit."

I saluted them from under the spray. "Nice to meet you both. I'm Scout."

I realized what I'd said, and almost said, *no wait, that's wrong, my name's Lenny,* when Joe immediately followed with, "I'm Joe." He shook both their hands, then added, "Now don't you worry, Rascal. You and Horse will have plenty of time together back in Tennessee."

Rascal grinned, revealing a missing tooth. "I sho' do hope yer right." He tightened his towel then raised a hand towards us. "Bye, we's best be gettin' back 'fore the sarge thinks we's drowned."

We both said goodbye then I turned to Joe. "My name's not Scout."

Joe wrapped his towel around his waist. "It is to me."

I grabbed my towel and rubbed it down my face. Was I Scout? And didn't I know my own name? My legs began to tremble as if the air was cold, except it was unreasonably hot. I didn't know who I was, but I did know that if I didn't straighten things out with the sarge, I'd be dead either by Wesley's guys or by a mission of certain death. Those were the options. It felt like a choice between being thrown into a VC tunnel, or into a pit of angry cobras. One thing I knew for sure was I could no longer think the way Lenny thought, that much was certain.

"You get all Billy's blood off?" Joe was picking at a small patch on his side.

I glanced at all the parts of me I could see. "Think so. Down the drain, along with tons of other jungle crud." I peered at the hole and felt a twinge in my chest. I covered my hand over the spot and stood as if ready to recite the pledge of allegiance, but instead uttered, "Rest in peace."

* * * * *

Walking back to the tent from the shower felt very different than the walk down. Watching Billy's dried up blood go down the drain and getting clearheaded about Wesley's fears, I knew there was only one matter of justice to focus on. My squad had to get home alive.

I saw Wesley about fifty feet before our tent, standing in a group of fifteen blacks and wanted him to be the first to know there was no need to worry about the sarge, I would take care of everything.

We approached and I tapped him on the back. "Hey, Wesley, good news."

He turned with a sudden jerk, then at the sight of me narrowed his eyes. "Keep on walking, man. You's not one of the brothers so don't butt your ass in." He turned back to his group as if he expected me to vanish the moment I was dismissed.

Joe began pulling my arm towards our tent but I yanked free of his hold and slapped it into Wesley's back. "Hell, man, I'm your squad brother, the one who's gonna save your ass no matter what goes down."

Wesley shoved his shoulder into mine and pushed me back a step. "You worry about saving your own ass because in the real world it's black against white. Now get on." The rest of the blacks already began moving away from me like I was an enemy intruder into their circle of secrecy.

Wesley backed away with them and I stood there feeling paralyzed.

Joe hit the back of my arm. "Come on. They don't want us around."

I watched the group close in its ranks then turned to Joe who was already headed for the tent. I caught up to him, feeling out of breath, though it was only ten steps. "It's not right." I paused to take in a deep breath. "All I wanted was to tell him I'm going to straighten it out with the sarge and polish the major's boots for a month if that's what it takes to keep us in the rear."

Joe picked up a rock from the ground and threw it into a tree. "No way he's going to hear that right now." .

We entered the tent nearly slamming into Moustafa who was on his way out. He let the flap close behind me, leaving us in dim light, and pointed his finger at my face. "Sergeant came looking for you. Says he's coming back at 1800 hours, sharp, and you're to be here, waiting for him. You got that?"

I stepped to the side and crossed my arms in front of my chest. "I got it, but what's it about?"

Moustafa's head tilted forward and his eyes widened. "Don't rightly know, but he was mad enough to chop down the cherry tree and lie about it, if you know what I mean."

I shifted all my weight on my right leg. "No, I don't know what you mean. You want to let me in on the secret?"

Moustafa raised his chin upward and peered at me through half closed lids. "I mean," his words were slow and deliberate as if talking to a stupid child, "that he ain't no model George Washington and don't care about no lousy truth. Is that easy enough for you to comprehend, mister big mouth white boy?"

"Yes, preacher," I emphasized each word, like he had done to me. "I read you loud and clear."

One side of Moustafa's mouth curved up then he turned and pushed his way out of the flap.

I felt like a lousy lying bunch of cherries hung in the air, only it was me, not the sarge that had to eat them, and then tell him anything that would keep us from getting sent into the middle of an enemy stronghold to get our asses blown up.

"Damn, Scout." Joe was looking at his watch. "It's 17:54. He'll be here in six minutes."

I dropped onto my cot, letting my boots slam into the floor. "What am I going to tell him?"

Joe sat opposite me, his blue eyes looking darker than usual. "Just make sure every other word is sorry. Can you do that?"

I propped myself up on my elbows. "Guess I have to."

"Good." Joe stood and took a uniform from my footlocker and dropped it next to me. "Now put this on and look like a Marine ready to serve his commanding officer."

I looked at the folded shirt then saluted it with a tight hand. "Yes, sir."

Joe shook his head as I slipped into the crisply laundered fatigues. Their tough, firm fabric felt powerful, even though they immediately dampened with my sweat. I was in the middle of tucking in my shirt when the flap opened.

"Private Belkin?" The sergeant walked in followed by Major Smith.

I jumped to my feet trying to get the pants button closed, but couldn't manage to slip it through the hole.

"Private Belkin." The sergeant walked directly in front of me and pointed to Major Smith. "Don't you know how to properly salute an officer?"

"Yes, sir," I said, leaving my pants unbuttoned and snapping my right hand to my head.

Major Smith looked around, as if he expected more troops to inspect. "At ease."

I let one foot ease out to the side.

"Private Belkin," the sergeant boomed as if he was a hundred feet away, "are you aware that insubordination is an offense for which you can be court martialed?"

"Yes, I am, Sergeant," I shouted, hoping it was clear and convincing.

"And, Private," asked the sergeant in the same loud voice, "Are you aware that failure to stay at an assigned post could also lead to a court martial?"

My throat tightened as I realized I had vacated my post in the hut, though I tried to keep my voice as steady as before. "Yes, I am, Sergeant!"

"Now, Private," his voice softened to a normal tone, as if we were having a mutual conversation, "I'd like to get a story straight for our major here to report. Tell him what happened in that village today so there can never be any questions in the future."

"Yes, will do, Sergeant, right away." My whole body tensed as the images of the day swelled in my head and I tried to pick the right ones. "We had to interrogate the villagers, sir, to find the VC tunnels, sir."

"Villagers or VC?" The major's voice had an angry edge to it that I feared was meant towards me.

I glanced at the sergeant knowing I had to get this answer just right. "They were living in a village, sir, but it was very clear they were all VC."

He wrote on his pad for a moment. "Go on, son."

"They resisted all our efforts, sir, though the sergeant and his interpreter were very forceful in their demands." I swallowed quickly, trying not to give any pause. "Then the VC came out of the jungle and shot mortars at us. We blasted back with grenades and M-16 fire, leaving a body count in the field of at least thirty or forty, maybe much higher, when the Hueys came and lifted us out, sir"

The major nodded into his pad as he continued to write. "Sounds like you men did admirably well for yourselves. And what was the business with Billy?"

Sweat gushed from my body and I hoped it didn't show through my clothes. "He got shot in the legs, sir, and Joe and I had to go back and carry him to the chopper, and we were lucky to get back in time, but we did, sir."

The major glanced up from his pad. "Is there anything else about Billy?"

The sweat soaked into my waistband and I feared soon it would look like I wet my pants. "No, sir, nothing more."

His pencil tapped the pad. "And the kids who got killed?"

I felt my shirt stick on my chest with each breath. "They wasn't no kids, sir. They were seventeen or eighteen at least, and they were VC. They would have killed us first chance they got, sir."

He nodded as he wrote. "I'm sure you're right about that."

I feared the next question would be why I left my post in the hut, but instead he looked at me and smiled. "Private, would you care to give a personal statement for *Stars and Stripes* that would do you proud?"

My flowing thoughts seemed to come to a complete halt. All I could do was utter, "I don't know what to say."

"Surely," the major pressed the eraser into his chin, "you must have some thoughts on being caught in such a dangerous situation that you could share

·with our readers. Tell me what a brave soldier like yourself is thinking in the heat of the battle."

"It's hard to tell, sir." I felt myself stumble over the words. "It all happened so fast, sir. There wasn't any time to think. All I could do was stand my ground and fire back when the mortars started."

The major raised his pencil into the air. "And save Billy."

"Yes." I fought against my increased breaths to keep my chest as still as possible. "That also happened too fast to think. All I knew was all three of us had to get on that chopper and I wasn't going to let nothing stop us, and we made it, sir."

"Yes, you did, Private." A smile spread on the major's face. "You certainly did. And I want to thank you for your enlightening story."

"You're welcome, sir," I said, hoping I'd said enough of the right things to save the squad, but fearing I hadn't.

"And," he tapped his pad against his chest, "I'm sure your parents will be very proud when they see their son's brave words in print."

"Yes, sir." I swallowed hard as I pictured my parents showing it to Aunt Eve, who would show it to Steve, who would probably show it to Naomi. How was I going to stop that!

The major turned to Joe, standing at the foot of his cot. "And I want to thank you, Corporal McCormack, for your brave actions under fire. The Army is proud of you and I'm sure your folks will be, too.

Joe saluted the major. "Thank you, sir."

My heart pounded harder as I knew Naomi would read right through it to the truth, no matter what was written. She would also know I was part of the cover up. I could already hear her cry of, *Imperialist mass murdering pig!*

I felt her furious eyes glaring at me and almost didn't hear the major say, "Keep up the good work. It's always a pleasure to meet genuine heroes."

Joe was the first to respond. "Yes, sir."

I immediately straightened my back and used my loudest voice. "Yes, sir."

Joe and I remained standing at attention while the sergeant began pacing in front of us. "Corporal, Private, I'm leaving it up to you to tell the rest of your squad they're on perimeter night duty this week from zero hundred to zero six hundred hours. I'll expect all of you to be at the bunkers on time, fully rested and alert. Any questions?"

I winced, feeling it a slap in the face when we had just come in from combat, then realized the sarge was directly in front of me. "Any problems with that, Belkin?"

"No, Sergeant." I stretched my back taller. "Perimeter duty at zero hundred hours."

"Very good." The sergeant dropped his hand from his hip. "Inform the others they have six hours to get rested and fed. See you in the bunkers."

"Yes, Sergeant." It came from Joe and me at the same time. We remained stiff in our positions while the major and sergeant walked out of the tent. I even remained still after they left, afraid that they might return.

Joe gave me a shove on the back. "You can breathe now."

I stumbled forward and fell across my cot feeling the edge of the frame dig into my side. "Do you think they believed me?"

Joe plopped down on his back and looked up at the ceiling. "Of course not. They know bull when they hear it. But what you said should convince them not to worry about you."

I sat up and looked around the empty room. "So you think they'll leave the squad alone?"

"Sure as I'd bet on a full house." Joe slipped his hands behind his head.

I jumped off the bed, feeling almost as high as that afternoon. "Great! Play you ten dollars a hand till the deck runs out."

Joe sat up and gripped his knees. "Damn, you're anxious to part with your money."

"Just feeling lucky." I began to pace the room. "Definitely lucky."

Joe went to his footlocker, retrieved his cards and began shuffling as he sat back on his bed. "How long you think your luck will hold out?"

I sat opposite him and watched him deal the cards face down in two sloppy piles. "Long enough to beat you."

Joe smiled and patted the space on the bed between us. "Ante up. Ten to start. Throw it away."

We both threw in a ten of Marine issue funny money then picked up our cards.

Joe tapped the deck. "What's your bet?"

I stared at my five cards and zeroed in on the two queens. I always liked queens, won a seventy-five dollar pot with a lady pair at Pendleton, but those were hearts and diamonds, this was hearts and spades. "Five dollars." I threw a five on the two tens.

Joe tucked his cards under his chin and looked at the bills on the bed. "I don't fall for your bull. Five and raise you five." He threw in another ten.

His eyes stayed fixed on his cards and I couldn't get a read from his face. I put in another five then threw down three cards to see what I'd get. Joe also took three new cards, so I guessed he had a pair like me, only lower than queens. My new cards were a six, a jack and a king. The queens were still my hand.

"Bet?" Joe's gaze shifted from one of my eyes to the other, as if looking for a reflection of my cards.

He was the one throwing the bull with that raise. I bunched my cards together and threw a twenty on the pile. "Raise that one!"

Joe's eyes widened. "You sure you want to throw all that away?"

I slapped my cards on my thigh. "Cost you twenty to see no bluff here."

Joe threw it in then flipped two aces over. "Can you beat that?"

I stared at the aces, stunned, and dropped my own cards at my side. Why had I been so sure? He knew I only had a pair, I should have seen it coming.

Joe scooped up the money and shoved it in his pocket. "You want to give the midnight assignment to the squad instead of going broke?"

"Makes more sense than losing my shirt." I pulled on it, realizing it had loosened from my skin and I buttoned my still opened pants.

Joe and I left the tent and started on the path we took before. "You think they're in the same spot?"

Joe pointed up ahead to the circle of black soldiers that seemed to have grown twice as large as it was before. "Looks like it."

Wesley, Moustafa and Leon were close together on the right-hand edge. I headed straight for them, shouting, "Squad orders from the sergeant."

Wesley broke ranks and walked towards me with Moustafa and Leon close behind. They stood in a row, forming a barrier between me and Joe and the rest of the blacks.

I looked across at all three. "Good news. I straightened it out with the reporter and the sarge and there's no talk of us being shipped out any time soon. Only..."

Wesley hands flew to his hips. "Only what?"

I felt my shirt begin sticking to my chest again. "Only the squad is assigned to perimeter night duty from zero hundred to zero six hundred hours, all this week beginning tonight. And Sarge wants us there pronto, on the dot."

Wesley's head started nodding as he turned to Moustafa and Leon, then the whole group of blacks, and raised his arms high. "We have a classic situation here of the black man's persecution in this white man's militia. There's one set of rules for these here whites and a whole other set for us down-trodden blacks."

I couldn't believe what he was doing, but the mass of stares from the group held me quiet and still.

He continued on, "Had it been a black man that accused a sergeant of doing wrong, he'd be court martialed and thrown in the slammer. But when a white boy does it, how does it go down?"

Wesley paused to sweep his eyes from one end of the group to the other. "I'll tell you what happens when a white boy does it. He gets away with it and who gets extra duty? Us darkies, that's who."

"I have the same assignment!" I shouted to the back of his head. "It's not just you."

"The point is," Wesley's arms pressed three times into the air like setting a beat, "the point is we have it because of the white boy's big mouth. They're down on him but the orders come down on us."

I rushed behind him and shouted between Wesley's and Leon's heads. "The orders came from the brass to the squad, not from the sergeant to you."

Wesley laughed as if amused by a child's funny words. "Wake up, Scout," he turned to me for a moment, then back to the group. "This is happening because they're down on you. You, being white, ain't used to how unfair treatment works."

I felt my shirt completely plastered to my body again, like it had been with the sergeant and major. I shouted as close to his ear as I could get. "What's that supposed to mean?"

"It means," Wesley turned, pausing towards me to glare for a moment before completing a full circle back to his group. "The sergeant doesn't like what you said about him. He gives you a chance to retell it so he comes out all patriotic for the politicians and reporters back home. Then he puts you on perimeter to keep you tired and busy so you don't go blabbing what he really did. But because you're white, he don't want to single you out, so he puts all the rest of us on duty, too."

I was stunned and unable to think of any way to refute what he said.

"Wesley." It was Joe's voice from right next to me. "Who you trying to impress with your big speech? I don't see no hot women here."

Wesley chuckled. "If there were, I'd have at least three on each arm, hanging on my every word. You can be sure of that. But you listen here, Joe." Wesley pointed his finger at him. "This ain't no personal thing. It's a miscarriage of justice, us getting an extra assignment because of covering up a white boy's mistake. The brothers are tired of that and we want it to stop. We do most of the hard contact in this stinking war and what are we fighting for? So we can keep being treated like niggers and assigned extra work to cover white asses? No offense to you and Scout, 'cause you is out there in the

107

jungle with us and putting up with the same hell we is, but the brothers is tired of having to cover more than our share. It has to stop somewhere and we have to take a stand."

I pushed myself in front of Joe. "Take a stand with the brass. They're the ones assigned it to you, not me."

Wesley stood looking at me, while everyone in the background remained silent when Moustafa called out, "We have to stick together or they'll kill us off one by one, just like they're doing to the VC!" He turned from the group to Wesley. "You can't cave in to no white boy. He has to take his own heat."

I grasped Wesley's arm but immediately let go. "I'm not getting any more breaks than you!"

The whole group moved closer to Wesley, who glanced across their mass as if taking in each face. I stood waiting, feeling my drenched shirt drip the excess down my legs. Wesley looked back at me. "There's no other way, Scout. You have to tell the sarge to give you your own punishment, and not have it assigned to the whole squad."

"He won't listen to me!" My shout set off a pounding in my ears that grew progressively louder. "Can't you see doing perimeter duty is better than being sent on a hump?"

Wesley thrust a finger towards me that came an inch from my chest. "You tell him, Scout, that this whole mess should come down on you, and you alone, and that the rest of us should not get nothing."

"You think I can make him do that?" Sweat slipped in my eyes and burned like tears. I swiped at it with my sleeve, but it merely smeared around my face.

"Hell no," said Wesley. "But if he don't to listen to you, then you'll find out what's it like to be a nigger, with nothing to gain but extra loads. Except you, Scout, you's white. You try hard enough, you can find a way to convince him, a deal, or your daddy can pull strings, anything to get him to make it come down on you alone."

I shook my head violently, not knowing how to make him understand. "I have no deals or strings to offer him, or even a way to get him to talk to me again tonight!"

Wesley leaned in close and spoke right at me for the first time. "Listen, Scout, we'll have to spell this out for you, so listen good 'cause I'm only saying this once. The VC are planning a full blown attack on base tonight."

"What?" Sweat gushed from my upper lip into my mouth, making me have to swallow hard. "Where'd you hear that?"

Wesley's voice stayed at just above a whisper. "Word gets around. There's ARVANS on base acting as patriots of the south by day who are VC by night, and word is, base is going to be hit tonight. That's why the sergeant gave us perimeter. He wants us in that line of fire."

"No, he wouldn't…"

Moustafa gripped my shoulders and shouted right in my face. "Yes, he would, and Scout, you're responsible if any of us buys it tonight. You got that?"

Joe came to my side and looked Moustafa straight on. "He's not setting no one up. Don't put that crap on him."

Moustafa leaned his chest towards Joe. "If it weren't for Scout's mouth, we wouldn't be on perimeter. You figure it out from there."

Joe threw his hands out to his sides and slapped them down on his legs. "You don't know that!"

"I know," Moustafa let go of my shoulders and pointed in my face, "that Scout's mouth put us there. And it's his job to get us off before zero hundred."

"Or what?" shouted Joe.

"Or we'll have to make sure he's no longer a risk!" Moustafa shifted his glare to me.

Joe stepped between me and Moustafa, holding his arms out like a shield. "Are you threatening him?"

Moustafa's hand took on the shape of a gun and pointed it at Joe. "It's a statement of fact."

Wesley shoved his arm between them and pushed Moustafa back. "Cool it. This is about education, not violence. Scout here has had his lesson on the ways of this here base. Now he has to get the heat off us before tonight. After that, if he's still drawing heat, might be time for another placement."

Joe turned to Wesley. "Transfers take weeks!"

Wesley shrugged. "He can always volunteer for some out there mission till his tracks are cool. Would be safer for everyone."

I was terrified and glanced at Leon before returning to Wesley. "You want me dead, don't you?"

Wesley shook his head. "You have it all wrong. It's me that wants to stay alive."

Moustafa pointed one hand up in the air. "And it's time for us brothers to stop getting set up."

"I want that, too," I began, but Wesley turned and started back up the hill with Moustafa one step behind. Leon lingered for a moment, placing his hand in his pockets. "Can't blame you for being mad. You is not the problem. It's the white brass. You been nothing but good to me. I'm sorry it came to this."

"I'm sorry, too, maybe you could talk to them…" but before I could finish, he turned to follow the others.

I watched Leon blend into the group then turned away and began long strides, with no thought as to where I was going, no idea where the sarge might be and no intention of finding him.

Joe caught up to me. "Those assholes got their enemies screwed up. Don't even know who to fight."

I quickened my pace. "They know who to fight, me. I'm the one out to get all the blacks killed. And I have to die to save them. Didn't you hear?"

Joe began to jog to keep up. "It's Moustafa. He's got their asses in an uproar over the desk job."

I kicked a rock out of my path. "This started because I cared that two kids got killed. Can you believe that? Now I'm public enemy number one. And what's this shit about me getting them off perimeter. How the hell can I do that?"

"You can't. That's impossible."

"Damn right I can't. But then which enemy do I fight, those in the perimeter or those outside?"

Joe turned to jog backwards, looking beyond me up the path, then turned forward again. "The outside enemy. The blacks are just blowing steam. They'll fight by your side when the VC attack. You'll see."

"And what about the ARVANS and villagers being VC. How do I know who's really the enemy?"

Joe pursed his lips for a moment, then loosened them. "The ones out to get you, they're the enemy. But truth is, that could be from any group or uniform."

"Yeah, well for me that's the VC, probably at least half the ARVANS and villagers, those blacks back there, the sergeant, the major, even Billy. I feel like this war has shifted to who can get Scout first."

Joe rapped me on the arm to get me to look at him. "Not as long as I'm alive it's not. You saved my ass, I'll never forget that. You're going to walk off that plane in Oakland and have a real life again. I'm going to make sure of that."

I recalled that patch of green that made me stop him from falling in the pit. But it was me that was the lucky one that he was still alive. Without Joe I'd be good as dead. I rapped his arm this time. "I think you're the only one I'll ever trust again. And all that bull I said about doing whatever I had to do to get the squad home alive, I must have been crazy. It's you and me. I'm going to get you home and you're going to get me home. The rest of them no longer matter one bit." A vision of Leon flashed in my mind, and I thought how awful it would be if he didn't get home to Dolores. I was almost ready to take back what I said—almost, but not quite.

We found ourselves in front of the mess hall, hearing the clamoring voices of men whose mission it was to kill other men, though who they considered the enemy felt frighteningly unknown. I hesitated and felt Joe's hand on my shoulder. "It's all right, Scout. I'll watch your back. We can't get home if we starve to death."

I looked through the opened door, seeing waves of olive camouflage and felt a churning in my stomach that wasn't from usual hunger. "You said the enemy could be any group or uniform. I've learned it could be a sergeant, a major, or anyone in my own squad judging me by the color of my skin. How do I know my real enemies?"

Joe scanned the inside crowd then looked back at me. "You keep alert at all times, and like that green leaf in the jungle, the enemy will always give you a sign."

~ CHAPTER 8 ~

Sniper on Base

Joe and I stood in line waiting for chicken, mashed potatoes, and the mixed together peas and carrots. I rapped my fingers on my tray, the smell of the food causing desperate pangs in my stomach. My fear of enemies around me was now rivaled by my building hunger.

I took one step closer, putting me about twenty back from being served. My eyes focused on the rolls behind the counter. Why didn't they give them out while we waited? I could almost taste one in my mouth with a thick hunk of butter in its middle. Saliva oozed from my tongue as I imagined delicious warm bread when a horrible smell of excrement made me suddenly wish all tastes were gone. I turned to see a man entering the mess who looked like he'd emerged from a putrefied swamp. The only clean things on him were an M-16 by his right arm and one strapped to his pack. He passed where I stood, giving me a close glimpse of his rancid uniform, roughly matted hair, and frayed belt supporting four ammunition pouches and three different knives. It was then I noticed the German Shepherd walking next to his left leg, following him to the front of the line where they stopped and faced the counter.

The man peered directly at the person serving the food and slammed his hand on the glass. "We're hungry. Two plates of food. Now!"

The server looked back at him and pointed towards the door. "Sorry, man, you have to get on that line. Those are the rules."

The filthy man flinched back his shoulders then raised, locked and loaded his M-16. "I don't think you heard me. Two plates, now!"

The entire mess hall became still. The server looked desperately around him as if expecting someone to come to his aid, though no one did. He put his hands up in front of his face and hunched his neck down into his shoulders.

"Man, I hear ya but they're not my rules and a whole lot of people will kill me if I don't follow the rules. Please, get on the line with everyone else."

"First," yelled someone from back near the door, "take a shower. Your dog, too. Your stink makes me want to puke."

A few laughs followed, then a shot went off, sending sawdust flying from the wall behind the server. The man lowered the gun to the server's heart. "This the last time. We haven't eaten in five days!"

I held my breath feeling the fear in the room like leaked gas ready to explode when a captain appeared at the man's side and shouted at the server. "Feed this man, on the double, his dog, too! Can't you see they're starving?"

"Yes, sir!" The server grabbed a plate so fast I thought it would propel through the air. But he held onto it and filled it with three times the usual portions before handing it to the man.

The man took it without a nod. "The dog?"

"Yes, sir!" The server this time looked from one warming tray to the next, then heaped on mashed potatoes and slices of chicken and held it up to the man. "Is this okay?"

The man reached for it, though it was the captain who grabbed that plate and said, "Fine," then carried it to the closest table. The captain motioned for the man to sit and set the dog's plate on the floor by the man's foot.

The man watched the dog take the first bite, as did everyone else in the room, then he scooped at his own chicken and potatoes with his hand, not waiting for anyone to bring him a fork from the utility stand.

I stared at him, guessing he must have been in the jungle for at least a month, maybe two, and felt compelled to know where he had been, what he had done, what he had seen, and more importantly, who he was. Without clear thought I left the line and approached his table. But the moment I came within ten feet, the dog raised his head and gave a deep, guttural growl that left no doubt in my mind he would lunge for my throat if I took another step. I froze and saw the man stare at me with the same threatening eyes as the dog.

The captain put his hand up and announced loud enough for everyone in the room to hear, "This man and his dog are to be left alone and given anything they ask. Is that understood?"

The only response was a respectful silence as I returned to my place in the line in front of Joe, unable to stop watching their jaws move at the same fast pace.

A corporal behind Joe spoke to the person next to him in line. "One of them snipers, you know, stay out for months, picking off Charley one by one.

Those guys are sick sonsofbitches if you ask me, living out in the jungle like animals."

Joe leaned back to the corporal instead of taking the next step closer. "Not sick, brave is what it is. They sneak into areas ARVANS have made off limits and report enemy locations we wouldn't otherwise know."

The corporal shook his head. "But months with no one to talk to 'cept a crazy dog? Man, he looks like he's gone mad."

We watched the sniper suck a lump of potatoes from his fingers as his eyes shifted back and forth across the room. Joe pressed his fist into his own stomach. "Gut instinct, that's what you're witnessing, survival in the raw."

I continued to stare at the sniper, though now instead of awe at his forceful presence, I saw him as the key to my own survival. He could get me out of here before I got set up by the blacks or forced on a suicide mission. There were organizations in Sweden that would assist American deserters once they fled the country. This man, who was ravaging his food while his eyes challenged anyone coming near him, had to know the trails out of this trap-infested hell. He could be my ticket out.

The captain who had demanded his food from the server, returned to the table with another filled plate. This time I could see the sniper speak a bit in between his chews. The captain wrapped his hand around his chin, but then as he listened for a while longer, scraped his fingers down his cheeks. It was clear that the reason the sniper walked in here wasn't just for the food. He also wanted to give information to the brass, obviously disturbing information. But the whole thing made no sense to me. Why would a man who could desert anytime and get himself written off as dead or missing and start a whole new life, choose to return? Suddenly, I was desperate to know that even more than I had to know if he would help me. It felt an essential key to my whole future, either on this base or off. I had to talk to him.

The sniper stopped speaking and listened while he pulled apart a piece of chicken from the second plate and held it down for the dog. The dog lapped it into its mouth quickly then rested his head on his master's thigh. The sniper offered more chicken to the dog, but this time he left it in his master's hand. The sniper then put that chicken in his own mouth and chewed slowly, keeping his focus on the captain.

The two men spoke for another minute when the sniper stood up from the table, and with the dog following one step back, headed out of the mess hall. I felt my chances at freedom disappear with each of his methodical, deliberate strides. I wanted to run after him but knew the dog would attack if I did. I stood watching him leave, in the same position I had been when he came, much closer to the food, but still fearful of what else might come down on me when I least expected it.

I continued staring at the door once he was gone, in case he reappeared, though he didn't. I considered following him but the wide perimeter he commanded around him and the dog was not to be crossed.

"You're next."

I turned, realizing it was the server talking to me. "Same as him," I said, meaning the sniper. The server placed the usual size mounds of potatoes and peas and carrots on my plate, then added three thin slices of chicken. I took it, disappointed not to be treated like the sniper, and walked towards the table he vacated.

I sat in his exact spot when Joe arrived with his tray and began waving his arms at the air. "Man, the stench here is awful. Let's sit somewhere else."

I placed a fork full of potatoes in my mouth and said in a mumble, "Doesn't bother me." I swallowed the sticky mass and started on the next forkful.

Joe sat opposite me, his nose crinkled from the smell. "If I was him, man, I'd get that brown soap and scrub myself raw. There must be every jungle rot in existence living on his skin."

I stabbed at my peas and carrots. "Maybe, but I bet he never caved into his sergeant or a reporter or his own squad. Damn, I feel dirtier than him."

Joe let his fork clink against his plate. "Don't kid yourself. Anyone looks at him wrong, he'll kill them faster than squashing a mosquito. That don't make him better than you."

I shrugged, pushing the peas and carrots into the potatoes. "At least he doesn't get messed with."

Joe laughed. "No one's crazy enough to do that."

I began to cut the chicken when Leon rushed up to us and leaned much of his weight onto the table. "Did you hear?" He paused, taking heavy breaths like he'd been running. "They're calling a beer fight for tomorrow noon, out on the big center field."

Joe jerked himself straighter in his seat. "That's impossible. They only do that back home."

Leon shook his head. "Tomorrow, noon. They's all talking 'bout it. There's fifteen grills gettin' set up and a guy in alpha company said they's assigned to unload a full Huey tomorrow and hump it to the field. Word is it's a hundred cases of Schlitz and twenty boxes of steaks."

I tapped my hands on the table. "It sounds good to me. What's so bad?"

Joe's forehead bulged over his eyes. "The food is only part of it. A beer fight is the Marine way of settling scores. If someone's bustin' your butt, no matter their rank, it's your chance to fight it out fair and square and get it out of your system."

My fingers throbbed picturing me and the sarge stepping into a boxing ring. But then the muscles I'd seen on his arms made me shudder. "Aren't we supposed to fight Charley instead of each other?"

"It's because," Leon's shoulders hunched higher around his head, "morale is so low with squads disputin' among themselves and what they see as unfair treatment by officers, some even stopped followin' orders. This beer fight's what Wesley says the Marine way of clearin' the air and gettin' us back to killin' Charley."

"Damn." I stared into my chicken and potatoes. "I'm not the only one can't figure out the enemy. The brass thinks we should kill each other."

"Not kill each other." Joe looked back over both his shoulders before continuing. "There's rules you have to follow, no guns, knives, or any kind of weapons. And no bars and stripes to show who's got rank. Just Marine issue tee-shirts and plain old fists. And if a man's down, you have to back off. No putting anyone in the hospital."

"Same thing I heard. They's real strict on the rules." Leon's gaze shifted from Joe to directly at me. "You gots to be prepared."

"Prepared?" I shrieked and dropped my fork to my plate.

"Keep it down." Joe's hands tapped the table right in front of me. "This isn't stuff you yell for everyone to hear."

My throat tightened as I whispered to Leon, "Prepared for what?"

Leon looked down at the table for a moment, then probed his eyes into mine. "Moustafa's talking about going for you, Scout. He's runnin' at the mouth about how you put the squad at risk and didn't care 'cause you knew you'd get off 'cause you's white."

Joe's elbows hit the table. "What's with him?"

Leon's gaze stayed on me. "He says you need to be taught a lesson you won't never forget, 'cause since you got away with it once, nothin' to stop ya from doin' it again, only next time we'll all be sent out on a hump where they's no return."

"That's crazy!" The buzz in the air quieted and I covered my mouth, realizing I had yelled too loud. I leaned closer in to Joe and Leon and said in an angry hiss that only the three of us could hear, "I did what Moustafa wanted. I lied to the sarge and the major. I did it for him and Wesley and the rest of the squad. How could he say I don't care if they get killed?"

"I know he's wrong about you." Leon's Adam's apple slid up and down his throat, ending in a slow gulp. "That's why I wanted you to know. It's only fair."

"Fair?" Joe's hands hit to the table, making it shudder. "What's fair about blaming someone for something they're not going to do?"

Leon straightened up then turned his head towards the food counter, scanning those waiting in line. I thought he was going to leave but he turned back, staring only at the table. "Look, that comes from him. I wanted you to know what he said, is all. Now I have to get back. You understand how it is."

Joe slapped his hand on Leon's before he could lift it. "Oh, we understand all right. You tell that mad man Moustafa that anyone gets their ass beat it's going to be him."

Leon's eyes shifted back and forth from one side of the table to the other. "Listen, I wanted you prepared, is all. Don't mean to start no fight between you and me and don't mean to be no go between." He stared down at his covered hand.

Joe pulled his hand back and dropped it in his lap. "Sorry. We appreciate the warning. I know it wasn't easy for you."

Leon's face winced, then he left for the door. I watched him walk away, and mouthed the word, "Thanks," wishing I could shout it for him to hear.

Joe tapped his fork on his plate. "Damn that Moustafa. He's got no business taking his desk job fight out on you."

I shifted uncomfortably in my seat. "He must figure stomping my white head is his best chance up the mountain to that job." I stared at the narrowed pile of potatoes on my plate, fearing I'd be smashed easier than that heap.

Joe shoved a piece of chicken in his mouth and chewed as he spoke. "We're going to get him good, Scout, don't you worry."

"We?" I pushed my plate to the side, the smell suddenly making me nauseous. "He's coming for me, remember?"

"Wrong!" Joe dropped both forearms to the table, making his fork and knife clank on the wood. "Don't think I'll let Moustafa break my promise to get you home in one piece. I'm going to help you get him right in his mouth, where he deserves."

I knew he meant well, but his tough talk annoyed me, since I was the one going to get the beating. "How you going to help me do that?"

Joe pointed at me with his knife. "I humped with him enough times to know where he's weak." He brought his face in closer to mine. "You ever see how Moustafa reacts to loud blasts?"

I shrugged one shoulder. "Not exactly but a blast jolts everyone. You can't help it. I do it too."

Joe shook his head. "Not like Moustafa. He hears a blast he cringes. I've seen it many times. You don't cringe. I watched you in the village. You hear a bang, you drop to the ground and lean forward with your gun pointed ahead. But Moustafa, his stomach caves in and his head bends down. That's your ticket."

I didn't know what he was talking about and screamed, "He's stronger than me and there won't be any blasts!"

Joe put his finger up to his mouth. "Hush, will you? Listen to this. You're right, no blasts from bombs or mortars or guns. But I'll be there, screaming at exactly the right time like a freakin' fire alarm. He'll cringe and you slam him in the face when his head goes down."

My right hand balled into a fist and thrust into my left palm. Was this possible? My punch was strong, I'd learned that at contact training, only I was easily hit. But this, if I could get him before he got me, there was a chance, the best chance I could hope for. My taut knuckles pressed harder into my palm. I looked back into Joe's eyes. "I can do that, man. That can work. Wham, smack on his chin!"

Joe grinned. "That's it. Go for the knock out. Break his jaw."

I pictured Moustafa bandaged from his chin around his head and slammed my clenched hands on the table. "That would shut him up. In fact, I'd like to do it right now."

Joe's cheeks lowered. "Now will get you locked up. Doing it at the beer fight will get you respect."

I anticipated Moustafa and me in a ring with a huge crowd around. The tension sent a chill up my back, but I was furious enough to beat him. I couldn't wait for it to begin.

Joe glanced towards the food line and pulled his lips in tight. I took a quick look and saw Moustafa's eyes focused on me. My chest pounded and I immediately looked down in my lap.

Joe snapped his fingers in front of my face. "You listening?"

I nodded, though the mounting fear made it impossible to speak.

"You ready for this?"

I nodded again, though I was thinking this was the suicide mission they had in mind for me. There was no choice but to go through with it because I couldn't live with myself any other way, but my chances of getting slammed were a lot better than of me teaching Moustafa a lesson.

Joe jabbed my arm from across the table and forced me to look up. "This is good. He's here. You can't let him get you rattled. You are in control of how it goes down. Keep your head and you can win. It's not a trick or luck. It's keeping your focus on what you have to do. You hear me?"

I let out a deep breath and felt a pulsing surge in my fists. I looked Joe straight in the eye. "Yes, I hear you loud and clear."

Joe pressed against the table and locked his arms straight. "Good, because this is serious. No drinking, no getting high, eat all of your food, and very importantly, get some sleep. There's no fooling around with your condition for tomorrow. You got that, Private?"

I snapped my hand into a salute. "Yes, sir, coach sir!"

Joe's hands hit the table again. "Damn right with that. I am the trainer and you are the trainee. Now finish up that plate and when you're done, carry my tray to the unloading stand. It will help build the muscles in your right hand."

"Roger, sir, trainer, sir, muscle builder, sir!"

We ate the rest of our food in silence then I took our trays to the garbage area in the center of the room. I felt myself being watched and fought against the tremble in my legs as I walked. I pictured how the sniper had walked, not a care in the least who watched or what they thought. It wasn't just that he was tough and ready to kill at a moment's notice. There was something he knew that made him sure of what he was doing. I had to know what that was, and I had to know soon, before the beer fight if I was to stand a chance. Joe came up to my side and we left the mess hall together, walking past Moustafa, Wesley, Leon and the others without looking their way. The only one I did want to see before tomorrow was the sniper. I hoped he was still on base and not already back in the jungle. I had to find him.

* * * * *

The two cobras slithered over the bloodied bodies of the boy and girl until they caught sight of me. They stopped and raised their heads, their eyes glowing in the dim background of the hut. They stared at me like vultures, waiting for their moment to strike, their tongues flashing like daggers in the hazy light. I went for the knife on my hip but found it missing. They hissed like steamy brakes on a train, taunting me for my defenseless state. I panicked and felt my body stiffen to stone, no longer able to move myself out of the

119

way. The hiss of the snakes turned to a mocking laugh, then they lunged for me, wrapped themselves around my head and jabbed their pointed tongues into my eyes.

"Get off!" I screamed, grasping my face for the snakes. Nothing was there as I jolted upright, finding myself in a shadowed darkness, on a cot, in a room with a long ceiling. I swept my fingers along my face, over my ears, through my hair, down my neck and body and onto the bed, frantic for any sign of the snakes, but there was none. I expected they must be in the air ready to lunge back onto me any moment, but all I saw were thin streaks of light illuminating empty cots, bare walls and plastic windows looking like empty tunnels to the outer world.

I realized I was panting through my mouth and sweat flowed down my body, adhering my clothes to my skin, like when the sarge had been here. Only he wasn't, just me, Joe, and a few of the squad. What mattered was there were no snakes. They were a dream, or a nightmare, like the others.

It had been a bad idea to try to sleep, always the same, the snakes or the kids, for only thirty minutes rest before they started, not even, fifteen was more like it. Joe's fist pounded his bed and I almost woke him, but then his hand relaxed and he seemed to become peaceful. I left him alone, hoping he was getting some real sleep that I couldn't get. It was our only chance for the night, then guard duty. I wouldn't have bothered, except Joe insisted I do it for tomorrow's fight.

I shook my head trying to make the image of the snakes crawling on the kids go away. Its lingering unnerved me. I should have waited till morning to shut my eyes, when it was light out and the dream demons weren't as strong. My head cleared enough to begin hearing the chatter from the whist game on Wesley's bed.

Moustafa's voice penetrated my thoughts. "Can't none of you fools beat my trump, so don't even try."

I wanted to answer, *I'll beat your trump tomorrow, right in the jaw.*

I looked over to see Moustafa at the foot of the bed, Leon to his right, someone I didn't know to his left, and Wesley at the head. It was Moustafa who spoke again. "All the good cards are right here in my hand so you all can pack it in now and put your money directly in my pockets. Save you all a lot of trouble."

I wondered if that's what he expected of me tomorrow, that I would just give up and not fight back. No way, Moustafa, I'm going in swinging. I've got nothing to lose. Fight you or be forced on a suicide mission, those are my choices.

I checked my watch, 2300 hours, sixty minutes to go. I picked up my M-16 and turned, my hand throbbing as I glanced in Moustafa's direction, but then I kept on going and headed for the door. A breeze in the cooled night air went through my damp shirt and sent a refreshing chill on my chest. My flashlight beamed into the darkness and landed on the path that led towards Joe's stash. I followed it, though I knew he'd be furious if I got high. I kept going anyway, not having anywhere else to go.

I reached the spot that had lured me and flashed the beam on the triangle of rocks. They were undisturbed, just as Joe had left them. I began to bend forward when I was grabbed from behind by overpowering strength. My arms were practically crushed into my body and a sharp metal edge was stuck under my chin.

There was a hot blast of air by my ear and the words, "Where are you going?"

The accent stunned me. It was American. I had expected the more precise pronunciations used by Vietnamese, but then realized the height of my attacker was too tall.

His hold on my body tightened and I struggled to keep from trembling, afraid to force the knife into my neck. I had no idea what was happening. Maybe I had walked in on a drug deal, which meant I could easily end up dead. I raised my chin, trying to speak, and he eased the knife enough for a bare whisper, "Nowhere, just going for a walk. I didn't see nothing. I swear."

He squeezed tighter around my middle and I feared my ribs would crack under the intense pressure. Again, his breath in my ear, "Who are you meeting?"

My chest felt ready to explode and I began gasping for air despite the ominous pressure of the knife. But instead of getting slit like I feared, he eased his hold enough for me to speak. "No one," I sputtered. "I'm alone, walking before I go on perimeter."

He slammed his elbow into my chest sending a throbbing pain that seemed to scream its way through me. He hissed louder this time, "Why over here?"

"No reason," I mouthed, too hurt to hear if it came out as real sound.

The knife jerked to the side of my face, its edge much too close to my eye. I inhaled only a drop of air at a time, afraid to move even the slightest bit, as he demanded, "Tell me!"

The pressure next to my eye increased and I shrieked, "My stash is here. You want to see it?"

He loosened his arm around me, grasping my left arm instead, then slid the knife to behind my shoulders. "Show me."

I fell to my knees and moved the rocks, then scraped at the earth, his breath on my neck. I continued to dig, feeling the knife shift sideways, allowing my arms to take longer strokes. A minute later I reached the plastic bag and held it up to the moonlight to show the eight joints.

He tightened his grip on that arm and raised it to take a closer look. "Anyone else know you're here?"

My head shook. "No one." I turned around to him, hoping he would see I meant it and let me go. But at that first glance I jolted backwards on my heels, nearly falling on my ass. It was only his grip on my arm that kept me from going over. I steadied myself, but with my ankles still shaking, I looked again into that partially shadowed face. It was those challenging eyes that were unmistakable. Except this time they were underscored by sharply angled cheeks and a blunt chin instead of a scraggly beard. But I would know him anywhere, the sniper, the one who I was desperate to meet, and now had been ready to kill me, twice.

He released his grip and crouched over the hole, his muscles bulging under his snug tee-shirt. He motioned to my stash with a flick of his chin, then in a whisper said, "Put it back and get out of here."

I nodded but didn't move, unable to take my eyes off him.

"Go on." He kicked loose dirt into the hole. "No one's allowed on this field tonight."

My eyes remained on him. "What are you here for?"

His finger went to his lips and I realized my voice had been louder than his. I covered my mouth to show my mistake, then whispered, "Someone's here?"

He pointed to his right. "Down the hill. I thought you came to give them signals."

I glanced in that direction but didn't see any movement. "Give who signals?"

His gaze shifted around my face, then stopped to look directly in my eyes. "VC. They're all over this base, day and night. This whole damn country's full of them, only reason we's still in this war is the napalm."

I pointed to my left. "They're out there now?"

The sniper gave a half nod. "ARVAN commander's been shuttling back and forth from this base to a tunnel past two days. Now I hears them down there, like a stream in April, could be as many as thirty."

I stretched my neck in that direction. "That's leaves rustling."

His eyebrows pulled closer together and he spoke to the air down the hill. "Leaves are scratchier."

I listened more intently, but couldn't hear any distinction.

"There it is again," he said, and remained perfectly still, only his eyelids twitched as if recording a code. It was then I noticed the dog sitting by his side, motionless as the sniper. He had been so silent I hadn't even heard him pant.

"They're turning our claymoors around to blast at us," the sniper whispered in my direction. "Most we have is an hour. Alert your sergeant. He must tell the captain."

At the mention of the sarge I panicked, knowing I hadn't told him the blacks refused to do perimeter and with an attack looming, this would come down on me even worse than before. "I can't. I don't know where he is."

The sniper silently swatted a bug on his face and then glared at me. "Get your squad to find him. The captain must know!"

I didn't know how to tell him my squad would refuse anything I asked. "It's not that simple."

He turned to face me full on. "What's with you? The enemy's coming!"

I swallowed hard and tried to answer without sounding weak. "They're not my only enemy."

He turned away from me and muttered as he stormed towards the path, "They's the worst enemy ever lived."

I rushed up behind him, jogging to keep up with his long strides. "How do you know that?"

He turned to the side and spit on the ground, then glanced back at me and spit on the ground again. "They killed my brother." He wiped his forehead with his sleeve. "Cut him up alive in a hundred pieces. Made my mother go so mad, she killed herself. No one's worse than that."

I opened my mouth but was too stunned to form even an "oh." All I could do was pant the way I expected the dog to do, but didn't. Finally I managed to gasp, "Sorry."

He didn't respond. I had to quicken my pace to keep up with him. He turned to go the opposite way of my tent. I stayed close behind, trying to figure out how to ask what I had to know. After a few more steps, I forced it out of my mouth in a rush. "Is that why you stay in the jungle?"

He stopped moving like he'd slammed on the breaks, and I stumbled to his side to keep from banging into him. His look at me was the same one he gave when I came too close to his dog in the mess hall. The dog was staring at me, too, growling a singular, deep, vibrating note. I was about to turn and run when he began to speak. "I've got nothing left but killing. And I won't stop till I destroy every last one of those bastards who tortured my brother."

I didn't know if I was more scared of his piercing stare or by what he said, but I still had to blurt out, "What about the kids? Do they have to die, too?"

His forehead wrinkled and his shoulders jerked backwards. "They's Charley, all of them, can't help it."

"But," words rushed into my mouth so fast I feared they'd suffocate me if I didn't get them out fast enough, "but we kill brothers and mothers like yours."

"I don't care about that." He spit on the ground, keeping a sideways glance on me. "I'd kill all of them to give decent, hard-working people a chance."

"But," I began, when he slammed down on my raised hand and pointed down the path we just came.

"Go back and listen to what they's doing. It could start faster than I expect. Stay out of sight, but don't leave till I show up. Now go, that's an order!"

He turned and continued towards the officer's club, the dog following at his heel.

I watched his purposeful steps surge onward over the packed down earth before heading back towards the field. I walked silently, hearing the sound of a very faint whistle in the distance. I wondered if it was wind blowing over leaves or if it was VC. And what would the sniper do if it was VC, rush at them with an M-16 blasting? And why didn't he do that down the hill? Was it 'cause he didn't want to get shot so he could keep killing? I shuddered, recognizing how his hatred made him want to kill them all, but unable to believe I could ever feel that way or even want to kill any of them. But the main disappointment was not gaining any insights to make me more forceful at tomorrow's beer fight.

I reached the opening to the field and entered, still hearing the whistling sound, though not any louder. I wondered if it was insects like cicadas back home that chirp all night, only these were quieter, like the people they lived among.

The plastic bag was lying the way I left it, uncovered in the hole. I crouched next to it and pushed the loose earth back in, then topped it with the three stones when a loud rustling occurred at the entrance. I looked up, assuming it was the sniper, but it wasn't. It was Joe.

He approached, his M-16 across his chest and his hand pointing to the freshly placed earth. "I was afraid I'd find you here."

I stood, holding my finger over my mouth and pointing down the hill. "We have to be quiet, 'cause he thinks they're down there. And I didn't smoke anything. The sniper was here when I came, only he thought I was here to give signals to the VC and made me show him the stash so he'd believe that's not why I came. He heard the VC positioning for an attack, and he's alerting the captain. I'm ordered to wait here and listen till he gets back."

Joe looked down at the three stones as if trying to see through them to count the joints, then gazed into my eyes. "Either you're so high you figure I'll believe that bull, or it's true 'cause it's too crazy to make up. But we got no time to play, Scout. We're due on perimeter now."

"I can't. Look it's true. I'm not high." I pointed to my eyes, opening them wider. "I have to stay till the sniper gets back. I can't leave. Really, and he told me about…" I was suddenly blasted off my feet, thrown forward on my stomach while a fiery explosion lit up the sky from down the hill. I grasped the ground, still feeling it tremble, then looked to the side, seeing Joe facing down hill about eight feet away.

I was scared he was hit but then saw him roll towards me. "Damn, the sniper heard right. We better get to the bunkers before we're blown apart." He began a high crawl to the entrance.

I hesitated, feeling paralyzed by my options of disobeying the sniper or disobeying the sarge.

Joe threw a rock at me. "Come on. The sarge is gonna kill you if you're not on time. Let's go! You want those charges of insubordination or leaving your post? You know he'll throw in failure to report!" That ended it. I had to go. I began crawling away from my sniper-appointed post, aware that the low whistling sound was getting deeper and louder, but its source and what it meant were still, as yet, unknown to me.

~ Chapter 9 ~

Base Assault

Joe and I ran towards the perimeter bunkers as more blasts shook the ground. Each step on the quaking earth felt uncertain, like it could either cave in any moment or throw us face first on the ground. Joe reached the dugouts first, lowering himself in, then I slipped down the five foot drop.

"Powerful glad to see more troops." It was a voice I recognized from the shower. I looked up to see the one with the hairy chest, though his chest was fully covered. The blond, who had been with him, was sitting in the corner hugging his gun straight up against his side with a radio on his thigh.

Joe squinted. "You're Rascal, right? From Tennessee? And you're Spit?"

Rascal waved. "Sure is right on all accounts. That's us, sittin' here like rats trapped in a snake's hole."

Spit leaned forward, using his gun like a crutch. "Told us there'd be four of you."

I hoped Spit wouldn't ask about it on his radio. "No, the others were assigned a different duty. Any instructions given before we arrived?"

Spit's mouth opened but there was a thundering blast and all four of us flattened on the ground. I gripped the earth, trying to hold fast within its trembling, and braced myself for another explosion. Others came, but they were more distant, and the quivering in the earth was not as severe. It quieted after a minute and I sat up seeing we were untouched, then peered over the bunker's edge. Farther down the hill were flashes of white mortar fire, like long fireworks. One hit the ground and an eruption of debris sprayed in the air. I couldn't tell if it was pieces of people or just pieces of the earth. More fiery flashes started then one headed in our direction. I dropped down, yelling, "Incoming strike!"

A blast boomed, jolting the earth with such force I was thrown into the wall, then a piercing shrill in my ears kept getting louder and harsher making it feel like my head held a bomb ready to blowup. Shards of metal clanged on my helmet, but they were like distant bells, as if miles away.

Rascal's muffled voice cried, "Sweet Jesus, oh lord and savior, if you see me through this alive, I will do whatever you ask!" I mouthed the same words, though not sure my promises would be believed.

There was another blast and more debris pelted down on us. I stayed pressed against the earthen wall, feeling harsh reverberations in my back. I pictured Naomi, angry and turning away, then my body in a casket and only my parents and grandmother leaning over my hole in the cemetery. Suddenly, this hole felt like that hole and I had to get out, fast. I looked for Joe, seeing his form in the darkness on his side, hugging tight to his gun. "Joe, we can't stay in here!"

His head raised when there was an alert from the radio. "Enemy ascending right quadrant hill, sixteen degrees. Direct all fire to that location immediately."

Rascal sat up, wiped at this face then looked at his hands. I had done the same thing, checking for blood. I flashed my light at his face. It was intact. "You look okay."

Joe straightened up and peered over the right edge of the bunker. "I don't see anything from here."

I went to his side and looked for myself. Smoke from the blasts was drifting like hazy clouds, giving an eerie sensation that Charley was hiding in its mist. I tried to see through it, but the smoke was too thick.

Joe looked with his infrared scope. "Man, looks like a swarm of locusts coming. Can't believe it. There must be a hundred of them."

I looked also, shocked at their numbers and their blatant thrust towards us as if our base held nothing to fear. I squeezed my hand around my M-16, feeling an uneasy throbbing all the way up my arm.

Joe began to shoot and I panicked. "Stop, they'll throw a grenade in here. We have to get out!"

Joe gripped the upper edge and lifted up while keeping his body flat on the ground. I did the same, hearing Rascal say to Spit, "Wish we had a root cellar here to hide in."

We crept like lizards, edging forward into the haze. All I could see was a filmy darkness that gave the false impression of empty space. A moving mob came into sight from the left, only it wasn't VC. It was our own men. I could see Wesley, Leon, Moustafa, and about fifty other Marines walking in a tight group with their hands held high in the air like they were under arrest, headed towards the top of the hill.

Joe inched sideways towards me. "What the hell are they doing?"

I put down my scope and wiped at my eyes, unable to believe my own sight. "Looks like those bastards are surrendering!"

The mob's hands tightened into fists and Joe put his gun down like it had suddenly become too heavy. "What are they doing now?"

But his answer came right from their own mouths, as a chant emerged from them like one voice. "1, 2, 3, 4, we don't want your fuckin' war."

I watched them continue up the hill, outraged that they were doing this, knowing we were being attacked. The chanting became louder and seemed to scream in my ears as if another mortar blast had hit. That chant suddenly ceased, then abruptly switched to, "Black power, brothers unite, black power, brothers unite."

I listened as though in shock and was about to ask Joe why they weren't being fired upon by the VC when a shrill explosion blasted into the already disturbed air. We immediately pressed our faces into the earth and I prayed it was one of our weapons aimed at the enemy. Nothing struck us or shook the earth so I thought we were safe and raised my head and saw a grenade hurling towards us through the smoke.

"Run!" I shrieked, rising to my feet. We tried to out-race it but when we were only ten feet ahead, its impact sent out a force that knocked us down like we were mere tiny dolls.

I lay still, throbbing where I had struck, hearing a barrage of firing from the gunners stationed high above us. I pressed every part of me into the ground, wishing I could burrow in deep enough to be safe. But then I had a sudden vision of being six feet under. No, that's not what I wanted and I became furious at the mob for not helping against the VC. Why were they doing this and why weren't they afraid of being attacked?

There were more blasts from both sides. My eyes, nose and throat burned from the smoke, feeling like I'd been forced to swallow smelling salts. I spit on the ground then more explosions came, each one feeling like a direct hit till I'd shake my legs to find out if I was okay, and each time, miraculously, I was. The blasts seemed to go on forever when suddenly I realized it was quiet. I stayed motionless, still braced for the worst, but the quiet remained. I waited some more, listening for sounds of people moving, or talking, or cries from those who might have been hit. But none of that came. I couldn't judge what had happened, even to me. I didn't know if I was paralyzed with no feeling and had fooled myself into thinking my legs could move, or if I was truly okay.

I lifted my head to look, but the burning smoke forced me to shut my eyes.

"Joe," I whispered to my right, hoping he was nearby. "Are you okay?"

No answer, just silence. I opened my eyes again, forcing them to stay open, but they swelled with so many tears I couldn't see. I felt desperate within my blindness, and called out again, in a louder whisper this time, "Joe, where are you?"

I anticipated his voice, saying something like, "I'm right over here." But nothing came. Then other noises began. I heard the rustling of people moving quickly, and one called out, "Over here. Bring a stretcher quick. This one got it in the legs."

And then fairly close to me, I heard a voice, "Check his vitals. I think he's gone."

"Who?" I called out, suddenly anxious. It couldn't be Joe. It just couldn't be Joe. I scrambled to my feet and pushed my way through the smoke to get to that voice.

It was hardly ten steps when I saw them, two medics crouched over a bloody body with a mutilated back. The body was still face down, but I stared at its shape and the shaggy clumps of hair on its head, and terror struck, piercing right through my chest.

"Joe," I screamed out. "It's okay buddy. You're going to pull through!"

One of the medics leaning over him said, "Nothing, no pulse on his neck and no breath."

From somewhere to the left came an alarming cry, "Quick, over here. I've got a big bleeder. Quick, I'm gonna lose him!"

The two medics jumped to their feet and were about to run when I screamed, "No, stay and fix him. He's still in there. I know it. He's alive. He's a fighter. He'll make it!"

One of them stopped and glanced from Joe to me. "I'm sorry, he's dead. We can't save him." He then ran after the other one.

I looked down at Joe, that horrible wound staring up at me, as if trying to tell me something.

"What," I yelled at it. "What did you do to Joe?" The wound was thick and dark, glistening from fresh blood.

"Get back in there!" I screamed at the blood. "He needs you."

I threw myself on the wound, hoping my body could act as a bandage to close it up. It had to work. It just had to.

"Please, don't die!" I cried at his cheek. The blood penetrating my shirt was still warm, but the body gave no resistance to my weight. I grabbed him around the shoulders and pleaded, "Speak to me, Joe. Tell me you're all right!"

A release of air came from his mouth. At first I thought he'd said something, but then I realized the Joe in my arms was totally limp, not breathing, not speaking, not anything.

I heard a medic scream. "I need light!"

A series of flares lit up the air, giving me a better look at Joe. I turned him over to face me and found myself staring into totally vacant eyes.

"No," I screamed. "No, it can't be!"

I rubbed the dirt off his cheeks, as if cleaning him would help, then the wracking in my chest began as I cried, "Joe, I'm so sorry. I promised to get you home alive. I should have done something. I should have given you my spot. Then you would be all right. You're the one that should still be alive, not me!"

A voice in the background came closer. "We got a load of them, Captain. Looks like a body count of at least a hundred VC. But no signs yet of live ones."

The loud staccatos of low flying choppers began filling the air with floodlights pointed to the ground. I wished I was gunning on one right now. I'd find them and I'd kill them all, blast them apart so there was no sign left of who they had ever been.

A commotion of chanting began descending the hill, "1, 2, 3, 4, we don't want your friggin' war."

But this time, instead of empty hands up the air, each one had an M-16 held high, like exclamation marks above their heads. Wesley, Leon and Moustafa were visible on the mob's left edge.

"Joe is dead!" I screamed out to them. I thought they'd want to know, they should know, we were all in the same squad. I waited for a moment but didn't receive a response. Maybe they didn't hear me.

I ran towards them, yelling, "Joe is dead!"

Leon's mouth opened wide and stayed that way, no longer chanting. Wesley returned my look with a hard stare, his forehead wrinkled to a tight line down the center. Moustafa looked through me like I hadn't ever been there. Whatever they each were thinking, they continued to move with the mob. I took a few more steps towards them when Wesley very clearly shook his head as a signal not to approach. I was in too much pain to argue.

I turned away and returned to sit next to Joe, the background chanting of, "Black power, brothers unite," felt almost as unsettling as the explosions had been. I looked down into Joe's eyes that could no longer respond, trying desperately to see into the mind of the one person who could help me sort through what was going on. The base seemed a whirling madness and I felt caught in a chaos I couldn't comprehend. First we were assaulted by our own weapons, then the enemy too easily entered and killed us on our own base, then a group of our own was spared enemy fire and refused to fight, and now a demonstration threatening the very military which provides us our only security within this ferocious war. I felt defenseless and frightened, with no sense of how expansive a mass of enemy there was.

"Joe, please, don't be dead!" I pleaded, looking into his eyes, anxious for a mere flicker of recognition which didn't come, but that I had to believe still had a chance. "You said the enemy was anyone who would kill us. I thought I understood that at the time, but does that also mean it's anyone who refuses to do their part to stop us from getting killed?"

I was desperate for an answer and angry he could no longer give it to me. Even dead, he was the only one in the world I could fully trust.

I brushed the dirt off his face then slid my arms under his body and began to lift. He felt terribly heavy and I struggled just to get him three feet off the ground. I tried a burst of energy to jerk myself into a full upright position, but instead lost my balance and fell backwards. Joe landed across my stomach and I lay there, the breath knocked out of me. I began pushing my arms against the ground.

"Take it easy, fella. I'll get him." I looked up expecting to see a medic, except it was the sniper and his dog staring down at me. Floodlights from the choppers gave me a view of him I didn't see before on the field. His rigid face had soft waves of hair overhanging his ears. He looked like a lion who, with the mere tightening of his jaw, could switch from tender to ferocious. The sniper's lips were now drooped at the sides, looking like he understood my grief, though his unflinching eyes made it clear he himself was beyond tears.

I pushed my back up with my elbows, but only managed a few inches. "He's dead, but I still have to help him."

The sniper gave a quick nod, then bent down and lifted Joe as if being careful not to wake him. Only losing the feeling of Joe was not at all a relief for me. If anything, it was unbearable. I wanted him back and jumped up to his side, taking his head in my hands and holding it steady as the sniper began to walk.

I followed the sniper's lead down the hill. "I promised to get him home alive."

The sniper's lip twitched. "I promised that to someone, too." I was going to ask if that was his brother, when he added, "But weapons are stronger than promises."

I looked at his straight-ahead stare, which avoided Joe or me, and felt suddenly angry. "You knew they were coming. You could have stopped them before this happened!"

The air between us grew taut while the bounce of Joe's head felt terribly loose. I tightened my grip wanting to make him as comfortable as possible.

The sniper increased his pace and blew out a harsh breath. "I first heard them only a few minutes before you came. Before that I knew something was planned, but not what or when."

The faster pace increased the bounce on Joe's head, adding to my frustration. "But you had time, that time you spent on me, you should have gone for the captain then!"

A deep, low, rumbling came from the dog, but stopped when the sniper began to speak. "I knew they were there but not the plan. I thought you knew it, that's what I hoped for, except you didn't. Then I heard them turn the claymoors. I told you, but you wouldn't go to your sergeant."

I wanted to scream, *Don't blame me,* when a loud commotion from behind us made me turn around.

A captain had a megaphone pointed towards the mob. "Put down your guns. Mutiny is not the answer. There are proper channels to handle grievances."

A voice from the center of the crowd shouted, "We're not your niggers anymore!"

The captain looked behind him. There was a line of fifteen Marines, all white, standing with their guns held flat across their chests. Rascal and Spit were among them, their eyes focused on their feet instead of the mob. The captain turned back to the crowd and called through the megaphone, "Put down your guns, immediately!"

There was silence. The sniper turned to face them and I squeezed tighter on Joe's head. My eyes shifted between the captain and the mob when an M-16 blast pierced the quiet and sent me to the ground. I peered up and saw the sniper hadn't moved, but now Joe's neck was stretched back farther than possible if he had been alive.

The blare of the megaphone filled the air. "This can be resolved peacefully. There is no reason to discharge your weapons. Put down all firearms and no reprimands will be issued."

A voice from the mob shouted back, "Damned straight you won't reprimand or you'll get your head blown off." A few of them raised and pointed their weapons at the captain.

The captain shifted his weight to one leg, placing his free hand on his waist as he yelled through the megaphone, "Let's be reasonable here. We're all on the same side."

A different voice came back from the mob. This one I recognized; it was Moustafa. "Same side in this Vietnam War because of uniform color, but different sides of the master - slave war because of skin color."

The captain's hand burst out from his side, hanging in the air. "Nobody here's a slave. Everyone's in this together."

Moustafa raised his gun high in the air. "Together, but not equal. Only choice to blacks is humping the fields putting their asses on the line while all the desk jobs is white."

"I don't make those assignments." The captain tapped his shirt then pointed at the crowd. "You want a desk job ask a colonel."

"I'm asking you." Moustafa stepped away from the mob and pointed straight at the captain. "Five desk jobs and we put down our guns."

The captain's arm holding the megaphone dropped to his side as he turned behind him, seeming to be searching for a face he expected to be there but wasn't. He turned back and raised the megaphone. "That's not my decision. That's up to the base commander."

Moustafa took a step forward. "Then get him over here, now!"

The captain turned the megaphone directly towards Moustafa. "He's in Da Nang. You can speak to him tomorrow."

A shout from the mob, "Get him now, get him now," then several others joined in, "Get him now, get him now." More voices joined in, then more and more, when the staccato burst of an M-16 hit the ground only fifteen feet from the captain's boots.

I called to the sniper to get down, but my words never reached him. He was already walking towards the area between the mob and captain. I jumped up wanting to stop him, but froze at the sight of fifty guns from the mob held in firm position at the captain. The fifteen men behind the captain had their M-16s pointed back at the mob, and the gunners in their towers higher up the hill were aiming straight into the crowd's center.

I wanted to yell to the sniper to come back when he raised Joe's limp bloody body high in the air and shouted, "Is this what you want? Is this what you want to look like?" His eyes pierced into each face within his vision as he turned to display Joe to both sides. "You kill each other, and this is how you'll go home! If you want to kill, kill those gooks that are killing our brothers!"

"The gooks are my yellow brothers," came a shout from the mob.

The sniper stared in the direction of the voice, his eyes opening so wide his lids seemed to disintegrate. "Then your brother killed my brother! He cut him apart piece by piece keeping him alive and laughing at his agony. Is that who you call your brother?"

"My brother doesn't call me nigger and keep me down like a slave," the voice shouted back.

"You think your yellow brother cares about you?" The sniper's voice was as piercing as his eyes. "Your yellow brother doesn't care one piss about you. What he did is trick you into not fighting back. Not because he cares about your black skin, he only tells you that to make it easy for him to get on base and kill us all. Once you've done what he wants, he'll kill you the same way he kills his own yellow brothers."

The same voice shouted again, "They didn't touch us, you saw that, let us be because they respect us."

The sniper walked closer to the mob displaying Joe's body straight out in front of his chest. "Look what they used you to do. You call this respect?" He paused to walk Joe's body right up to those at the mob's edge. "They only tricked you into thinking it was respect. If they respected you, they wouldn't trick you into standing by and doing nothing while they killed your real brothers, like this fine Marine right here. He could have been the one to save your ass next time you're sent out." The sniper raised Joe's body high in the air, again. "You sure you call this respect?"

The mob remained eerily silent.

"Tell me," the sniper shouted into their restrained stillness, "did this Marine try to kill you or was he on the line trying to save your life?"

An angry voice from the mob yelled, "Hold up a dead black Marine. Let's see how much you care about one of us!"

I ran up to the sniper's side and screamed at the mob, "Joe would have run back to save any of you, same as he did for Billy, and you all know that!"

Wesley stepped to the side, pointed his gun up and faced the sniper instead of me. "We don't have any problem with Joe. He was a good man and I'm sorry he's dead."

I wanted to scream back, *Then why did you stand by and let him get killed?* but the sniper responded faster. "You deserted a man who would have saved your ass, and it's exactly his not saving your ass that could get you killed tomorrow, or the next day or the next. Is that what you want?" He paused to another still silence. "Is it?"

Moustafa stepped forward. "No, man. What we want is desk jobs, but they're only for whites and the officers won't listen."

The sniper looked at him without changing expression. "And you think a VC officer will offer you a desk job?"

Moustafa thrust his gun forward in the air. "No, but you don't listen either. We deserve desk jobs just like whites!"

My anger at Moustafa was too much to restrain. I looked up at him and screamed, "Then take it up at the beer fight with an officer!"

Moustafa pointed his gun above my head. "There's all kinds of oppression on this base to fight."

It was clear by his glare that he intended to pound me tomorrow, and without Joe, I had no chance. I turned my back on him, not able to look him in the eye. All I wanted to do now was hold Joe one more time. I reached out to the sniper for Joe's body. He carefully placed him in my arms and, for a moment, our arms held him together, like two vines crossing paths. He removed his hold and I nodded to him, keeping my chin pointed in his direction. "I'm sorry about your brother."

He nodded back, while keeping his gaze down on his dog.

I pressed Joe tighter against my chest, hoping to somehow feel his heart beat, though I knew there wasn't one, and cried into his face, "Joe, I should never have let this happen!"

"Not your fault, Scout." Wesley's voice startled me. I looked up to see him approach with Leon by his side. "It's no one's fault, but this damn war, making us fight the wrong people."

I felt the first of actual tears swell in my eyes. "He didn't deserve this."

Leon looked at Joe and winced, shaking his head as he spoke. "Sorry, man, it's a damned shame."

I pressed Joe tighter into my chest, his bulk feeling too much for me, but at the same time there was no way my arms would let him down now that I had him in my grasp.

The sniper turned to leave and Wesley stepped in his path. "You've got nerve man, really laid yourself on the line. You're the kind of brother we need."

The sniper's jaw tightened and he peered directly in Wesley's eyes like he was looking directly at his brain. "My brother's dead. The VC took him away. And now another American's brother is dead, too."

Wesley took a step back, nodding. "I hear you, man. I hear you."

The sniper turned and began walking to the left, in the direction of the field. I felt abandoned and scared, not sure I could handle Joe without him.

I called out to him. "Thanks."

He didn't show any signs of hearing me, and I called out, louder, "for Joe."

His fingers went up in a "V".

I didn't know if he intended it as a peace sign or a victory sign and if it was meant for me, him, the base, or this whole war. I took it as all of them and looked down at Joe. "You stopped the worst war of all, my friend, the war among ourselves."

Wesley's voice rang in. "That you did, Joe. You saved a lot of asses from getting shot up tonight. But when you're carted away, heaven help this base of fools."

Two medics ran up to me with a stretcher, one saying, "Sorry, but the chopper has to take off in two minutes. There's a lot of wounded won't make it if they don't get to the hospital fast."

They positioned the stretcher under me and I let Joe down gently while I whispered, "Goodbye, you're going home now. I'll look you up as soon as I get back."

I realized as he was rushed away that it was a strange thing to say, but it felt perfectly natural as I said it. I watched him taken out of sight then looked down at my empty arms, my eyes feeling as vacant as his had been.

Wesley tapped my arm. "Losing Joe is tough, man. Real sorry. I mean that."

A vision of him in the mob with his hands in the air while Joe was shot surged through my head and I found myself screaming, "You let them up here. That's why he's dead!"

Wesley gripped my upper arm. "Now hold on. They was coming up anyway, no matter what we did. Only thing is they promised we wouldn't be touched if we didn't fight back. And they was true to their word. But they was coming anyway."

I pulled my arm against his grip except he held on. "So you saved yourself and let Joe die!"

Wesley shook my arm. "The only plan was to get the sons of bitches brass to take us seriously, not for no one to die, just scared."

I yanked my arm free and took a large step back. "But Joe was killed!"

Wesley glanced at my blood soaked uniform, his head shaking. "That was not 'cause of us. They was attacking no matter what we did. Couldn't have stopped that even if we was on perimeter. Joe was in the wrong spot. That's how it is, bad luck. Others been killed in this war, and others who knowed them a lifetime suffering, too."

I crossed my arms in front of my chest, feeling Joe's fresh blood seep into my palms. "I know I should care about all the others, but right now I only care about Joe."

"Surprises me, Scout." Wesley raised his eyebrows and tilted his head to the side. "You acted so high and mighty when two gook kids were killed, but you don't give a damn about thousands of your black brothers getting destroyed in this honky man's war. If you was hip to it, you'd know it's mostly blacks killed here, and you know what that is?" He paused for only a second, then went on. "Genocide, my man, master race purification. And you just said it yourself, you don't give a damn about any others, and neither do any of the other whites here. Us blacks are the only ones care enough to straighten this out. If the white brass is so hot on this war, let them send their white sons out to get killed. I'm sorry about Joe. He was a good guy. But we all could get killed at any time. There's no stopping that and it's not our fault."

I had listened, though the pounding in my chest resounded over half the words. Wesley kept looking at me, waiting for a reaction. I understood what he'd said, and felt bad that the blacks were killed more than the whites, but I had no reaction to give. I couldn't feel all that right now. I could only feel the misery of Joe's loss.

Leon stepped in front of me, his glances shifting from my shirt to my face. "May not be the right time, but wanted you to know what Joe told Moustafa about the blacks he saw get killed. Said he had three different blacks he followed to teach him point, 'cept one after the other they always got sent out on a fool's mission and got killed. Then he had to take over point hisself, 'cept the missions he got didn't kill him, least not the point missions."

Every part of me seemed to throb as I looked back at Leon. "I know it's unfair, but where does that leave me? Dead 'cause I did point with Joe, or dead by Moustafa 'cause I'm white and whites like Joe don't get killed?"

Leon's head shook, "That's not…"

But he was interrupted by Moustafa's call. "Wesley, Leon, over here."

They turned to see their group forming again. I couldn't bear to look at it and turned away.

I heard Leon's voice behind me say, "Another time, man," and then their footsteps tromped into the dirt up the hill.

I stood alone, staring off to the field where Joe was airlifted out when

Rascal came up to me. "It's a crying shame, Joe being called to his maker, what with no reason and all."

Spit stood by his side and all I could think of was if they had been better Marines, they would have been the ones to jump out of that hole and run where we ran. Then one of them would be dead now and Joe would be alive.

Spit kicked at the dirt, sending a dark cloud above his boots. "It's all those niggers' fault."

My hands squeezed into fists as I glared back at him. "Words like that are what set it off in the first place."

His shoulders shrugged and his hands went in his pockets. "They's always making trouble back home, too."

I had to get away from him and without knowing where to go, began walking towards the field where the sniper had gone.

Rascal called after me. "You want some company?"

I shook my head without turning around and walked away fast. The path heading to the field was dark, though I could see moving lights up ahead in the sky. I was looking for signs and thinking of Joe with every rock, leaf and hum of insect I passed. I couldn't believe Joe was dead, even though I had his blood all over me to prove it. How dare they do that to him, to me. Who was this enemy that infiltrated our very own base, friends by day, murderers by night, who filled villagers with so much fear they wouldn't speak to save their own children? I wanted to kill them all, kill them for what they did to Joe, for what they made happen to those kids, for what they're doing to me.

The clatter in the air became louder. I entered the field and saw two choppers with searchlights pointed into the brush on the edges. It was clear they thought VC were still hiding. Those bastards, were they waiting to attack us again? Was that it, they didn't kill enough of us for one night? Or were they trying to escape after what they'd done? Did they really believe they were going to get away with this?

"Joe, buddy, I'm getting those bastards. That's one promise I'm going to keep!" I gripped my M-16 and charged onto the field.

A spotlight from a chopper beamed on me as I ran. I waved to them to show I was one of theirs. A voice called down through a megaphone, "Get out of the area. We're gunning anything that moves."

"Don't shoot," I screamed up to them. "I'm going down to the barbed wire."

They called down again, "This area is being patrolled. Return to the camp."

This time I remained quiet and pointed straight ahead while continuing to run.

They called down again but when I failed to respond, followed my lead, illuminating my way with enough light to see the perimeter barrier up ahead. The six foot mass of razor wire imposed itself upon the shrubs and grasses with a dominating savagery. It was impossible to imagine a person trying to cross it with all those sharp edges tearing at their skin. I wondered how the VC had penetrated to make their attack when I saw a slim dark figure slithering on the ground towards its edge. His head began to disappear and I knew he was entering a tunnel, right under our own defense. I immediately aimed and shot off a five second burst. The chopper turned its beam to follow my tracers and lit the spot. The figure lay motionless, its bloodied back reminding me of Joe. I ran up to it, screaming, "You lousy gook," and yanked it out from the tunnel's entrance, hoping he was still alive to be tortured for information.

I twisted his face towards me, ready to slam my fist between his eyes, but suddenly became nauseous and fell to my knees. It was that kid, Tuan, who had been on the base that afternoon. That same boy who had seemed so sweet with his big smile and polite manner, that I gave him two chocolate bars. And here he was, lying before me, killed by my own gun. I didn't know if I was more furious or horrified. He had helped kill Joe, maybe even did it himself. I wanted to slam the butt of my gun into his skull. I swallowed against the thick clog in my throat then looked down at the small face, not yet fully grown, and began to tremble. Behind my swelling eyes, Billy had the dead village boy in one hand and his bloody knife in the other.

I stared into Tuan's fixed eyes feeling an enraged scream from my stomach push up through my throat. Its shriek resounded through my head and throbbed in my brain like it was splitting it in two, one part to hide what I could no longer bear, the other for what I needed to do to stay alive.

A voice came up behind me, shouting above the noise of the chopper. "Good catch." I looked up to see the sniper with a dark ball in his hand. "Get away from him. I'm ready to fire up the hole."

I grabbed the body under its shoulders and began to pull it with me when the sniper swatted my arm. "Leave him. He would have left you." He held up the grenade then waved it in his hand towards the chopper, shouting, "Evacuate the area."

The chopper tilted left and veered off in that direction. The sniper tossed the grenade in the hole, gripped my arm and began running. He pulled me faster than I ever ran on my own. We were at least sixty yards away when the blast came, throwing us flat down onto the earth.

The gritty soil pressed into my face as the ground trembled and a gust of heat swept across my back. I had no sensations in my legs and feared I'd been hit like Billy. I shuddered then felt my knee bump against a rock. I banged it again, harder. It hurt, but that was good. It meant I was all in one piece.

The sniper tapped me on the back. "Let's go. There's more out there."

Suddenly Tuan's smile rushed through my mind and without realizing it, I pointed my gun to my head ready to squeeze the trigger.

There was a piercing yell above me as my M-16 was yanked out of my hand. Next thing I knew I was pulled upright by the back of my shirt. "Don't let them do this to you. You're not the enemy, they are!"

I shook my head and he gripped my jaw, pressing in hard on each side. "Listen to me. They twist your mind by sending kids out to fight. They know that hurts you enough to make you think you're the enemy here. But you're not. The killer of these kids is them!"

A cold sweat dripped down my chest and sides. I looked into the sniper's steady eyes and cried out, "I can't take it anymore!"

His hold on me tightened and his eyes probed into mine. "Stop it, you're doing your best for all the Americans they killed and you have to keep doing that. You killed that kid because you had to, otherwise he would have killed you."

"But he's a kid," I screamed. "He's just a kid!"

The sniper gave me a hard shake then screamed back. "Listen to me and listen good. He helped kill your friend and he'd kill hundreds more friends and brothers first chance he got. You stopped him the only way you could. You're a credit to your uniform and to your friend back there. Now stop this and let's go get more of these bastards."

I pressed my heel back into the ground. "No, I'm done with all this. I just want to get the hell out of here!"

He shoved the front of my shoulder. "You can't give up. It's not over yet."

"It is if you get me out of here!" I looked into his piercing eyes that attacked whatever he didn't like and repelled what he didn't want to see. I suddenly hated him and his clear vision. Who was he to criticize me? I was doing my part and I had done my share of killing. How much more did I have to do?

A chopper hovered overhead and dropped a rope ladder down to us while a voice shouted, "Climb up, everyone off the field."

That familiar sound to the orders stunned me. I stared up, feeling a mixture of relief and terror. It was my sergeant, shouting, "Scout, what you doing down there? Get your ass up here, now!"

The sniper pulled on the ladder, holding it tight, while I grasped it and climbed with my hands. The vibration in the rope seemed to shake me loose and I thought I was going to fall when the sarge clasped his hand around my arm. I looked up at him hoping he didn't want to drop me as I let go of the rope. His grasp tightened and my other hand was able to latch onto his extended wrist. Our combined holds were my only chance.

His arms pulled me up and, with my elbows on the chopper's floor, he hauled me in the rest of the way by my belt. I rolled to the center, seeing the sniper pulled in next, except he stayed at the opening, sitting on the edge, leaning out to see the field.

The sergeant looked out over his shoulder. "What about the dog?"

The sniper waved both hands in the air as if saying goodbye. "She'll find a place to hide till I get back. She knows the drill, not the first time."

I wondered if he knew he was lucky someone wanted him to return, as he leaned into the arsenal that was behind the pilot's seat, choosing a grenade launcher and three grenades. I looked at the array of weapons then pressed my M-16 against my chest, stroking the trigger with my fingers, thinking it had the same smooth curve as Naomi's toe.

The sarge yelled above the clatter, "Shell the crap out of them!"

The sniper nodded and looked through his scope towards the next hill, two hundred yards ahead.

The sarge peered in that same direction. "See anything?"

The sniper scanned to the left. "There's caves in these mountains, but no gooks is headin' for them. Probably all went deep in their tunnels."

"Damned moles." The sarge looked straight down through binoculars. Can't see 'em but they all know where each hole is. When are we gonna get smart and blow them apart?"

The sniper shifted his gaze to the right. "Don't kid yourself. Half the south Army, the friggin' ARVANS themselves, they're the ones protecting the tunnels."

The sarge slapped his thigh. "And for every VC we kill there's a hundred in their place the next day."

The sniper scanned across a field. "All I know for sure is every dead VC is more of us get to stay alive."

I crept up behind them and stayed crouched on my ankles. "What's the plan, Sarge?"

"Plan?" His lower jaw twitched to the side before straightening out. "Let's see. The base commander wants a body count ten times higher than the fifteen of ours killed on base. That's a hundred fifty dead, minimum. You want to crawl into a crowded tunnel and make him happy?"

I didn't know if he was mocking me or if he was still mad. But at that moment I was so angry at the VC for killing Joe and for forcing me to kill that kid, that throwing myself in a tunnel and killing them all didn't sound bad. I looked out the side of the opening to the rolling hills below. "You got a tunnel in mind?"

The sniper pushed his arm in front of the sarge. "No one goes near a tunnel tonight. Moon's too bright, you'd never get close. You want something, look'a yonder."

We followed his pointing arm straight down. "See it? There's a hooch in that set of trees. We blow it up and watch for retreats down a shaft. Then we know coordinates for a strike."

"I see the hooch, Sarge. You want me to take it out?" It was the gunner, quiet all this time, seeming to blend in with the multi-barreled machine gun he sat behind. We all turned to take notice.

The sarge raised one hand. "Wait on that. First an M–79, then you gun 'em."

The sniper steadied the launcher with his arm. "Got it right in my sights, man. Give me the good word."

The sarge peered down with his binoculars. "Go ahead, fire that baby."

I moved to the opening on the other side of the chopper and watched the 40mm grenade hiss its way to the hooch then smash right through the roof. A huge blaze burst upward and flaming debris came shooting up. Its brilliance mesmerized me as it flared to the staccato of the gunner's bullets.

My eyes strained for signs of VC through the wafting smoke. It seemed almost impossible, but then against the lighted backdrop of fire, I saw it. A black moving line, gliding quickly through the field.

"Over there!" I leaned out of the opening. "They're running to the trees."

"Turn left," the sergeant yelled to the pilot. "And lower her down."

The chopper began to change direction when, suddenly, I saw a missile headed straight towards us. "Incoming missile. Get down!"

The sergeant turned to look through my side. "Raise this bird. Missile at forty degrees!" he began shouting into his radio. "Charley launching grenades at Chinook at forty-nine and seventy. Send immediate strike, then bomb tunnel directly below."

The chopper angled sharply to the right, holding its tilt as it retreated higher into the sky. I saw the missile approach and hastily aimed my M-16. I started blasting, feeling the release of bullets as if they were slow motion cannon balls. I watched them fly through the air fifty feet towards the missile, then hit, sending brilliant flashes of flame in all directions, including ours. The chopper veered the opposite way, but the blast seemed to chase us, sending a heat through the air I thought would set the chopper on fire.

Joe's face flashed before me. "You have to get home alive, Scout. That was my promise to you. Don't let it be broken."

I expected our helicopter to blow up any second and cried back to him in my mind, "I don't know if I can, Joe. I let you down once, it might happen again."

The chopper jolted as if pushed by conflicting hundred mile an hour winds. I hid my face in my hands, sure we were ready to explode, when all of a sudden it became silent, except for the chopper's clattering blade. I lifted my head, seeing the sergeant, the gunner, and the sniper all lying near me on the floor. The sergeant's head raised. "Damn, Scout, that was fast shooting."

The sniper grinned and slapped the floor. "Shot that bad boy right in the kisser. Saved us all a one-way trip to hell." His sights then went beyond me to out of the opening. "And look at that, a F-4 Phantom, sent us the good stuff."

I turned in time to see the fighter-bomber make a sudden forty-five degree angle downward. We all pulled ourselves to the edge just in time to see it drop its load right on the tunnel. It blasted into the air in fiery arches and a sudden elation filled me that it was them and not me. I pictured Joe in my mind and thought, "I'm alive, Joe. Your promise is still safe. I just might make it home."

~ Chapter 10 ~

Know Thy Enemy

The helicopter landed the sarge, the gunner, the sniper, and me back on base fifteen minutes after watching the tunnel get blown. I hurried out onto the landing zone weary and wanting to get some rest, even if it couldn't be a real sleep. I began walking towards my tent, not sure if I'd end up there or by Joe's stash. Naomi was in my mind, saying, *How could any decent person get excited watching others get bombed?* when a deeper voice overpowered hers.

"You kept me alive up there. I owe you."

I continued walking, feeling the sniper's presence an intrusion. "I kept myself alive. You just happened to be there."

"As I recall," he adjusted to my exact pace, "you didn't want to stay alive."

I felt an unsettling throb in my chest. "You changed my mind on that one."

He tapped his chest. "Lucky for me. And an unlucky night for the VC."

My mouth turned suddenly bitter. I spit the awful taste on the ground before I could speak. "If anyone was unlucky, it was me."

"Your friend." He placed his hand on my back, holding it there for a few moments. "That's agony, man, the worst torture ever was. But you struck back hard. Don't forget that. You were the one found their tunnel on base, the other tunnel out there and you blasted their missile right out of the sky. You gave those bastards a payback they won't soon forget."

I knew he meant well but it didn't lessen the pain of losing Joe. I wondered how many he'd killed to avenge his brother and if it ever helped when I spotted my tent up ahead and, not ready to go in there, started in another direction. "Are the VC the only enemy you have?"

He kicked a rock out of his path, propelling it into a shrub. "None that's worse. They don't come worse than them."

I kicked a rock downhill towards the bunkers. "But they're not the only ones responsible for Joe's death. Our own troops let it happen. Maybe they should be killed, too?"

He grabbed my arm and forced me to look sideways at him. "There's only one enemy here and that's the VC and their brothers, the North Vietnamese Army. Every American here does their part to keep you and me alive. Believe me, if they turned enemy, we'd be dead now."

My arm throbbed under his hold and I yanked it free. "But Joe was killed and his number shouldn't have been up!"

He put one foot forward, crossing his arms over his chest. "You think it was my brother's time? No, but it happened!"

I felt attacked and wanted to get far away from him, but there was one more thing I had to know. I squinted as if the question hurt my eyes. "Does it, I mean the killing, does it help?"

He took a long inhale then let the word come out slowly, "Yes." It lingered in the air for a while till he added, "It's the only thing that does help. It's become my life."

His answer scared me, but not just for him, for me, too, as my hand gripped some crusted blood on my sleeve. "That's not life. That's just revenge!"

He uncurled his fingers from his upper arms then squeezed them in place again. "No, there is no more." His eyes reflected like steel from the moonlight, not seeming at all upset by what he'd just said.

"But there's always more to life, like friends, family, movies, comics, restaurants, concerts, anything."

He licked his lips and let out a hard breath. "Not for me. My home back in the world has been destroyed. There's nothing for me to go back to and no one waiting for me to arrive. Only place I have is here, and only one I have is my dog, and she belongs in the jungle same as I do."

I stared at him for a minute, not sure I heard him right. "Here? You mean here in Vietnam? You consider this your home?"

He shrugged, his eyebrows rising and falling with his shoulders. "This is all I have."

We walked for a few steps while I tried to understand what he said. "Maybe that's all you can think of, but you can find a place to live back in the world. You can choose anywhere you want. And your dog will go wherever you go. There must be some relatives or friends from here that you would want to see when you return."

His gaze scanned the ground around him before looking back at me. "What I have to go to and what I have waiting for me is my dog. That's it. We think the same and go up against the same enemy, the VC and anyone else trying to threaten us."

"You mean like the black mob?" I raised my eyebrows and looked directly in his face.

He glared back and pointed his finger at my chest. "They was never a real threat."

"I felt threatened." I turned away from him and quickened my pace.

He rushed ahead of me and turned to stop me in my path. "Did they shoot you?"

I folded my arms in front of my chest. "No, but…"

He cut my answer short. "If they were VC with guns, would they have shot you?"

I shifted all my weight to my left foot. "Yes."

He leaned in closer and looked down at me, his three inch advantage making me tilt my head back. "Those who would kill you on sight, no hesitation, no questions asked, are your enemy. Anyone that lets you live is not."

His stare pressed on me and I shifted my weight back to both feet to get a firmer stance. "In the mess hall," I began, feeling a quiver up my back, "I thought you were going to kill me."

A wrinkle formed at the top of his nose as he studied my face. "I could have, but did I?"

"No." I stepped back and faced him straight on. "I guess I wasn't much of a threat."

He hooked his thumbs in his belt. "No threat at all. In fact I thought you wanted my damned autograph for nearly shooting the cook."

I couldn't judge if I was insulted or not but decided that didn't matter right now. "I wanted to know what you see out there, hiding out alone in the jungle for weeks at a time."

"You want to know what I see?" His hand slid up the side of his head and clasped into his hair. "I see bugs survive their predators and turn rotten wood into a place to hatch their eggs, like they're showing me if I can survive and keep on my mission, all the rot around us will benefit those to come. And I see snakes hanging from trees waiting in absolute stillness like perfect snipers for as long as it takes to snag a bird in mid flight, reminding me that keeping still gets its reward. And I see huge, thick leaves that can hide anyone, giving me as good a chance as Charley to stay out of sight and alive. And then I see VC stalking through the thick growth with silent steps, ready to blow a platoon away."

My arms pulsed with the feel of the jungle. "What do you do then, shoot or call it in to headquarters?"

The sniper wiped his sleeve across his forehead. "First I listen for how many there are. If it's less than seven, I unload fast, aiming right near their eyes. If I miss, I pitch a grenade and hightail it out of there. Usually I get them, but once me and the dog were chased for three miles before I found a cluster of fallen logs to hide under. It worked. They passed us, but those bastards came back and kept combing that area all night. They sure did want to kill me real bad."

"What do you expect?" The words seethed out of my mouth. "Not only do you try to kill them but all of us. We're invading their land and they want it back."

His forehead wrinkled into thick wavy lines. "It's the VC trying to take land that belongs to the South Vietnamese. And if we let them get it, they'll keep going for more till they start shooting their guns at the good old U.S. of A."

I held out my empty hands, except they felt heavy as if the air on the palms had condensed into solid lumps of soil. "They want back what was taken away from them. Is that too hard to understand?"

He stared at my opened hands, and for a moment, I thought he was going to spit. But instead, his words sprayed out like a harsh rain. "You're wrong. They're power vultures! They want power over more land, and they'll kill anyone for it. Look at Hitler or Genghis Khan or Napoleon. They kept wanting more land and taking it. They would have gone to Texas if they had modern-day bombers. And the VC are no different."

"What about the ARVANS?" I was annoyed he only saw one side. "They're not innocents here. They torture and kill their own people, same as the VC. Why defend them?"

"Are they killing people to take their land?" He turned, making his eyes glare at me from their pointed corners. "Or are they killing those who are helping the VC?"

"Who the hell cares?" Sweat trickled down the back of my neck, irritating a spot I had scratched yesterday. "Killing is killing. The VC are only the enemy because we're on the side of the south. If we were fighting for the north, the ARVANS would be the enemy."

He grasped his temples and turned away. I thought he finally understood me. He then turned back and spoke as low as he had on the field. "Try to see what I see." I quieted my breathing to hear him better. "Who's trying to take over more land, the North Vietnamese or the south?"

I hesitated, not sure if I was being tricked. "The North Vietnamese. The south is defending what they have."

His lips pursed forward then he nodded. "That's right, the north. They want to take over people's land then force them to submit to their power. But soon it won't be enough. They'll want more land and more power over more people and go after it again and again and again."

"How do you know?" Bitter sweat dripped into my mouth.

"I know," the sniper tightened his lips showing more of his teeth, "because it's the way of greed. Once someone sets their sights on another man's land, there's no stopping them. Not in Vietnam, not in Germany, not even back in Texas."

"What's Texas got to do with this?" I was annoyed by his argument as well as by the sweat that kept irritating my tongue.

"You want to know?" He glared directly into my eyes like he was staring at a flame, half looking and half mesmerized. "I'll tell you what Texas has to do with this. It was ten years ago, 1960, just four years before I was sent here, and seven years before my brother was told by a judge that it was either go join the Marines or go to jail for seven years. Poor Rattlesnake." He paused and let out a long breath arching his shoulders forward.

"Was that his name?" I was really more interested in what he'd done to get sent to jail, but didn't feel it the right time to ask.

"That's what I used to call him." The sniper stiffened his shoulders back again and slipped his hands into his pockets. "It was from when he was a baby. He used to slither on the floor with a rattle in his hand." He smiled for a second then his mouth pulled together in a tight circle before he spoke. "I told him it was a wrong deal, but no, he wouldn't listen, and now…"

His gaze lifted to over my head like he was watching for a chopper in the distance before returning to my face and continuing. "Anyway, there we were, ten lousy years ago in the grand state of Texas. It was one of those situations same as we have here with the VC where the enemy tries to trick your thinking, confuse you into believing they're really your friend. Oh, those sneaky bastards pretended to be nice, but my father understood clear as day what they were doing. One of the big cattle ranchers had his sights set on my father's land. There was a good stream on it, flowed most of the year, even when all the others went dry. Except my father didn't want to sell. He didn't care how much money they offered. That was his land and he wanted to live on it like he'd done his whole life."

The sniper pulled his hands out of his pockets, looping his thumbs into the openings instead. "The big cattleman figured he was entitled to that land no matter what my father wanted and gave big payoffs to the town council to raise taxes ten times over on land with all year running water. Every one of them men bought new pickups that year and my father could no longer afford to make the payments on his taxes. Oh, he took out loans, as many as he could get, but times were hard and he fell behind. Then one blazing hot day, when it finally came time for those bastards to take over the land, my father stood at the gate and raised his gun like any man would do to defend his home. But the sheriffs, with a paper in their hand stating he had to leave, started yelling at him and when my father fired his rifle above their heads, they shot him down like he was some rabid coon, ten bullets in the body before the smoke stopped."

The sniper paused and narrowed his eyes into thin slits. "Those that want your land will kill you and take what you have unless you stop them before they get there."

My throat squeezed together as I pictured his father shot right before his eyes. Then I swallowed hard trying to clear enough voice to speak. "I'm sorry, there's no excuse for that, ever."

The sniper kicked the ground in front of him, sending a clump of dirt into a dispersed brown haze. "The enemy can pretend to be on your side or the side of justice, but they are always planning to take what they want any way they can get it. The VC are masters at that, playing on American sympathies, trying to make us forget they'll kill their own people for their land."

"But," I swiped at the sweat on my lip with my sleeve, "how can you tell who's VC and who isn't?" The laundry kid had fooled me though I didn't think the brother and sister had.

"I know by watching," his thumbs shifted from his pockets to his belt. "I look for those that wear ARVAN uniforms by day and Charley black pajamas by night. I watch for those setting the traps, those that steal food from innocent farmers and those that trample across another man's land as if they already own it. Then I know who the real enemy is."

"But what if it's hard to tell?" His explanation felt uncomfortably simple. "What if someone sees you murder?"

"There's a difference between a warrior and a murderer." His shoulders pulled all the way back. "The warrior knows that to save the innocent he must stop the enemy. The murderer kills for personal greed."

"You think the sheriff did it for greed?" I watched his chest lift with his breath.

"Sure did. He knew the cattle rancher would have him fired if he didn't get rid of my father. He chose his paycheck and a new GMC over right and wrong."

I shifted all my weight to my left leg, feeling it stiffen under the strain. "But what about us. It's not greed, but it's still murder. We can't see from base who's the enemy and who isn't, like you do in the jungle."

The sniper released the tightness in his shoulders. "You can't know cooped up on a base like cattle, never getting to think for yourselves, never knowing if you had to destroy the life you just took."

I was about to tell him I agreed when his gaze shifted toward the field and he crouched low. The next moment, his dog rushed up to him, her tongue licking at his now smiling cheeks. I watched as he ruffled her fur and rubbed his nose into the back of her neck, wishing I could get a welcome like that from Naomi. Her embrace would be the only thing that could get the feel of being a murderer out of my head.

"You think your dog understands the difference between a warrior and a murderer?"

"Utah?" He brushed his hands in long strokes down her sides. "She knows faster than lightening if someone's ready to blow us away."

I watched her ears straighten up suddenly, then relax. "Even when you're in the air?"

He raised one eyebrow. "Don't know. Never had her up. But you sure enough can do it in her place. Don't forget, I owe you, and I always pay a debt."

"I'll remember," I said, wondering if he'd help me go AWOL, or if he'd get mad like he did before. He stood and began walking, the dog moving precisely at his leg. My gait matched theirs as I leaned sideways to stroke her back. "Why do you call her Utah?"

He looked down and grazed his fingers along the tops of her ears. "It's a place I once thought of going, but never did."

I tried to picture that state but all that came was desert. "Why Utah?"

"Why?" He leaned more to the side to scratch her head for a moment. "It goes back to when I was ten. In school they told us that Utah was named after the Ute tribe and it means people of the mountains. I was from the mountains so it seemed a natural place to see where I would feel right at home."

I shifted my picture of a desert to one of mountains, and it looked nicer. "Better reason than most. How come you never went?"

"If I recollect right," his eyes squinted into the moonlight, "my mama claimed our mountains in Texas were same as the mountains in Utah which meant we were Utes right where we lived and I didn't need to go anywhere else to be what I already was. So I stayed in my own mountains until Uncle Sam saw fit to send me here."

I looked at the shadows on the mountain in the distance, wondering how the mountains here compared to Texas or Utah. "Uncle Sam, the travel agent no one wants."

The sniper laughed. "The relative that offers you apple pie, 'cept when you go to take a bite you find it's filled with flies."

I spit at the thought, but then laughed. "He's more joke than anything. Just because his initials are U. S., I can't believe they still use him."

The sniper pointed a finger in the air. "If they were smart, they'd use Davy Crockett. At least that's a name that fought for this country in battle and in Congress. He even gave his life defending the Alamo. That's a name people could respect."

I wondered if my name could ever be one to receive respect and realized I wasn't even sure what my name was, or which one I preferred. There had been too many to answer to, Lenny, Belkin, Private, Kid, and Scout. "You think a name's important?"

He swiped at the sweat on his forehead without slowing up his pace. "It tells who you are."

I looked at him, thinking his designation was clear, the sniper, or was it? "What's your name?"

"William Tell." I almost laughed, but then he didn't show any signs of amusement and continued on. "My father's favorite story. One thing it taught me clear as all get out is not to make myself no target. Couldn't stay alive in the jungle if I didn't learn that. Only targets out there is them, not me. I picture an apple on their heads then aim three inches lower."

I shuddered. "Remind me never to put an apple on my head!"

He stopped walking and turned to face me. "From what a major tells me, the only things on your head are dead faces that you can't shake off."

I was stunned he knew about that, and I guess my startled expression was funny because he pointed at me and laughed. "Don't be shocked. I could tell by the reporter's description it was someone like you. You're the type, a protector more than a warrior, except a lost one. You're not sure who to protect, but you'll find out soon enough."

A pounding started in my chest making each word feel like it echoed as I asked, "Do you know who I'm supposed to protect?"

He saluted with a smile on his face. "No less than everyone you see. It's noble, but a curse. It's simpler to be a warrior. Protectors have too big a job."

The pounding in my chest became harder. I rubbed at the spot, trying to soothe the ache. "I couldn't protect anyone, not the kids and not Joe."

The dog jumped up on him, placing her paws on his chest. He rubbed her back while looking at me. "The kids were a casualty of their village. You couldn't have changed that. As for your friend, he could protect himself as much as you could, but his location got hit. It happens, except you believe you should have stopped it."

The pounding increased, making the spot even sorer. "What's the point in being a protector if you can't protect?"

"The point is," he tapped himself on the chest, "that most important in your heart is to keep people alive."

The pounding became louder, making it almost impossible to hear my own question. "And that's not important in yours?"

His hand dropped away from his chest. "I'm a warrior. I take the lives that need taking." He paused for a moment to check a spot on Utah's head, then looked back at me. "You have a much larger task than I do. It's much harder to protect than to kill."

The pounding heightened to a sledgehammer. I pressed my whole hand on my chest hoping it would stop. "And I'm supposed to protect everyone in the world? How the hell can I do that?"

He took hold of Utah's paws, gently lowering her down while still looking at me. "You can't. There will be a number, one, five, twenty-five, maybe even a thousand in your lifetime. You'll be able to protect them. And those dead faces in your head are your direction to help you do it, just like my family's faces are mine."

I shook my head as much from the unrelenting pain in my chest as from the confusion I felt from his words. "You're crazy."

He nodded and smiled. "Many people have called me crazy. But whether we admit it or not, it's dead faces that steer our course."

He turned and began walking, the dog at his side. I stayed back for a few moments, watching the fluid rhythm of their strides. But when I started again it felt like each rock in the ground was a dead person who wanted to push me in their intended direction. First was the boy then the girl from the village, then the laundry boy, followed by Uncle Morty, my grandfather, and the mass of faces from photographs that were Grandma's relatives killed in World War II. I found myself walking on my toes, shifting my feet to different spots till I finally found an unbumpy patch to press on with all my weight.

The sniper and his dog continued to get farther and farther ahead, turning in a direction that went farther and farther away from my tent. I had to take my own path back to the place where I could lie down for a few hours, even if I might not be welcomed. At least I couldn't be turned away. I began for the tent feeling a sudden exhaustion overtake me and had to force my legs to keep moving. It was important that I get there. I needed to close my eyes for a while even if I didn't expect to sleep. Rest, that's all I wanted, even if it was short lived.

* * * * *

A hot-tempered outburst shook me from a grayish haze where the sniper was dressed like Superman, except there was a "W" on his chest instead of an "S," and he'd handed me a shirt with a "P" that I'd thrown on the ground. The voice boomed again, forcing my eyes open to misty light and dim shadows moving on the tent wall.

It was unmistakably Moustafa. "They said it's not called off, man, and I'm telling you, it better not be. It's making me bust inside, I want to kick that cracker's ass so bad."

"Keep yourself cool, man," came a whisper, though it was clearly Wesley. I turned on my back to hear him with both ears. "Sit your ass back down and play your cards."

I glanced at my watch, four-eighteen, then turned to the left to see five of them gathered on Wesley's bed, cards in their hands. Moustafa waved his cards in the air towards Wesley. "I'm tired of being hushed. He has it coming and I'm going to hammer him to a pulp. He gets that skinny-assed white boy to hold Joe's body in the air and all of a sudden dead Afro-Americans are not supposed to matter."

I bolted up from my bed and yelled across the room, "You have a problem with me, Moustafa?"

He stood and put his hands on his waist. "Why looky that. You mean the white devil himself has a guilty conscience?"

I walked a few steps in his direction, stopping at the edge of Joe's bed, letting its edge dig into my shins as I pointed to my chest. "That my ass you want to kick? Because if it is, you can have your chance right now!"

Moustafa raised his arms, his cards dropping in silence to the bed. "It's you, Scout. You the one thinks you's better than us 'cause you's white. You the one telling the brass we's savages, killing kids, then you clean it up for yourself like you the only one who's good."

"What?" I slammed my knee into the cot, scraping its legs on the floor. "I cleaned it up for everyone!"

Moustafa pointed up in the air. "Then why are you up in the helicopter kissing the sergeant's ass while the rest of us are left on the ground?"

I was stunned, not only that he knew about the helicopter, but by how he saw it. "The sarge picked me up from the field. He didn't even know it was me!"

"Not what I heard," Moustafa crossed his arms in front of his chest. "Pilot from that bird told me the sergeant's going to transfer you to another squad and the rest of us are being sent with Company B to the thirteenth valley, home of gook headquarters."

"What?" My own shrill scream felt like a mortar blast in my head. "Why would he do that?"

Moustafa pointed a finger up in the air as if he were instructing a class. "First and foremost the sarge's main concern is to get his ass-kissing white boy someplace safe. After that," he paused to raise a second finger, "is to get us black boys blown away so he don't worry we'll tell how he let those kids be killed."

"I don't believe this!" I kicked the leg of the cot, frustrated that neither Wesley nor Leon told him how absurd he was being. "The sarge didn't say anything to me about a transfer, and he has no reason to think you'll talk about that village!"

Moustafa's eyes enlarged. "Wouldn't treat us like untrustworthy niggers, would he?" He placed his hands on his hips and leaned forward. "Nobody wants to take no chances on uppity niggers."

I pointed at Moustafa's barreled chest. "He has no reason to see you as a threat!"

"No? Don't you?" Moustafa's eyebrows jolted to high arches.

I wanted to slam my fist into the curved line above his nose and shoved my hands into my pockets. "We're not enemies, Moustafa. In case you forgot, we're in the same squad and supposed to keep each other alive!"

Moustafa smiled like I had just told a joke. "Oh, is that what we're here for, keeping each other alive, like you did for Joe?"

Sweat rushed into my eyes, burning harsher than tears ever could. I went to wipe them when I heard, "That's enough, Moustafa."

It had been Wesley, but I was too deeply wounded to stop now. "You want to get it on, Moustafa? We'll settle this right now, just you and me!"

Moustafa began for the aisle, pushing through the air with his fists. I stormed towards him, planning to scream loud enough to make him flinch. Except, before I could get a solid footing, he lunged his head into my neck, knocking me down on my back. I coughed, trying desperately to catch my breath when I felt a series of punches on my head and everything within me began to throb and spin.

Only thing I could see was rounded shapes that blobbed larger and smaller, then a voice demanded, "Get off him!"

I couldn't tell if it had been Wesley or Leon or one of the others, but a heavy weight was lifted and a blurred version of Leon's face peered down. I felt him slap my cheeks, hearing, "You all right, Scout? You still in there?"

Moustafa shouted from close by, "He's not hurt. He's faking it. That's what white boys do, play possum 'cause they's too scared to fight."

There was a scuffling sound and I turned my head to see blurred images of Wesley and the two others holding Moustafa up against the wall while Wesley said, "Knock it off, Moose. It's over. You hurt him enough."

Moustafa glared at my flat-out position on the floor. "I'm not done with you yet, boy. I'll finish you off at the beer fight."

I tried to scream though it came out weak and raspy, "I wasn't your enemy before, but I am now."

Moustafa smiled and I pushed myself up on one arm.

Moustafa's voice pierced into my ear like another punch. "I'm okay. I won't touch him. You have my word."

Leon grasped under my shoulders and pulled me up. I let him at first, but then he began to walk me to my cot and I shoved him away with my elbow. "It's okay. I don't need help."

"Let…"

But I pushed myself away from him. "No, just leave me alone."

I sat on the edge of Joe's cot and slumped my head forward into my hands.

Moustafa muttered under his breath, "Look at the white boy, wants everyone to feel sorry for him."

I forced myself up on my feet and threw my right fist towards him in the air. "I'll be waiting for you, Moustafa. Don't be late!"

* * * * *

Reveille's shrill call throbbed in my head. I pressed my hands over my ears, feeling the soreness that went down my left side, not letting me forget the fight less than two hours ago. I lay there, hearing the rustlings of people sitting up, even the shuffling of boots on the floor, wondering if I should run before the beer fight, though there was nowhere I knew to go. I glanced at

Joe's bed thinking of the words in the helicopter, *You have to get home alive for me, Scout. Don't let my promise be broken.* I shook my head, thinking there was no way I'd be able to manage that today.

Moustafa stared at me from three cots down, his lips pressed tight like he was disgusted just by looking at me. The throbbing in my head became matched by a pulsing in my arms and hands. I squeezed my fingers into tight fists as I muttered under my breath, "I'll try, Joe. I sure as hell want to beat that bastard real bad."

The sergeant entered the tent, though no one stood like we did at boot camp. I slid my boots out from under my bed as he announced, "New orders have been issued so listen carefully. Scout, you're transferred to the Fifty-First squad. Wesley, Leon, Moustafa, you're going to Company B. Transfers take effect tomorrow morning 0700. My advice, rest as much as you can today. You're going to need it. Your humping orders are already placed. If you're smart, you'll catch as much sleep as you can. All previous assigned duties today are cancelled. This, men, is your day of R&R."

I felt Moustafa glare at me from across the room and lay back down. The beer fight didn't begin till noon. Maybe I should just lie on my cot till then.

The sergeant left the tent, his message leaving a stillness in the air behind him, till Moustafa threw what sounded like cards on the floor. "See, told you I know what I say. You have to admit I's right. Can't never say no different."

No denial followed, only silence and rustlings of arms and legs going into clothes. Ten minutes later Leon, Wesley and Moustafa left for the mess hall. I remained on my cot, planning to go to breakfast in fifteen minutes, giving them time to get through the line before I entered. Last thing I wanted was to listen to remarks about me or grumblings about the transfers. I shut my eyes then opened them, feeling it all of a sudden hotter and brighter than a few moments before. I glanced at my watch and was shocked to see 11:30. I couldn't understand how there had been no noise in here to wake me before. I sat up and looked around, but there was no evidence that anyone had returned from breakfast.

I dressed quickly, feeling my heart begin to pound, thinking about what was to come all too soon. It crossed my mind not to go since it wasn't officially ordered. But if I didn't, the blacks would see it as my automatic guilt to everything Moustafa charged, and I couldn't stand for that. I squeezed my M-16 for a moment, then put it under my cot, hoping Moustafa had done the same, and began the walk to the field where Joe's stash was buried and I had killed the laundry kid barely ten hours ago.

There were arguments going on in my head between Joe and the three kids about what I should have done to keep them alive when I heard someone call, "Scout, wait up."

I turned to see Rascal rushing towards me, with Spit by his side. "Scout, do you know what the hell is going on here?"

The stench from their morning on garbage detail made me hold my stomach as I continued to walk. "Yeah, you got a gripe with someone, this is your chance to slug it out."

I quickened my pace trying to get distance from the smell, but Rascal persisted by my side. "Lordy be, I wish it was simple as that. From what I can figure, it's one damned, confounded hoe down. You gots your fights that's allowed, but then you gots the darkies with the guns. It's asking for trouble."

"That was last night." I assumed that's what he meant. "But today's different. There's MPs to make sure it doesn't get out of hand."

We reached the field where about two hundred Marines had already arrived, with more entering from the different paths and ten MPs on its perimeter. Rascal slapped his leg. "Hells, bells, nosiree. It don't look like enough MPs for what I seen."

Spit rapped him on the arm. "What's a down-home barbecue without a spat to rile things up and a heap of chili sauce to flare up the meat like the Fourth of July." The smoke from grilling steaks made its way to where we stood and my stomach ached with hunger. He pulled out a small reddish-orange bottle from his pants pocket and held it up in front of his face. "Want to try it? Puts hair on yer chest thicker'n a buffalo's."

I looked at his lanky frame, thinking how in the shower it was Rascal with all the hair on his chest while Spit's was kind of sparse. I shook my head. "Not hungry yet. I'll get my steak later."

Spit tilted the bottle in my direction, "You know where it's at when you's ready," and began walking into the field.

Rascal turned to me before following, "Watch yourself, Scout. Bad blood's brewing. I's can smell it."

I was thinking he was smelling his own stench from garbage detail as I looked across the field for Moustafa, scrutinizing the groups of Marines clustered around its edge, most dressed in fatigue pants and tee-shirts, some in cut-offs and bare feet, others with no shirts at all. Their faces seemed blurred, like the glare of the hot sun had distorted them and I strained for a better look. But as far as I could tell, Moustafa was not among them. I searched for signs of other fights, though all I saw were movements to and from the grills and the nearby unattended cases of beer. The center of the field remained empty. No one had yet dared to venture in its midst and no brewing disputes were obvious from the sidelines.

Wesley entered the other side of the field with Leon rushing up behind him. He began flailing his arms as he talked. I would have given anything to be able to read lips. Then Wesley's hands went palms up, seeming to say, *Where?*

Leon pointed back from where they had just come and immediately they both turned and left. I considered following them, fearing it had something to do with Moustafa and anxious to know what it was, when a hand unexpectedly clamped down on my shoulder and the sergeant's voice boomed in my ear. "Come on, Scout, no one deserves one of these steaks more than you."

My eyes stayed on the empty space where Wesley and Leon had been. "I'll get one later."

His grip tightened. "No, you'll get one now. That's an order. We have to talk. I don't think you're aware of what's going on."

"You're the one not aware..." I began.

He gripped my other shoulder and forced me around to face him. "I'm telling you, there's things you have to know."

There was no question how his hold on my shoulders would look to Moustafa. I had to end that as soon as possible. "Okay, Sarge, a steak sounds good." I looked towards the closest grill, starting to turn.

His hands dropped from me and we began to walk side by side, though my eyes went back to the empty spot Wesley and Leon had been. "Scout, you need to be prepared for what's going on."

"I am. I know..."

His hand raised to stop me. "There was a fight, an hour ago, outside the mess. Words were exchanged among the squad on garbage details, racial remarks."

I braced myself for an accusation against me.

The sarge continued. "It got way out of hand and the two blacks threw the other two, white southern boys, out of the truck."

My ankle twisted as my foot hit the ground. "What? Do you know if it was Rascal and Spit?"

The sergeant's hand raised at his side. "I don't know their names, but I know two blacks took over the truck then picked up two more blacks. Four of them on the truck, riding around the base screaming at whites, calling them cracker, or whitebread, or Wallace boy. They even pointed their guns at a captain demanding office jobs and entrance to the Officer's Club."

In my head I heard the shot fired from the black mob last night and shuddered, knowing what it would mean. "Did they shoot?"

"Not yet, but this is where it gets worse." The sarge stopped walking and turned to me straight on. "Moustafa jumped on their truck about fifteen minutes ago. Word is he has a grenade launcher and they're going to ride it right up here to the beer fight."

My arms flew up in the air. "Isn't someone going to stop them?" I scanned towards the empty spot where Leon and Wesley had been, noticing that many of the blacks were missing from the field. Were they all out there getting machine guns to blast the rest of us away?

The sarge hit my chest with the back of his hand. "I'm trying to tell you. This is the situation. They're too hot headed to talk down and the brass is afraid shooting them outright will start a revolution. They've decided to take them down one by one at the beer fight."

My chest began pounding and my whole body was suddenly drenched with a chilled sweat. Moustafa was gunning for me with a grenade launcher and I didn't even have my M-16.

The sarge continued. "I know about you and Moustafa. The best thing is for you to get off this field before he shows up."

My heart pounded harder as I looked towards the path Leon and Wesley went down, expecting to see the truck storm its way in any moment. "The best thing for me is for someone to stop him. If I'm not here, he'll come for me. At least here there's other people."

The sarge emphatically shook his head. "You can't be up here against their guns."

My hands squeezed into fists, pulsing as hard as my chest. "My leaving won't stop anything. If you want to help, stop Moustafa. He's the one gonna start a blood bath!"

The sergeant's eyelids tightened into slits. "That's precisely what I'm trying to do. Get you out of the way so we can get Moustafa. And I don't want you to end up dead."

"Why?" The pulsing in my fists shot up to my arms. "What's the difference to you?"

His lower jaw pushed forward, showing a gap in his lower teeth. "Listen, Scout, I look out for my men. I don't get thrills writing parents that my men are dead. And I sure as hell don't want it on me that one of my men was killed by another in my squad."

I squeezed my knuckles together, feeling them crack. "No, of course not, you'd never get promoted to captain with those stats!"

He grasped my shoulders and gave me a harsh shake. "Shut it, Scout. Your mouth is your worst enemy."

"You're wrong!" I shoved at his chest and he let go. "My worst enemy is anyone who would stop me from defending myself!"

His arms crossed in front of his chest. "You calling me your enemy?"

I hunched my shoulders backward. "No, not you. Not even Moustafa. If you were my enemies, you both had plenty of chances to kill me outright. But if you put me in a position where I can't defend myself, that's as good as killing me yourself."

His fingers tapped on his arms. "Maybe, except I don't get it. If Moustafa's not your enemy, why do you want to fight him?"

His eyes were half shadowed by his forehead as I peered in. "To show I'm not afraid. If I back off, he'll keep shooting off his mouth about me, blaming me for every black problem in the whole damned military. But I don't want to kill him. I just want to show him I'm not afraid."

The sarge glanced down at his feet and shook his head. "I still don't trust him." He looked up. "You're ordered to KP."

"What?" My head jolted like I'd been punched. "Order him to KP. He's the one you're worried about!"

He reached out to grab my arm, but I stepped back, leaving his hand pointed at my chest. "I can't order him at this time, and you know it. But by tomorrow he'll be in the brig, and you'll be free. That's the best resolution on the table."

"Free?" I laughed. "For what, to be out in the jungle with no one watching my back 'cause my squad thinks I'm out to set them up? Tell you something, Sarge, I'm not leaving this field. I don't care what the hell you do to me."

His jaw jutted forward and his hands flew to his hips. I suddenly feared being sent to prison for insubordination and tried one last thing. "Tell me if I'm right, Sarge." I paused to look hard into his furious eyes, and gave a toothy grin. "You're now so angry at me you're thinking it would be a good idea to leave me here for Moustafa to kill, and that if he doesn't do it, you'll do it yourself."

One of his cheeks slid into a half smile. "Not far from wrong, Scout. Tell you what. If you're fool enough to want to stay that bad, go ahead. But don't get yourself killed, you hear?" He then pointed towards the nearest grill. "May as well get that steak. Might be our last meal."

160

I was happy to get to stay, though not looking forward to what would come. It wouldn't be pretty, I knew that, and it was likely I'd go off the field in a stretcher. I took a paper plate and plastic fork and watched as the cook lifted a steak for me off the grill, dripping its fat on the ground before getting it on my plate. I walked only three steps away when I stabbed it with my fork and brought it straight to my mouth. It singed my lip, but I huffed on it as I chewed and swallowed as fast as I could get it down.

"Damn, Scout," the sarge appeared at my side with his own steak. "You're worse than a cave man."

I smiled, blew on one corner of the steak then shoved it back in my mouth for another bite. The sarge cut at his meat with the plastic knife making blood ooze onto his plate. I looked away, not wanting to think of the blood from Joe or the kids or anyone else and scanned the other side of the field. Still no sign of Wesley, Leon or the truck with Moustafa, or any fist fights in the vacant center of the field. Just a lot of smoke rising from the grills, and lots of Marines standing around eating steak. I chewed faster, wondering if the only score to settle on this whole base was between Moustafa and me. I then bit off another piece, thinking it was much too peaceful for what was expected to happen, when my mouth stopped.

A truck plowed onto the field, bouncing hard into the ruts and bumps of the rough terrain. Several Marines were forced to run out of its way while five faces pointed guns and yelled at them from the opened back. Wesley and Leon, along with about thirty other blacks were running behind the truck. Some of them shouting, but it was impossible to distinguish what they said.

The truck started going in circles, making passes by groups of Marines that were holding up their beers and steaks and shouting, while offering them glimpses of the grenade launcher leaning in the truck's corner. It finally stopped right in the middle of the field where Moustafa stepped onto the side panel of the truck, holding up an M-16, his voice booming over all other clamor on the field. "My fellow compatriots in arms, the revolution has started. It's time for the black man to pick up his guns and demand his due. First in Vietnam, and then back in the world. The revolution is now!"

The stationed MPs around the field raised their guns. Seven of them were black and three were white. I wondered if the black MPs were in on Moustafa's plan and were waiting for his signal to turn against the whites. I swallowed the meat in my mouth, forgetting it hadn't been chewed. It lodged in my throat and I began to gag. I feared Moustafa would react with extreme insult at my coughs and shoved my hand in my mouth, pulling the hunk of meat loose. My throat was sore, but as least I was able to breathe. I gasped for air, trying to do it quietly when there was a roar from the crowd. I looked up and saw Moustafa's M-16 aimed directly at my head. My brain told me to hit the ground, but all the stares from the crowd kept me unable to move. I stared back at the truck, my focus as far off Moustafa's gun as I could manage, counting the seconds till an explosion would blow me away.

Moustafa shouted. "Oppressors are all around who will set you up to take the fall for wrongdoing done by whites."

A voice from a megaphone shouted. "Put down your guns and come off the truck peacefully."

Moustafa went on. "But no time to teach you your lesson today, Scout. We's got bigger things to do. Taking over a plane and bringing a whole blasted arsenal back stateside to use on anyone trying to stop us from getting what we's owed."

I swallowed hard, tasting the lingering bitterness of the coughed up meat.

Moustafa raised the gun straight up in the air and I felt my body shudder uncontrollably. "My fellow Afro-Americans, this is your wake up call. It's time to let the white establishment know you're not going to be their niggers any more. Come join us now or be kicked and spit on for the rest of your lives!"

About fifteen blacks moved towards the truck, but most didn't.

Moustafa began waving his gun in the air like a flag. "Fellow brothers, this is your chance to act, or stay at the bottom of the mountain till your dying day!"

There were some grumblings around me when suddenly, I felt myself propel off my spot. Next thing I knew I was running towards the side of the truck, screaming, "What's the matter, Moustafa? You afraid I'm going to beat your ass?"

Moustafa raised his foot like he was going to squash me with his boot. "I ain't scared of you or your honky kind, boy. We's ready to do Allah's work and take our future in our own hands."

I jumped up at the side of the truck. "Then I'm coming after you!" I climbed on the tire, grabbed onto ruts in the side panels and began scrambling for my next foothold.

The sergeant's voice blared. "Get down from there!"

But all I really heard was Moustafa's voice. "Your puny white ass can't do nothing to me. I's ready for the big man now."

I was only about two feet from the top of the truck. "You're making a mistake, Moustafa. The only fight you have around here is with me. Just you and me, remember?"

Moustafa raised his gun like he was ready to smash it on my hand if I got any closer. "Not no more, Scout. I'm too busy to waste time on you."

I gripped the top of the truck and began pulling myself up. "You can't just drop it like that, Moustafa. I'm challenging you. You'll have to fight me first before you fight everyone else."

The sergeant's voice screamed in the background, "Scout, get down!"

I felt someone pull at my legs and I began kicking. "Get away, Sarge. Stay out of this."

But what came back was Wesley's voice. "Scout, what you think you're doing? Get yourself off of there. You going to get yourself killed. Can't you see he's gone mad?"

"I've gone mad?" Moustafa held his gun up high to the crowd. "I've come to my senses is what I did. Desk jobs don't go to no niggers so it's time to stop acting like one. You want to kiss their asses, go ahead."

I kicked my legs free from Wesley's hold then managed to pull all the way up on the truck and swing myself inside.

Moustafa pointed his gun at me. "Get him off this truck!" Three guys began to come for me.

I stood on a high box inside the truck, screaming out to the crowd. "This is between him and me. We were supposed to fight today and as far as I'm concerned, it's still on. We have a score to settle."

Wesley began climbing up, and turned to the crowd. "That's right. If Scout's fool enough to still want this, let them get it on."

The crowd started roaring, "Settle the score. Settle the score!"

The others in the truck stepped back to give us room, but Moustafa raised his gun to my chest.

I jumped down to get out of range, then slipped on something slick and fell on my back.

Moustafa lunged for me, his fist coming for my nose. I slid to the side, sending his fist into the floor. But before he could scream, I hollered in a piercingly shrill voice, "Save the farm!" The sudden blare of my voice made him cave in at the stomach and my fist propelled into his face.

Moustafa fell back on one of his cohorts, who shoved him back towards me, saying, "Don't let that whitebread do this to us!"

Moustafa lunged for me as I heard Wesley yell, "He's got a knife!"

I glimpsed the blade about ten inches from my face and threw up my arms, feeling the sharp edge break my skin. Wesley jumped in and grabbed

163

Moustafa's arm, but Moustafa angled the blade back towards Wesley's neck, screaming, "I'll kill you, too!"

"No!" I shouted, charging into Moustafa's arm. He fell back into his cohort again, while I fell on my side.

There was a roar of yelling and then I saw it. Moustafa's blade high above me on its way down. I was sure my life was over as I screamed a desperate, "Joe!"

A quick blast of shots rang out and Moustafa's eyes suddenly focused away from me to the side of the truck. He began to fall forward and I was pressed between him and the side of the truck with nowhere to go. The knife continued to come down at me and thrust through my skin. It burned like I'd been struck by a branding iron, flaming waves surging through my chest.

Moustafa was pulled off me and there was Leon, looking down. His eyes shifted to my chest, then back to my face. His mouth spread wide but didn't curve up as he said, "Hang in there, Scout. You'll be all right."

"What happened?" I choked out the words. But then Leon was pushed aside and a medic appeared above me, saying, "Don't talk. Breathe lightly through your nose." He then glanced around him. "Back off. He needs space."

I looked up into his face and saw another face peering down above him. It was smudged with a dark grease, blacking out all features, but the gripping stare was unmistakable. "What was cut?" he demanded.

The medic worked on me as he spoke. "Upper chest, near the collar bone, could be deep."

An M-16 was propped against the sniper's arm. I raised my hand and pointed at it, then at Moustafa.

He nodded as he said, "A warrior can never let a protector die. They're too important and too few."

His words drifted into my mind like sparks in a fog, then distinct images began to blend till there were only dim moving shadows. It seemed that the sniper saluted me with his right hand, but then everything went blank.

* * * * *

"The jugular could be nicked, and tell them he's had the maximum morphine."

"Yes, sir, doc."

I opened my eyes, seeing a medic peer down and felt him pull me onto the floor of a chopper. The vibration under my back made the pain in my chest

164

spread everywhere except to my left arm. At first I was glad my arm was fine, but then I realized there was no sensation at all. I panicked and struggled to raise it, but it felt like there was nothing there to lift. I raised my right hand and pointed to my left side, uttering as part of a gasp, "My arm!"

The medic looked down at me, his forehead wrinkled in thick, brown bulges. "It's there, son. Don't worry. I see it."

I tried to lift my head to look, but the pain forced me to stop. I managed to gasp, "What...?"

His gaze shifted to my shoulder and his chin twitched from side to side. "Sorry, son, can't rightly tell those things. Don't look too bad, like some I seen."

I turned my head, trying to see if it was bloody, when I saw the black body bag only two feet away, its rubbery substance quivering from the chopper's tremors.

"Who...?" I choked out the word.

The medic's shoulders shrugged as he reached for the tag hanging from the zipper. "It says here Tyrone Williams. He's the only bag on this flight. You know him?"

I couldn't think of anyone by that name, and the only one I knew who got shot was, oh no, Moustafa! Was that him? I stared at the bag, trying to figure if it was his shape. The height was right and the outline of the body looked like his stocky build. I gasped, "Mous..." and then my throat tightened, feeling like it was being strangled by his large, powerful hands.

Terror and hate pulsed with my pain as I had the impossible urge to rip open his bag and scream, *Why did you try to kill me? You didn't have to do that!* I managed to utter a barely audible, "You bastard," then my head went to spinning and I shut my eyes trying to keep still when I saw the bag float in space above me. The zipper opened and Moustafa's face pushed out with teeth that looked too large for his mouth as he screamed, "You tried to stop the revolution. I had to stab you!"

My eyes squeezed tighter as I heard my voice scream back, "Damn it, Moustafa, it wouldn't have worked. You would have been killed!"

His teeth glared like they were in the sun. "I was killed being Allah's messenger. He will grant me my rewards."

I wanted to choke him but then remembered I only had use of one hand. "Why did you take away my arm!"

Moustafa clucked his tongue in mock sympathy. "An arm is an honorable sacrifice for one of Allah's soldiers."

There was an increased glare from his teeth that made me squeeze my eyes tighter. "I'm not one of Allah's soldiers!"

Moustafa began to laugh when suddenly the sniper flew in, black grease on his face and a large "W" across his shirt. But instead of taking my side against Moustafa, he hovered in the air next to him, looking down at me in silence.

My right arm throbbed with the Morse code S - O - S as I screamed up at him, "What are you waiting for? He's the enemy! You could have saved my arm if you shot him sooner!"

The sniper's "W" expanded then deflated, his breath blowing warmth in my face. "I had to wait while you defused the revolt. You had a job to do that couldn't be done with a bullet."

My heart began pounding to the same throb as my arm. "But he almost killed me!"

The "W" swelled and remained enlarged. "A good warrior never lets a protector die. They're too important and too few."

I wanted to reach up and rip the "W" off his chest, but at opening my eyes his image was gone and Moustafa was back on the floor in the body bag. The rubber quivered from the vibrations and my own throbs felt like razors surging through every part of me. That is every part except my left arm. I would have given anything to feel that piercing pain in my left arm!

~ CHAPTER 11 ~

Field Hospital

"Anyone else?"

"No, only him. Too late for the other."

I was pulled off the chopper and rushed by two medics to a gray barracks with a Red Cross on its side. I was closer to help, but I was also closer to the truth about my arm. I tried to lift it one more time but there was no sensation, like it wasn't even attached.

The medics slid me onto a table and a woman's face appeared. Her lips curved up more on the left side than the right as she began to speak. "Hi, I'm Susan. There's no call to worry. We have the world's best docs. They'll see you in a jiffy, soon as I can get you prepped." She began cutting my shirt with a scissors and I strained to see what she exposed. There was a broad dressing spanning my left chest and shoulder. She lifted it halfway but then placed it back down and turned away towards the doctors. I panicked that what she saw was a completely severed arm and feared it was lying there, unattached. "Can't feel my arm," I gasped.

"Over here," she called across the room then turned back to me. "Don't worry. A doctor will be here in a jiffy."

"Is it..." I gasped, unable to say any more.

A man in khaki scrubs came to my side, and without a word or a smile, lifted the dressing. "Shrapnel do that?"

The nurse pushed a strand of hair off her face. "No, a Marine knife fight."

"Of course." The doctor nodded his head dramatically then looked again under the half-lifted bandage. "Not enough violence here for you, son? You have to make more?"

"No..." I gasped.

But the doc had turned away. "Where's the other one?"

The nurse's eyes winced slightly. "Dead."

My chest began pounding, like my severed arm was slamming on it in a fast beat. I wanted to tell him what happened, but only a choking sound emerged.

The doc pointed to my face. "You settle down and stay quiet. You're lucky it wasn't an inch closer to your neck." Then he turned to the nurse. "Sedate him."

I had to ask before I went under and managed to utter, "My arm?"

The nurse took hold of my good arm, beginning an IV. The doc looked down at me and shook his head. "You have muscle, nerve and artery damage. But don't worry, son, you'll be holding a knife again in no time."

I was desperate to tell him, *I didn't start it, I was protecting others,* but the words choked in my throat.

The nurse placed her hand on my good shoulder. "Count backwards, starting from one hundred."

I could only barely utter, "One-hundred, ninety-nine, ninety-eight," when everything suddenly went blank.

* * * * *

The light was so sharp I had to squint, allowing only a narrow band of vision. But what I could see was a pole of tubes by a bed a few feet away, and a body lying on its back with a thickly wrapped leg raised at a forty-five degree angle in the air.

My eyes began to adjust and I opened them further, seeing the blanket lying flat against the mattress where his other leg should have been. I shuddered, triggering a sharp, piercing pain across my chest. I held myself absolutely still, trying to stop what felt like a knife slicing through my insides and took a deep breath, but that made it feel worse.

I glanced back at the flat space where the leg should have been, then reached for my own legs and arm, making sure they were there. The movement hurt, but at least I knew I was whole as I collapsed back on the mattress.

There was a rustling sound from the man without a leg. "You all right, Lenny?"

The familiar voice made me scared to turn and look.

"I hear they call you Scout now. You all right, buddy?"

All I could think of was standing on my own two feet and getting the hell out of there. I slid my legs over the edge of the bed, felt a few toes touch the floor, and stood, expecting my feet to support me. But instead, I collapsed on the wooden floor feeling immense pain in my chest.

"Nurse!" I heard Billy call.

The pain surged from my body to my arms. My arms! I'd felt a fleeting pain in my left arm, but then it went away.

The nurse arrived with two Vietnamese men who slid their arms under my body and lifted me back onto the bed.

A nurse with the name Susan on her shirt peered down at me. "Oh my goodness." Her voice had a melody like the children's song, "Three Blind Mice," recalling a long lost time of comfort in the midst of horrible pain.

"I wanted to stand," I gasped, barely able to get the words out.

"You're all alike." Another sweet, soft melody rang above me. "You can't wait even a few hours to heal. No, you have to jump right up as if the world depended on it."

"It does," I uttered under my breath, glancing at Billy's legs, then back at her.

She draped the sheet over me, letting it fall loosely around my feet. "Now you listen to your nurse and stay in bed." Her finger touched my good arm. "Is this going to be a struggle between us?"

Her concerned eyes made me want to please her. I forced the words, "No more standing." The raspiness of my voice annoyed me, especially compared to her musical tones.

Her lips blossomed into a delicate smile and she placed a hand on my shoulder. "Very good. You'll heal, but not today."

I looked at her, admiring her straight brown hair and her smooth pale cheeks that glistened with sweat.

But then she turned to Billy and, in the same sweet voice said, "And how's my best patient feeling today?"

He squawked like a threatened vulture. "Hanging like butchered meat, but this place don't give me no choice, do they?"

I was about to tell him not to take it out on her when she said, "It's good you called on him. I didn't hear him go down."

Billy slapped his hand on his wrapped leg. "Hell, he once saved me when I couldn't get up. It's only right I return his bad judgment."

I looked at him, surprised he remembered. But why shouldn't he? It was only two days ago.

"He did you a favor," she said, smoothing his blanket, then began for the next patient down the line. I strained my neck to keep her in view, though it pulled against my bandages.

"Hit in action?"

I turned to Billy, annoyed that he pulled my attention away from Susan and pointed up towards my shoulder. "Stabbed."

His forehead wrinkled down the center. "Tough break. Anyone else hit from the squad?"

I swallowed hard, feeling it pull against my stitches. "Moustafa's dead." My face went suddenly hot. "Joe's dead, too."

Billy whistled a long, deep note then dropped his head back against his propped pillows. "Damn, the squad's practically wiped out. The sarge is going to have to pull in a whole new load of cherries."

I looked back at Billy, thinking much of what I had to say was his fault and he should know what he did. "The sarge is out, transferred to the Twenty-Sixth. Richard took a parachuting mission. And Wesley and Leon," I paused, stopping before I said Moustafa, then continued, "they're being sent with the Sixty-Seventh to the thirteenth valley."

"Thirteenth valley!" Billy twisted his upper body to face me, holding onto the bar at the side of his bed. "Damn, that's death row. Hell, we'll be the only ones left from the Forty-Fifth. How's that for a kick in the ass—you and me, old war buddies."

My voice was down to a gasping whisper but I had to answer. "No way. Can't let that happen."

Billy pulled himself closer to the bar. "What, be war buddies?"

I shook my head though that was on my mind, but something else was more pressing. "Wesley and Leon, I have to keep them alive. They saved me."

Billy hunched over the bar, glancing at my left shoulder before he spoke. "People you save don't keep you alive. Only ones keep you alive is doctors. And only reason they do it is to keep the body count down. Otherwise, it don't make no sense."

I also agreed that things didn't make sense, especially that the sniper kept me alive but no one kept Joe alive. I looked back at him. "What you expect to make sense?"

Billy pushed against the bar, raising himself up higher. "Keeping us alive like this. What's the point? I ain't gonna have legs."

I brushed my hand against my own legs before pointing to his bandaged one in the air. "What about that one?"

Billy pushed himself back from the bar, flopping back on his pillow. "It's a crap shoot. Doctors give it a fifty-fifty chance of working again."

I squeezed my toes, unable and unwilling to imagine no legs as I uttered, "I can't feel my arm."

170

Billy didn't respond and I turned away from him, catching sight of Susan, five beds down unwrapping a bandage from someone's head.

"They sending you home?"

His voice intruded on my thoughts of Susan and I was going to snap back when I realized I hadn't thought about home. "I don't know. You?"

Billy tried to adjust his sitting position with his hands but, after much effort, remained in the same place. "In three weeks. First to a carrier hospital, then the last place I want to get sent back to, Columbus."

I turned to him too quickly, feeling a harsh pull from my stitches. "You're from Columbus?" My throat suddenly went completely dry making the rest a barely audible gasp. "Joe's from Columbus." I swallowed hard, feeling furious that Billy didn't appreciate his chance when Joe had so many plans that were now shattered. He was going to open a business, marry Marie, have a house with a swimming pool, have me visit him, and have barbecues for the squad.

One side of Billy's mouth twitched into his cheek. "I knew that but it's a good thing I didn't know him there so I won't have to face his folks."

"Lucky for you. You get the choice. He doesn't!" My stitches pulled tighter making me want to scream, but I wasn't sure if that was more from pain or anger.

Billy turned to me, shaking his head. "It's not what you think. I wouldn't know what to say to them. How do you talk to parents whose kid has been killed?"

"With a lot of sadness, I suppose!" My outburst felt harsh against my throat, like it had been scraped by a razor.

Billy hit the pole next to his bed, making it ring. "You think it's great going back like this?"

I looked over at the blunt edge of his missing leg, trying not to think that it could have been me. "You have to do a long stint in the hospital?"

Billy's hand dropped where his leg should have been. "It better be forever, man, that's all I can say. Those bastards did this to me and now it's up to them to take care of me."

I felt more sorry for his doctors and nurses than for him, as I mumbled, "I'm sure you'll make certain of that."

A metal pan slammed against a metal post ten beds down to the left. I jolted my head upright as a man with thick gauze wrapped around his head began to scream at a small Vietnamese man in hospital khakis, "You're gonna die for this, you and your whole friggin' country!"

171

Billy's chuckle startled me. "Perkins from the Eighty-Fifth, head trauma. Should have seen him yesterday when that gook tried to change his bed pan. Knocked it over on his feet. Served that gook right, too. He don't belong here. Can't trust him not to kill us."

The man didn't look any larger than the twelve-year-old laundry boy. "Has he killed anyone here?"

Billy gripped the metal bar on the side of his bed and pulled himself forward a half an inch. "Poor bastards in this torture chamber are dying all the time. How can you tell what caused it?"

"Keep him away from me!" shouted Perkins, waving his hands in the air.

A doctor and three nurses surrounded him. Susan was one of them, trying to push his left arm down, while he flailed against her restraint.

"Don't hurt her," I gasped, trying to raise myself higher for a better view, but my one working arm buckled under the pressure. Susan gave out a yell and I felt frantic, wishing I had a grenade to throw onto Perkins that would hurt only him. But then there was sudden quiet. I peered down towards his bed to see Susan and another nurse easing him down on his back.

"He's out," said Billy, pushing both hands into the stubbed hair behind his ears. "Enough morphine does it every time."

I watched impatiently for Susan to leave his bedside. "I'm glad they shut him down."

Billy turned towards me with his elbows sticking out from both sides of his head. "Don't think you're any better. It was only a few hours ago you was screaming when they wheeled you in."

"Me?" I felt a sudden gush of sweat down the back of my neck. "What did I say?"

Billy grinned and looked up at the ceiling. "Let's see, it was something like, *'Watch out he's going to kill everyone!'* And then there was the, *'What are you waiting for, shoot now!'* " He paused, looking directly at me. "Scout, you was one raving maniac coming in."

I didn't want to believe him but also didn't believe he could have made up something that close. "Did I say anything else?"

Billy's left cheek bulged, showing his uneven teeth on that side. "Something about a Naomi and an Anna. Are you planning to introduce me any time soon?"

The soreness in my chest began throbbing heavily. I avoided his eyes, staring only at his one tooth that stuck out farther than the others. "What did I say?"

"Don't worry about it." Billy's lips pressed down over his teeth then popped apart. "This place is full of whacked out, screaming freaks. You fit right in."

I thought of Perkins with Susan fighting against his arm. "Who stopped me?"

Billy's head tilted in Perkins' direction. "The gook. He held you still while the doc shoved a needle in your ass. They had you down in less than two minutes."

All I could think of was how it looked to Susan and if she acted nice to me because she feared I might go crazy again. I raised my gaze to Billy's face. "Did it happen to you?"

"Me?" His mouth stretched wide. "No way. I don't keep no ghosts in my head. When something's over, it's over."

I suddenly saw the girl with the knife at her throat and felt it pressing against my own. "You don't think about the village?"

"Hell no." Billy's head shook, his hair rubbing against his pillow. "Only thing I think about is you and Joe getting me on the chopper. You didn't leave me. I owe you."

He must have heard me want to leave him, but he didn't mention it. My mouth flooded with spit as I said, "You don't owe me anything."

Billy bolted his head upright. "Oh, I owe you all right, don't kid yourself. But 'cause of what those damned gooks did to me," he slapped the bed next to his stump, "I got no way to pay up."

A Vietnamese man in the same hospital khakis as the nurses placed a tray of food on the stand next to Billy's bed. Billy hit the tray making the fork and spoon clatter. The man didn't react and began to walk away when Billy demanded, "Hey, you, which part did you poison?"

I watched Billy's eyes narrow like he was watching the man leave through a scope. "Why would he want to kill us? We're no threat, the condition we're in."

Billy glanced at my legs, their outline prominent under the sheet. "I'm not, but you are. Hell, I wish they would poison me. It would be better than this."

I flexed my legs, not minding their harsh pull. "You'll come out of this okay. You can get a wheelchair or a wooden leg, maybe even a plastic one. I'll bet they have new plastic legs that work good."

Billy chewed on his upper lip as he stared at his missing leg. "Could be, if you only need one. But two is total gimp time."

The man placed a tray on my stand with a cup of red Jello that looked too close to what was oozing out of Billy's bandage. I raised my hand to push it out of view when Susan appeared, placing two paper cups next to it.

"Swallow these after you've eaten." She pointed to the cup with three pills in it, and the cup of water next to it.

I wanted to keep her near for as long as I could. "What are they for?"

She tilted her head to the side and moved it as she spoke. "To fight off infection, inflammation and pain, and you better take them 'cause I have to get you healed fast."

"You trying to get rid of me?" I hoped it sounded like a joke, but feared it was true.

She leaned in closer, the warmth of her breath like a tender touch on my cheek. "In a way." Her smile revealed a thin scar on her left cheek. I wanted to reach up and touch it when her face lifted. "Really it's for Lieutenant Tell. He called and said he's coming in four days to take you on R&R to Da Nang. When I told him you wouldn't be in good enough condition in that short a time, he said he'd take me along and set me up first class if I got you healed fast enough and that's when I told him you'd be ready." Susan winked, like it was our secret, and I felt a throb in my groin.

I imagined she was getting ready to bend lower and kiss me on the lips when Billy asked, "Who's Lieutenant Tell?"

I was suddenly struck that I didn't know and feared she had confused my name with someone else.

Susan's eyebrows arched, waiting for my answer. My shoulder began to pound and I went to touch it when the sniper's face popped in my head. I thought he'd been kidding about the name William Tell, but it had to be him. And it was possible he was a lieutenant. With his missions he could easily have earned enough promotions.

My fingers tapped the bandage. "Must be the sniper."

"Sniper?" Susan lifted my hand off the bandage and placed it halfway down my stomach.

She let go of my hand, leaving the spots she had touched feeling empty as I struggled to find a way to describe the sniper. "He saved my life and I saved his."

"We got us here a veritable war hero." Billy's voice intruded into what I had hoped was private. "What's next, Scout, you gonna show us your "S" for Superman?"

Susan stepped to the right, blocking Billy from my sight as if she could read my mind. I looked up, hoping for some melodious words which soon came. "For Da Nang first class, I'm going to make sure you're ready."

I wanted to raise both my arms to her and draw her in close, but could only raise one. It lifted stiff and she stepped back, as if afraid she would get hit. I didn't want her to think I was crazy like Perkins and moved my hand slowly forward. "Let's shake on that and I promise not to let you down."

She took my hand and I felt her tempting warmth within her fingers. "No, please, don't let me down." She pulled her hand back and pointed to the cup of pills. "Don't forget."

"No problem. I'll take every one."

She smiled, her eyes half-closing, making me unsure whether she was looking at me or the floor. I tried to slide lower, to see her eyes better, but she turned and moved on towards Billy, placing his white cup of pills next to his can of peaches.

Billy leaned in her direction, his hand reaching for hers, but fortunately, it was an inch too short. "You wouldn't go to Da Nang without me, now would you, honey?"

I jolted upright, feeling the severe pull in my chest as I yelled in my pathetic rasp, "Sure would!" She looked towards me and I winked, though instead of receiving an expected smile in return, her lips tightened into a straight line. I had made a mistake, though I didn't know what it was. I had to make it up to her. At least we'd be alone on the R&R. If she couldn't smile at me here, she'd have plenty of chances in Da Nang, I'd make sure of that.

The next three days I spent my time watching Susan and trying to make her laugh every time she walked past me by calling out, "I'm almost healed," or "Countdown to Da Nang," or "There she goes, the fastest healer in the east." She would smile briefly but then turn away fast, making me fear she still thought I'd turn into Perkins. I tried to deal with that by keeping the different ways she smiled in my head. There was the one where all her teeth gleamed in a smooth semi-circle, or the one where her cheeks seemed to dance into her eyes or the one where only her left cheek pulled back in what looked like a cresting ocean wave. I played them over and over in my mind when she wasn't around, pretending each one was only for me while we sat on a deserted beach at night. But the truly best times were when she came to change my dressing and her warm fingers, with their usual thin layer of sweat, brushed against my chest. She would smile at those times while she dabbed at the wound with the brown disinfectant, saying, "The sting is good for you, remember that."

I'd answer with, "Anything from your hands could never give me pain." Billy had grumbled one time, "You two are disgusting."

175

She had winked and I took that as a sign she did want the R&R with me, no matter how quickly she looked away the other times.

The third morning, she came to my bedside accompanied by a doctor. He tapped a small rubber hammer on several spots of my unfeeling arm and then rubbed the full length with his hands. I felt nothing and held my breath, waiting for the words, *It will be good as new by the time you get to Da Nang.* But looking at Susan instead of me, he said, "The muscles are beginning to atrophy. They need to be exercised."

Her eyes flashed on mine momentarily, but then turned quickly away as she said, "I'll get right on that, doctor."

"You can start now," I said, taking her wrist with my good hand and moving her hand towards my left arm. The doctor looked into my face, which was pleading up towards her, and said, "Sometimes the cure is worth the pain."

Susan had stayed and lifted my left arm, flexing every joint in my hand and wrist, and I imagined feeling every bit of her touch. She flexed my elbow all the way, making my fingers touch my shoulder. "Feel anything?"

"Not in my arm, but you're heating up the rest of me." I moved my good arm to her waist and felt the momentary uplift of her breath.

She shoved my hand off of her and squirmed away on the bed. "None of that, you hear me?"

"In Da Nang?" I whispered, looking up to her face for any sign of assurance.

Her eyes turned away from me as she placed my unfeeling arm down at my side, and whispered back without any hint of smile, "I think your lieutenant has other plans for you in Da Nang."

I moved my good hand closer to her, though made sure I didn't touch. "He'll change them. He owes me."

There was a bare hint of a smile as her eyes softened and her cheeks twitched, but then she looked back at my unfeeling arm and said, "We'll see." Suddenly I was afraid the tender desires I had imagined had only been from me. Her sweetness could merely have been that I was her ticket to R&R in Da Nang, and nothing more.

My wound suddenly felt stabbed all over again, only much deeper and with a much broader dagger. "You don't have to be nice to me if you don't want to. You only have to get me healed enough to sit in a Jeep."

Her left cheek eased into an uncertain smile. "I know what I have to do, Mr. Marine, and I know who to take orders from."

176

I was almost afraid to ask, in case I'd find out about some other man in her life, but then couldn't hold it in. "Who's that?"

"The doctors, for one." She shrugged without finishing.

I checked her hand one more time for a wedding ring and saw only a silver band. "And there's someone else?"

She turned away, crossing her arms in front of her. "The only other orders I take are those that come from my heart."

My stitches tightened to the point of agony. I wanted, more than anything, to know if I was in her heart.

Billy's voice felt like a gunshot. "What are you two whispering about? Still plotting to desert me in my time of need?"

I tried to ignore him and leaned forward, getting as close to her ear as I could. "Promise me we'll be together in Da Nang."

She closed her eyes and didn't answer, her lips starting to tremble.

"Please," I whispered, desperately wanting to touch her with my right hand, but afraid she'd get mad and leave. "What is it?"

"Nothing is worth starting. There's too much pain," she uttered so softly I could barely hear it. "Don't worry. You'll get sent home and then you won't care anymore."

Her quivering lips made me even more anxious to wrap my arm around her, but I was too afraid of her reaction. "I'll stay. I promise."

She shook her head vehemently. "No! No one who can go back should stay!"

"Might be worth it." I leaned in closer. "I can also take orders from my heart."

She stood abruptly, bouncing me back against my pillow. I desperately wished I could jump up next to her and take her some place where we could be alone.

She angled her shoulder towards me but her face remained turned away. "I'll inform Lieutenant Tell that you can manage without me."

"What?" My chest felt stabbed all over again, only this time with jagged glass. I wanted to scream out to her when I realized all the noise in the room had ceased and all eyes had turned on me. I tried to ignore their persistent stares and whispered, "If you stay here, I'm not going."

She turned around with her arms crossed. "You'll go, all right." Her fingers fidgeted on her arms. "And you'll have a good time and never come back."

"No," I yelled, not caring who heard. "I'll need you. My dressings and my walking's not steady."

177

Her forehead wrinkled and cast a shadow over her eyes. "I'm sure your Lieutenant Tell will know where to find plenty of nurses in Da Nang."

I began to yell, "I don't want other nurses," but she turned and rushed away, her sight focused way beyond the rows of watching eyes. I shut my own eyes, unable to bear seeing her leave. I hoped for a vision of what I could do to change her mind, but all I saw was total darkness.

Susan didn't return the rest of that day, and I feared she'd left. Another nurse came to change my bandage and I asked about Susan.

"She's taking a break."

That made it sound like Susan would be back in a little while. But she wasn't, not the rest of that evening or even the next morning when the other nurse came back in to give out medications with breakfast. I couldn't bear her absence another moment as I turned to Billy. "How long do nurses get off?"

Billy scratched the stubble on his cheeks. "All I know, Scout, is you chased her out of here fast and ruined it. She was taking to me real good, even said she'd escort me back to Ohio when the time came."

I began coughing, my stitches feeling like they were ripping into my skin. How could she? Billy had to be deluding himself, right? Or was I the one deluded, imagining she felt something for me? I closed my eyes, trying to recall every look she ever gave me, every word she ever spoke to me, every touch against my skin. There had to be something real meant only for me in those gestures, or was there?

A deep voice startled me. "Scout, wake up. You's lying there like you been thrown by a bull." I opened my eyes to see the sniper with his arm extended to my right side.

I lifted my hand into his when I realized Susan was standing behind him. I stared at the only part of her face not hidden by his back, her right eye. It shifted from my face to my bandage and then towards Billy.

The sniper squeezed my hand while holding it still. "Susan tells me you're ready for Da Nang."

I glanced at him then back at her, though she was looking down the row of beds. "You coming with us?"

The sniper turned from me to her. She looked back at him and answered as though he had asked, "I arranged with the other nurse to take my place."

I slammed my hand on the bed. "No way. It's Susan or I won't go." The sniper looked at me with one eyebrow raised high.

Susan turned towards the door. "I'll let her know you're ready."

But before she could leave, the sniper grabbed her arm. "Wait a minute, darling, this is my call. I arranged with the commanding officer for three days of Nurse Susan to accompany my wounded Marine, and Nurse Susan it will be."

Susan stared at the ten pins of bars above the pocket of his uniform then glared at me. "The other nurse is more experienced."

But before I had a chance to yell that it had to be her, the sniper shook his head. "Sorry, darling, my plans don't get changed by anyone but me. It's an occupational necessity." He let go of her arm and held his hand out for her to shake. "Truce?"

She looked at his hand without offering her own, her right shoulder shifting forward. "I'll get his meds and dressings, but I won't be forced into anything I don't want to do in Da Nang."

The sniper left his hand extended at waist level. "Fair enough, as long as my Marine is given proper medical care."

She nodded at his empty hand and walked away, leaving me afraid she wouldn't talk to me the whole trip.

The sniper turned back to me, his not taken hand shifting to his waist. "You ready to travel?"

I almost said, *I still have my legs,* but then realized Billy was listening and switched to, "Yes, but why the R&R?"

His gaze moved to my limp arm and bandage before settling back on my face. "I should never have let it get that close. I owe you."

"You don't owe me. You saved my life." I was uncomfortable as to what my responsibility was in return. He stared directly into my pupils, making me shift in my bed. "Why are you looking at me like that?"

He shook his head then smiled, his lips pulling mostly to the right. "Didn't know I was walking into a lover's spat." He winked, then added, "Don't scare her off. She could be useful."

But before I could ask what he meant, he commanded, "Be outside in my Jeep in fifteen minutes."

"Yes, sir." I snapped my right hand to my head. He returned the salute and I realized that's what he was doing the last time I saw him, in the truck, and felt more like I was returning that salute than saluting for the order I just received. The sniper turned and walked out of the barracks in long, purposeful strides.

Billy watched him leave, breathing loud as if accompanying the strides, then turned to me. "Who the hell is that?"

"A sniper, lives in the jungle for weeks at a time with only a dog, watching and destroying the enemy. I think he knows who they are and what they are doing better than any man alive."

179

Billy looked back at the door the sniper had passed through. "Why's that?"

Air gushed from my mouth like I'd been holding in too much. "Because he has reason to hate them more than any man alive."

"Not more than me." Billy slapped his elevated cast. "I'd like to nuke this whole country."

I shifted in my seat, tilting towards Billy. "He only hates the enemy. He doesn't want to kill innocents."

Billy laughed. "They're all the enemy."

"Even those kids?" I blurted out.

Billy leaned forward a few inches, the muscles in his neck bulging with strain. "That's right. Don't think they wouldn't have killed us if they had the chance."

I pictured the laundry kid with a gun in his hands, but then I saw the boy and girl chasing the chickens and taking care of the baby. "You had no reason to suspect those kids."

Billy dug his knuckles into the mattress and pushed himself up another half inch. "Don't be stupid, Scout, they would have killed me and you and the rest of us if I let them live after holding a knife to their throats. Someone did that to me, I'd want paybacks, too."

A pounding inside my chest started right under my wound. "And that makes it okay?"

Billy squinted and his mouth tightened. "I saved the guys in our squad. That makes it okay. Don't forget that."

Susan entered the barracks with fatigues draped over her arm. I wanted to smile at her and try to make her happy about coming to Da Nang, but the image in my head of those kids getting their throats slit was too overwhelming. I turned back to Billy seeing he had collapsed on his back and was staring up at the ceiling. I mumbled to myself, "Don't worry. It's something I won't ever forget."

Susan arrived and laid the fatigues across my legs. "I'm under orders to get you ready. Your lieutenant is used to getting his way."

I wanted to say something funny to her but those kids faces were still in my head. And by the looks on their faces, Billy was right. They would have killed all of us first chance they had. But that was only because we made them that way.

"Come now and cooperate. We only have eight minutes." Susan's pronunciations were short and precise with no hint of melody. "Raise your arm and help me put on your shirt."

I lifted my good arm, anxious for the feeling of her touch, though still seeing those kids. She gripped my wrist and guided it towards the short sleeve. My fingers got caught in the entrance and I squeezed them together in a fist. "Sorry, I was thinking about something else."

Her eyebrows flinched higher for a moment. "I noticed. You seem to be a thousand miles away."

I looked at Susan's averted eyes. "'Fifty miles, maybe, but it's someplace I never want to go again. All I want to look at is you."

She jerked the shirt upward, making it pull on my hand. "You want to look at something, look at this sleeve and get your arm through it."

I glanced at the shirt seeing my fist pressed into the cloth like it was ready to punch right through, and angled it straighter to slip out the proper opening. "Better?" I hoped she would at least smile.

She didn't, but merely draped the shirt across my back and began to raise my limp arm. I leaned in closer hoping that would help, desperate to feel her touch on that arm and be able to guide it through the other sleeve. A few of her loose hairs touched my cheek and, without thinking, I began towards the rest of her hair, my lips brushing along her neck as I moved. It was a moment of tender bliss that felt like I was on a deserted beach alone with Susan. But then, as if I had approached too close to a pit of snakes, I was suddenly pushed backwards and found myself in a horrible panic.

"Stop it!" Susan propelled up from the bed. The shirt fell off my unfeeling shoulder, and she threw my pants and socks on the bed. "Get dressed yourself!"

"What did I do?" Each of her steps away was a harsh stomp on my wound, throbbing with the fear I wouldn't see her again. "I didn't mean to upset you."

She turned just enough to show a thin stream of tears from her left eye. "You think this is a joke, don't you? I'll let your lieutenant know he can dress you himself!" She turned towards the door and ran like she was being chased.

It was eerily quiet as I sat up in bed, dangling both legs over the edge, knowing I couldn't catch up with her if I tried.

Billy chuckled then pulled himself closer to me, stretching his neck so his face was only three feet from mine. "Blew it that time. You sure have a lot to learn about military nurses."

"Like what?" I snapped.

"Face it, man. Everyone in here is trying to get them in bed. They have to put up a tough front or they'll be grabbed every second of the day."

"But I wasn't…"

Billy raised his hand in a stop gesture and grinned. "Sure you were, Scout. We're all horny bastards. We can't help it."

My eyes glanced at the closed door hoping to see it open, but it didn't. "It's different with me. I love her."

"We all love her. She makes us feel better, laughs at our jokes, cleans our wounds…"

I punched on my bed. "It's not that way with me. Mine is real."

I began fumbling with my clothes when another nurse appeared. She slipped my limp arm through its sleeve, buttoned the front, and then put on a sling. Her touch felt nothing like Susan's and I wished I didn't need her help. But I had no choice. I wanted to get out to that Jeep as fast as I could. Susan would be sitting in it and I hoped that, once on the way to Da Nang, she would stop being angry with me.

The nurse held the pants low for me to step inside. I did and began to bend for them, but she already had them coming up to my waist and then snapped and zippered before I could ask any questions about why Susan was crying. She held out her arm to me, which I took, hearing Billy say, "Find some pretty gook bitch and leave Susan alone."

I held up my hand to him, hoping it was goodbye forever, then walked without taking hold of the nurse. She stayed at my side and I could see her hands ready in case my legs became unsteady, but she was not the one I wanted to lean on and if I couldn't have Susan, I wanted to go it alone. I stepped outside anxious for the look of her smile, but was immediately blinded by brilliant sunlight blazing in my eyes. I squeezed them shut and stood still, feeling my chest heave in big breaths. The air felt hot enough to scorch my lungs, but as I became used to it I realized it didn't have the rancid smell of decay I'd become accustomed to in the last few days.

The nurse's hand grasped my arm. "Are you all right?"

"Yes, I'm fine." I opened my eyes slowly and only twenty feet away was the Jeep with the sniper in the front and Susan and Utah in the back. I began for them, taking care to get a firm footing under each step before going for the next. Susan watched me for a few moments but then turned away as if preferring to see some distant tree.

I approached the passenger door of the Jeep and pulled on the handle with my good hand, but my strength wasn't enough to get it opened. I wished she hadn't seen that but then remembered it was because I was weak that she was there at all. The sniper came around and opened the door, then helped me in. Once seated, the sniper slipped back into his seat and turned to me. I wanted to turn around to Susan and smile, but before I could, the sniper leaned right in front of my face. "Susan will come only if you promise not to kiss her."

"That's not fair…" I started.

Susan jumped up, gripping the back of the sniper's seat. "You see, I'm not going!"

The sniper slammed his hands on the dashboard. "Hold it!" He turned back to Susan, then at me. "You have to promise. I told her you would."

I wanted to turn around to Susan, but the Sniper's stare prevented it. My throat tightened, but I had to speak. "Okay, I don't like it, but I promise."

"Good, that's settled." The sniper started the engine and pointed forward. "First destination, Marguerite's, the only restaurant in this whole damned country that grills a steak fit for a Texan."

The Jeep lurched forward, accelerating slowly, bucking at each shift in gear. Dust from the road made me stay at a squint and also forced me to keep my mouth shut. I tried to talk once but bits of grit coated my tongue and all I could do was spit instead of speak anyway. I leaned back and braced myself the best I could against the ruts. Each one was a nasty jolt to my wound, but there was a particularly horrid one and I screamed.

The sniper rapped the back of his hand on my unfeeling arm. "Sorry, Scout, there's not much smooth road out here in this unappreciated territory."

I nodded and covered my mouth to mumble a few words. "My stitches don't appreciate it, either."

Susan's fingertips touched my shoulder, feeling like drops of comfort on the burning pain. I wanted to press her whole hand down on my shoulder when she extended her reach to in front of my face, exposing two blue Darvons in her palm. "Here, take these."

She tilted her hand waiting to drop them into mine, and I wished I had a choice and could choose her touch instead of the pills. But there was no choice and I opened my hand watching her drop them without letting her fingers touch my skin. The capsules fell forming the top of a triangle and reminded me of math homework I never wanted to do. I shook my hand to make them move but they were already stuck in that position from the sweat on my skin. I shoved them in my mouth and swallowed, expecting liquid to push them down except all I had was a coating of dust keeping them at the top edge of my throat. I began coughing, feeling panicked by the choked feeling.

Susan's hand extended a canteen in front of me. "Here, drink this."

I grasped the canteen, swallowing long gulps of water as fast as I could. The pills went down and after a few minutes, the coughing subsided.

I turned to the sniper, keeping my mouth covered by my hand. "How much more of this torture did you have in mind?"

The sniper shouted above the engine's noise. "Two hours, if we're lucky."

The Jeep jolted over another series of deep ruts. I wondered what I was doing out of a hospital bed and was ready to scream, *Take me back!* when Susan's hand grasped my bad shoulder and her fingers stroked gently just above the throbbing wound. Her touch was like cool rain dousing a raging fire. I breathed deeper, feeling the pain worth the price of her touch, if only it would stay there. I sat perfectly still for fear she would retreat if I moved. My eyes shut and I felt like I was in a dream, driving on a deserted island alone with Susan. My head leaned towards her and rested on her forearm, when in the midst of momentary comfort, the Jeep lurched to an abrupt stop.

~ Chapter 12 ~

Da Nang

I bolted upright in my seat, feeling my shoulder throb now that Susan's hand had retreated. We were stopped at a checkpoint being approached by four MPs. Three had M-16s held across their chests and one had his hand extended. "Your traveling orders, sir?"

The dog growled but the sniper raised his hand and she quieted instantly, leaving the clacking of the Jeep's engine the only noise in the air. The sniper scrutinized the faces of all four guards then pulled the papers from his shirt pocket and placed them in the waiting hand. I wanted to turn around to Susan and ask her to put her hand back on my shoulder but the silence demanded absolute respect. After a minute the MP handed the papers back and saluted the sniper. "Good luck with the mission, sir."

The sniper returned the salute then pointed to their gate. "How far to Da Nang?"

"Ten kilometers. I'll radio ahead for them to let you through at the line."

The sniper saluted again. "Thank you, much obliged."

He put the car in gear and began again on the dirt trail. More dust seemed to be kicked up than before as I watched his jaw shift from side to side.

I angled sideways to speak closer to his ear. "Mission?"

The sniper scratched at the side of his face. "General's words. I cashed in a favor."

I was impressed with the long reach of his pull but then became concerned at what this was all about. I had never asked for a trip to Da Nang and even the sniper doesn't go to a general for regular R&R. "Something you expect of me?"

His lips pushed forward before relaxing. "Not yet."

After that my wound seemed to scream at every bump. I kept sending quick glances back to Susan, but she'd immediately avert her eyes towards

185

the dog. Finally, I shut my eyes against the dust and tried to will away the pain. It worked for a short time, then voices called out, "You're clear, sir, go right through."

I realized we had passed the second checkpoint and were finally in Da Nang. We drove past huts that looked like they'd blow away in a strong wind, on into a section of one-room stone houses, and then into an elegant area of multi-storied homes with elaborate stone carvings.

The sniper double-parked the Jeep outside a glass-fronted restaurant with a gold Eiffel Tower and the name *Marguerite's* painted on the window. He tightened the brake and looked up at the sun's glare on the window that made it possible to only see shadows inside. "At last, real meat. I can smell it already."

He stepped out of the Jeep, pulled a leash out from under his seat, and buckled it around Utah's neck. "Sorry, girl, you know the rules in there."

I opened the Jeep's door with my right hand, held onto the car's frame and stepped down. Susan took hold of my feeling arm and helped me up the five steps. Her touch, though far from the wound, soothed much of the throbbing from the drive. If only she would hold onto me long enough, I was sure it would all fade away.

The inside of the restaurant held at least thirty tables, most of them round, but a few rectangular. The sniper was already at a round one by the far wall, with Utah lying on the floor by his feet. We approached and took two of the three seats. Susan sat to my left, my unfeeling side. I looked at that arm, hoping to see her touch it, but she had both hands on the table and began to straighten the arrangement of spices in the center.

The sniper held up his finger to the waiter, a frail Vietnamese man in black pants, white shirt and a black bow tie. He began towards us, glancing from the sniper to the dog as he came. "Utah well, yes?"

The sniper leaned forward to rub the dog's head. "Yes, fine and hungry like the rest of us. As fast as you can we want four steaks, rare, and a huge bowl of those mashed potatoes Marguerite makes in the kitchen back there."

The waiter tapped his pencil on the pad without writing anything down. "Yes, sir, steak and potatoes, very American. Will tell Marguerite is for lieutenant." He turned for the kitchen and the sniper leaned back in his chair, gazing at the black and white photos of Paris on the walls.

"Stop in here before your jungle trips?" I turned around to take in the full restaurant. The blue and white checkered tablecloths glowed in the window's sunlight while the rest of the room was dim from the dark wooden walls.

He looked first at Susan, then at me. "I was stationed in Da Nang for six months. I lived right nearby."

My mouth stayed opened for a moment, struggling with the image of him in this elegant area, before I could finally speak. "What were you doing in Da Nang?"

His hands gripped the edge of the table. "Special advisor. We were all special advisors back in 1964."

"Damn." I slapped the table harder than I meant to. "You been in country six years? Why so long?"

His eyebrows pulled to the center as he stared back into my eyes. "I was under the impression your memory wasn't affected by that stab. I've told you before, there's nothing for me back home. All my business lies here."

It was clear he didn't want to discuss it. Maybe it was because it was in front of Susan. He glanced at her and I looked quickly to see her response.

Susan leaned closer towards him, her head slightly tilted to the right. "Did you come here as a private?"

His cheeks eased to the sides forming an attractive smile I had never seen on him before. I didn't like that he directed it at Susan. "Not hardly. I was part of a special recon unit. Damned good at it, too, but that didn't last long once we set out in the field."

I dropped my hand on the table wanting to get his attention away from Susan. "What do you mean?"

His lips tightened into a straight line as he turned to me. "I wasn't their kind of team player. I refused to follow orders to torch an innocent village and was insubordinate to my officers. So it came down to a choice, either go to the stockade or go on what they considered a suicide mission to blow up a VC tunnel. Only thing is, I survived the suicide mission and they didn't know what to do with me. So they gave me a medal and sent me to blow another tunnel. I survived again and they gave me a medal and that time felt they had to promote me. That happened eight more times till I became a lieutenant. But still, no one in the higher brass could trust me to follow their orders, so when I offered to stay in the jungle they jumped on it, figuring every gook I killed added to their body count. And I could get them information on Charley they couldn't get any other way. It kept me out of their hair and I was able to stay in the jungle and do what I had to do. It's worked out best for everyone."

Susan's nose twitched. "You like it in there?"

He tapped his fingertips together a few times before answering. "In there I can get back at the bastards that destroyed my family. Out here I'd end up in jail."

Susan watched him clasp his hands together in a combined fist then looked up to his face. "If you'll end up in jail, why are you here?"

The sniper shifted his gaze between Susan and me before settling on Susan. "It's simple really, I need Scout's help."

My good arm that I was leaning on gave way but I caught myself before falling forward onto the table. "My help? With what?"

The sniper and Susan both stared at me, but it was the sniper who spoke. "You're the only one could do this."

I pointed to my bum arm in the sling. "How can I help you like this?"

The sniper placed his two pointer fingers on the tablecloth and began to slide them apart as he spoke. "It's from when I lived in Da Nang." His fingers traced lines that moved towards him. "I had a woman, Hooang," her name came out in almost a whisper. "She took care of me during my time in Da Nang, did my laundry, fixed me meals, and comforted me in the only way she knew how. That was before I was assigned to missions in the jungle."

Susan's hand moved towards one of his. "Do you love her?"

His head shook once, still looking at the table. "No, I'm not meant for love." He retraced his fingers back together then looked up at me. "But there is a complication."

I shifted in my seat, feeling a sharp twinge in my chest. "What kind of complication?"

His eyes locked on mine, making me feel completely fixed in place. "A child. We have a son."

"You have a family right here in Da Nang?" It was Susan's voice, though his stare remained steady on my face.

"No." His eyebrows raised higher as he continued to focus only on me. "It's not like a family. I'm a warrior, a destroyer, a killer, not the sort of man who can be a father."

Susan moved her chair right next to mine as if trying to get in his line of vision. "But you must help them. He's your son."

He looked down at the table and I felt myself released to gasp for air.

"I send Hooang money, but that's no longer enough." His gaze came back up at me, only this time, his eyes shifted like they were searching mine from different angles. "The boy, Chim, is hated by his own people, all because he has my hair and my eyes. They won't ever allow him an education or a legitimate way to make money. His only chance for a decent life is back in the states where he can be educated and accepted, at least more than he can be here."

"So take him back." I felt sweat gush under my arms and wished I had a way to make it stop.

His head shook without changing the fix of his eyes. "I can't. There's no going back for me. But you, Scout, you can take him with you."

"Me?" I screamed, then realized I was too loud for the restaurant and lowered my voice. "Take on a kid? I can't even take care of myself? Remember, I'm wounded. I can't even feel my arm!"

The sniper wiped his forehead with the back of his hand, but a few trickles remained down the side of his face. "You'll be sent back home. You can take him with you. It won't be hard."

"And then what?" I wanted to get up and run, but had nowhere to go. "What do I do with him there?" I stared back at him, realizing he had set a good trap bringing me here. I couldn't escape him and he knew it, but I wasn't going to fall for his scheme.

"Maybe there's someone in your family…"

"No! Absolutely not!"

At that moment Utah jumped up, placed her paws on the sniper's leg and looked behind her. We turned to see what had her attention and saw the waiter, only two feet away, standing still with our plates cradled in different parts of his arms.

Susan tapped the table. "Please, put them down. Their yelling has nothing to do with you."

He hesitated, looking first at the sniper, then at me, as if giving us a chance to protest. When we didn't, he approached and placed the four steaks on the table, including one by the empty chair, and set a bowl of mashed potatoes in the middle. He turned to leave when the Sniper said, "Please, three beers, and a dish of water for Utah."

The waiter nodded from his half-turned position, then walked back towards the kitchen.

The intoxicating smell of the steak melted into my anger. I became suddenly ravenous, anxious to feed my famished body. I stabbed my fork into the steak then realized I didn't have use of my other hand to cut it. I lifted a corner of the steak off the plate, bent down, and took a bite. The hunk was too large for my mouth but I worked at chewing it while watching the sniper cut the steak from the fourth plate into several small pieces and place it on the floor. My mouth was still overly full, but I couldn't hold back what I was feeling. "You take care of your dog. Why can't you take care of your son?"

The sniper glanced at me without giving any response then began chewing a piece of his own steak, his eyes shifting from one picture on the wall to the next. I was going to demand an answer when Susan's voice broke in, "This is delicious. I haven't had steak in months."

I realized my last steak was at the beer fight, which I didn't want to bring up, but I couldn't stop the thoughts of Moustafa and my stabbing and the sniper's too long a wait before he shot. I put my fork in my steak and began to lift it again.

"Not like that." Susan took hold of my fork and began to cut my steak with her knife. She raised the first piece to my mouth, which I took, wishing that the fork touching my lips was her fingers. She proceeded to cut the rest of my steak, leaving the pieces pushed back together, resembling the whole it had been.

I wanted to savor this piece she had given me before demanding an answer from the sniper when he dropped his fork on top of his steak and stared directly at my eyes. "Utah's different. I can take care of her 'cause she's already a killer like me. But my son, I don't want to pass down the hate I have inside and make a killer out of him."

The meat in my mouth should have been chewed enough to swallow but some of it stuck in my throat, making me gasp out the words, "He's your son. Get rid of the hate for his sake."

I cleared my throat and gulped down the rest of the meat as he said, "I can't, the hate is what keeps me alive in the jungle. If I start worrying about him, I'll be dead in no time."

His lips twitched like they were being pushed by something from the inside as he continued to stare at my eyes. I knew he was waiting for my answer, but I wasn't the one to take on his kid.

I stabbed another piece of steak, put it in my mouth and began to chew. The sniper nodded as if he understood my silence and scooped at the mashed potatoes, putting a big heap on Utah's plate, then one on his own. He looked down to watch Utah eat and stroked her back while he said, "She and I can't do anything but what we're doing. We've gone too far and we're in too deep to ever change."

I swallowed, then stabbed into another piece of meat and put it in my mouth. The sniper glanced at the food on his own plate without making a move to touch it, then looked straight back at me. "I'll send you all my paychecks for him as long as I'm alive, and you get the insurance when I die. That's the best I can do."

The steak I was chewing turned to glue, holding my mouth firmly shut. I began to breathe heavily through my nose. His stare continued and I felt like

I would stop breathing all together if I didn't escape his look. I covered my face with my hand, picturing when my cousin brought her little boy to visit my mother and the kid screamed the whole time, my mother had told my father she never wanted a child visiting again. I worked on the meat in my mouth for a while, finally feeling it loosen from my teeth and slide down my throat. I was breathing again through my mouth and dropped my hand to get more air.

The sniper's stare was still coming at me, but this time I was able to talk. "I can't do this. It's impossible. You'll have to find someone else."

The sniper nodded, his eyes shifting to Susan, then back at me. "You don't have to decide, yet. We'll meet them tomorrow."

"Tomorrow?"

The waiter suddenly appeared, placing glasses of beer before each of us and the bowl of water on the floor. I grabbed my beer and gulped it half down, wishing it would wash away what I had just been asked.

The waiter left and I placed my glass back down on the table, stretching my arm to the sniper. "What do you mean we'll meet them tomorrow?"

The sniper didn't respond, instead taking the plate handed to him by Susan and bending low to scrape the pieces of her leftover steak onto Utah's dish. I turned to Susan, surprised she had given up that much food, and saw lines of tears sliding down her cheeks. My throat tightened, forcing all the words I wanted to say to get trapped. I reached over, barely touching her arm, when she abruptly pulled away. My hand dropped to the table as I watched her wipe away tears, then lean her face into her hands. Was she that upset that I touched her? But no, it was something from before. Was it the child, because his father didn't want him? But she was upset with me, not the sniper. Was that it? Was it because I didn't want the child? Why wasn't she crying about the injustice of being asked to take care of someone else's mistake?

The sniper scooped at the potatoes, putting a heap on Susan's plate and then on mine. "Try these before they get cold." He dropped a second scoop on my plate then looked at me. "Don't worry about tomorrow, Scout. I mean this. I have to stop in and see them, and then you can say yes or no. It's up to you."

I put a fork full of potatoes in my mouth and chewed, feeling a tingle on my tongue as I swallowed. They were tasty and I took some more, only after the third mouthful, the tingle turned harsh. I swallowed them fast then grabbed the beer which helped cool it down, but afterwards my tongue felt like it had been badly burned. I turned to Susan to warn her, seeing her pat her potatoes into a neat mound with her fork.

191

"Don't eat them. They're filled with chili or pepper or something."

Susan's eyebrows raised. "Probably my mother's recipe."

The sniper put more potatoes on Utah's plate and I was shocked that she'd eat them.

"Did you live on this street?" Susan stopped playing with the potatoes and dropped her fork to her plate.

The sniper turned around towards the window and pointed. "No, a few blocks that way."

I sucked at the inside of my mouth trying to remove the pepper from my skin as I looked out of the window in that direction.

"Did you like it there?"

The sniper rubbed at his chin. "Had to bend down every time I walked from one room to the other. Banged my head more than I didn't. I get banged less times in the jungle."

The waiter brought the check and the sniper slapped it with his hand and slid it onto his lap. I began to lean forward but he raised his hand, then stood and left for the register.

I turned to Susan, seeing her stare out of the window. "You all right?"

Susan let a loud breath rush from her mouth. "Are you kidding? Eating in a restaurant is the most human I've felt in a long time."

The sniper motioned to us from the cash register and we followed him out to the Jeep. The drive was quiet except for the rumbles of car engines and the music of other people's radios. I kept shifting in my seat unable to get comfortable, feeling the soreness in my mouth as well as the throbbing in my wound from every little bump. But mostly, I was feeling the emptiness of having to give up those few moments alone with Susan in the restaurant. It now felt like we were miles apart in the car. I had to find another way we could be alone. And I had to know what had made her cry.

* * * * *

It was two in the morning and I was nowhere near sleep. I lay in the hotel bed wishing I could go into Susan's room. I kept imagining the careful way she had removed my old bandages only three hours before, and dabbed my wound with a betadine pad. And then the tender way she positioned the new dressings. And how her fingers pressed into my arm as she wrapped new gauze around my chest to hold it all in place.

The sniper and his dog shared a bed six feet away from mine, both lying absolutely still, with neither one making a sound. It must be something they learned to survive in the jungle. But for me, the stillness and the quiet brought images to my mind I couldn't bear, except for Susan. As long as I was thinking of her, the disturbing visions stayed back.

A crack on the ceiling turned into the stream in the village where the kids had played. Next thing I knew I saw Billy holding a knife to the girl's throat and her mouth opened wide in a silent scream. I bolted upright in the bed, my wound feeling the pressure of the air like an angry punch as I screamed silently in my head, *No more, I can't bear to see it again, please, stop!*

I placed my hand on the bandage hoping it would help stop the pain and tried to picture the way Susan had touched me as she put it on. The pounding slowed and I slumped forward, facing my knees. If only I was able to go into Susan's room, I wouldn't even touch her. I would just want to watch her sleep.

I glanced around towards the door seeing Utah's eyes opened, watching me. I nodded to her and brushed my fingers back through my hair, feeling the damp sweat on my head begin to cool. The filmy curtains over the window fluttered and a slight breeze reached my face. I lay back down, trying not to focus on that same crack. There in my mind was Susan, her smile the way it had been that first day in the hospital. Stay with me, Susan, please, don't turn away.

Three more hours of dark shadows, trying to keep Susan's smile in my mind, then streaks of sun slowly stretched across the floor. I began to breathe heavier, thinking how I would soon see her, not just in my mind, but for real, in person. I looked to the door, wishing it were now.

The sniper sat up on the edge of his bed then went for the bathroom without looking in my direction. There were sounds of water running, then of a razor scraping against his face. I imagined Susan doing that for me, her fingers on my chin and my cheeks, even on my neck.

I heard a knock at the door and sat up straighter. "Come in."

The door opened and there was Susan in a yellow dress with little flowers dotting the long skirt and fitted top. I stared at the straps that tied around her neck, leaving her shoulders bare, and wished I could run my fingers along her smooth skin. "You look fantastic."

Susan smiled, though didn't make a move to come closer. "Thanks, I can't remember the last time I dressed for a day in the city. You ready?"

"Ready?" I grabbed the center of my wrinkled tee-shirt and pulled it straight forward. "I'm not dressed yet."

Her eyes shifted to the sound of running water in the bathroom before looking back at me. "No problem, we can take care of that in a jiffy."

She went for my duffel bag on the floor next to the bed and opened the zipper.

"I was thinking of a shower and shave," I began, but Susan instantly shook her head.

"No, the wound can't get wet. The scab needs more time to dry and thicken if it's going to heal right. A clean shirt and you'll be fine."

"What about a shave?"

"Why?" she asked, looking in the duffel instead of at me. "You think the kid will care if you have a beard?"

I wanted her to care, to want to rub her hand on my cleanly shaven face, but instead she placed a buttoned down shirt and a pair of pants on the bed, then reached towards my shirt. I raised my good arm, feeling her get the stretchable material over my head and off my good arm, then saw her grasp the unfeeling arm and remove it the rest of the way. Her fingers lingered on that arm and I tried desperately to feel each of those spots she touched, but couldn't.

Susan backed up and stood next to the bed. "Come to the edge, it's easier from here."

I slid across the mattress while she worked at opening the buttons on the shirt. She held it up and I slipped my arm through the sleeve then she guided my bad arm into its opening. I had hoped she would button my shirt and be close enough for me to smell her hair, maybe even brush up against it with my face, but she turned away and went for my pants, bringing them to my feet. I slipped my legs into them and watched her lift them halfway up before stopping.

"You're set. You can do the rest without me." She brought my hand to my waistband and let go.

I pulled at my pants with the one hand while watching her walk to the window, push the curtain aside, and peer down from the second floor. The pants came up to my thighs but then I had to stand to raise them the rest of the way. I managed the zipper but was struggling with the button when the sniper came out of the bathroom.

"Can you," I began, when he glanced at Susan and let out a long, slow wolf whistle.

She turned from the window with her mouth set in straight lines above and below her teeth. "You guys are all alike. Don't care how much you embarrass a lady."

Utah jumped off the bed heading for the sniper. The sniper bent down towards her but kept his gaze on Susan. "Sorry, it's been months since I've seen anyone that beautiful. Won't happen again."

He turned his full attention to Utah and Susan leaned back against the window before turning to me. "The stands are all set up. You ready yet?"

I was still fumbling with the button. "My pants…"

Before I could finish she turned to the sniper and pointed at me. "Could you?"

He turned and focused on my hand's inability to close my pants. "Sorry, Scout, didn't mean to make you struggle like that. Ten seconds faster would have prevented that, but then they would have called it murder, a very different kind of kill."

I wasn't too happy about that ten seconds myself but then I never would have met Susan. He reached for my waist, when in that split second, I managed to slip the button through myself. I stepped back to show him, then looked straight ahead at his clenched jaw. "A save is a save."

His lips protruded forward then separated. "True enough. And I have to remember that my previous officers are anxious to slap a court martial on me."

Susan came across the room and took hold of my arm. "Come on. I promised him I'd take you with me and there's so much we need."

Her touch was on my bad arm, though I imagined its feel, soft and tender, even loving. She pulled gently and the pressure made me step sideways towards the door. I turned towards the sniper and nodded, feeling my wound begin to pulse with a warm pain.

"Let's go, we have a lot to get." Susan pulled on my arm and I realized I was staring at the sniper and not able to be moved.

I let her take me out through the door and into the hallway. "Who's we?"

"We nurses, who else? We're out of makeup and hand cream and stationary and film and we need hats and sunglasses and we want canned fruit and nuts and champagne."

"Champagne?" I suddenly feared an unsuspected romance in her life. "For what?"

Susan's grip jerked my arm up and down in a fast motion. "You know, champagne's for everything, welcoming new people, saying goodbye to old friends, birthdays, promotions, or even for sad news."

We were almost on the steps when the sniper's voice called from behind us. "Should I bring champagne to Hooang?" He was fully dressed in pants, shirt, and boots, with Utah at his heel. I couldn't imagine how he did that so fast but he looked calm like he hadn't had to rush.

Susan's cheeks bulged almost double in size as he caught up to us. "Of course, she'll love it."

I hoped her smile was for the champagne, but feared it was for the sniper as I followed her the rest of the way out of the hotel, and he followed behind me.

Once outside she let go of my arm and stepped between the sniper and me. He assumed a one step lead down our street, past several small stalls that he glanced at, uttering in Vietnamese to the merchants, getting responses that made him nod, smile or spit on the ground. It was on the next block that he stopped in front of a stand, told Susan to pick what she wanted, then argued with the man before handing him an American ten dollar bill. It seemed very low for what she chose, getting everything even the champagne, but it was accepted and Susan was given two filled bags. We moved on to the next street, stopping in front of a restaurant, with a sign in red and black letters that read Enriqués.

The sniper pointed to the red door with several small glass panels. "Best breakfast in country I ever found, makes eggs just like my mom used to. Hungry?"

Susan peered into the frosted window but it was impossible to see through. "Is it expensive? I can't have you paying…"

The sniper raised his hand then stepped to the door and held it wide opened.

Susan crossed her arms in front of her chest and stood still.

The sniper waved his arm into the opening. "Entrez-vous, s'il vous plait."

Susan turned to me, then back to the sniper. "But…"

The sniper reached for her arm and pulled her to the door. Susan didn't resist his urging and I followed, entering inside a spacious room with a cherry orchard mural on the far wall. We walked past ten small round tables, none large enough for more than four chairs, till the sniper stopped at one in the corner by the window that offered no outside view, but spread a glow across the red tablecloth that made it appear to be lit from underneath.

"This is where I last sat with Hooang and Chim." He stared at the glow like it held their photographs. "Two years ago, or maybe more." He sat in the corner which faced into the center of the room, and we sat facing him, though my attention was on Susan's shadow that streaked across the table like one of the smooth tree trunks from the wall.

A waiter approached and placed paper menus on our plates, which I recognized as written in French on the left, from three years of it in high school, and what had to be Vietnamese on the right. The sniper gathered them together before I could try to figure out the French and handed them back to the waiter. "Not necessary, we'll have the American special number two."

The waiter nodded then pointed to the floor by the Sniper's feet. "And zee usual for le chien?"

The sniper reached down to stroke Utah's head. "Yes, her usual."

I looked at Utah, wondering how she knew when it was necessary to kill for her food and when it was only required to wait. And for that matter, how did the sniper switch from constant surveillance and readiness to kill, to social familiarity with shopkeepers and waiters. I watched him stare at the window as if he were able to see outside. "How often do you come here?"

The sniper looked back into the glow on the table. "Not for two years and before that another two years."

"But everyone seems to know you."

He glanced around the room as if looking for someone he feared might appear. "They know me from when I was stationed here, a time when my American face brought hope."

Susan's shadow on the table stretched long as she leaned forward. "They still seem happy to see you."

"Happy?" He looked back at Susan with his left eyebrow tensed into a straight line. "I was a good customer and they're a loyal people. But a new American face is like dirt."

Susan's palms opened upward like a blossoming flower. "Why? Don't they still want our help?"

The sniper's forehead tightened into a thick crease down its center. "Not after six years of more torture and devastation than they bargained for. Now we're mere dollar signs to make up for a small part of what's been destroyed."

My heel bounced up and down, shaking my knee. "If they don't want us here, and we don't want to be here, why don't we all pack up and go home?"

The sniper's hands slapped down on the table and he pushed back, locking his elbows into a straight line. "Too much unfinished business. You can't just leave."

My heel began to rap harder onto the floor, causing a tremble in my chair. "I could, in a second, there's nothing here worth staying for except for one thing." I turned to look at Susan.

Susan shoved her chair several inches away from me. "Stop that! And don't stay here for me. Go home while you can get out alive."

I steadied my feet and pressed my heels hard into the floor. "I would if it wasn't for you. But I don't want to leave you. Would you go with me?" Sweat rushed down the sides of my face as I wished she would look back into my eyes and say, yes. But instead, she turned to stare out of the frosted window, talking more in the direction of the sniper than to me. "Don't be ridiculous. I can't leave."

"Why?" I heard myself shout, then swallowed hard and forced my voice lower. "What's keeping you?"

She focused on her hands and squeezed them together. "I'll go home when the time is right."

I leaned on the table, pointing my good arm towards her. "When's that?"

She glanced at my hand, seeming to glare at it with anger like it was set to attack. "When there's something more worthwhile there than here."

The sniper raised an eyebrow then gave a sharp salute against his forehead. "Yes, ma'am. I roger that, nurse, sir!"

She looked up and smiled. He gazed back, his lips curving up on one side. She loosened her hands and stretched her fingers towards his direction. Sweat poured from my forehead. I swiped at it with my sleeve then scuffed my chair on the floor, shifting it closer to Susan. I wished I could see what they saw in each other's eyes. Was it whatever pulled them both to this country? But what was that and how could they not be anxious to leave? And worse than that, how could Susan be attracted to a jungle sniper who wants to keep killing VC for the rest of his life?

I moved my hand next to Susan's arm, tapped it ever so slightly with my fingers. "What's so great here that you can't leave?"

Susan slid her arm a few inches away from my touch and turned only enough to see me through one eye. "Us nurses, we're in desperate demand. There's not enough of us to do the job needed."

"That's not what I meant." I pressed my hand flat onto the table. "You could help sick people anywhere. Why here?"

Susan's hands squeezed together like they suddenly held something tiny and precious she was afraid to lose.

"Leave her alone." The sniper's sharp voice forced my gaze away from Susan to him. "She's where she's needed. What more do you want? Aren't you glad she was here to help you?"

"Of course, but," I glanced back at Susan before returning to him, "I don't understand the attraction to Vietnam. What is it?"

"For me," Susan's voice was so soft I almost didn't hear it. I leaned in closer to her whisper. "Being here is less scary than being home."

"Are you kidding?" My chair squealed on the wooden floor as I slid it an inch in her direction. "Home has to be better than this."

Susan pushed herself back from the table to where she could easily stand to leave. I leaned back from her, afraid I had made her uncomfortable.

She grasped her knees and squeezed, wrinkling the yellow dress that covered them. "There are some things better not to go back to."

"But what could be worse..."

The waiter appeared, blocking my view of Susan, and placed a plate in front of her. "Mademoiselle, c'est bon?"

I looked at the plate he placed in front of me, listening to Susan say, "Who back home would ever make fried rice with drippy eggs for breakfast?"

The sniper was already stirring the eggs into his rice with the fork that came on the plate. "My mother, she liked to experiment on us, said it would help us adapt in the real world."

I noticed there were no knives or spoons on the table and everyone else in the room ate with chopsticks as I picked up the fork that came on the plate and followed his lead with the eggs.

"Not my mom." Susan pulled herself in towards her plate and took a closer look. She picked up the fork and began flattening the mound of rice. "She wouldn't touch anything new, had to be the same biscuits with homemade jam every morning. And eggs were scrambled in bacon grease so they came out thick and browned or else they weren't fit to be chewed."

I knew it wasn't her mother's unadventurous cooking that kept her here, but as I was about to ask one more time, the sniper said, "Imagine you haven't eaten in three weeks and your only other choice is live worms. Which would you choose?"

Susan lifted a forkful of rice towards her lips and hesitated. "Is that what your mother said?"

The sniper laughed and looked at Susan's face instead of his plate. "No, mama said shut up and eat before I pour it down your throat."

Susan smiled, slipped the rice in her mouth and began to chew.

I took my first taste, chewing slowly at first, afraid they would be too spicy like the potatoes last night, but was pleased to find them tasty like my grandmother's mushrooms. My stomach responded with a quiet gurgle and I scooped into the rice and eggs for more.

Susan's fork clinked against her plate as she looked from her plate to the Sniper. "Will we meet Chim right after breakfast?"

My teeth suddenly bit my tongue and it was all I could do not to show the pain.

The sniper looked at his watch as he lifted the slice of bacon to his mouth. "In one hour."

Susan's eyes widened. "Good, I can't wait to see him."

I swallowed too fast, gulping again to try to get it down.

"Are you all right, Scout?" Susan's hand began to pat my back.

I gulped again, then took the glass of water by my plate and drank a long swig. I put the glass down seeing their concerned faces. "I'm all right, just swallowed wrong."

I put another fork full of rice and eggs in my mouth, chewed slowly and was glad that it went down without any trouble. I ate faster after that, managing to get pieces of bacon on my fork which tasted good with the eggs and helped keep me from thinking only of the kid.

We finished eating and the sniper stood, handed a few bills to the waiter on his way to the door, then kept going. Susan ran after him, her hand in her purse, trailing ten steps behind. I stood and followed, but didn't have the strength to go at their speed. I caught up to them at the Jeep where the sniper was closing the back door on Susan and, at seeing me, immediately went to open the front passenger side. I entered, feeling like we were back the way we had come yesterday, only I hoped Susan would be more friendly than angry this time. We drove past Marguerite's, then through an area of banks and office buildings that soon gave way to a series of outdoor markets.

Susan grabbed hold of the back of the sniper's seat and pulled herself forward. "Are we close?"

I twisted around towards her, though the pull on my wound made me almost sorry I did.

The sniper's right hand dropped from the steering wheel, landing on his knee. "Soon, another ten minutes.

Suddenly, five dogs ran in front of us and the sniper slammed on his brakes. I was knocked into the back of my seat and my wound began to throb, but I couldn't take my eyes off these dogs as they rushed for a stand on the other side of the street, straight for a cage of live chickens. I thought they were going to knock it on its side, but a man at the stand swung at them with a long stick. They scrambled back out of reach, then fanned out, making almost a semi-circle around the man. I had never seen wild dogs like that, especially in a city, as threatening as a pack of wolves. I turned around wanting to know how it would end and saw one dog leap for the chickens while the others went for the man, then the jeep turned to the right and they were out of sight.

I glanced at Susan, seeing her looking through her bags for the nurses, and decided not to mention it.

We drove another half mile when the road turned to dirt and the small one-room homes changed to run down shacks with gaps in the walls and odd pieces of tin for roofs.

Susan grabbed both our seats and pulled forward, her nose only an inch away from the sniper's ear. I feared she was going to rest her head on his shoulder when she poked him on the back with her hand. "What's she doing living here? You said you were giving her money!"

The sniper placed his right hand back on the steering wheel and squeezed. "I am, don't think this is my idea, it's hers. She moved from the place we had 'cause they were stoned every time they left the apartment. Then six months ago, a big rock hit Chim in the head and they wouldn't treat him at the hospital. She moved here where she says it's easier to live with your sins."

Susan slapped the back of his seat. "How could you call your boy a sin?"

The sniper shifted into neutral, letting the engine roar, then put it in third. "I don't. That's how they think!"

"But how could you…"

A pack of seven small children, each only partially dressed, ran up to the jeep, chanting like it was well rehearsed, "Chocolate, Coca-Cola, cigarettes?"

The sniper jerked the car forward, driving fast to get ahead of the kids. "That's why I'm," he glanced at me, "we're here."

A pulsing started in my chest, throbbing into my wound.

"Hooang wrote that it's too dangerous for both of them, even here. She gave me one month to make good on my promise to move them stateside. It's that or return to her parents' village, but they won't take the boy. He would have to go in an orphanage, which means by the time he's eight he'll be sent out to live on the street."

I suddenly felt like those trapped chickens in that cage. Why had I ever agreed to this trip and how long had the sniper calculated this plan? I was ready to bet he let Moustafa stab me on purpose. He could have shot Moustafa sooner, he was threatening enough. And what was that salute after I'd been stabbed? Was that his way of showing it was now my time to obey his orders and pay back my debt? Was I that big a sucker, or was this all coincidence?

The jeep came to an abrupt stop. The sniper jumped out and ran to the side of a hut where a gang of small boys had another kid surrounded. A young woman was behind the crowd, hitting the ones closest to her with her hands. One turned around and struck her with a rock. She shrieked and stumbled backwards, putting her hands to her forehead. The sniper yelled in Vietnamese as he shoved his way into the center of the crowd and yelled words I didn't understand. Whatever he said, there was no doubt it was frightening and the gang quickly ran away. The sniper then crouched low and put his arms around the boy and the woman, holding them close.

"That must be Chim and Hooang!" Susan pushed her door open and ran from the Jeep.

I opened my door, watching Susan reach them with her hands extended, then look at Hooang's forehead. I approached, taking a good look at the boy in the sniper's arms, with his smudged face, rounded almond eyes, flat cheeks and small nose that came to more of a point than the usual round tip. But it was his hair, coarser and much lighter that set him most apart from the others in his homeland. He stared up at my face the same way I was scrutinizing his while the sniper stroked his hair and Hooang had her hand on his shoulder.

"Don't fret, dear. We've come to take you away." It was Susan's melodious voice, while Hooang talked back to her in soft desperate sobs.

Susan placed a hand on her tiny knee. "You're in our care now, dear. This won't happen to you again."

Hooang turned to the sniper and yelled. He was quiet for a moment before yelling back. She stood and walked into the closest hut, and he followed but stood outside with the boy in his arms.

The boy pointed inside and whimpered a string of words, then pointed to where the gang had surrounded him, and next to his hair that was cut short but stuck out instead of lying flat. I wondered if he knew how different he looked from the other boys, or if he was trying to find out why they hated him so much.

Something rubbed against my good shoulder and I flinched, then realized it was Susan, wiping away her tears on my shirt.

"It's horrible," she whispered in my ear. "Most horrible thing I've seen since I've been here. An innocent little boy, branded for life, I can't believe how awful this is." She took hold of my arm, pulling it against her body, and I could feel her shaking.

The sniper stepped aside from the door and Hooang emerged carrying two soft woven bags and a rolled grass mat under her arm. She seemed too small and thin to manage those bags, and I expected her to put them down, but she didn't. Instead she raised them higher in the air and turned to the sniper who nodded and began for the Jeep. She followed, her eyes shifting between him and the car, as if afraid if she stopped looking at either one, they would disappear.

I stepped towards them, Susan moving along with me, like we were driven by the same thought.

The sniper held open the front passenger door for Hooang and positioned Chim on her lap. Susan and I went in the back on either side of Utah, who I realized had kept quiet through the whole ordeal. Chim was the one yelping as he pushed up from Hooang's lap and tried desperately to reach Utah.

Susan stretched out her arms towards him. "Here, let me have him. He wants the dog is all."

Hooang's hold only tightened. The sniper spoke to her softly in Vietnamese and a moment later, Chim was climbing onto Susan's lap.

Susan settled him in place and then brushed Chim's hand along Utah's back, saying, "Doggie, see, nice doggie."

Utah raised her nose up to the boy's face and sniffed. Chim giggled and slapped his hand on Utah's neck.

Susan grabbed his hand. "No, not like that, like this, nice, make nice, no hitting only make nice. See how nice?"

Chim pulled his hand out of her hold and rubbed along Utah's back himself, giggling with delight. Utah's nose went up closer to Chim's face and licked his cheek. Chim squealed and pushed himself back into Susan, but a second later, returned his face by Utah's nose. Utah licked him more this time, as if purposefully cleaning the dirt from the scratches on his face and I wondered if she could taste or smell that this boy was the son of her master.

Chim began to squirm and strike out at Utah's face. I pulled her closer to me and rested her head on my lap while Chim kicked and cried out something in Vietnamese. Hooang turned around and responded, but it was Susan's words in his ear that I understood, "We'll get you out, Chim, you and Hooang, you'll see."

I didn't know who she meant by we. Did she mean us, her and me? Maybe with her help I could, but that would be the only way. I began to scrutinize his American hair, a despised trait in his own culture but a welcome one in mine, and then the rest of his features which made him an enemy in mine. A sharp twinge emanated from my wound that seemed to be as much his pain as mine.

Hooang cried a long string of words, her hands moving wildly as she spoke. The sniper turned to her, one hand reaching towards her arm. "Slow down, I don't understand," then his mouth stopped in its opened position for a second before switching to Vietnamese.

She paused, then startled me with English, as she shouted, "Worse now!" then lapsed back into Vietnamese.

Utah lowered her chin onto Chim's lap and Chim's attention shifted from his mom to the furry head as he shrieked and dropped his hand on her neck, stroking quickly down her back.

Hooang turned around, the hard lines under her eyes softening as she watched his excitement. I thought she was going to reach out and touch the dog herself, but then her gaze turned to me and a line formed down her forehead, seeming forged by the dreaded question. My wound constricted into a taut throb as I shifted in my seat, wishing there was a way to get out of her sight. I looked back, trying to smile, but could feel the line across my mouth as tight as the feeling in my chest. I turned to Susan, only her eyes bulged with the same expectant hope.

Chim's hand hit my arm, "Look, woof-woof, nice."

~ Chapter 13 ~

September, 1970
Kennedy Airport, New York

My mother's face said it all, the fallen jaw, the curled lips, and the cheeks that sagged as if burdened with sudden tears. I shouldn't have been shocked, not having told them about Chim, though I had hoped for something closer to a smile. Our five-minute phone call had been just long enough to say I was medically discharged, would need periodic visits to the VA hospital to regain the full use of my arm and that I'd arrive at Kennedy airport in three days, on September nineteenth.

The fatigues I'd been wearing for the past sixty hours felt uncomfortably rooted into my skin. There had been no chance to change since departing Saigon for Oregon where I was checked through military customs, had to sign affidavits with three different officials that Chim's papers were authentic and agreeable to me, and afterwards had only fifteen minutes to board our flight to New York. I wiped my forehead with my damp sleeve as I walked though the roped off area for arriving travelers, duffel over my right shoulder and Chim holding onto my pants leg. It probably would have been better to let them know about Chim in advance, there had been time for a two-minute call from Oregon.

I looked down at Chim in the embroidered blue silk shirt and matching shorts that Hooang had bought for him to look his best for his trip to America, and began waving his arm as I pointed to my parents. "See, Chim, that's them, over there, Sol and Sylvia, the ones in the matching white shirts with blue collars."

Chim waved in the right direction, jumping up and down saying, "Solsylvia," as if it were one word. I thought of Susan showing him their pictures and teaching him their names. My mother would have to be at least a little pleased he knew her name.

We entered the waiting area and I heard my father's voice, "Lenny, is that you?"

"Yes, Pop!" I began moving faster, feeling Chim's feet bumping into mine as he began squealing, "Chocolate, cigarettes, Coca-Cola!"

I peered down at him. "Remember, first say hi, chocolate comes later." I pictured Susan instructing him in, *Hi, my name is Chim,* and *thank you,* and *you're welcome* and the piece of chocolate she gave him every time he said it right. I hoped his education would come through today.

Sylvia ran towards me, her hand pressed against her chest as if holding in her gasps for breath. "Ach, Lenny, look at you." Her speaking stopped as her eyes focused on my left arm that was held in a sling.

"It's fine, Mom. Don't worry. Just needs time."

Chim enclosed both arms around my leg and bumped his face on and off the side of my thigh.

"Of course it will be fine." Sylvia stretched out her arms, while keeping her eyes rigidly on my face. "Come here and give me one of your big boy hugs."

"I can only hug with one arm, Mom." I let the duffel down on the floor and wrapped my arm around her back.

"Wonderful, just wonderful." Sylvia pushed back from my hold, then grabbed Sol's arm to push him towards me. "Doesn't he look wonderful, Sol, the picture of heath, no?"

Sol extended his hand towards mine. "Wonderful, Sylvia, he looks simply wonderful." We shook quickly then his hand slapped my unfeeling shoulder and began to squeeze.

Sylvia swatted at his arm to push it down. "Sol, the boy is hurt."

I smiled, though it was as much from Chim's shake on my leg as from the fuss over the slap. "It's all right, Mom. I wish it did hurt. A little pain would be good."

She raised her pointer finger at first, then tucked it into her other hand as if that was her intention all along. "That arm is nothing to joke about. More pain you don't need."

Chim's hands squeezed harder into my leg and I felt uncomfortable that we'd ignored him so long. I leaned over and patted his back, whispering, "That's Sol and Sylvia," then looked up at my parents myself. "Mom, Dad, this is Chim, a friend of mine from Vietnam."

Sylvia's eyes widened as she bent forward towards him, then glanced back at me. "Friend?"

I wondered if I made a mistake saying it that way as I tried to explain. "Son of a friend, his name is Chim." I raised his arm as if to wave, then realized that was silly and kept it still. "Chim, say hi."

Sylvia leaned in closer and opened her purse revealing the corner of a Hershey's bar. "You want some chocolate?"

Chim yanked on my pants leg and began bouncing up and down. "My name Chim."

Sylvia smiled and opened the wrapper and broke off a small square. "That's very good. You know English. Here try this wonderful food from America. Bet you never had anything this tasty before."

Chim took it and shoved it in his mouth, gripping that hand back on my leg.

Sylvia put the chocolate back in her purse and snapped it shut. "And who's meeting you here? Is your mommy coming to the airport?"

Chim swallowed the chocolate and peered up at her, mumbling, "You're welcome."

Sylvia looked up at me, her eyebrows hunched towards the center of her forehead. It was clear she wanted an explanation and I couldn't delay any longer. "He's coming home with us," I began, then continued fast at seeing her mouth open. "It's just for a month, till the sniper makes another arrangement. He saved my life. I owe him this." I hoped that would satisfy her and also seem convincing, though I myself was uneasy with the sniper's plan. The only reason I agreed to take Chim was Susan's promise to visit us in New York on her R&R next week, if it was us.

"Mede? Mede?" It was Chim's voice, and he was pointing up towards the people walking by, jerking his arm from one to next.

Sylvia crossed her arms in front of her. "He sure looks like he's expecting someone here."

"Mede," I said, fearing the explanation would get used against me, us, but knowing I had no choice, "is the word for mother. That's who he's looking for, Hooang, except she's back in Vietnam."

Sylvia's hand pressed against her upper chest. "You mean a mother that's still living and breathing sends her son away with a total stranger? What kind of mother is that?"

"She couldn't get out!" I shouted, though I hadn't meant to. Chim hid his face in my leg and I toned down to a whisper. "It's too dangerous for him

207

there. She had to send him away. But getting her out is harder 'cause she's not his wife."

Sylvia pressed her hand deeper into her chest and shook her head. "Whose wife?"

"The sniper." I placed my hand on Chim's head and began to stroke his American hair. "Chim's father."

"You hear that, Sol?" Sylvia nudged him on the arm. "This boy's father pawns off his kid on our son and leaves his girlfriend stranded in the middle of a war. What kind of a man does that?"

"The kind of man that saved your son's life," I said it loud enough, but she ignored it and bent down in front of Chim.

"You poor skinny little thing, sent far away by your mommy and daddy. But they'll come. You'll see. They're not just going to leave a cute little boy like you."

Chim's face was rubbing on my leg, but I could see he was keeping one eye on her, then he glanced at her pocketbook and his lips spread in a sweet smile.

Sylvia's face smiled in return and she reached out her hand to him. "Of course I'm right. What a shame, no one taking proper care of you. Come, let's go get you some good American home cooking. You must be starved."

He looked up at me and I nodded. "It's okay Chim, that's my mede."

He smiled back, let her take his hand and began to walk. The straps from her purse fell down her wrist to in between their hands. Chim looked up at her with a big smile. "Thank you."

Sylvia looked towards Sol. "Isn't he darling?"

I glanced down at Chim and saw him looking at the purse. I rushed up to his side and held out my hand. "Come on, Chim. Come back to me."

Sylvia pulled his hand closer to her. "Leave him alone. He's a smart boy, figured out what a real mother is."

Sol elbowed my good arm. "The best mother in Brooklyn. Best cook, too, no one makes better pot roast and a blackout cake that puts the bakeries to shame. Baked one this morning, just for you, Lenny. Chocolate cake, chocolate filling, chocolate icing…"

"Chocolate, cigarettes, Coca-Cola!" Chim began jumping up and down, then grabbed the purse off her hand and began to run.

"No, Chim, stop!" He kept running, and I went right after him, but he slipped through the crowds easier than I could. I watched him getting farther ahead of me and pushed harder against people in my way, when I saw him headed for the doors. I screamed in that direction, "There's a kid running. Don't let him outside!"

No one responded and I began to shove harder, hearing bits of nasty remarks as I tried to get to him fast. Next thing I knew I fell flat on the floor and realized I'd been tripped. I immediately pushed myself up and was about to dash after him again when a young woman in a gauzy print dress blocked my path, screaming, "You didn't do enough harm in Vietnam. You have to beat on American civilians, too?"

I strained to see Chim through the crowd, spotting the bright blue shirt only ten feet from the door. I pointed to him and screamed, "Stop that kid!"

A man in a red shirt grabbed him and I could see Chim's new white shoes kicking in the air as the man lifted him off the ground. My chest pounded as I went after him, watching Chim try to hit and kick his way out of the man's hold. I was anxious to get to him fast before he hurt the guy and got away.

"It's okay, Chim," I called as I ran, "it's me, Scout. Everything's okay. No one wants to hurt you."

He was almost in my reach when a voice behind me yelled, "Didn't kill enough babies over there, you have to grab more here?"

I turned to see that same woman in the gauzy dress standing only three feet from me. My face flushed as I turned back to Chim and tried to get him to come willingly into my one good arm. But Chim hit me with the purse, sending its contents onto the floor, then began crying out in Vietnamese.

That woman's voice shouted at me again from behind, "No wonder he's screaming. You raped his mother and now brought him home as your trophy!"

"What?" I screamed, turning towards her but not wanting to lose sight of Chim. My parents were right next to her, and suddenly I was ashamed they had to hear those charges, even though they were false. I would have liked to see them tell that lady to shut up, but instead they seemed to be gaping at me which upset me even more. Did they agree with her? Did they know about the village kids and the laundry kid? People walked by, peering at me with sideways glances. I wanted to shout at them all, almost wished I had my M-16 in my hands when Chim's shouts turned to cries of, "Mede, mede!"

I called out to the crowd while I stretched my arm towards Chim, "I'm taking care of him for a friend. He deserves a good life and because of me he's going to get it!"

Chim slipped into my arm, his sobbing body trembling against my chest.

The guy in the red shirt patted Chim's back and looked me in the eye.

"Don't worry, buddy. The crazies have big mouths, but they're scared of their own shadows."

"Thanks." I pointed with my chin towards Chim. "I appreciate it." I also meant for the comment. At least one person wasn't against me.

My mother began gathering her personal items from the floor, looking up for a quick moment to say, "Don't listen to that lady. She had no right to say those things to you."

I watched her attention return to the floor, left with the uneasy feeling that she meant it wasn't right she said them, not that they weren't true.

My father bent down helping her pick up the rest. They stood and I extended the purse, which Sol held open while Sylvia placed the items inside. Chim had been watching with one eye, then pushed his face into my shoulder as soon as the purse was snapped shut.

My father pointed to the revolving door that was only ten feet away. "Let's get out of here before another crazy hippie complains about what responsible people have to do. I'm surprised she didn't panhandle for money while she was at it."

He pushed me towards the door and I went through, turning around to him as soon as he emerged behind me. "It's not like that, what she said."

He pointed to the light at the crosswalk and answered while steering me in that direction. "Of course not, those people are nothing but leeches on decent people who hold real jobs and pay their bills while all they do is go to college and cause trouble."

I wondered if he was thinking of Anna when he said that, or only of that lady. But he said no more about it and didn't ask any questions as to what I really did. It surprised me that he didn't want to know, or was it that he was too afraid to hear the truth?

He rushed a couple of steps ahead, taking unusually long strides to the end of the fifth aisle where our olive green Dodge Dart with the black vinyl roof awaited amidst a sea of neatly arranged cars. But upon seeing that one, it felt like I was looking upon the Huey that evacuated us from the village.

I began to take a deep breath when Chim pulled from my arm and I heard my mother's voice say, "Lenny, you sit in the front. This naughty little boy can sit in the back with me and learn some manners."

Chim tightened his grasp on my shirt and I began to protest, but she opened her purse and took out the chocolate bar, holding it in front of Chim's face. "And I'll bet no one's fed this poor hungry boy for hours."

Chim let go of my shirt and followed the waving chocolate bar right into the back of the car. I couldn't blame him for that. I settled into my seat hearing my mother in the back. "It's bad to steal someone's purse. Didn't your mommy in Vietnam teach you that?"

I turned around to see her ripping the chocolate bar wrapper and breaking off a piece for Chim.

Chim grabbed the piece, put it in his mouth, and mumbled, "Thank you."

Sylvia patted his arm. "Very good. You're not completely bad."

I winked at Chim though he didn't notice, focused only on the chocolate. "He'll learn our ways," I began, "but over there the war has forced kids to steal food or else go hungry."

Sylvia gave a soft tap to Chim's knee. "Now he's in the good old U. S. of A. where kids don't have to steal for food."

"Yes," I nodded, "but it will take him time to adjust."

I gazed out of the window finding myself scrutinizing each car for signs of weapons. I had never done that before I went, that was for sure, but now it was impossible to stop. Chim's hands suddenly gripped my neck and I realized he was pulling himself over the top of my seat.

"No!" It was Sylvia and I could feel him pulled backward.

Chim cried in my ear, "Mede, mede!" hanging on tighter to my neck.

I took his hands and began to pull him forward, knowing he really wanted me to get his mother for him, but at least I was a closer connection to her than Sylvia. "Let him go, Mom. He's used to me. He'll get used to you later."

His body no longer had resistance as I pulled him over the seat and settled him into my lap. He squirmed his face into my chest and I wished Joe was right next to me where my father sat, and Susan was placing her hand on my shoulder from the back seat. Tears pressed behind my eyes, almost pushing their way through. I held tighter to Chim, pressing his quivering body more firmly against my stomach.

"He's not hurting your arm, is he?" It was my mom from the back seat.

I brushed his sweaty curls back from his face with my good hand. "No, he's fine. We're both fine." Chim began whimpering and I whispered into his ear, "You'll get used to it here soon enough, we both will."

It seemed uncomfortably quiet in the car and I realized my father hadn't said a word since he began driving. Had he always been that quiet in the car? I couldn't remember. I watched the familiar stretch of highway that was taking us home to our apartment house on West 12th Street off Stillwell Avenue, feeling it bumpier than I recalled and the cars around us much closer than they had been in the past. The saltwater marshes to the left were strangely devoid of rice paddies and the dark green water of the bay beyond the marshes seemed empty without warships, same as it was odd that there were no military road blocks set up on the parkway. A loud roar came from above and Chim's head pushed hard into my chest.

"Get down!" I shouted, leaning my body over his.

"You haven't been away that long." Sol pointed to a 707 low in the air above the highway. "Remember how you used to jump up and down in your seat every time a jet came in for a landing?"

"I remember." I sat up straighter. "But it all seems different now." I looked out of the side window surprised none of the cars had driven off the road for cover, or that no drivers were looking up through their windshields for attacking aircraft. All eyes were straight ahead and all cars were moving at least at fifty miles per hour with no concern for tripping a mine or encountering enemy fire. It felt as unreal as watching a movie. And where were the convoys of Jeeps and transporters?

Chim strained his neck to see out of the window, his grip on me tightening. I felt his heart pound faster than before, and realized mine was going at the same speed, like we were both reacting the same way to our new surroundings. Only I, at least, knew this world, even though it was feeling like a long ago dream. Chim, poor thing, had never seen anything like this before.

He began to shriek, pointing out of the front of the car to the towering Coney Island Wonder Wheel with the Parachute Jump right behind it. He squeezed my arms with the force of a vise grip and I realized he thought those rides were massive weapons.

The car slowed up and began to exit the parkway. Chim smashed his cheek into my chest while still keeping his eyes focused on those monstrous steel forms.

"They won't hurt you," I whispered towards his ear. "They're rides, made for fun, though I know it doesn't look it to you."

Chim shrieked like I had hit him instead of trying to soothe him, and his arm stiffened as it pointed to the structures still getting closer.

I held him tighter and leaned in closer to his ear. "No one is going to hurt you. You're safe. I promise."

The car turned right and began driving away from the rides. In a moment, they were completely out of sight. His body continued to tremble against my chest and he began crying, "Mede, mede, mede."

Sylvia leaned over my shoulder from the back seat. "What's the matter with him?"

I swallowed hard, not wanting to mention the frightening structures, even though he wouldn't understand the English, and only said, "He misses his mother."

Sylvia's hand stretched over the seat and her fingertips grazed the top of Chim's head. "Poor little thing, let's take him for a hot dog at Nathan's to cheer him up."

"No!" The word burst out of me before I realized it would be frightening. Chim began quivering as if he expected to get hit. I squeezed him closer and stroked his back as I whispered towards my mother, "We can't go to Nathan's. It's right by the Wonder Wheel and Parachute Jump and that's what scares him. He thinks they're bombs."

Sylvia turned around as if trying to get a look at the rides, but fortunately, they were out of sight. "What are we going to do, Sol? You can see them from our apartment windows."

Sol rubbed his hand down his thick five-hour stubble, making a scratching sound on his face that sent Chim cringing deeper into my chest. "Don't worry, Sylvie. We'll keep the Venetian blinds closed. If we have to, we'll use the electricity in the middle of the day. It won't kill us."

His use of, *It won't kill us,* made me shudder, though it never used to in all the times he'd said it before. But this time it made me picture Joe's dead body, and Diego's, and then a battlefield in the middle of the thirteenth valley. I wanted to cry out for Wesley and Leon, but didn't want to alarm anyone. Instead I sat quietly and stroked Chim's back.

Sol parked the car in the middle of the next block and I whispered to Chim, "This is it. We're home." He didn't smile or make a move for the door when I realized this was my home, not his. He was nine thousand miles from home, though looking at the familiar tree-lined street, I felt nine thousand miles away myself.

We walked to our corner apartment building, Chim holding my hand, my mother on his other side, and my father two steps ahead, carrying the duffel. We came to the front of the brown brick building and Sol held opened the heavy glass door encased by iron scrolls. "You think the elevator will scare him?"

I was surprised that Sol thought of that and a little annoyed at myself that I hadn't. "It could, Dad, I better not take the chance. We'll take the steps and meet you in the apartment."

I began running with Chim towards the wide staircase, hearing him giggle at our fast pace. It felt good to use my legs after all that sitting, probably to him, too.

I found myself letting go of his hand, leaping up to the sixth step, then quickly turning around. "Come on, Chim, you can do it."

He came bounding up behind me, climbing with both hands and feet, prattling a string of Vietnamese words with a big smile on his face. It reminded me of how I used to play on these steps, imagining they were a space ship or a cave or a fort. I wondered if Chim could ever see them in the same way, or if he'd imagine them as something totally different, like the hut where he had lived with Hooang, or an underground tunnel of the Viet Cong, or even the Jeep where he last rode with the sniper.

He pranced up the stairs, his noises switching to barks, as if he were a dog. He followed me up to the top then turned around, pointing down, screeching as if excited though a little scared that he had come up this high. I wondered how many staircases he was ever able to play on before, and guessed it was probably none.

I rubbed my hand on top his hair. "Guess what, Chim, there's three more of these to go."

Chim jumped up and down and I feared he'd stumble down the flight he just climbed. I grabbed his arm and made him run around the landing with me to the next staircase before I stopped. The rows of steps seemed to beckon, like they were a helicopter lifting up to a better place. I bounded upon them, taking them three at a time, hearing Chim scampering behind me, barking like before. I wondered if he was playing Utah and if that would continue when we entered our home sweet home in only a couple of minutes.

There was the rumbling of the elevator door opening two flights above and my mother's voice could be heard muffled but clear, "You know how my migraines are, Sol. I can't have him here for more than a few days, even if he was well behaved."

Sol's voice was fainter, like he was whispering. "Don't worry, Syl. We'll have a nice dinner and talk about it later."

Chim's hands grabbed my legs and his face pushed in between my calves. I let him spread them apart and crawl through then watched him rush on all fours for the next staircase, his knees slipping out from under him on the smooth granite floor. He reached the next flight of stairs and began up, but slower than before, as I stayed behind him, taking only one step at a time. He stopped halfway and turned to me, pointing up as if asking if he should go farther.

I looked up at his eyes, realizing he had no sense of where we were headed. For all he knew we could settle right here in the middle of these steps and stay. "Up is right, Chim, keep going. This flight and one more. That's where home is." But as I said it, I knew it wouldn't be a real home for him, and I also feared it would no longer be a real home for me now, either.

214

~ Chapter 14 ~

Homecoming

The pine-scented cleaner my mother used weekly was thick in the air as Chim and I entered the apartment. I walked the two strides of the hallway trying to regain that feeling I used to have of entering a cocoon, safe from all outside dangers. Only this time the protective walls felt paper thin instead of thick pillars of strength.

Folk music played faintly in the background as my father said, "Come in, come in, that was a big climb for your little friend here. He looks tuckered out. Better help me get the cot ready."

I looked down to see Chim crawling slowly across the floor, making his way towards the kitchen, whether he realized that or not.

"Sure, Dad." I accompanied him to the closet next to Anna's room, the one without shelves that held the ironing board, vacuum cleaner and cot. The folk music became louder, clearly coming from behind her door. It was Bob Dylan, singing "The Times They Are A Changing," making me angry that things changed so much she wasn't even required to come out of her room when her brother came home wounded from the war. Hell, she never wrote and my parents never mentioned her in any of their letters, so I thought she had run away and they didn't want to tell me. But here she was, hiding in her room, pretending the rest of us didn't exist. I felt like smashing her door down with my military boots, just as a way of letting her know I was home. But I didn't want to start a scene in front of Chim who had crawled next to my feet.

My father and I brought the cot into my room, which at first seemed like a mirage that would disappear any moment, same as on those sleepless nights in Vietnam where I'd pictured myself back in this exact place, but as soon as I reached out for a touch, it vanished. But here I purposely knocked my leg against the bed and was happy to feel its solid steel frame jab into my skin.

215

And the rest of it remained in place also, my poster above the bed of a big day-glow orange peace sign with the words, *Make Love, Not War*. I thought of how Naomi had insisted if all mankind heeded those words, it was possible. If only I had been able to stick to it, all would be different. But I had strayed too far away from its message to ever look at it again without thinking of the personal wars that trap you, like the sniper and his war that started back in Texas, and mine that started when my best friend was killed and made me shoot a kid.

I helped my father set up the cot, purposely bumping into my dresser that held my radio and turntable on top, and also my desk with the globe on it that I had spent hours spinning instead of doing homework. But then I noticed, under the globe, a newspaper sticking out with the extra large letters that read *Stars & Stripes*. My heart began pounding as I feared what Major Smith had written and what my parents had read. I was ready to grab it and read it right then when Anna's bedroom door slammed opened and she appeared in my doorway, grasping its molded frame.

She looked up and down my uniform, shaking her head. "Went right along with the massacre, no protest, no nothing." Her chin pointed in the direction of the newspaper, feeling to me like a poisoned arrow projecting across the room.

I stared back into her chin, seeing it as more angular than I remembered, and her whole face tighter, as if her skin had shrunk while I was gone. She stared back at me, her mass of hair like a jungle thicket poised to conceal a trap. I wanted to tell her what happened with the reporter when she raised her fist in the air and began chanting, "Hey, hey, what do you say, how many kids did you kill today?"

Sol stamped his foot on the wooden floor. "We'll have none of that in this house!"

Chim grabbed my leg and I could feel his trembling, but I couldn't stop from yelling, "It's not like that. People aren't running around killing babies!"

She jabbed her shoulder into the air between us. "It's all over the papers so don't pretend it's not happening!"

"If it's happening," I yelled, feeling Chim pull my leg backwards and having to pull against him to keep my balance, "it's not from me!"

Her lips curled out, showing the flash of her tongue. "If all the soldiers refused to fight, all this senseless killing would stop!"

"Mede, mede, mede." It was Chim, whimpering into my leg.

I turned away from Anna and stroked Chim's hair, furious at not just what she said, but also at scaring Chim. "It's all right, boy," I whispered down to him, "No one's going to hurt you."

Anna stretched upward to see what was on the floor behind the cot. "Who's that? Some slave you won in the war?"

I wanted to leap across the room and slap her when Sylvia's voice shouted, "That's enough out of you. If you can't keep a civil tongue, don't open your mouth!"

Anna spun around and glared down at her mother who was three inches shorter than her five foot six. "What's the matter, Mother dear, can't face the truth?"

Sol slammed a fist on the desk, sending the globe close to the edge. "Stop this!" Chim's face burrowed deep into my calves as Sol continued shouting, "There will be peace here. All this fighting must stop!"

Anna crossed her arms in front of her chest. "Peace doesn't come by force."

Sol smacked his hand on the *Stars & Stripes*, sliding it forward. "In this house it will!"

"Fascist pig!" Anna kicked the doorframe then stormed towards her room and slammed her door with a force I felt in my feet.

It was suddenly quiet and still except for Chim who was shaking my legs so hard I lost my balance and fell backwards on my bed. He kept hold of my legs and pulled himself up on my thighs, hugging them as if afraid to let go.

Sylvia entered the room and stood looking down at Chim. "Oh, that poor boy, having to listen to all that. Lenny, take him in the kitchen and give him a piece of cake while your dad and I put fresh sheets on the cot."

"Yes, do that." Sol was looking at his feet, his voice still tight.

I had expected them to talk about Anna, or at least to offer an apology to me, but there was nothing, as if she didn't exist. It was all right with me if she didn't exist, but truth was, she was only a few steps away. I would have said something about that except right then, Chim's trembling concerned me more than Anna.

I placed my hands on the sides of his face and lifted it to look at me. "You want some cake?"

Chim's lips trembled, but he nodded as if he understood, or maybe he thought I was asking if he was okay. In either case it didn't matter. I lifted him up to my chest, then stood and carried him to the kitchen, hearing Sylvia tell Sol she wanted the green linens with the fish on them for the boy.

The cake was on a tall, porcelain serving dish in the center of the table. I pointed to it with Chim still in my arms. "See? Chocolate blackout, my favorite, chocolate cake, chocolate filling, and thick and sticky chocolate frosting."

He stretched out his arm and I brought him closer till his hand was only two feet away from the circular swirls. He jerked sideways within my hold and swiped at the cake before I could yank him back, leaving three long tracks in the frosting. He looked at me, smiling through fingers in his mouth and chocolate smudges on his lips.

"No." The word jumped out of me but felt wrong as soon as I said it. It was my fault he was that close and also how was he supposed to know what's right and wrong with a cake like that? He probably never saw one before.

Chim reached towards it again, his quaking body pressing on my arms while he uttered cries like birds do when a squirrel gets between them and their crumbs. I let him swipe it quickly once more then sat him in a chair and held up a finger in front of his face. "That's the last time you get to do that, you understand?"

Chim slumped back in the chair, his chin on his chest and his eyes only on the fingers lingering in his mouth.

I put my finger down, slipping my hand in my pocket. "You don't move while I get you a plate, okay?"

Chim didn't respond, though I couldn't expect him to and stepped away for a mere few moments. His whole body straightened up at my return and stared intently as I cut a triangular slice and tipped it sideways on the plate. I placed it in front of him and put a spoon next to it, which he ignored. Instead, his fingers scooped into his cake and carried a hunk that was too big to all fit in his mouth. It smudged into his cheeks and chin and I turned to look for a paper towel, when I saw Sol standing in the doorway. I wanted to explain about Chim's manners, only he spoke first.

"Your mama made a pot roast that has to be heated." He headed straight for the refrigerator and removed a heavy covered roasting pan.

"Not for me, Dad." I patted my stomach. "I'm not that hungry. I ate on the plane."

Sol was already at the stove turning on the flame under the pot. "That was hours ago, son. Believe me, you get that first whiff and you'll be hungry on the spot."

Chim sucked on his fingers, making a kissing sound. I began to laugh and Chim giggled, but when Sol didn't, I feared my mother would yell at Chim for that sort of offense, or worse, force him to leave. I watched as Sol used the old stained potholder to lift the lid.

"When's grandma coming back from Miami?"

Sol reached for a spoon and began to stir something in the pot. "Another month, at least, probably longer. You know your Aunt Becky has cancer. That's her last surviving sister and Grandma won't leave while she's in the hospital. She felt awful not being here when you returned but we told her that you're not hurt that bad and Aunt Becky needs her more. Still wouldn't hurt to call her and tell her yourself."

I looked at the phone on the wall, then turned to Chim who stuck his finger in the chocolate filling. I was going to stop him but he pushed his finger in his mouth and began sucking, looking so peaceful, I decided to leave him alone. "I'll call now. The book in the same place?"

"Same place." Sol was back at the refrigerator, leaning inside.

I removed the address book from the kitchen drawer it had been in since I was little and looked under G for Rebecca Goldman. The long ago Bronx address had been crossed out and the Florida one written sideways in the margin. I dialed the ten numbers, remembering Aunt Becky only vaguely from when I was six, though not able to picture her now. The phone rang five times when it was picked up. "Hello?"

The voice was weaker than I expected. "Grandma, is that you?"

"Lennichka!" There was almost a squeak to her voice that made it louder for a moment, but then it became uncomfortably frail again. "Tell me, my boitshick, how is your arm?"

I hesitated, not wanting to add bad news to what sounded like her fragile condition. "Not bad, Grandma. Doctors expect it will heal fine. How's Aunt Becky?"

There was a faint moan she may not even have heard herself. "Oh, not so good I'm afraid. Cancer's a slow, tragic death, but maybe not so terrible as what you saw in Vietnam, no?"

I felt my throat tighten and couldn't respond.

Grandma's voice continued. "But no more of this morbid talk. You're home and that's all that matters. Tell me, Lenny, what will you do now that you're back?"

I took a deep breath, trying to figure out what to say. "I'm not sure, Grandma. There's Chim I have to take care of. He's five years old, the son of a friend from Vietnam, a lieutenant, who's going to send the mother here soon."

Grandma gave a soft laugh. "You brought home a little boy, Lenny, so wonderful of you, and maybe it will do everyone some good."

I knew she meant Anna as I glanced back at Chim and saw his hands on the table, leaving chocolate streaks on the wood. "I don't think so, Grandma."

"Ach, don't worry about sour grapes," she said, but then she coughed and when she spoke again, I could hardly hear her say, "Lenny, I need some water. Send mein regards."

"I will, Grandma. Send my regards to Aunt Becky."

She gasped the words, "A dank," which I knew meant thank you, then a click and the phone went silent.

I hung up, the faintness of her voice ringing in my head as I looked towards my father. "Grandma doesn't sound good."

Sol had just lifted the cover to the pot roast. He glanced at me for a quick moment then looked back into the pot as he stirred with the big wooden spoon. "I keep telling her she should talk to Aunt Becky's doctor about herself. But no," he shook his head while scooping the juices from the bottom and dripping them over the top. "She insists it can wait till she comes back to her own doctor. So stubborn your grandma is, afraid if she asks about herself he won't have enough time for Aunt Becky."

Chim called out, "Scout," then held up his fingers covered with clumps of chocolate.

I turned towards him and smiled at first, then feared my mother would walk in. I moistened a paper towel and held it out towards him, saying, "What a mess you are!"

Chim giggled, then raised his hands up higher and called louder, "Scout!"

Sol covered the pot and turned around. "What's he saying?"

I grasped both of Chim's hands with the paper towel trying to rub off the gooey chocolate. "Scout. That's me. My name in Vietnam."

He dropped the spoon onto a saucer, but kept his hand on it. "Tell me, Lenny, did they give you a hard time because your name's Jewish?"

I looked up from Chim's hands, squeezing tighter to keep him from getting loose. "No, it's not that. Joe gave me that name, out of respect because I could read signs in the jungle."

Sol's eyebrows pulled closer together. "The jungle, is that where your heritage lies?"

"No." I felt Chim's hands grab the towel and begin to rip it apart.

Sol crossed his arms in front of his chest and stared at me with his head angled down towards the floor. "Your mother will think you're ashamed of her father's name. Is that what you want?"

A sudden burning in my wound made me loosen my hold on Chim. He started to slide off my lap, but I held onto him as my father continued to look at me with his head tilted down. "My name's still Lenny. They just gave me another name for there. Doesn't mean I'm ashamed of you or your father or that they came from Russia."

Chim slid all the way down to the floor then pressed his face into my legs like he was trying to hide. He had done that to Hooang at the airport, as if that would protect him from having to go off with me. But now he was using me, hoping for that same loving protection. I looked down, almost envious, not able to imagine that I had ever pressed my face into my mother's legs, and saw his still chocolate smudged hands grasping my pants. I feared what my mother would say and glanced towards the kitchen door. "What happened to mom?"

Sol's chin dropped down to his chest as his focus switched between me and the floor. "You know her headaches. She's lying down. Not getting any younger, your mother, and it's been too much strain for her."

I began walking towards the paper towels, dragging Chim along with my steps. "What has?"

He turned to the pot on the stove then at the paper towel I held under the faucet. "Worrying about you getting killed, or worse."

The word *worse* disturbed me. What did they think would happen to me that was worse than getting killed?

I almost asked but was afraid of what he'd say, when he continued, "She hardly sleeps, and then the fighting with Anna." He pressed a hand onto the top of the stove as if to steady himself.

I squeezed the wet towel into the sink. "But I'm home now. She can stop worrying about me, and maybe she'll feel better."

He took hold of the spoon and smeared the thin gravy around on the plate. "Maybe, but…"

"Sol, let's get dinner started." Sylvia's voice rang into the kitchen as the shuffle of her slippers was heard from the hallway. "Heaven only knows how long it's been since Lenny had a decent meal."

Sol quickly turned to face the stove and lifted the lid as she entered the room. "It's already heating, see?"

"You know, Sol," she paused to stare at Chim's hands, then the smudges on the table before taking a deep breath and going on, "there's more to dinner than a pot roast."

I immediately grabbed the sponge along with an extra paper towel and dragged Chim with me back towards the table. Sylvia opened the refrigerator and pulled out three Tupperware containers, one blue, one yellow, and one green, and put them onto the drain board next to the sink. I was rubbing the moist towel on Chim's face when she motioned towards him with her elbow. "That boy has to have more than chocolate." She leaned into the low cupboard, emerging with a double boiler that she brought to the sink, and proceeded to spoon the contents of the yellow container into its top.

The familiar orange circles that dropped slowly off the spoon made me salivate, as I said, "Mmmm, honeyed carrots."

Sylvia glanced at me. "You think I wouldn't have all your favorites on your homecoming? Look at this?" She opened the long green container and held it out towards me. "See, fresh celery and radishes." She took out a radish and stepped closer. "Remember how you used to beg for these?"

Those red-hot globes, as I used to think of them, had been a matter of honor with my friends in elementary school, to see who could eat them without crying. I had begged for my mom to buy them to practice, then stopped asking when I was twelve. I took the one handed to me and bit into it, expecting it's bitter flesh to make water run from my eyes as it had in the past. But this time it only tasted spicy, not nearly as harsh as it used to.

Chim watched me chew and tried to push his fingers in my mouth. I turned my head to the side to make it out of his reach. He then began to bounce on my lap and pointed anxiously towards the container.

Sylvia shook a finger towards him. "No, no, no, not for little boys, only big boys and men."

Chim started shrieking and reaching for the container.

I held his arm tighter, feeling him almost jump off my lap. "No, it's not good. You won't like it."

Chim wriggled himself down from my lap and began jumping up and down with his hands flying in the air. Sylvia raised the container, but then at his persistent shrieks, lowered it. "All right, don't be so head strong. We have enough of that around here. Take one. That will teach you."

Chim reached inside, grasping one half the size of his hand, and popped it in his mouth. He kept it still for a minute, and I was sure it was too big to get between his teeth when he began chewing. Little dribbles of clear liquid dripped from his lips as his nose scrunched up tighter and tighter. A moment later his eyes were practically closed and I expected him to spit it out on the floor. But he didn't and he chewed on like it was gum that he didn't dare swallow, then a tear dripped from his right eye.

"Sol, quick, a cup." Sylvia was at the refrigerator pulling out the orange juice.

Chunks of chewed radish began oozing from his mouth as Sylvia was just in time with her own quickly grabbed paper towel. He spit into it, then she handed him the cup of orange juice. "That'a boy. This will help."

I crouched next to him. "Drink it, Chim. It's good for you."

He held it up to my lips, the little slits of his eyes not hidden by his scrunched face staring right into mine.

I understood he didn't trust it, not after the radish. I sipped it then gave a big smile. "Mmmm, delicious, try some," and held it back to him.

He took a quick short gulp, then another and another. A bit of orange mixed into the thin line of dribble that continued from the corner of his mouth.

"That's right. It's good for you, makes you strong." I raised my good arm into the air and made a fist.

Chim imitated, using only his right arm.

I reached for his head and messed the top of his hair. "You can raise two arms, you little squirt. I could, too, till I went to your country."

Chim jumped at me, the cup spilling on the floor and began punching my legs with both fists.

"Stop that. You don't have to rub it in!" I pushed at him, not meaning to do it so hard.

Chim fell backwards and bumped his head on the table. His mouth opened all the way, showing bits of radish still on his tongue, before his pitiful cry, "Mede, mede!"

I almost said, *Serves you right,* but then realized he had lost much more than I did, his mother, his homeland, every shred of security he ever had. He could never go back, had nothing to go back to. His only hope was that Hooang would come here. He was desperate to believe that, and I realized I was, too, as I reached out to him and pulled him back on my lap. "I'm sorry, Chim, really. I didn't mean it."

Sylvia came next to me and put a hand on my bad shoulder. "Of course you didn't, dear. It was all an accident. Those things happen."

Chim's whimpering stopped and I could feel his heart beating through his back. His hard, frantic rhythm was twice as fast as mine, making it more apparent that whatever I felt, his was much worse.

Sylvia stepped back and looked from me to Sol. "Dinner won't be ready for an hour. If it's all right with everyone, I'm going to lie down for a half hour and rest."

Sol put the wooden spoon he had been holding back on the dish. "Yes, dear, you do that. I'll bring you some Excedrin to help you rest."

My mother put her hands on her cheeks, as if they were sore, then walked out of the kitchen and turned towards my room instead of the living room where she and my father slept on the high riser that converted to a couch. I wondered if she now considered my room hers, and if so, how she felt about it coming back to me.

My father followed her with a glass of water and I remained with Chim in my arm, thinking about the countless meals I had eaten in this room where I used to feel I belonged as if it were an inalienable right. But now it felt like I no longer had claim to it, as if it was only for the old Lenny and the new Lenny was an imposter. I wondered if the new Lenny, or Scout, would ever be accepted, and if they'd want to know what I lived through that turned me into the military pawn I never thought I could become. So far, they showed no sign of interest at all.

I stood and carried Chim towards my room, peering in at my mother lying on my bed, my father opening my desk and removing a bottle of Excedrin, and then handing it to her while he continued to hold the water. It was like they were in a space that was only theirs, not mine.

I cleared my throat that had suddenly become choked, feeling it still half clogged as I spoke. "I'm taking Chim out for a walk. I'll be back before dinner."

My father's shoulders sagged forward as he glanced at me and nodded. I turned away, starting for the door hearing Sylvia call after me, "Careful with him in the street, Lenny. You know how crazy the drivers are around here."

I nodded to myself, though more because it felt good to be heading out than in agreement with her. Chim began pushing against my chest and wriggling out of my arm. I let him down and watched him bolt ahead to the door as if he understood everything I'd said. He gripped the handle but his hand slipped around its smooth surface, unable to make it turn. I grabbed it and yanked it opened with more force than I planned. It used to seem to take a lot more strength than it did now.

Chim ran out of the door and right for the steps that led to the floor above. I started for the ones to go down. "Come on, Chim, over here."

Chim grinned at me and began running up with hands and feet, barking like a dog. I chased him, planning to grab him by the waist and take him back down so we could go outside. But as soon as I got close enough to touch his shirt, he charged up the stairs, his shoes scuffing in fast progression.

I continued to chase, my arms outstretched but not quite able to reach. "Come back, you little rascal!"

He only ran faster and then around to the next flight of stairs. I planned to grab his feet and pull him down if I had to, when I found him stopped at the bottom of a narrower staircase, darker and dingier than the others. I realized that yes, we had already reached the top, at least the top of the inside.

My own fears of these same steps when I was five came back, as did the threats of older kids to tie you to these rusted railings if you interfered with their games of dice. The barely lit enclosure reminded me of a VC tunnel. Chim's sudden tight grip on my leg made me suspect he had the same thought. I peered up to the top, seeing the door that I used to believe led right into a witch's oven. It wasn't till I was seven that my friends and I pushed it open and found it led to the roof instead. We had felt like great explorers that discovered a whole new land.

I began to walk up, feeling Chim's grip on my leg like an anchor trying to hold me down. I pulled against his weight, lifting him with me. His grip pinched into my calf as I took another step.

"Mede!" he cried.

I didn't want to upset him, but I felt drawn to that door and couldn't stop. "It's okay, Chim. I'm with you. You're going to like this."

We reached the top, Chim's heart pounding against my leg though he had become absolutely silent. I looked down at him and smiled as I pointed to the door. "See this, Chim?"

Chim shook his head and cried, "Mede!"

I touched the top of his head. "Don't worry. No one will hurt you. You'll see. It's magic. Here, take a look."

I turned my good shoulder to the dull metal door and shoved against it, feeling it resist at first, but then with another shove it opened, letting a shimmer of sunlight rush into the dim stairwell.

I pulled my leg up towards the opening and took the first step through the door. "Chim, see this!"

Chim had his eyes pressed into my knee as I looked across the flat roof covered by tar paper that sparkled in the sun's glow. Warmth radiated into my feet while at the same time there was an intense heat on my head, as if the sun was only inches away.

Chim reached down and touched the sticky black surface but pulled back fast, holding his finger as if it had been burned.

"Are you all right?" I asked, but then he touched it again, longer this time, rubbing his finger along its rough surface that contained embedded bits of gravel. I watched him, remembering the first time I walked on tar paper, hearing it scrunch under my feet and feeling myself stick to it like it had been coated with drops of glue. After I'd heard kids talk of a boy who had fallen off a roof a few blocks away I had concluded that the parents in my building had made our roof sticky to keep kids from falling off. It made perfect sense at the age of seven.

There was the crackling of small quick steps and I turned to see Chim running for the edge. There was a four-foot wall around the rim but that didn't stop my horror as I began to charge after him, screaming, "Stop!"

Chim kept running, but I nabbed the back of his shirt in three leaps. He shrieked and fell on his side. I held him down, feeling his body heaving for big breaths of air as I glanced to the edge that was only six feet from where he lay.

He then bounced up and slapped me in the chest, crying, "Mede, mede!"

I took him into my arm and stood, looking at the panorama of buildings, the tops of trees, and a sky that seemed to go on forever. Chim became quiet and still, moving only his head to stare in different directions. He pointed to a bird and I noticed a cut on his hand, though he wasn't crying from it. It was like when I was twelve and had been hurt in a fistfight. I came up here to cry without anyone seeing me, but then I caught sight of the world from the top, and everything looked so big and grand making me feel that way, too. It made me forget how hurt I was for that time and become a part of something much greater and too magnificent to be concerned with mere cuts and bruises.

I looked in the direction he pointed. "Bird, is that what you see? Bird in the sky?"

We watched it land on someone's television antenna on another roof. "See that, antenna, for better television reception. You like television?"

Chim's arm and gaze didn't move as I wondered if he'd even had a television in his shack in Vietnam. I figured he didn't when his arm shot straight up and his whole body began to bounce as he cried, "Mede, mede!"

I looked up to see an airplane and pulled him closer to me, saying gently in his ear, "No, Chim, Hooang is not on that plane. She'll be on another one, another time." His jumping diminished, but his heart thumped hard against my arm and didn't begin to slow down.

I lifted him higher and began walking towards the other side of the roof to what had always been my favorite view, the ocean. Its huge expanse made me believe that one day, if I looked hard enough, I would be able to see where it touched the shores of another continent. I thought that would soothe Chim as it used to do me, but as we neared, his shrieks made me realize I was forcing him to see the rides that caused him so much fear. I quickly turned and moved from their sight. His feet kicked against my thighs, but then stopped, like he had lost his strength.

I surprised myself by singing what had popped into my mind so many times in Vietnam, though never expected that same song to push through my mouth at home. "We gotta get out of this place. If it's the last thing we ever do. We gotta get out of this place. Boy, there's a better life for me and you."

Chim went limp against my chest, though I could feel my own heart thumping frantically into him.

I headed back through the doorway to the steps, though once on them, descended slowly, not anxious to go back to the apartment, or to let Chim out of my arms. I took them one at a time, moving to the rhythm of the song, which I had reduced to a half speed hum. We reached the bottom at the same time as Mr. Goldberg stepped out of his sixth floor door.

"Lenny, that you?" He stood, dressed in an undershirt, slacks and slippers, a paper bag of garbage in his hand. His body faced the incinerator while he looked over his shoulder at me. "Look at you, in uniform like a man instead of that pipsqueak you used to be. One thing I am is proud of you boys for kicking butt, like we did to the Japs in the big W. W. Two. We'll show those chinks who's boss."

"They're not chinks, sir," I began, surprised that the sir slipped out, "they're Vietnamese. North Vietnamese to be exact."

"Same thing." He waved his hand in the air. "We have to keep them in their place." Chim lifted his head from my shoulder and looked at Mr. Goldberg, who took a step back but kept his eyes solidly on Chim. "He yours, Lenny?"

I was tempted to say yes, to see if it would make him see Chim as something other than a chink, but instead told the truth. "No, I'm watching him for a friend."

His under chin swayed as he nodded. "Good, those GI marriages don't last. Glad you didn't get roped in by one of them. All they want is to shop at the PX."

I started for the next flight of steps feeling Chim shift within my arms for a parting look at Mr. Goldberg. The steps echoed with a hollow resonance as I descended slowly, not in a hurry to reach the apartment any time soon.

A female voice called out from above, "Papa, don't forget I'm staying at Amy's." It sounded like Mr. Goldberg's daughter Tina. I looked up to get a glimpse of the girl who had been two years ahead of me at school, seeing the frayed bottom of her jeans and hair that was squiggly bunches down her back.

Mr. Goldberg answered, "I remember, I remember. Don't worry about me. Hey, you know who's back? Lenny Belkin from downstairs."

Wooden sandals thumped against her heels as she started for the elevator. "He was gone?"

Mr. Goldberg stayed near his door and called after her, "Sure he was gone, in Vietnam, like an upstanding citizen. Not like those freeloading friends of yours."

The elevator button clacked several times against its metal plate. "Only ones go there are those too stupid to stay out."

My knee buckled and I sat down on a step to keep from falling forward. Chim pushed against my hold, but I tightened my grip, not wanting to let him go.

The elevator clanked to a stop on their floor. "Papa, remember,"

"I know, I know. You're staying at Amy's."

The elevator began to rumble its way to the lobby as Mr. Goldberg's door shut and there was the clicking of locks. I collapsed back, letting my elbow slide onto the step behind me, when Chim broke out of my hold and began running down the rest of the steps. I scrambled after him, hearing him run around the landing where I expected him to stop at the doorway of our apartment. But instead, he ran right past it and onto the next flight down.

"Stop!" I screamed after him.

He kept going but began babbling like he was singing a nursery rhyme. I caught the word, mede, and was scared he was going to run outside by himself to look for her.

My chest ached from harsh pounding and my left calf began to cramp. I stopped for a second to catch my breath, calling down to him, "Chim, come back here!"

He didn't respond, just kept on going, and I began running again, seeing him one and a half floors below.

"Chim, stop, damn it. I can't keep this up!"

I pushed myself to run faster, starting to gain some ground on him, but he was still a floor ahead and I was ready to collapse when I yelled, "You may be the first Vietnamese baby I have to kill!"

A young woman I'd never seen before with a baby carriage half out of an apartment door, stopped short and stared at me, her mouth opened though she didn't say a word. She quickly turned away and pulled the carriage back inside, slamming the door behind her. I felt awful and considered knocking on her door to explain it wasn't as she thought, but Chim was now in the lobby of the building and I was afraid he'd run outside and get hit by a car or almost as bad, lost.

The front iron door creaked and I flew down the last flight of steps, not feeling any touch my feet. I then charged outside, my gaze shooting in all directions at once. Chim was a few houses down, stopped in front of a boy holding a large beach ball. He was talking in Vietnamese and pointing to the ball when I appeared behind him. Only at that exact moment the other boy's mother appeared behind him, and without a glance at me or Chim, picked up her son and whisked him away.

Chim began to follow, shrieking like a wounded bird. I grabbed him and lifted him in my arm, feeling his soggy shirt spread its dampness straight to my skin.

I put my mouth close to his ear to whisper, "People around here are scared of us. You because you look and talk different, me because they fear I've been turned into a killer."

Chim looked up into my face, his eyes wide while his lips pinched together. I went on. "The scary part is I'm afraid they may be right about me. You, well, you don't deserve this. You haven't done anything wrong."

He blinked then rubbed his eyes in my shoulder. I kissed the top of his head, glad he was at least in my arms and safe. I swayed from side to side, wanting to soothe him while looking at the familiar street that now felt so strange, wondering what had happened to the joy I'd expected to find at this end of the journey.

I raised him higher and he looked up, his lids only half opened like he'd come out of a long sleep. "You know what, Chim? You and me are going to take a walk to the playground and go on the swings. Forget everyone else. It'll be just you and me and a whole lot of fun." Chim smiled and I was pleased. "But one thing. You're going to have to hold my hand the whole way, 'cause I've had enough running after you for one day, you understand?"

Chim put his fingers on my lips like he was trying to feel my words.

"I'll take that as a yes, my boy. Let's go have a good time."

We walked hand in hand with our arms swinging. I found myself humming the melody of "Soldier Boy." Chim had his own song going of the same note over and over. A breeze blew straight in my face and I turned to the side. Chim had done the same and we caught a glimpse of a sporty car driving by.

"Cool, isn't it?" Chim giggled and I did, too. For the first time since we landed in New York, I was happy to be here. "Everything is going to be all right, Chim. You'll see, we'll both be fine."

A boy on a bicycle rode past us and Chim jumped up and down as he pointed.

The memory of how badly I had wanted a bike when I was five flooded back as I looked down at him. "Someday you'll have one, you'll see."

His finger retreated into his mouth as he watched it get farther and farther ahead. We continued walking another block then crossed the street entering the concrete path to the park lined with iron railings that enclosed long grassy areas on each side. Women with baby carriages sat on benches against the rails as we closed in on the play area with the jungle gym that teemed with screeching children, and the see-saws that landed with thumps at each switch of who was on top. The swings were all taken, the kids on them gliding through the air reaching various heights. We stood behind the fence to keep from getting hit by a lunging foot.

Chim pulled on my arm in the direction from where we had come and I looked down, surprised to see his teeth digging into his lower lip. "Come on, Chim. We just got here." I crouched to his height and pointed to a kid who was swinging towards us, then soared upward above our heads. "See? See how much fun? You pump your legs back and forth and go as high as you can. See that? Swing, swing, swing."

A ten-year-old boy a few feet away from us with his canvas sneaker wedged into the linked fence, turned to look at us. "What's the matter with him? He a retard or something?"

I placed my arm around Chim. "No, he just never saw swings before."

His eyes squinted as he scrutinized Chim's face before glancing at me. "Why not? He just digged his way from China?"

If Chim hadn't stepped behind me, holding tight to my back, I might have laughed to hear that kids still thought they could dig all the way to China. But as it was, this boy strained his neck to keep staring at Chim and I felt Chim's tremble against my back. "He never saw them before 'cause he just came today from Vietnam."

The boy pulled his sneaker out of the fence and angled his neck for a better view behind me. "He one of those killer kids?"

My left foot buckled and I began to fall to the side. My hand slammed against the cement to catch my balance. "What?"

"You know," the boy pointed a finger at Chim's face which was peeking from around my shoulder, "those kids they show on the news who run around with grenades and guns. You seen them."

I jerked myself up straighter, trying to make a taller barrier for Chim. "No, he's not one of those. Most kids there aren't!"

The boy slapped his hand on his hip and pushed his chest forward. "My dad says they are. He says you can't ever trust any one of 'em 'cause as soon as you turn around, they'll get you in the back."

I felt my face flush and swiped at the sweat rushing from my forehead. "Your dad been there?"

"No." The kid shifted his weight from one foot to the other. "Says he wished he could 'cause those people deserve to get bombed, but he's stuck here putting bread on the table for his hungry family."

I wanted to scream at the kid when Chim's arms latched around my chest and squeezed. I gripped his fingers as I looked back at the kid and exhaled a deep breath. "Do me a favor. You tell your dad that I been there and that there's lots of fathers in Vietnam who want to put food on the table for their hungry family, too. And their kids are not going around killing."

The boy's glare turned to Chim, who had leaned to the side for another peek. "Really? Is his father one of those?"

My foot buckled again, but this time Chim's hold held me in place. "No, his father's not a killer. He wants him to go to school and go to playgrounds just like you."

The kid tilted his head as he continued to glare at Chim. "He looks like one of those killer kids to me. I don't want him in my school."

A girl screamed and the boy and I turned to look, seeing her being told by her mother that she had to get off the swing. I jumped up, grabbed Chim in my arms and ran for it, not responding to the boy's shout, "Don't put him in my sister's class, you hear?"

I kept my focus on the swing, reaching it the moment the girl was pulled away by her mother. I tried to place Chim on the seat by himself, but with only one arm to hold him in place, and his not knowing how to hang onto the side chains, he kept sliding off.

The kid we spoke to before watched from the other side of the fence and yelled, "I told you he was a retard! A retard and a killer!"

Two kids on swings next to us started to laugh and Chim threw himself face first into my legs. I scooped him up as gently as I could, then slowly and carefully sat down with him on the swing, holding him firmly against my stomach. But not being able to hold onto the chains, I couldn't swing. I let it rock as far as it could with my foot pressed into the concrete. It swayed on a crooked angle rather than going straight forward and back.

The boy on the other side of the fence began jumping up and down and pointing at us. "Look, they're both retards! Retard killers, retard killers!"

231

The kids next to us joined in on his chant. "Retard killers, retard killers!"
I began shouting, "Shut up, all of you. Shut up and leave us alone!"
But they continued, even louder.

It made me wish I had my M-16 and could blow every one of those rotten kids away when Chim started crying and kicking wildly against my legs. I had to get him out of there. I stood, hanging onto him in my arm, and began walking away. Jeering voices behind us continued and I quickened my pace. After we were fifty feet away, Chim peered back at them over my shoulder. They were still laughing and I couldn't even imagine what he was thinking. I was surprised that he wasn't screaming and kicking and crying. But he was absolutely still and silent. Maybe he had learned to stay that way to keep from being noticed by the bullies around his shack.

We reached the park entrance and I scanned the street carefully for signs of traps or sites of ambush. It seemed clear but I didn't trust it at first. I looked again before venturing out to the curb then checked both ways for cars, parked and moving, that might have machine guns sticking out of their windows. It seemed safe but at the least I expected another assault from a nasty kid or mother to hit us any moment. I tightened my hold on Chim, wishing that could protect him from any and all of it, though it was clear it couldn't. I began in the direction of home wondering how I would tell Hooang and the sniper that Chim's chances of growing up happy and safe in the United States did not seem possible.

Chim's small hands pressed into the back of my neck as he buried his face in my shoulder. "I'm sorry, Chim," I whispered in his ear. "I'm afraid it's as bad for you here as it is back home."

His body gave a sudden tremble against my chest then began to loosen its grip and slide downward.

I tightened my hold, afraid for him, afraid he would fall, or if he ever got away he would disappear into an alley where he would be attacked by bigger kids, or even dogs. I had a mere glimpse of what it must be like for him, having felt unwanted since we landed myself, but I had a place to live I could count on. He had nothing except me, and I feared I wasn't up to that task.

Sweat gushed down my cheeks and I felt frustrated at not having another hand to wipe them dry. Suddenly a small hand reached up and rubbed at the drips, pushing them to the side. I looked down seeing Chim's wide-open eyes focused right into mine. Tears swelled and spilled on my cheeks as I lifted him higher so his head was on level with my whispering voice. "We'll find a place. You'll see, somewhere safe where you'll be wanted and loved and grow up happy. I promise." Chim smiled like he understood, and I added, "And maybe even a place where I'm wanted, too."

A candy store on the next corner came into view and I had a sudden urge to buy Chim some Good & Plenty, which had been my favorite treat as a kid. I carried him inside, purchased a box and noticed the phone booth jammed in the back corner of the store. It looked like a tiny protected oasis and I took Chim back there placing him on the seat. He looked around at the narrow, wooden booth and I feared he would scream, thinking it a trap. But, fortunately, Chim's focus shifted to the candy box in my hand, which I shook and held up in front of him.

"Want some?"

Chim bounced in the seat and reached for the box. I opened the top and tilted it in his direction. He pushed his hand inside and I could hear the candy rattle before he pulled out a single pink one. He grinned and held it up to me, like he was proud of what he found, and I expected him to then shove it in his mouth. But instead, he extended it closer to me and began to press it between my lips. I let my lips part and the candy slipped in, along with the tip of his finger. I nipped at his nail, pretending it was something I was supposed to eat. He pulled it back with a laughing squeal and pointed to my mouth.

I made noisy sucking sounds, then a loud, "Mmmm."

Chim giggled and looked to the box. I pulled out a white one and put it to his lips, which he opened immediately. He tried nipping at my finger, but I pulled it away too fast. He giggled harder this time, showing the white candy against his tongue like a beam in a dark cave.

"Watch it there," I pointed to his mouth, "that candy's gonna fall out."

Chim clamped his lips shut and began humming a tune he had done before on the steps. I shook the box to the rhythm when a voice startled me from behind.

"Hey, buddy, you making a phone call?"

I turned to see a man with a cigar in one hand and a dime in the other. He looked old enough to be retired and I resented that he didn't just go home and make his call instead of wanting us to give up the one peaceful place we found all day. "Yeah, we need the phone. We have to call the kid's mother."

He stuffed the cigar in the side of his mouth and bit down. "How long's that gonna take?"

The dank stench of the already snuffed out cigar felt as threatening as rotted debris on the jungle floor. "Long, real long, about an hour, maybe two."

"Hey, sonny," the man took a step closer, "you being a smart aleck with me?"

I knew I was and I knew it wasn't right, but something inside of me couldn't stop. I took a step closer to him when the man behind the counter called out, "Yo Benny, use the phone at Louie's barber shop down the street. He has two of 'em, no waiting." I turned in time to see the man behind the counter put his finger to his head then tilt it towards me. I knew what that meant. He thought I was crazy. I stared back at him but he kept his eyes averted from my direction as I watched Benny leave the store.

I almost yelled, *I'm just back, but I'm not crazy* when the rattle of candy in my hand made me remember why I was here. I turned back to Chim, finding him huddled in the corner of the seat with his head hunched behind his knees. Had he been scared by Benny? Or was he scared of me? No, it couldn't be me. That would be too hard to bear.

I crouched in front of him and placed my hand on his knee. "It's okay, Chim. No one's gonna hurt you. No one, believe me. I'll never let that happen."

He raised his head but then lay his cheek on my hand.

"Oh, do you look tired. Why don't we rest here for a while? No one will bother us, that's for sure. May as well take advantage of people thinking I'm crazy. Come, take a nap on me."

I lifted him and positioned him on my lap, feeling the phone receiver rub against my head as I rocked Chim in place. "I wish we could call Hooang. It would be nice for you to hear her voice. Too bad her parents' village doesn't have a phone."

Chim slumped down in my lap, leaning into my unfeeling arm. I was a little nervous at that, but it seemed to hold him in place and I decided he could stay there when Naomi's phone number popped into my head. I glanced at the circular dial, thinking of the hundreds of times I used to call her. If only I could do that again.

I fumbled in my pocket for a dime, slipped it in the slot and dialed. Chim's head kept shifting to different parts of my chest as I listened to the ring when I realized he was looking for the Good & Plenty. I handed him the box, listening to the third ring, wondering if she was home or maybe she was with Charles. Chim reached up to my mouth and pressed a candy into my lips.

"Not now," I said, keeping my lips tight, as I listened to the fourth ring. But Chim slipped it in at the same moment Naomi's voice said, "Hello?"

The candy propelled straight back to the top of my throat, forcing me to cough at the same time I said, "Hi."

"Hello?" The hopeful voice of the first time turned to distrust.

I cleared my throat and spoke quickly. "Hi, it's me, Scout."

"Who?" The distrust was turning to anger.

The wrong name screamed in my ears as I tried again. "Me, you know, Lenny."

"Lenny?" she sounded irritated. "What kind of joke is this. The only Lenny I know is in Vietnam."

"I was," I said quickly, afraid she might hang up. "I'm back. Came back today."

"Today?" She let the word trail on for a long time. I waited for her to say more, like how nice it was that I came back, or I'm glad you're alive, or how are you, or something. But she remained silent.

My throat began to throb where the candy had hit. "Naomi, you still there?"

There was a pause, then, "Yes, but I have to go in a minute."

I swallowed against the soreness. "You want to go to a movie sometime?"

"No, I can't," then a five-second silence. "I'm engaged, to Charles."

I felt choked again but fought hard to speak through it. "We could all go." I knew that was a stupid idea, but wanted it to not seem a big deal that she turned me down.

"Lenny," she said my name like she was scolding a child, "stop this. We wouldn't have anything to discuss. Besides, Charles is president of S.D.S. at Brooklyn College and we're too busy arranging anti-war rallies to have time for movies."

I wanted to say, *Roger, I read you loud and clear. You're too wrapped up in yourself to even consider that I might be anti-war. Hell, most everyone in Vietnam is anti-war. What makes you think you're so special?* But instead I said, "Have a good rally. Give 'em hell."

"Thanks." She paused, then hung up.

At that moment, Chim pushed another candy on my lips and I shoved it away, yelling, "Not now!" It fell out of his hand and he began to cry.

"Don't cry, Chim, I'm sorry. It was a mistake, I didn't mean it. I don't know what happened to me." I hugged him closer and rocked from side to side within the cramped seat. The big mistake was calling Naomi at all. What did I want with her anyway when I was really in love with Susan?

Chim took another candy out of the box and stared at it, holding it in front of his stomach.

I pointed to it and then pointed to myself. "Can I have that one? I promise I won't ever knock a Good & Plenty away again."

He looked at me with a wide-open mouth, like he was showing me what to do. I opened my mouth and he slipped it in.

"Mmmm," I said, making sucking noises like I had done before. "This is yummy."

Chim smiled.

I opened my mouth wide again and pointed to the box.

Chim giggled, picked out three and dropped them into my mouth one by one, his eyes wincing after each one as it clinked against my teeth.

I rubbed his stomach instead of mine, saying, "Mmmm, this is the yummiest candy there ever was in the whole wide world."

Chim leaned his head back, opened his own mouth and tilted the box towards me. I took three candies and purposely clanked each one against his teeth, saying, "Kerplink, kerplank, kerplunk!"

Chim stuck his hand behind his back and rubbed my stomach. "Mmmm."

* * * * *

I was about to knock on the door when it was pulled open from the inside by my father. He placed a finger to his lips. "Mom's resting. Anna woke her when she slammed the door on her way out. That child, so much noise, and can never join us for a meal. Good thing you're back in time. Dinner will be ready in fifteen minutes."

"Good," I said, thinking both of no Anna and the food. I was hungry.

Sylvia appeared in her bathrobe and leaned her hand on the wall for a moment before standing up on her own. "You and the boy can watch TV in the living room while I finish in the kitchen. Or there's the new *Life* magazine, did you see it? Such a shame, that lady, Angela something, the one that's a Black Panther and wanted by the FBI? Can you imagine? Going from being a college professor to a criminal? Ach, the nonsense of some people. They don't know when they have it good."

She turned and I listened to her slippers scuff along the floor to the kitchen while I led Chim to the TV and turned it onto channel five for cartoons. Chim put his hands on the screen and leaned into it, trying to see inside. I didn't know if he'd ever seen one before and pointed to Deputy Dog. "Cartoons. Just picture, not real dog."

Chim pressed his face right up to the screen and I guessed it was better for him to see what he could on his own since he didn't understand me.

I stepped over to the coffee table, picked up the *Life* magazine, and read the headline, "Angela Davis, the Making of a Fugitive" with underneath it,

"Suspected Murderer on the Run." For a moment, I pictured my name in that headline, "Lenny Belkin, the Making of a Deserter," with underneath it, "Kid Murderer on the Run."

I shuddered and threw the magazine back down on the table, not wanting to see more, especially since the last *Life* magazine I had seen upset me more than I wanted to remember. It had been at Camp Pendleton, two days before, and its cover was a picture of a girl screaming over the body of a student shot by the National Guard at Kent State. The article had blamed the murder of four students on the invasion into Cambodia by U.S. troops from Vietnam. It hadn't made any sense to me at that time, everyone in the military knew we were fighting in Cambodia and had been in there a long time. That had never been blamed for killings back home before. As bad as what we were doing in Vietnam was, why blame the soldiers for killings in the United States? Except, now that I thought of it, in the few hours since I'd been home, I'd been accused of being a baby killer by a woman at the airport and by my own sister, and received fearful looks by the mother with the baby carriage, the mother with the young child who was holding a ball, and the guy in the candy store. And even my own parents were afraid to ask me what I did over there because they also assumed what I did was so terrible, it was unbearable to know. So if everyone seemed to think I was responsible for unspeakable brutality, why not blame the killings at Kent State on me, too?

I sat down on the floor behind Chim and pulled him into my lap. He slumped right in, molding his body into mine. We both stared straight ahead at the screen, watching dogs dressed up as bank robbers. Chim pointed at the dog that rushed in, wearing the star.

"That's Deputy Dog, fastest gun in the west. See him. He's a good guy catching all the bad guys."

Chim's finger went to his mouth making him seem focused on the action, but then his head slumped to the side and his breathing became faster and deeper. I lay all the way back on the carpeted floor, Chim rolling with me, staying on my chest. My eyes closed and it felt good to shut them and not be on alert for attacks. At least we were in a safe place for now.

I drifted into what felt like thunderstorm clouds, my skin prickling with electricity while my body bounced off of soft, thick cushions. There was a voice, my mother's voice, that almost brought me back, saying, "Dinner's ready, Sol. You think we should wake them?" But then the response, "Let them rest, Sylvia. They must be exhausted," released me to return to the suspended space.

The hazy air began filling with faces, angry faces, that all began shouting at once. Blasts of M-16 fire resounded in the background and then chopper clatter so loud I wanted to scream, when suddenly, everything went quiet, eerily quiet, and I saw those two kids, their throats slashed, drifting towards me dangling from strings. I became frantic and cried out, "Hold still, let me cut!" But they didn't stop and there was Joe, standing in front of me. He held up a scissors. "Here Scout, this will help you cut them loose." I took the scissors from him but then he started to fade. "No, Joe, don't go away, you have to tell me where to cut!" But just as I finished the words he was gone. I started after him, then found myself lying on my parents' living room floor, panting, my whole body covered in sweat, Chim still on top of me, sleeping.

I let my arms flop back to the floor and took deep breaths against Chim's weight. There were beeping sounds from the TV, a cartoon, Road Runner. I put my hands on Chim's back and began to stroke gently, feeling his shoulders loosen under my touch.

My father entered the room, stepped over my outstretched legs, and switched the channel. A news story began as he seated himself in the overstuffed chair. I peered up at a screen to an F-4 phantom and Walter Cronkite saying, "Fifty-four Viet Cong were counted dead today in Thua Thien Province by the ARVAN first infantry division after the U.S. 101st Airborne conducted bombing raids in that vicinity. Four American casualties were reported."

I raised my head, feeling my stomach tighten. "Thua Thien! That's just north of our base. I hope Wesley and Leon are all right."

Sol slapped the arm of his chair. "They always make it sound worse than it is. The U.S. has the best fighting force in the world and that enemy can't hold out much longer. Don't worry about your friends, they'll fend for themselves and make it, just like you did."

Chim's weight on me suddenly made it hard to breathe. I propped myself part way up and slid him into my lap as I looked towards my dad. "The worries are different in Vietnam, Dad. It's not like World War Two. There's no clear fascist enemy like you had. We've got the VC and the North Vietnamese Army and the South Vietnamese Army infiltrators, and village people and people on your own base and people in your own squad, all potential enemies."

Sol's foot began tapping the floor, rapping a soft, impatient rhythm. "Nonsense, those South Vietnamese are a freedom loving democracy who don't want that communist Ho Chi Minh taking over their country. That's a clear enemy to me, son. There ain't much clearer than that."

Chim's body jerked, like he'd been jabbed. I patted his back, but it stayed stiff as I said, "It's not simple as democracy versus communism, Dad. The news doesn't tell you everything. It's really about who's more scared of who and who's unfortunate enough to get caught in the middle. And there's also the whole black power thing. Some of our soldiers are backing the VC and not only that, they're turning on each other. Do you know how I got stabbed?" I peered up at my father, but his glance turned away the moment I did. I had to say it, whether he wanted to hear it or not. "Moustafa did it, a guy in my own squad!"

He turned back to me and leaned forward. "What are you talking about? Your sergeant sent a letter saying you got hit on a battlefield."

I wanted to laugh, but was afraid if I let my stomach shake too much, it would wake up Chim. "He lied! I'm setting the record straight. It was a U. S. Marine in my own squad, pissed off because he didn't get a desk job."

My father raised his finger like he did to scold me as a kid. "You listen to me, Lenny, before you act so highfalutin like you know more than everyone else. There are people here who think you boys all get turned into crazed savages. That you go over there and rape whenever you want, that you keep count of the innocent people you slaughter by wearing their ears around your necks and that you come back like explosive time bombs ready to kill at the drop of a hat. But I know that if my Lenny was over there that he was fighting the good fight just like I did in W. W. Two, and that you wouldn't do anything out of line. You got that?"

I snapped my hand to my forehead. "Yes, sir, I got that, sir, loud and clear. The good fight, your Lenny, yesiree."

"Yesiree is right." He stood then looked straight down at me. "And there won't be any more of this kind of talk, especially near your mother. She has enough headaches. She doesn't need any more."

I dropped my saluted hand back on the floor and nodded, wondering if she already heard it and what she thought. But I got my answer a moment later when she stepped out of the kitchen. "I thought I heard voices. It's about time you woke up. Everything's getting cold. You feel good after your nap?"

I nodded, knowing it was best not to upset her with the nightmare, especially for Chim's sake. She was having enough trouble accepting that he was around as it was. Having to accept anything new or difficult from me would be too much.

Sol walked towards her. "Anything left to do?"

"No, it's all done. And I was on the phone with my sister, told her for myself that he's fine and I have my old Lenny back. You know how she gets."

"Yes, I know." Sol walked inside the kitchen with Sylvia.

I stayed on the floor, feeling Chim begin to squirm, knowing he didn't want to get up, same as I didn't. For me, I was weighted down not just from Chim, but from the feeling of having to keep everything quiet. But if I didn't it was clear they'd fear the rest of what they'd heard about vets and believe I'd come back a crazed dog, ready to kill at the drop of a hat. And maybe that was the truth. I had killed a twelve-year-old boy and I stood right nearby and let two other kids be killed. How could I tell him what I did and still be normal in their eyes. The good fight, that's what it had to be for them, that or nothing.

I felt so alone and found myself shaking Chim's arm to wake him up. I could have left him on the floor to sleep, but strangely, I needed him at the table with me. I needed someone near me who understood.

Chim opened his eyes then shut them again. "Come on, Chim. That's it. Wake up. We're going to have dinner now."

Chim squirmed but then went limp. I patted his back. "Dinner, boy, you know, that home-cooking that the guys on the hump would kill for?"

Chim's eyes popped open and I was sorry I said that word even if he didn't understand. But maybe he did. I hoped not, at least not this time.

I stood, lifting Chim with me, and carried him to the table. Anna's seat was set and I placed him in it, taking my usual seat at a right angle to him.

A platter of pot roast was held in front of me. "Here, Lenny, you take the end pieces, before your father gets them."

Sol tapped his fork on his plate. "I would never deny my son his favorite food on his homecoming."

The steaming aroma made me dizzy with memories of the times in Vietnam I had wished for and tried to recall the taste of this exact meat. I took three thick slices and smothered them with the onions and mushrooms my mother stewed in the roast's juices. There was a momentary impulse to grab a handful and shove it in my mouth, but then my mother's hands appeared between the food and me, heaping a big portion of honeyed carrots on my plate.

I noticed she placed some carrots on Chim's plate also as I cut a piece of pot roast and shoved it into my mouth.

"Oy, such an appetite. It's a good thing I made a rice kugel." Sylvia lifted a baking pan from the stove, holding it up at an angle for me to see.

"Mmmm, looks delicious," I mumbled through my mouthful.

Sol chuckled. "The boy missed your food, dear."

I glanced up at her and smiled with the meat bulging in my cheeks. "Sure did, Mom. This is the best."

"Don't talk so much and eat." Sylvia began to cut a slice of meat on Chim's plate into small pieces. Chim picked up a piece and placed it in his mouth then scrunched his face together like he had with the radish.

Sylvia stopped cutting and stared at him. "What's this? You don't like my food?"

I swallowed my own mouthful and pointed my fork up in the air. "It's not that, Mom. He's probably not used to meat. Try the rice. He might like that better."

Sylvia put a square of kugel on his plate, then scooped some onto Chim's spoon and held it in front of his mouth. "Open up for the best rice you ever had, not like that pasty stuff at Tung Wong's."

Chim opened his mouth and closed his lips around it, but instead of taking it off the spoon, his face froze like he didn't know what to do next.

Sylvia shook the spoon in his mouth. "Like it?"

I reached for the spoon and took it from my mother's hand. "Maybe he's not used to sweet rice. Let me try." I shook the spoon and said, "Mmmm."

Chim smiled, loosening his mouth from the spoon and said, "Mmmm." But then he began to push the rice out of his mouth along with the spoon. I quickly removed it and wiped the rice from his mouth on my napkin.

"Guess not." I used his spoon to scoop up some carrots and put them in my own mouth. "Mmmm, Chim, these carrots are good. Want some?"

Chim's mouth opened slightly and I slipped some in. He chewed and smiled at the same time. Bits of chewed orange dribbled from the sides of his mouth as he said, "Mmmm."

Sol tapped his fork on the table. "The boy likes your carrots, Sylvia. You gotta give him that much."

I slipped some more carrots in his mouth, then handed him the spoon. "You do it yourself, Chim, eat."

He took the spoon, but held it flat on its handle.

Sylvia began to reach for it and I put my hand up to stop her. "No, let him hold it any way he wants. He'll get used to it in a few days."

I watched him try to get more carrots on the spoon and finally pushed some on with his finger. "He'll be fine, Mom. Maybe he's not that hungry. I bought him some Good & Plenty before."

Sylvia's hand dropped on the table. "No wonder he doesn't want the meat. You ruined his appetite!"

I shoved some more meat in my mouth and said through my chews, "Sorry, it won't happen again."

Sylvia gave a big sigh. "Poor thing has no idea what good food is."

"Don't worry, Syl," Sol, paused to swallow, "with your food around it won't take long." Then his focus switched to me and he let his fork slip onto his plate. "There's an opening in the hardware store, full time, Tuesdays to Saturdays, ten to six."

At first I thought he was just mentioning it, but then his gaze stayed on me like he was waiting for an answer. The meat in my mouth suddenly felt dry as I thought of that dingy place I worked in during high school, with the two old guys and the same jokes they told day after day and still thought they were funny.

I shook my fork in the air. "I don't really…"

"Hardware store?" Sylvia's voice cut in. "He should go to college. Lenny has to finish his education, remember?"

"Wait a minute." I dropped my fork and raised my hand. "Only thing in my plans right now is getting my arm back and seeing Susan when she visits on R&R."

Sylvia's hands gripped the table. "Susan? What's this about a Susan?"

"A nurse," I began, hoping this didn't cause another problem, though it wasn't anywhere near as shocking as bringing home Chim. "The one who took care of me in the hospital. She's coming next week to New York."

Sylvia's arms stiffened, pushing back from the table. "Is she your girlfriend?"

I almost let slip my true feelings, then decided against it. "No, just a friend."

Sylvia leaned forward, relaxing her elbows. "It's nice that she's getting home. Her parents must be very happy."

"No, it's not like that." I tried to quickly decide how much to tell. "She'll be Billy's transport nurse to Columbus, then she gets R&R before going back."

"Going back?" Sylvia's head shook. "Why would any decent girl go there in the first place? She one of those floozies?"

I wanted to scream, but knew how my mother was, and you just had to let her speak her mind no matter how hurtful. "No, Mom, she's wonderful, sweetest girl I ever met." Then before I could stop it, "I love her."

"Love?" Sylvia clasped her hands together, straining her wrists in right angles. "You love her because she took care of you when you were hurt. All wounded men love their nurses, but it's not real love. Real love is with a decent girl who doesn't run off from home to be with soldiers in Vietnam."

I pushed the dry meat in my mouth into my cheek, feeling it pull on my mouth as I spoke. "Susan is decent! She went to Vietnam because she wants to help people."

Sol placed both hands flat on the table. "Of course she's decent. She took care of our Lenny, didn't she? Tell me, son, what part of Brooklyn is she from?"

"She's not," I began, not understanding why he thought that. "She's from Virginia. She's coming to New York just to see Chim and me. And I promised I'd show her the sights. The military is paying for her to stay five days at a Manhattan hotel."

Sylvia pressed all the way back in her chair. "Manhattan hotel? That's a place for a decent girl?"

My jaw tightened, forcing my words to push through my teeth. "Should I invite her to stay here?"

"Don't get upset, son. Your mother is only looking out for your best interests. No question Susan will be more comfortable in a hotel instead of our small apartment. She's welcome to visit, of course, and we can see her for ourselves."

I swallowed the wad from my cheek, feeling it scratch my throat going down as I knew there was no way I would bring Susan here.

Sylvia shifted in her seat but remained quiet.

I gulped whatever liquid was in my mouth, trying to soothe my throat, wishing Joe was here to talk to and calm me down. Joe, how I missed him, but feared mentioning his name in case something bad was said about him. I had a pressing urge to bolt from the table, hop a bus to Columbus and speak to Joe's parents. And Susan, she would arrive there tomorrow. I wouldn't have to wait till next week.

I sat up straighter and looked at Chim who was sticking his finger into the honeyed carrots, then licked whatever sauce stuck to his skin.

I shoved a hunk of kugel in my mouth and mumbled through my chews, "I promised I'd see someone in Ohio as soon as I got back, tomorrow probably."

"Tomorrow?" Sylvia's chair inched back on the floor. "Why so soon?"

I didn't want to mention Susan again, or Joe, then it came to me. "Billy, from my squad, was hit bad, lost both legs. We were in hospital beds next to each other and shipped back at the same time. I promised I'd visit as soon as I could. It would mean a lot to him."

"Of course it would." Sol leaned closer to Sylvia. "Squad mates are a strong bond."

Sylvia glanced at Chim, then at me, her eyebrows pulling tighter together. "When are you going?"

The kugel's sweetness dissolved in my mouth as I watched her eyes continue to shift back and forth between us. "In the morning. Don't worry. He's coming with me." I half stood to leave, then sat back down, realizing it had been too abrupt and I couldn't go without Chim.

I was about to look towards him when Sylvia said, "Now what's he doing?"

I turned and saw Chim with his hands in a praying position and his head bowed forward. I was suddenly very proud of him, as if I had taught him to do that myself. "That's how they end the meal. It's a gesture of thanks."

Sylvia put her loose fist to her chest. "Oh, you're welcome, and you can be thankful that your mommy is going to raise you in the United States instead of that awful Vietnam."

I didn't want to tell her that the thanks was to Buddha and not to her as Chim slipped from his chair and began to pull on my hand.

I clasped my fingers around his and started moving away from the table. "We're going out for some fresh air before we pack."

Sol stood, pulling his wallet from his pants pocket. "Wait a second. Here, buy him an ice cream on the corner."

I looked down at the five-dollar bill he held in front of me, knowing it was much more than was needed. I wasn't sure if it was meant as a way of saying welcome home, have a good time, or, get the kid an ice cream and bring me the change.

Sol's eyes shifted from my hand holding Chim's to my hand in the sling, then pushed the money in my shirt pocket. "Go, you and the boy have a good time."

"Thanks." I smiled, pleased with his gesture though he probably figured it would keep Chim and me out of the house a little longer, then turned and began for the door.

Sol called after us. "Breyer's flavor of the month is caramel almond crunch."

"Sounds good," I called back, then glanced down at Chim, wondering if he'd think that as awful as it sounded to me. There were much better things five dollars could buy than caramel almond crunch.

Chim hopped down the stairs, singing to himself in Vietnamese while I trailed behind, one step at a time, Joe's words playing in my head: *Scout, you and me, we'll get each other back in the world and everything will be all right, like this never happened, except we'll have each other.* I wanted to yell out,

You're wrong, Joe, every second there's a reminder of where I've been and that no one will ever let me forget it, and Joe, I don't even have you!

Chim's jumps echoed in the lobby and I rushed to catch up with him, grabbing his hand just as he opened the heavy metal framed door that led outside. We stepped into the dense, heated air with the faint music from the rides in Coney Island playing in the distance. The melodies drew me towards them, though I knew that would upset Chim. But all I wanted was the momentary thrill of that first steep drop on the Cyclone, then the flying around the tracks so fast, the gushing wind would blow everything out of my head.

I began rushing in its direction, pulling on Chim's arm. "Come on, you can move faster than that."

Chim shrieked and I realized I was dragging him, his body having gone limp.

I yanked him upward trying to get him on his feet. But in that yank, Chim's hand freed and he took off, running down a long, narrow street. I chased him on the sidewalk, fearing he'd rush into a shadowed alley between the two-family homes. I was only five steps behind, when he slipped between two parked cars and rushed straight into the center of the road. A car engine roared towards him and I scrambled over a parked car, landing a few feet behind him, waving my arm, screaming, "Stop!"

Car breaks squealed though it never fully stopped and all I saw was Chim going down on the other side of the car. It sped away and I rushed across its vacated space, pulling him up by the arm. "Chim, are you all right?"

His eyes were shut and his face had thick dark streaks. I grabbed him around the waist and lifted, pressing him hard into my chest. "Are you hurt? Talk to me!"

His heart pounded into me, then his body writhed like the snake in the pit. He whimpered for Hooang, then grasped hold of my hair and cried, "Scout!"

I felt like crying out that name, too, for Scout to appear and help me, also.

"Scout, Scout!" Chim's cries grew louder as I sat him on a car to get a closer look at his face. His eyes opened. One had scratches around it, though there was no sign of blood. He grabbed onto my arms and began whimpering "Scout," over and over, directly into my chest. It seemed to vibrate right into my heart, feeling like it was pushing all traces of Lenny out of my skin. Who wanted Lenny here, anyway? No one, not now that he had been in Nam and been turned into murderer. Who, if the truth of what he did is denied long enough, might one day become civilized again. I kissed the top of Chim's head and whispered, "Don't worry, Scout's here and will make sure you're all right."

The rumble of a car engine approached and I squeezed my arm tighter around Chim. His chest heaved as the noise became louder. I was counting the seconds till it would be gone when it stopped behind me and a voice said, "That you, Lenny?"

I turned and was stunned by the flashy yellow Camaro with the 457 engine insignia, then peered at the partially bearded face looking through the opened window. It took a few moments before I realized it was the guy whose gym locker was next to mine in high school. "Brian?"

He slapped both hands on the steering wheel. "That's me, keep tryin' Brian, remember that?"

I turned sideways to face him more directly. "Sure, who could forget? Mr. Fazio had the whole class yell it every time we did push ups." My lips pulled to one side while I glanced across the hood of the car, wondering how Brian ended up with an expensive car like that.

"Still can't do those damned push ups," he said straightening his arms so he pressed farther back in his seat. He grinned, then tilted his head towards Chim. "Is the kid all right?"

I squeezed Chim closer in to me. "Appears to be just shaken, almost got hit by a car. We were lucky."

Brian leaned towards us, taking a closer look at him. "He yours?"

My hand patted Chim's back. "No, I'm watching him for a friend."

Brian's jaw shifted from side to side. "He don't look like any kid I ever saw."

I wiped at the smudges on his face. "He's not. He's from Vietnam. We just got off the plane today."

Brian's hands dropped to his knees. "You were in Nam?"

I nodded, not wanting to elaborate.

Brian grabbed his opened window frame. "Drafted?"

I nodded again, then turned to Chim, looking for new signs of blood on his face, but didn't see any.

Brian whistled, sounding like a bomb falling through the air. "Bad break, man. I'm making damned sure I keep my student deferment. I even fail one course a term to stretch it an extra year. No sense getting out sooner than I have to."

My heart began to pound in my chest as I scanned my eyes across Brian's car. "No sense in that, man."

Brian rapped his fingers against his metal door. "Hey, you want to go to Nathan's?"

The faint music from the rides suddenly recurred in my ears as I swallowed the impulse to say yes. Instead I uttered, "No, I can't, the kid freaks out at seeing the rides."

Brian shook his head. "Too bad. Could have gotten high and munched out, man."

Suddenly, Sol's voice calling out caramel almond crunch rang through my head like a siren. I looked down at Brian and whispered, "You got dope on you?"

Brian's lips widened, showing his broad expanse of teeth. "One joint, man. You want to light up? Step right in." He pulled the release lever on the door.

I picked up Chim, slid into the black leather seat and settled Chim on my lap.

Brian looked behind him, then back at me. "You want to do it on the boardwalk at Brighton?"

"No, the kid could still see the Wonder Wheel. Let's stay in the car out of sight from Coney Island."

Vibrations shot up my legs as Brian revved the engine. "Kings Highway good? Plenty places to score if we want more."

"Fine." I took the joint from his outstretched hand, squeezing its center as I lit it with a match. My fingertips almost touched making me concerned there wouldn't be enough to even begin obliterating my uneasy feelings since landing. I sucked in hard, hoping the harsh heat on my throat would burn the day's accusations and unsettling stares into ash.

My lungs were nearly ready to erupt as I released the smoke and passed the joint back to Brian.

He held it in front of his teeth as Chim coughed and I waved the lingering cloud out of the window. "How's this stuff compared to Nam?"

I swallowed, feeling only increased irritation. "Rougher, and not the same kick."

Brian began to cough then exhaled in a gush. He handed it back to me, speaking in a higher pitched voice. "Heard that stuff is so pure, one puff puts you out."

"Almost." Chim shifted in my lap as I inhaled a long stream, feeling the heat of the tip too close to my fingers.

Brian reached for the joint and pointed it at me. "You must have a connection to that stuff, man, get me some."

247

The burning in my throat flared in my head. "What do you think I was doing over there, dealing?"

Brian stopped at a red light and waved the joint, leaving a jagged trail of smoke in its wake. "You gotta have a number, man, someone with a line."

"Not me, you got me figured wrong!" I watched his cheeks suck in as he dragged. "You want some, go over there yourself and get it!"

Brian's eyes squinted as he exhaled hard. "Cool down, man. I was looking to score some good stuff. You bring any back?"

"Hell no!" I shifted Chim more on my left thigh. "With my luck I'd either get busted by the MPs or the sniper would shoot me for taking the chance when I'm watching Chim."

Brian held the remaining stub towards me. "Who?"

I touched my chin to Chim's head, watching the lit edge burn closer to Brian's skin. "The boy's father."

Brian's hand shifted, making the smoke drift towards my face. "Not enough left to get busted for."

The rank smell made me wish it was the Vietnam stuff as I took it and dragged hard enough to almost finish it. Brian's hand snapped in front of mine, grabbing for the last toke. He inhaled then flicked the last bit out of the window, speaking through his clamped teeth, "Don't know how you put up with that military crap, man. They get their hard-ons sticking guns in people's faces."

The brackish taste on my tongue turned to foul spit as I glared at Brian. "You know what that's like?"

"Hard-ons, sure..."

"No!" I screamed, "Sticking guns in other men's faces. You done that?"

"No, but..."

My voice shrieked, "Don't say nothing, man, 'cause you don't know! There ain't no hard-on in shooting to save your life!"

Brian's hands went up as he pressed back into his door. "Don't do it, man, I didn't mean nothing. Just shooting my mouth off is all."

My heart pounded, its force pushing up to my head. "Shoot your mouth off at someone else, Brian, 'cause I got news for you, it ain't no hard-on, nothing close to it. It's a damned war!" I yanked the handle down and kicked at the door with my foot, then turned back to Brian. "Thanks for the lousy joint!"

I stormed out of the car, Chim in my arms, slamming the door behind us. Two girls crossing the street glanced at me over their shoulders and ran.

Brian's tires squealed, then made a hasty right turn and sped away.

I began walking back in the direction of home. "Bastard! Where does he come off thinking Nam's about hard-ons from guns and dope connections? Doesn't he have any idea?" My lips pressed down into Chim's hair and I whispered more to myself than to him, "Doesn't anyone have an idea what I've been through?"

Chim grasped tighter to my back then looked up into my eyes.

His breathing intensified against my hands and I looked back into his eyes that now were sloped downwards instead of up. "I know, Chim, you lived through it, too. I think we're the only ones around here who know."

~ Chapter 15 ~

Columbus, Ohio

The sign for the first rest area in Ohio on Interstate 80 said one mile. Chim's head banged into my chest one more time, same as it had at each bump since he fell asleep three hours ago. I flexed my toes, hoping the cramping in my legs would soon be relieved. We slowed up for the exit, though my vision remained blurred from too much rubbing against the images of the village kids each time my eyes shut.

The bus pulled into an angled parking spot that faced a small gray stone building and a line of people began a slow procession past our seat. I jostled my legs, hoping Chim would waken and we could stretch for ten minutes, though I knew he was better off sleeping and feared that he'd be awake for the last three hours, same as he was for the first six. He shifted on my lap, his head sliding down to my forearm and it was clear he didn't want to get up. My leg throbbed under his move and I regretted my choice to save the money needed for two separate seats. I slid Chim onto our seat while slipping out from under him, positioning his head on the armrest. He rubbed his face into his hand then lay still.

My legs resisted straightening at first, keeping me huddled over Chim for a minute longer before stepping into the aisle. But then each muscle's stretch felt great as I went down the steps and walked the path into the little house. Once inside I squatted before the vending machine, bouncing in place while I chose a Hershey's for Chim and a box of Good & Plenty for me. People from my bus began heading back and I quickly went to the bathroom and headed back myself.

I lifted Chim to slip under him and his eyes opened to thin slits, gazing only straight ahead at the Hershey's sticking out of my shirt pocket. I wasn't sure if he was awake or asleep till he began to grab at the candy.

I placed my hand over his to remove his hold. "No, we'll have it later."

He didn't resist as I put his hand down to his leg but looked up at me and asked, "Mede?"

For the first time I realized he thought we were on our way to see his mother. I hadn't told him anything, thinking he wouldn't understand anyway. But now I knew I had to try, whether he understood or not. "Not Mede, not see Mede." I shook my head, hoping that would get it across. "We go to Joe's mother and father, Mr. and Mrs. McCormack." He reached again for the Hershey's and this time I let him have it as I went on. "They're very nice people, you'll like them." But then I suddenly feared I could be wrong. Maybe seeing a Vietnamese kid would only make them angry since it was Vietnamese who killed their son. Or me, maybe they'd be angry at me, too, for not saving Joe. Why didn't I think of that before? If only I had pulled together enough nerve to call them last night to explain who I was and that I was arriving today so they would be prepared for me, for us. But for some reason I didn't know how to explain, calling them terrified me. I could only meet them face to face. That scared me, too, but that's how it had to be.

* * * * *

The clock inside the Columbus bus terminal read 7:30 p.m. I looked down, noticing my military khakis that I purposely wore for meeting Joe's parents, were sweated and crumpled and Chim's face and shirt were smudged with chocolate. Chim jumped up into the aisle and pulled on my arm. Surprisingly, as cramped as I felt, I wasn't anxious to get up.

"Wait a minute, Chim, from here on we have to scout our terrain. We can't just go busting out into Columbus."

I looked through the windows seeing the luggage from the bus getting placed on the pavement. My olive drab duffel with Belkin stenciled on it was like a mound of moss next to all the boxy black, gray and brown suitcases. I stood, keeping my eye on it on the way off the bus, then went for it, swinging my arm around to get hold of Chim with the same hand, except it bumped into the bus driver and Chim was not there. I looked around frantically, seeing Chim running towards a pretzel stand twenty feet away.

"Chim," I called, as I began to run.

From behind me I heard the bus driver say, "Viet vets don't care who they knock down, that dirty war turns them all mean."

Chim stopped in front of the pretzel stand and was pointing up when I arrived.

The vendor looked at me. "How many?"

I reached down to take Chim's hand as I tried to catch my breath. Part of me wanted to yell at him, but the other part was just glad he was okay.

"Tell me, man. I ain't got all day. How many you want?"

I was only going to say one, but then it slipped out, "Two."

The vendor grabbed two off the stick inside the glass case. "With or without?"

I thought he meant with or without a napkin. "With."

"With, you got it." He began to spread mustard on top of the salted side.

"Wait," I yelled, grabbing the pretzel away from him. "Not with that!"

The vendor held up the broad knife with mustard smeared on it. "But you said."

I dropped the duffel in between my legs and held up my hand. "I know, just leave the other one plain." I gave the plain one to Chim who giggled with excitement as he put it to his mouth. I looked back at the vendor. "This mustard thing, that something new?"

The vendor wiped his hand on his white apron. "Not that new, man. Where you been?"

I didn't answer and then saw him take notice of my clothes and step back.

I almost said, *Don't worry, I'm not going to hurt you,* when someone else came for a pretzel and I left, pulling Chim's arm to follow me. Chim hardly moved and I looked down to see him stuffing a big hunk in his mouth, unable to bite it off.

"What's with you?" I asked, and pulled Chim a few steps farther, then dropped my duffel and sat on it. "Listen here, kid," I pulled his pretzel out of his mouth, "this is too much at once. Take little bites, like this." I bit into my own pretzel, at first annoyed by the mustard, but then not minding it. In fact as I sent my jaw up and down about ten times to show Chim, the taste seemed rather good. I swallowed with a loud gulp. "See, Chim, small bites, lots of chews. You got that?"

Chim took a bite, yanking on the pretzel to break it off. I helped him tug and it worked. He was left with a mouthful he could manage and I waited for him to swallow. A big clock above the outside exits read a quarter to eight. It was almost night and we had to get going if we were going to find the McCormacks. And I didn't even know how far they were from the bus terminal. In fact, I didn't even have their address. I looked around for a phone booth and saw one nearby.

Chim was easier to pull this time, as I managed him and the duffel together. He was happy to sit with his pretzel while I pushed the phone book pages with my right hand until I found McCormack. But there was a whole column of them. I looked for Joseph because Joe was Joseph McCormack Jr., and there were three listed with three different numbers and addresses. I looked at the phone receiver, but couldn't get myself to lift it. Instead, I reached into my duffel for a pen and wrote the three addresses on the back of my bad hand. At least it now had a use.

I turned back to Chim, watching him bite off another piece of pretzel. I bit into mine and chewed as I said, "Ready to go visit Joe?" But the moment I said it, unexpected tears burned from behind my eyes. I squeezed them shut and swallowed, the taste of the mustard suddenly bringing to mind that stew Joe made me that first night. I smiled at remembering how he cooked it over the flaming blue cube then handed it to me with a spoon. I opened my eyes slowly, seeing Chim watch me with his pretzel resting on his cheek. "What do you say, boy? Should we go?"

Chim's finger swiped at my mustard, brought it to his tongue then sucked it for a moment. His nose scrunched up but his lips spread in a wide smile.

I ruffled his hair. "I'm with you, Chim, that's exactly how I feel." I grasped Chim's hand and the duffel with my mine, and led him to the terminal exit. The door opened automatically, bringing us outside where a line of buses waited by the curb.

I looked around, trying to get my bearings, but the only signs were for bus routes that didn't help. A black cop stood guard near the curb and I walked to his side. "You know which one of these places has a back yard?"

His right eye looked me up and down while the other one stayed straight ahead. "What places you mean?"

"These." I tried to point to the back of my hand without letting go of Chim.

He glanced down at the scribble then gave a nod to Chim. "You just back?"

"Yesterday," I nodded. "I have to find my buddy's house, see his parents."

His head bobbed up and down slowly as he leaned closer to my bad hand. "Try the one on Rosewater Street. You take the Potter's Avenue bus right there about fifteen minutes to Highlawn, and then walk four blocks east. You roger that?"

I grinned at the familiar word. "That's a ten four."

He tapped me gently on the shoulder. "You take it slow, real slow, you'll get there."

I tilted my head towards the addresses on my hand, saying, "I'll find it," even though I knew he meant more than that. I was tempted to ask him more questions, like where he'd been stationed, what he saw, what he did, how long he'd been back, and mainly how long it took him to adjust, but then he turned his attention to two teenage boys starting a fight. I squeezed Chim's hand and headed for the Potter's Avenue bus.

* * * * *

The night air was dark and thick with bugs. The last of Chim's pretzel was in his mouth as we headed in the direction the bus driver had pointed as east. Rosewater Street was four blocks down, like the cop said, and I began to look for number 165. The one story square brick homes resembled the green plastic houses of the game Monopoly, with lawns front and back.

There was no light on at the door of 165, like at most of the other houses, and the two front windows seemed dark behind closed shades. It looked deserted and I feared they'd moved after the news of Joe's death.

We walked up to it and I knocked on the door, shaking Chim's arm as I muttered, "Please be home."

There was no response and I knocked again. The house remained silent, though a man came out of the house next door, carrying a bag of garbage to his pail by his fence.

I left Chim and the duffel by the door and ran across the lawn. "Sir, can you tell me, did this family have a son in Vietnam?"

He dropped the garbage in the pail but held onto the cover, pressing it up against the fence. "You know the boy?"

I grabbed onto the fence, above where the cover pressed. "If it's Joe McCormack, I served with him."

The metal cover scraped as he let it slide down a few feet. "Then you know he ain't come back alive."

I kicked the fence, then regretted it, hearing it rattle against the metal cover. "I know, I was with him when he got killed."

The man stepped back and placed the lid on the pail, keeping his hand on its handle. "Then what do you want?"

I removed my foot from the fence and stood up straight. "I want to speak to his parents."

The man shook his head and scratched the right side of his face. "They ain't been right since it happened. They's probably at the grave right now. You can't hardly get Mary to leave it and come home no more. My nephew's in the Nam and my wife prays for him all'a time. Ain't a day goes by she don't call her sister for news. And she can't neither look Mary in the face without the two of them bustin' out in tears. It's tored us apart something awful."

Chim came running over and grabbed onto my leg like he was scared. "I hope your nephew comes home soon. It's not fair what's happening because of this war."

He began fitting the garbage cover securely onto the pail. "Sure ain't fair one bit."

I leaned over the top of the fence. "Can you tell me how to find the cemetery?"

His whole body turned around and pointed to the left. "A mile that away, straight down Highlawn. That's where they is. Don't usually return till midnight. That's when we hear Mary wailin' up the path."

Chim pushed against my thigh. "Thank you, sir. I should be able to find them."

I decided to leave the duffel by the McCormack's front door, took hold of Chim's hand and began heading down the street.

"Hold up," the man called, running up behind us. "That boy's too little to walk all that way. I'll get me keys and give you a lift."

I stopped and turned to him, grateful that I wouldn't have to carry Chim most of the way. "Thanks, a ride would be great."

He opened the doors to the blue Malibu in front of his house and I entered, pulling Chim on my lap.

He extended his hand to me. "Family named me Augustus, but to friends I's Gus."

I grasped his hand and shook. "Nice to meet you, Gus. I'm Lenny, or Scout to friends, and this is Chim."

He pointed straight ahead. "Cemetery's up there a piece, but it ain't a place I likes to go. Back in West Virginia everyone just had family buried on they's own land. Cain't get used to all those strangers put to rest in one place. Don't seem right. You know whats I mean?"

Chim leaned back on my chest, staring straight at the Jesus statue on the dashboard. "I guess I never thought about it. In New York you live near a lot of strangers when you're alive, so it doesn't seem to matter when you're dead."

He slapped his knee. "Don't seem right. Kin is kin, alive or dead. Had to pry me away to come all this way for work when the mine shut down. My mama cried her heart to pieces when they sent me out so's I could send home money for food.

I watched the statue shake on the dashboard as we hit a bump. "You get to see them often?"

Gus pulled up to the curb by the open field dotted with gravestones. "Christmas, Easter and August when the hay comes in." He pointed into the center of the cemetery. "That's them way in there."

I noticed a light, like a flashlight or a lantern about a hundred yards in. "I see it. Thanks, sure appreciate your help."

He waved his hand in front of him. "Neighbors is near to kin, cain't bear to sees them so broke up."

I exited the car with Chim and waved to Gus, watching him make a u-turn and head back. Chim's arms wrapped around my leg and we stood there, listening to the fading hum of Gus' engine and what seemed like an increasing buzz in the air that began to take on the sound of distant moans coming from the direction of the light. I turned around to face it and stared into the small beam in the distance. That glow, that was Joe in there, on that spot.

I began towards it, feeling a shudder shoot up my back then go through my good arm and into each finger like trembling worms. I squeezed my hand to make it stop, but the moment I stepped onto the grass, it shot back up my arm to my neck and rushed all the way down to my legs. I tried to stay steady as I walked on the soft earth, but my feet began to buckle in. It was Chim's hold that kept me from falling. I rubbed his head in appreciation and he looked up with his arm outstretched to the light.

"That's the spot, Chim, you're right on target."

The earth grew softer, feeling like fresh graves. I suddenly feared I was surrounded by dead bodies and began to step higher, feeling into the air in front of me before stepping down. Chim thought it was a game and began to hop and jump instead of walk. I kept focused on the light, feeling sweatier as I approached. The sobs that were part of the air I was breathing rang louder in my ear. Ten more yards, I was almost there, then the cries suddenly stopped, leaving a silence that shook me worse than the pitiful moans.

I looked down at the two figures sitting on a blanket, facing flowers at the head of the grave. "Mr. and Mrs. McCormack?"

The man's arm flew up in the air. "What do you want from us now? If we want to stay here, we'll stay. We're not bothering anyone."

My legs trembled and Chim tightened his hold. "No, sir, it's not that." My eyes wandered to the flowers and I suddenly flashed back to the moment I first realized Joe was dead. Sweat gushed into my eyes, mixing with the swell of tears. I wiped at them and went on. "I'm Scout, Joe's friend. We were close buddies, closest one I ever had. We did recon together and he told me about you and his girlfriend and his house he was going to have. I promised him I would never let anything happen to him. But then it happened and there was nothing I could do to stop it. I was right near him when he died."

The woman's hands grasped her face and she fell sideways into the man. He glanced at me, nodding. "Thank you, son, appreciate you came."

I nodded back but then there was too much pressure from Chim behind my legs. They buckled under me and I fell to my knees. I found myself staring over his grave and grasped the earth. I knew he was down there, I could almost see him, looking like he last did when I held him in my arms. I began to utter into the dirt, "Sorry, Joe, but I made it back like you made me promise. And I came like I promised you. Only wish I could talk to you direct." Tears dropped from my chin to the soil as I felt Chim leaning across my back. "I wish I hadn't let you down. I should have done something to keep you alive. You taught me so much, and there was nothing I knew to stop that mortar. I let you down, Joe. I'm so sorry I didn't know how to save you."

A hand bigger than Chim's gripped my shoulder and I suddenly sat upright.

"It's all right, son." The voice had the same soothing depth of Joe's, and my chest started heaving hard for breaths. "We know it's not your fault. You would have kept him alive if you could. And we know he would have done the same for you. He wrote us about how much he wanted us to meet you."

I grasped the center of my pounding chest. "He didn't mean like this."

The hand on my back lifted. "No, none of us meant like this. But it was decent of you to come."

He kneeled next to me as I felt Chim's grasp on my arm on the other side. "I would shake your hand, but the boy," I tilted my head to the right, "and my other arm," I pointed my chin down to my sling.

"No matter, you're a welcome guest wherever and whenever." He moved back to his wife, putting his arm around her then pulled her closer into his side.

Her head tilted in a short nod towards me. "Nice of you to be here."

"Thank you," I began, when Chim started pulling on my arm and cried, "Mede, mede, mede."

Mrs. McCormack put her hand on her chest and focused completely on Chim. "And who are you?"

I felt him peering over my shoulder. "This is Chim. Please excuse him. He doesn't understand much English."

"My heavens," said Mrs. McCormack, leaning forward to get a closer look. "Is he...are his..."

"Yes, Vietnamese, half that is, and half American."

Her lips began to quiver. "Did he know..."

Her voice stopped and I filled it in. "Joe? No, they never met. Joe was already killed."

Her hands immediately raised to her face and I was sorry I'd said what I did.

She slowly slid her hands to the side of her face. "Was it, I mean, did he, suffer?"

That last word was so soft I hardly heard it, but there was no question what it was. It was the same thing I kept asking myself when I thought of not being able to see him in all that smoke. I looked into her face knowing I could never tell her the horrible details of that night. "No, it was instant. He never knew what hit him."

Her lips quivered as she said in a mere whisper, "He didn't say anything?" Her hands slid over her mouth but she continued staring at me.

A breeze blew some of her hair across her eyes, as she remained absolutely still, keeping her gaze intently on me. I knew she wanted to know his last words and I had none to offer. Her eyebrows lifted and her eyes opened wider. I tried to remember anything he'd told me about her. "He said you were the best tennis coach because you knew when to play hard and when to let him win. And that you made a lasagna so delicious, people always tried to guess the recipe but no one ever figured out every spice. And that you let him drive you to the store when he was only thirteen, and that you were the only mother he knew who was great enough to do that." I could see the shadows of her cheeks twitching to the sides and I wasn't sure if she were going to smile or cry.

Her hands brushed over her eyes and then dropped in front of her where she clasped onto her own arms. Her head leaned sideways onto Mr. McCormack and her face seemed to have taken on a soft, almost serene smile.

She let her gaze drift down to Chim and in a soft voice began, "It must have been horrible there, for everyone. He never wrote what it was really like. I wanted to know, even if it was terrible. I wanted to know what he saw, what he had to do, no matter how awful it got. He was my son. I wanted to know from him, not from reporters who are looking for a story that makes good news. I only wanted to know what the war was to Joe."

Her gaze was now on me and I shifted all my weight on my left side. "None of us wrote that stuff home. There was no point getting in trouble with the censors and when we had a few moments to write, we'd want to forget about the war and just think about people back home. That's what Joe was doing, acting like he was back home when he wrote, 'cause that's where he wanted to be."

She sat up straighter. "Is that why? I thought he was afraid to admit if things were bad for fear we'd think he wasn't a man enough."

Joe placed his hands on her shoulders. "Now stop that nonsense, Mary. I told you he just didn't want to worry us."

She placed her own hands on his, but talked towards me. "I was so worried. I couldn't watch the news or even glance at the newspapers because I was too scared about what it was really like for Joe. When that *Stars and Stripes* came with the article about how you two saved that other Marine and Joe sounded so brave and so proud of what he was doing, I felt better. But then that awful telegram came and all I could think was what was it all for?" She held her hands out to me, like waiting for me to fill them.

I wished I had something to offer then something he'd said came. "Joe once told me that we were there to learn what it takes to keep our loved ones safe and to keep bad things from happening to them when we come back."

Mrs. McCormack's shoulders sagged and her fingers pointed down to the earth. "He often promised to keep me safe. That was my Joe. But he also promised to come back. How am I supposed to go on now that he's gone?" She covered her face and collapsed into her husband's chest. I watched, feeling helpless, as sobs shook her whole body.

Chim grasped tighter to my arm and began crying, "Mede, mede!"

She looked up from her crying and began watching Chim, her mouth opening and her arms spreading apart. "Come here, you poor boy. Come let me hold you."

Chim squeezed into me even more, pressing his face into my shoulder.

Mrs. McCormack sat forward and crossed her legs, tapping on her thighs. "Come on. It's comfortable. I'll hold you."

Chim peeked towards her from the side of my leg, and then looked up at me. I nodded and he walked one step at a time, looking into her eyes same as she kept looking into his. She nodded as he came closer and once he was within reach, she wrapped her arms around him and huddled him into her lap. Joe leaned in next to her as she rocked Chim forward and back, a soft hum flowing from her barely parted lips.

Her tune drifted into the rhythm of the crickets' chirps as though they were part of the same song. I watched her rock, then my eyes shut and I heard the buzzes in the air and rustlings from the breeze mix together with her melody as part of a vast harmony.

I felt in a trance somewhere between Vietnam, Brooklyn and where I was now, Joe's grave. The places blended together same as the outer sounds. It was as if I was suspended within everything that happened to me since I was drafted, when Joe's voice broke in, "Mary, look, he's fast asleep."

I moved to in front of her, seeing Chim's head resting on her elbow and his chest rising and falling in a quick rhythm.

I held out my arm thinking she would want to return him now but she turned partially away. "No, he's fine right here. This child needs to be put to bed." She looked up at me. "Where are you staying."

I pushed my foot into the loose dirt of Joe's grave. "I don't, I mean I didn't…"

She turned to Joe. "They can stay with us. We have Joe's…"

Her head bent down and Mr. McCormack stood to face me. "If you don't mind his room."

My hand squeezed into my leg. "That would be fine, thanks. I appreciate it. We didn't…"

Mr. McCormack waved his hand to stop me. "Our pleasure." He glanced down at Mary with Chim. "Joe never mentioned you had a boy."

I looked down at Chim with Joe. "He's not mine. His father's a lieutenant who wanted to get him out. The Vietnamese are not nice to mixed kids. I'm watching him for a while."

Mary stroked the hair on his forehead away from his face. "Where's his mother?"

I feared it would sound like Hooang abandoned Chim and didn't want them to think that. "She'll come as soon as the lieutenant can arrange it. Right now she had to return to her family's village."

Mrs. McCormack stared down at Chim and I wondered if she was thinking it wasn't fair that this son got out when hers didn't. She gently brushed some dirt off his face. "It must be very hard on him to be separated from his mother."

His cries for Mede rang in my head. "It is. And everywhere we go he thinks she's going to be there. Even here."

"The poor little boy." Mary shifted her position, raising Chim slightly." Joe, take this sweet child from me without waking him."

I stepped in to help, but Joe already had him in his arms. "Okay, Mary, you can let go now."

She dropped her hands to the ground and began to push onto her knees. I held out my hand to her which she took, and I gently raised her to her feet.

Joe turned to me. "You have a car?"

I looked down at Chim's squirming body in his arms, surprised that Joe showed no signs of the burden. "No, we took the bus."

I held out my arm for him to pass Chim onto me, but he turned to the path we had entered on and began walking. "Good, you'll come with us."

Mary walked next to him and I followed, grateful that they had accepted us and were taking us in so graciously when I suddenly realized I'd be staying in Joe's room, sleeping in his bed. I turned back to the grave and whispered, "Sorry, Joe. I wish it were you sleeping in your bed, not me. I didn't want it like this, believe me. I'll try to make it up to you if I can figure out how.

* * * * *

The screaming pierced into my heart as I ran frantically, hearing it get louder and louder. There it was, a fresh grave, three horrified voices shrieking from the bottom, "Scout, get us out of here!" It was the kids and it was all up to me. If I could dig them out fast enough, I could save them. Otherwise, they were dead in two minutes.

All I had were my hands and I dug wildly, desperate to get to them before it was too late. But deep as I went, they were still further. I put my face low in the hole to see how much more I had to dig when two snakes lunged for my eyes. I was terrified that any moment their teeth would pierce into my vision and frantically tried to grab them, when all of a sudden I was in a dark room with a thin line of light on a wall. But I still had to get the snakes before they got me and slapped against my shirt, legs, face, hair, but didn't find them. Maybe they were back in the grave, had to find it. I bolted upright, confused by the strange room and the empty bed across from me with the crumpled blanket on top. I stared at it trying to get it in clearer focus, when it came to me, that's where Chim had been and I was in Joe's bed.

I turned around to the window, remembering gazing through it most of the night and the five a.m. pink streaks that I had become used to waiting for, my sign that I survived another night. The clock on the desk read six thirty. Had it been that long? Ninety minutes of sleep was rare, something to be appreciated, even if it did end in a nightmare.

The crackling of bacon in a pan came from outside the room, followed by a high pitched voice. "My name is Chim, you're welcome."

There was a short rustling of slippers on the floor. "Call me Mary. Can you say Mary?" Her voice was cheerful, not anguished like last night.

Light feet jumped up and down. "Thank you, chocolate."

"Chocolate?" Mary laughed. "Silly boy, not for breakfast. Do you like cereal?"

There was a shaking of a cereal box, and Chim's voice. "Thank you."

A deep creaking of a floor, then Joe McCormack, Sr. "The boy does have good manners."

"Yes, very polite." There was a pause, then, "You ever have Wheaties before? See the box?"

Chim squealed, "Scout!"

"Scout? Is that a picture of Scout? No."

Another squeal. "Lutent!"

"Lutent? Who's that?"

She couldn't have known he meant the lieutenant, his father. I heard Chim begin speaking in Vietnamese, using *mede* a few times, and I quickly slipped on my pants and joined them in the kitchen.

Joe raised an inch out of his seat. "Good morning, son. Sleep well?"

For a moment I feared he confused me with Joe, but then remembered how Major Smith had used son, as an underling to sir. "Yes, sir, best sleep in a long time."

Mary put a bowl by an empty chair at the table. "Here, have a seat. Chim's been trying to tell us something. Maybe you can interpret."

I watched Chim's fingers touch the face on the Wheaties box. "I only understand a few words. Mede is mother and anything that sounds like lieutenant is for his father. The rest I only guess."

Mary placed a container of milk on the table and a spoon next to my bowl. "Oh, the poor boy, so far away from his parents. When are they coming?"

I looked at the Wheaties box, as if it had an answer. "I don't know, but they may send more word with Susan. She's a nurse bringing an injured soldier to Columbus."

"Oh." Mary's voice choked, and she coughed to clear it. "Someone you know?"

I hesitated saying the name, wishing, as I knew she did, that it was Joe. "It's Billy. He was in my, I mean Joe's and my squad. They're supposed to arrive today."

Mary went back to the bacon pan and gave it a stir. "Today, how nice for you. What time are you going?"

Actually, I had no intention of ever seeing Billy again, but knew that would sound cruel under the circumstances and didn't want to mention that. "I don't know exactly where I'll see Susan, or when."

Mary drained the bacon onto paper towels. "Invite her here. I want to meet her and I'll see if Marie wants to join us."

Joe stood and went towards her. I thought to help with the bacon, but he stopped next to her and put a hand on her shoulder. "Now Mary, you know Marie said she finds it too painful to be around here. Said she's going to live with her aunt in Kentucky for a while."

Joe took the pan from her hand and Mary leaned on the counter. "That's right." She stared at the floor for a moment and then looked at me. "Did Susan know Joe?"

I wished I could say yes, but couldn't. "No, she never saw Joe. He never made it to the field hospital."

"But Billy did, and you." Her voice took on the anguish of last night.

I stared straight at the Wheaties box and shifted in my seat. "Yes, but we were all hit in different locations at different times."

She hastily turned to the sink, wet her hands under the faucet and pressed them against her face. Joe put his arm around her shoulder. "Would you like me to make the eggs, dear?"

I could see the back of her head nodding, then Joe said to me, "It's all very hard on us, son. We don't know what to do with ourselves."

Johnny Bench's smile on the Wheaties box seemed wrong. I pictured Joe there instead as I replied, "I understand."

Joe pulled a carton of eggs from the refrigerator and started cracking one at a time against a bowl. "Of course you do. That's why you're here. The key is to stick together and help each other through."

It sounded exactly as if it were said by Joe, my Joe. I looked up expecting him to be there then saw his father with the same sideways pull of the lips. I nodded to its familiarity. "Yes, stick together. I'd like that."

He cracked the next egg too hard and it oozed all over his hand. He grabbed a paper towel and wiped one finger at a time as he stated each name. "You, me, Mary, Chim, Susan and Billy."

I turned away at the mention of Billy.

"It's the same Billy, right?"

I wasn't sure what he meant and tapped the table.

"In the *Stars and Stripes*," Joe continued, "it says you and Joe saved Billy's life."

"Oh, yes, that's the Billy." His name felt like it needed to be spit out of my mouth, but that would be too crude.

Mary took the bowl from Joe and reached for the whisk. "I'll finish the eggs, dear. You do the toast, and keep it set to light so it doesn't burn."

I stood, pushing my chair behind me. "Can I help, get plates or something?"

Mary's left cheek pulled back as she lit the fire under the pan. "Yes, they're in the cupboard behind Joe, and the silverware's in that drawer below it. But no knife for Chim."

I recalled how Chim picked up the sniper's knife in our Saigon hotel room and stabbed at the bugs on the floor. He wasn't quick enough, but he had no fear of its use. "Don't worry, Mrs. McCormack, no knife for Chim."

She turned to me as I placed four plates on the table. "I hope you'll stay for a while, as long as you like."

I glanced at Chim.

"Chim, too, of course."

My eyes momentarily flooded, making everything go blurry. I blinked trying to clear them, wondering how she knew we needed this? I slid my hand on Chim's shoulder and turned back to her. "Thank you. That would be a big help."

* * * * *

It was my fifth call to the veteran's hospital. At least this time they answered and transferred me to admitting. Except ten minutes on hold was enough to make me want to give up. Finally, there it was. "Hello?"

"Susan!"

"Hi Scout, I had a feeling this was you. How's things in New York?"

"Fine, I guess. I mean I'm here in Columbus with Joe's parents. We arrived last night."

"We? Chim's with you?"

"Of course, I couldn't leave him with my parents. Besides, we're getting used to each other."

"At least that part's lucky, because I didn't know how to tell you this."

"Tell me what?"

"It's the sniper." She paused and I felt my chest begin pounding into my bad shoulder. "They sent him in to blow up tunnels in the valley. It happened right after you left. He was told he owed them for the strings he pulled to get Chim out."

"When's he coming back?"

"I don't know."

The stab in my shoulder suddenly throbbed, as I didn't mean to yell, "He has to know. He's got to get Hooang here. What's he going to do with Chim?"

I held my breath while a loudspeaker blasted in the background, then Susan's voice again. "You have Chim. You taking good care of him?"

I pictured her angry with me, except I was angry she didn't understand my side. "He's fine. As a matter of fact, half an hour ago he ate Mrs. McCormack's bacon and eggs, a bowl of Wheaties and a donut for dessert. But that doesn't…"

"My little Chim ate all that?"

My hand holding the phone got sweaty and I squeezed tighter so it wouldn't slip. "I ate all of mine. You excited for me, too?"

A loud sigh came through. "Come on, Scout. No one has to look out for you. But Chim's a kid, out of his element, far away from home, with no one."

"Hey, I'm doing my part. Doesn't that count?"

"Scout!" At first I thought she was going to say I was doing great, but then she added, "What's with you?"

"I'm feeling a bit out of my element, myself, and could use some sympathy from a beautiful woman like you."

There was a long pause and I feared she had hung up. "Scout, you have to stop that."

I was relieved she was still there. "All right, I'll be good. Can we meet somewhere?"

There was a heavy exhale. "I can't leave Billy, but if you two want to join us while we get the paperwork settled, it would do Billy a world of good."

My knees began to cave in, but I locked them in place. "I wanted to see you, alone. And Mrs. McCormack doesn't think Chim should be around the…" I stopped myself before using the word gimps that Susan hated, and slipped in the word, "wounded."

There were voices in the background and I feared she'd have to get off. I began talking faster. "Listen, Mrs. McCormack wants you to join us here for dinner. She wants to meet you and you could see for yourself that Chim's doing fine. They even offered me their car to come pick you up."

The other end was silent, then finally her voice. "I have no idea when I'll be done. They're not even close to admitting him." Another silence and I feared she'd decided not to see me no matter what.

"Susan," I began, when she interrupted.

"And what could I possibly say to her? She just lost a son and I have nothing to say about him."

"That doesn't matter," I said fast. "What matters is that you were in Vietnam and could tell her what you saw. She wants to hear that stuff. Really, it would mean a lot to her."

My hand pulsed hard against the receiver. It pounded in my ear until she began to speak.

"I can't leave Billy, and that's that. You don't know the half of it. He's talking suicide every five minutes and I'm at my wit's end. I called his mom and asked her to come visit thinking that would make him feel better. But then he became even more agitated, accused me of butting into his life and that if I wanted to help I could get him a gun to blow his brains out. Scout, I don't know what to do. You have no idea how bad it is."

I wanted to blow Billy's brains out myself but that was not what she wanted to hear. I had to swallow hard before saying, "You want me to talk to him?"

"Scout!" It was the first time she sounded happy I was on the phone. "That would be wonderful!"

I shook my head, not able to believe what I was doing. "Okay, Susan. I'll be there as soon as I can."

"Scout, you don't know how much this would mean to him."

I had hoped she would say how much this would mean to her, but she didn't. "No problem, I'm on my way."

"Great. Just ask for admitting."

The phone clicked and I whispered into the phone, "I love you, Susan. This is only for you."

* * * * *

The inside of the hospital was as gray as the pouring rain outside. The man behind the desk had a cluster of ribbons pinned above the pocket of his khaki shirt. I approached then noticed his wheelchair and my gaze flashed to the flat drape of his pants. I looked up, embarrassed at what I had done, and asked, "Admitting?"

"You looking for that Billy Langdon feller?"

I nodded, for a split second hoping he'd tell me he was dead.

The man tapped on the paper in front of him without looking down. "Seems to be right popular already. Follow that lady over yonder by the elevator. He just been moved up to 242."

I glanced towards the elevator, seeing the woman in tight black pants and bouffant blonde hair crushing a cigarette butt with her heel. The elevator door opened and I rushed towards it, entering as she pressed the button for two. Thick black eye liner reflected back in the stainless steel of the door. They were almost full circles, the same shape as Billy's eyes. The elevator opened and she stepped out, turning to the left. I followed, but slowly, hoping that if Billy was busy with his mother, Susan would come out in the hallway and we could be alone. The smell of pine scented cleaner made me think of my own mother when Billy's voice exploded out of his room.

"I'm over here, Mom! She's just a lousy nurse who doesn't know crap about how I am. Why don't you ask me?"

I ran for the room wanting to grab Susan and pull her out of there when a woman's loud cries stopped me at the door. I peeked in to see the woman facing Susan as she ranted with her hands waving wildly in front of her. "He blames me for everything, especially losing his father who was an unfaithful pig, but he doesn't care about that. And he's convinced my second husband Bob is out to kill him all because Bob once said if he was bad he was going to slash his throat. But, of course, Bob didn't mean it, just an expression, you know, to keep Billy in line."

Billy slammed his hand on the bed rail, making it ring like an alarm. "He meant it, Mom. Don't kid yourself. That bastard would have cut my throat if he wasn't convinced I'd slit his first."

Billy's mom threw her hands up to her cheeks and rushed for the door, then stopped and turned to Susan. "I thought he wanted to see me. You tricked me!"

I took two steps away from the door, expecting her to rush out, except she didn't and there was Susan's voice. "Please, won't you try to talk to him? He's lost both his legs!"

There was a snapping sound on the door handle. "I wish I could. Don't think I'm not sorry this happened, but there's nothing I can do. He hates me and talks to me like an animal. You see what he's like! You blame me?"

"No, I mean stay and we'll talk to him together."

Billy's scream cut in on Susan. "She's scum, a whore, you expect a whore to care about her own son?"

This time she rushed from the room, running right past me without a glance while Billy's voice screamed, "You see what she's like? Now stay out of my life. You don't know what you're doing!"

I burst into the room seeing Susan grasping her own arms and her mouth quivering. "Shut it, Billy. You've already said too much!"

Billy grinned like he was amused at my entrance. "Look who's here, the third cavalry come to the rescue." He switched his glare to Susan. "You call him to blow my brains out or to cry on his shoulder?"

Susan's whole body trembled and I was furious. "You watch how you talk to her, you stinkin' gimp!"

Billy laughed. "Finally, someone willing to say what I am!"

My hand itched for a gun, wanting to grant Billy his wish. "A heartless runt is what you are, dumping your crap on Susan!"

Billy raised a hand in my direction. "Look at you, a regular hero going to save Susan from the likes of me. Well, I got news for you, Scout," Billy's hand dropped down to the bed, "you're in on this, too. You saved my ass in that village and in Vietnam that makes you responsible for me for the rest of my life. So go get a gun and make my life short. It'll save both of us a lot of misery."

My good hand throbbed as I slammed it on my hip. "No way I'm going to jail for you, man. You can live your gimp life and you can damned well be responsible for yourself. I don't want any part of you."

Billy's arms crossed in front of his chest. "You mean you don't want any part of the parts that are left."

My hand clenched around my waist. "You have more than Joe's got, so shut up with that self pity!"

"Joe's lucky!" Billy's fist slammed into the bed. "He went fast and easy. I'm the one stuck with pain and no legs."

"Joe would be grateful to be alive!" I yelled, seeing that first vision of Joe's dead body flash in my head. "It should have been him who's alive, not you!"

Billy's lips spread and his head nodded. "That's right. Why don't you take care of that right now. You want to slit my throat?"

My fist began to throb. "Like you did those kids?"

His lips pushed forward before bursting apart. "Those gook kids were better off dead than stuck in that stinkin' village with Viet Cong breathing down their necks."

My chest pounded, resounding in my ears. "That wasn't your decision to make. It wasn't your life!"

He pointed a finger right at my gut. "Bet you wish I'd slit my own throat 'stead of theirs."

I started to nod, then stopped myself and stuffed my hand in my pocket. "Would have saved Susan a lot of trouble."

His finger lurched forward at me. "You want me dead. Go ahead, admit it!"

I stepped back, almost losing my balance then leaned forward on my solid foot, my head tilting in a short nod.

Billy slapped his stump. "See, I knew it. You wanted to leave me there to die. Well, here's your big chance, man. Do it now!"

Susan rushed to my side. "Stop this. He's weak. It's making him worse." She pulled on my arm, trying to move me away.

Any other time I would have turned to look in her eyes. But my legs locked in place and all I could do was glare back at Billy, feeling my voice hiss as I said, "Every time I close my eyes, I see what you did to those kids!"

Billy shrugged then looked to where his legs should be. "Hell, every time I open my eyes I see what those gooks did to me." He grasped his fingers on the ends of his stumps. "I could have left them alive to blow off your legs, too. Would you have preferred that?"

"No!" The word jumped out of me like I'd been struck on the back. I shuddered then realized it had been a touch, Susan's touch. I leaned back into it, hoping to feel it press harder and deeper, but it dropped away. I glared back at Billy. "You know that's not what I want, but those were kids who didn't…"

Billy's hands clapped over his ears. "Get the bleeding heart out of here. He's making me sick."

Susan's hand wrapped around my left arm and pulled. I followed it, this time more interested in being close to her than in what I could say to Billy. My arm tingled where she touched and I realized it was the arm I hadn't felt in four weeks. I stopped for a moment, making her increase the pressure to see how it would feel.

She did, but Billy's voice overwhelmed the excitement. "You got legs, man, both legs!"

I turned back to him wanting to shout, *Yeah, and arms, man, both arms!* But he looked so pathetic lying there, unable to move, I just shrugged and continued out with Susan, feeling the pressure as if it was the most thrilling sensation ever known. We stopped in the hallway where I put my hand around hers and squeezed. She began to pull away, but I clasped harder. "My arm. It's coming back!"

Her eyes widened then shifted to my sleeve. "What? Let me see!"

She grasped my arm with both hands and pressed her thumbs into the crease of my elbow. "You feel that?"

"Yes!" It was all I could do to keep from throwing my arms around her and kissing her on the mouth. But then the pressure began to fade. I looked at her thumbs turning white from pressing hard, but couldn't feel them. "No, now it's gone!"

She grasped my upper arm. "Anything here?"

I was desperate to feel it, but couldn't. "No, press harder!"

Her thumbs slid down to the inside of my wrist. "You feel this?"

There was a vague tingle that I wasn't sure was real. "Maybe, like you're pressing through a thick cushion."

Her eyebrows arched higher. "Try this." Her fingers bent down towards her wrist.

I attempted, but my hand stopped at a right angle. "I can't!"

She rubbed at my upper arm, though as desperate as I was for her touch, I could hardly feel it. "A doctor has to see it right away. There may be something we can do to bring it along faster."

"We?" I stared directly at her eyes, though she was focused on my arm.

She looked up. "You don't want me to help?"

"Oh, I do." My chest started heaving with fast breaths.

"It means exercising all the muscles to return you to full flexibility and strength. We don't want any more atrophy settling in."

I began to smile but then turned serious to match her expression. "No, we don't."

"And..." she paused, glancing in Billy's direction.

I feared she was thinking of going back in with Billy. "Yes?"

She looked up at me. "It means no situations where you can sustain more injury."

I reached out with my right hand and lightly touched her arm. "I promise."

She pulled her arm back, leaving my hand suspended in the air. "I mean it, Scout. It has to be protected, at all costs, against any further abuse."

My hand dropped to my side finding no comfortable place to land. "This isn't Vietnam. What kind of abuse could happen here?"

She covered her mouth and turned away.

I wanted to pull her into my arms but was afraid she'd push me away and run. "What? What is it?"

She looked down at the floor and shuddered. "It's being back here. I'm so scared!"

"Scared, here?" I put my hand on her arm for comfort, surprised that she let me leave it there. "Did Billy try to hurt you?"

Her head shook as she wiped at tears with the back of her hand. "No, you don't understand."

"Understand what?"

She turned away from me and leaned the top of her head into the wall, talking directly into her chest. "It's my husband."

My legs started to shake and my shoulder fell against the wall. "Husband?"

She looked sideways at me, tears rushing down her cheeks, and nodded.

I leaned harder into the wall, trying to grasp whatever steadiness I could find. "Where is he?"

She covered her face with her hands, her voice quivering. "I don't know."

I watched, wanting to reach out and pull her in close with my good arm, but no part of me moved. "Doesn't he know you're here?"

She slipped her hands under her eyes and focused directly on my sling. "That's what I'm scared of, that he'll see me."

I glanced down at the end of the hall half expecting him to appear, but at the emptiness shifted back to her.

She looked up at my eyes and went on. "I knew I'd never cross his path in Vietnam, but here…" Both her hands rushed up to her face and her whole body began to tremble.

I took hold of her arm, wishing I could take both. "What? What's he going to do to you?"

She grasped her hand over mine and whispered as if afraid to speak out loud, "He'll kill me. This time he'll really do it!"

I squeezed harder on her arm, desperate to protect her. "No, believe me. I won't let anyone hurt you. Trust me on that."

Her shoulders hunched around her neck and shuddered. "You don't know him. If he sees me, he'll get me. All I know is I have to get out of here. As soon as Billy's settled, I'm heading back."

"No, don't go. Stay here with me!" The words gushed through my lips before I knew I was speaking.

Her gaze shifted to the sling. "I don't think…"

"My arm will heal faster than you think. You'll see. I'll protect you. I'm a trained fighter, Susan, a killer." My mouth suddenly flooded with spit, but I swallowed without a pause. "I mean it, I did when I had to, I'd do it for you. I'll keep you safe. No one will ever hurt you again."

She looked up at my eyes for a moment, then immediately down at the ground. I feared she didn't believe me. "You know how I got the name Scout?"

She glanced up and I hoped I still had a chance.

271

"A scout sees the signs and senses when the enemy is near. I have that, saved Joe's life and Diego and Moustafa my first day out." I realized all three were now dead and my legs began to shake. I fought to steady them as I went on. "I promise, Susan, I'll be there for you, always. If he's near, I'll know it."

Her lips quivered like they were struggling, then finally the words, "You sure?"

I locked my knee against a quaking in my leg. "Positive, you'll be safe around me. No one will ever touch you again."

She looked steadily into my eyes and smiled. I felt my heart begin to pound and smiled back, adding, "Unless of course you want them to."

Her lips tightened and her eyes darted away. "You needn't be dragged into my problems."

"Susan." I let my hand fall lightly on her shoulder. "I was dragged through the worst you can imagine in Vietnam. There's no return to an easy life after that. Let me prove I can do this for you. I'll keep you safe, Susan, please."

Her face went into her hands and her head shook from side to side. I feared she was still planning to go back to Vietnam the next day and stay there as long as she could. If she did, I'd have to follow, even if it meant going back with Chim to the country where we would both be unwanted as is.

Susan wiped her hands down her face and gazed at my chin before making her way up to my eyes. "Okay, Scout. You can keep me safe."

I wasn't sure I heard right, but then the way her eyes looked up at me, with a longing that I wanted so much to believe, her words rang again in my ears. I wrapped my arm around her and pulled her in close. She moved in easily, pressing her face into my chest. The wetness of her tears spread into my shirt. I leaned down, my lips grazing her hair. "I love you, Susan. I'll take good care of you."

She wrapped her arms around me and pressed her whole body into mine with a soft firmness that made my breathing stop. Protecting Susan would be the most important mission of my life, one that I couldn't fail. I closed my eyes wanting to feel only us in each other's arms when I was hit by a vision of the village kids with slit throats, then Joe's mutilated back, and Moustafa's horrified eyes as he fell from the sniper's shot. Cold sweat gushed down my sides. I hoped Susan couldn't feel it as I whispered into her hair, "You'll be safe. You won't ever have to worry again." The drips of sweat stopped at my waist, trapped in the thick band. *Please, Susan, don't feel that sweat, I'll do whatever it takes, I promise.*

PART II
2~1/2 YEARS LATER

~ Chapter 16 ~

March 29th, 1973
Columbus, Ohio

.

"Scout, the helicopters!" I was stunned by Chim's words as I walked through the door. Susan would never buy him helicopters or guns or anything that resembled a war toy. But then I heard them, clattering, real ones, from the TV.

"Chim, you know you're not allowed to watch..." I entered the living room shocked to see Susan watching with him. It was the news, only she never allowed the news on when he was home.

Chim jumped up and pointed. "Scout, look, helicopters taking people out! You see Hooang?"

I hadn't heard him use her name in almost a year and clutched harder at the textbooks I didn't get to drop on my desk. "What's going on?"

Susan's upper body shivered. "They slammed the gate on all of them, Scout, only Americans can get out!"

I turned to see an overcrowded chopper try to lift off the roof of a white building while the words *American Embassy, Saigon* flashed on the screen. Two from the mob on the roof grabbed onto its landing gear and caused the chopper to tilt.

I crouched in front of the TV and grasped the sides of the screen. "What the hell?"

The two men continued to hang from the landing gear, keeping the chopper from gaining height. Four Marines aimed their guns at them, though I only heard one shot. The two men dropped to the roof and the chopper immediately lifted straight up. We followed its ascent when abruptly we were shifted to the mobs of Vietnamese locked outside the embassy's gate.

Susan pushed into my side as she joined me right in front of the TV. "Look at them all! Why won't anyone help?"

Chim pushed between us and slapped his hands flat on the screen. "You see Hooang?"

Susan threw her arms around his shoulders. "No, honey, but it's impossible to tell."

I was afraid the tremble in her voice would make him more nervous. I forced mine to be as reassuring as possible. "The lieutenant wouldn't let her in this mob. She's in her village, waiting for a better time to leave."

Chim's fingers curled and slipped down the screen onto the table that held the TV. "What about the lieutenant? He there?"

I tapped my fingers on the side of the screen. "You can be sure he knows what's going on and has his own plan to get out."

Chim's hand grabbed my wrist and looked up at me. "With Hooang?"

I leaned my face right in front of his. "If there's any possible way, he'll find it, like he got you out safe with me. Soon as he can get Hooang out, he will."

Susan leaned her face on the other side of Chim's. "He loves you, never forget that."

"I love him, too," Chim began then his fingers slammed onto the screen. "Look!"

An American in fatigues was climbing the outside gate. A Marine threw a rope over for him while four others pointed their guns at the Vietnamese trying to grab it for themselves. The American hauled himself to the top in a few quick grasps and jumped to the ground. We watched him roll on his side then spring upright, his familiar wiry build making it hard for me to breathe. The camera focused more directly on the side of his gaunt, scraggly face before he sprinted into the embassy.

Chim began jumping up and down. "Is that him?"

I wished they had shown his eyes, his hardened stare that penetrated whatever he looked at like cutting through steel. "Maybe, Chim, I can't tell for sure." I put my face closer to the screen hoping they'd show him again.

Susan moved in closer, too. "It resembles him. Don't you think?"

The screen suddenly switched to the anchorman. "This concludes our special report. More coverage will follow on the six o'clock news."

Chim hit the top of the TV. "Not fair, show him again!" The TV screen returned to *Huckleberry Hound*.

Susan glanced at me with strained eyes, then placed her hands on Chim's shoulders and began massaging. "Don't worry, Chim. They make it look much worse on TV than it really is. And if it was the lieutenant, you could tell by what little we saw that nothing will stop him. Now come, let's go look at that new book you have on stamps."

A siren rang and I grabbed Susan by the arms and pushed her and Chim to the floor. I stared out the window expecting to see bombers charging through the air, but then it rang again and I realized it was the phone.

Susan shrugged off my tight grip, shot me an angry glare, then rushed to the hallway and lifted the receiver. "Hello?" There was a few moments pause. "I know, we just watched it, too. It's so..." she glanced at Chim before going on. "The television makes it so dramatic." There was another few moments pause. "I know what it means, Billy."

My jaw tightened. This wasn't his usual check-in time. It was bad enough that every Monday and Thursday Susan spent an hour on the phone calming him down about either incidents that upset him on his job at the post office, or problems between his mother, step-father and him. He received enough of her time, why did he have to talk to her now, also? I was going to signal Susan to hang up when all of a sudden the village kids appeared before me, laughing and splashing each other like they had that time in the river. I stared at them, my heart slamming harsh beats into my chest. I didn't understand what was happening. They hadn't come out in the day in over two years.

I turned to Susan, her foot tapping the floor as she stared into the wooden planks. "Billy, calm down. They don't leave Americans behind...No, you're wrong. No one's dropping a nuclear bomb...No, you're not going over there...Yes, I heard you, but...Scout saw it and he's not talking nuclear bombs...Listen Billy, you have to promise me you're not going out to get drunk tonight. You stay home and...Yes, I said he was here, but first you have to promise me. Okay, wait a second, I'll get him." She covered the receiver with her hand and looked at me. "He wants to talk to you."

The village kids' mouths opened wide, their tongues writhing like snakes. I turned away, starting for the bedroom. "No, I'm not taking it."

She grabbed my arm. "Scout, please!"

Chim arrived at Susan's side, a book in his hand. She smiled down at him and pushed the phone in front of my chest. I hooked my thumbs in my belt, refusing to lift my hands. "You know to tell him I'm not home."

Thin creases pulled at her eyes. "It's different this time. I'm really scared he'll do something crazy."

"Let him," I stepped back from the phone, "that's his problem." I glanced at Chim, upset that he had stepped into the same spot where I'd seen the village kids a moment before, as if reminding me it could have been him.

Susan followed me, holding the receiver between two pleading hands. "For me, Scout, talk to him for once. He needs you right now!"

Chim stepped up to us and pointed to the phone. "Uncle Billy needs help?"

His eyes looked into mine, then next thing I knew, I reached for the phone and put it to my ear. The rough pounding in my chest echoed back to me as I turned my sights to the TV and took a deep breath. "Billy, you see that chopper? Man, I thought they were going rear end on the roof!"

"It's not the choppers I'm worried about, Scout. It's those crazy gooks! Don't kid yourself, they're going to break through that gate and kill every American they see. I know you like them cause of that kid, and I ain't got nothing against Chim, but if we don't drop the bomb now they'll get hold of one and drop it on us. And they'll do it, man, right here where we stand, in the good old U. S. of A. We got to get them first. It's our only chance."

I squeezed the phone, feeling my arm bulge as if it was ready to burst. "Get a grip, man, nukes is death to the world. Everyone knows that and no one's going to use them."

"You're wrong, Scout. It's happening and the generals know it. That's why they're pulling out. They're gonna push the button and end it all. But we gotta get the sarge, man."

My tongue scraped along the rough edge of a tooth. "The sarge? What are you talking about?"

"Don't you know? He's MIA man, POW if you ask me. We can't just leave him there to get nuked. It's not right, man. We gotta get him out. If we can't go, we can at least petition the Pentagon. They'll listen to his squad. They got respect for that."

"Why would I want to do that?" I pictured the sarge's face when he forced me to change my story to *Stars & Stripes*.

"He was our sarge, that's why. You have to call the squad, Scout. They're the only ones who will do it."

"No way. I'm not calling nobody. You're the one told me Wesley's got shrapnel in his head too dangerous to remove and Leon lost half his hand. You don't think they blame the sarge for sending them to that thirteenth valley?"

"It's not the sarge's fault. It's war. Hell, I lost my legs, that's worse. And you know I would call except when I did, they said they don't want no pals shooting the breeze about Vietnam. But you got along with them, Scout. You can call. They'll listen to you."

I had wanted to call, at least a hundred times, especially Wesley, to ask why he helped me against Moustafa. But the guilt that he was sent to the thirteenth valley because of me was too strong.

"Scout, you're the only one who can do this. You have to do it for the sarge."

"I don't have to do anything for him. I'm discharged, a civilian, h - o - m - e, and I don't care if the sarge is stuck back there or not. You copy that?"

Chim pulled on my arm and looked up. "Uncle Billy going back?" He stared into my face, his eyes growing larger.

I shook my head as Billy went on. "Scout, all you have to do is make the calls. Best thing is if we demonstrate outside of the White House and get the *Washington Post* to notice. The right headline will force them to go back and get him out."

Chim reached up for the phone, "Let me talk. I want to go back with Uncle Billy!"

I turned away, wanting this ended with Billy and to explain what I'd meant to Chim. "Okay, give me the phone numbers, I'll do what I can." I glanced down at Chim. "And I'm sorry for saying I don't care if the sarge is stuck back there or not. I do care."

I quickly scribbled down the numbers, then turned to Chim whose mouth was tight and eyes narrowed into slits.

Susan grabbed my arm. "Did he mention doing anything violent?"

My gaze stayed on Chim. "No, but he wants me to help get the sarge out."

Chim's mouth stretched sideways, showing the bottoms of his upper teeth. I was about to explain that I cared who was stuck back there but that the sarge had been a cruel man and that's why I said I didn't care, when the village kids appeared behind Chim. They had long, jagged wounds on their necks, shining with a red rawness that made my own throat throb.

"You hear me, Scout?" It was Susan's voice. I jerked my eyes to her face seeing her jaw shifted to one side.

I blinked my eyes to be sure I was seeing her and only her. "What?" I hoped the village kids would stay away, back in their hidden shadows I forced them into at night.

"What do you mean get the sarge out?"

I looked back at Chim, knowing I couldn't mention what Billy said about dropping the nukes. "He wants me to organize our old squad to force the Pentagon to bring back our sarge from a POW camp."

Chim looked up at me. "And Hooang, too?"

I gripped his shoulders and swallowed hard. "Only the lieutenant can get her out."

His eyes began to glisten and tears rushed down his cheek. "He'll do it?"

I put my arms around him and pulled him into my chest. "When he can, he will." I thought to myself, *or he'll die trying*, when Susan crouched low by the other side of Chim and wrapped her arms around the two of us.

"You see, Chim, you have to trust your father. You know how it's up to me and Scout to take care of you?"

Chim nodded and Susan continued. "Well, it's the same thing. It's up to the lieutenant to take care of Hooang. You understand?"

Chim pushed his face into her shoulder and began to tremble. I rubbed his back, wondering what I could say to soothe him when the village kids appeared next to him again and began to laugh. I wanted to scream to leave Chim alone, except I knew Susan and Chim would think I was crazy. I was the only one who saw them. They were mine alone, though to me they were horrifyingly real.

"You'll be all right." Susan's voice was soft. "Scout's here, and if you need me, you can call."

My head jolted up from the taunting kids. "Call?"

Susan leaned Chim's head onto my chest and began to stand. "Yes, you know I have to cover Roseanne's shift tonight."

The kids began jumping up and down as if getting ready to pounce on Chim. I wanted to swing my arm and knock them down, but instead just squeezed my hands into fists.

I watched Susan take her sweater from the closet. "Don't go! Can't you call in?"

She slipped her arms into the sleeves. "Wish I could but you know how Roseanne covers for me when Chim gets sick. She'd get in trouble if no one showed and I owe her."

I wanted to be reasonable, but the laundry kid now joined the village kids. The three of them whispered among themselves then pointed at me. I turned away from them and up to Susan. "You'd stay home for Billy if he needed you."

Susan's mouth opened, taking a few moments before she could speak. "Are you still jealous of Billy's calls?"

"No, not that!" I suddenly found myself panting. "Susan, don't go. The vets are condemned anyway. No one else cares, that's clear."

"I care and I have a job to get to." Susan turned and started for the door.

"Listen to me," I ran after her. "First we're destroyed, then we're blamed, and now we're told it was all for nothing."

She turned around to me and stood with her hand on her hip. "It wasn't all for nothing. They're airlifting out, but that doesn't mean it's over."

280

I gripped her arm. "But Joe, what about Joe? He gave his life and they're pulling out!"

She tried to yank herself free but I gripped harder. "Let go of me. What's the matter with you?"

Suddenly, the laundry kid flashed in my head, saying, "Without the war it's murder, cold blooded murder!" My whole body shivered.

Susan's nails dug into my hand. "Let go of me this minute!"

I feared the moment I let go she'd bolt through the door. I grabbed her other arm and pushed her back against the wall. "You're staying!" My lips slammed into hers and kept pressing harder. She tried to slip out from under me, but there was no way I would let her loose.

I felt her pushing against my chest then heard muffled wails, like a cat trapped in a closed trunk. It seemed far away and she seemed even further away, though I had her in my grasp. I wanted her closer, holding me, whispering soothing words into my ear.

She pushed against my chest, but I wouldn't budge. Her lips tried to slip to the side, but I pushed into them harder, feeling my skin split, then a few drops of blood on my tongue. It was bitter and I was about to release her when there was a sharp sting on my tongue. I jerked my head back and at the same moment she jabbed a fist into my stomach. I jumped back, hitting the opposite wall.

"Stay away from me!" Her voice screeched like a stopped train. I suddenly realized what I'd done when the door yanked open and immediately slammed.

I pulled at the door and heard her footsteps rush down the steps. "Come back, I didn't mean..."

"No!" Her shriek felt like a mortar strike, making me fight to keep from stepping back. "You come after me, and you'll never see me again!"

Her feet clamored down the second set of stairs and I panicked. "Susan, please, I can explain. I didn't mean to. I'm sorry!"

She clattered across the tile floor then an angry, "So am I!" The front door slammed and the framed pictures trembled out of their proper placement.

I ran down the steps and pushed the door's curtain aside. Susan was already two blocks away. There was no question she would run the full eight blocks to the hospital. My watch read 3:45, which meant she wasn't even late. She was running to get away from me.

"Susan!" I pressed the side of my face into the window. "I don't know what happened, but I promise it will never happen again!"

A door startled me from behind. The old woman from the back apartment peered at me through squinted eyes. I glared back and took a step closer. She immediately shifted behind the door as I heard another woman shout from inside, "Sis, get in. Those vets were loony before, but now…"

The door slammed and I kicked the bottom step. "That's right, lady, shut the crazy vet out."

"Scout?" I looked up in time to see Chim's eyes disappear behind the rail.

I reached upwards. "Chim, come here!" I leaped the steps, anxious to hold him in my arms. But when I was within ten steps, he ran inside and shut the door. I grasped the handle ready to jerk it right through its hasp if it was locked, except it opened easily and I went inside trying to keep my voice under control. "Chim! What's with you?"

Chim was clutching the couch, his back trembling.

I rushed towards him. "Chim, what's the matter?"

He rolled away on the floor, pressing something in his hand against his chest. "What is it?" I reached out my hand. "Show me."

His hand flew behind his back. "No!"

But I saw the familiar worn edges jutting under his fingers. It was the photo of the sniper, the only one we had.

I held up my hands. "It's okay. I'm not taking it. What are you so scared of?"

He scampered a few feet farther away, then stopped suddenly and peered over his shoulder. "You hurt Susan!"

My arms dropped hard against my sides. "No, not true!"

He lurched back like he'd been hit and I clasped my fingers in a tight squeeze. "It's not like that. I told her I'm sorry. You know I'd never hurt her."

Chim turned away and clutched his knees. "Stay away from me, Scout!"

I reached over and rapped the top of the TV. "You wish I'd left you back there?"

His body shook and my vision split in two, then three, the three Vietnamese kids, huddling in a heap, their arms entwined while they stared back at me. Acid churned in my stomach and vile spit filled my mouth. I felt myself kneel down, then lay still on the floor, fearing any movement would make me vomit. The laundry kid pointed at me and screamed, "Child killer!"

The horror of those words thundered in my head as I tried to shout over them, "You wanted to kill me!"

I braced for another dreaded accusation, though the response was surprisingly soft. "Why would I want to kill you?"

I looked up, seeing the laundry kid turn into Chim with his mouth still moving. "All I said was stay away."

A rush of sweat ran into my eyes and a flood gushed down my cheeks. My lips trembled and I tried holding them stiff. But the shaking spread to my jaw, then down in my shoulders, till the next thing I knew I was face down, grasping at the rug to try to keep me still.

Something touched my back and I lashed out with my arm. It retreated and I felt a foot push into my side. I looked up to see Chim on the floor, leaning back on his hands like he'd just fallen.

I grasped his leg and looked up at his squeezed eyes. "Chim, I'm sorry, I didn't mean to hurt you." His eyes opened slightly, letting a thin flow of tears slip down each cheek. I caressed his leg. "You all right?"

He looked at me with pupils only half exposed. "Are you?"

I pushed on his leg and lifted to my side, a wave of nausea almost forcing me back down. "No, not yet."

Chim leaned forward, gripped his knees and glanced at my hand on his shin. "I don't want you to die, Scout. I didn't say that."

My stomach twinged with a sharp stab, but at least it wasn't nausea. "It was someone else wanted to kill me, I know that. I shouldn't have yelled at you."

He didn't look up at me but continued to stare at his shin. "And Susan? Did you mean to hurt someone else?"

I almost collapsed on his foot but managed to lock up my arm in time. "No, with Susan, I couldn't bear to have her leave. I don't know what happened to me, something terrible, as terrible as all those people left behind the gate."

Chim pointed to the TV. "Like Hooang and Lieutenant?" He turned to the screen as if they'd be there.

My eyes suddenly burned and my vision blurred. I crawled next to him and wrapped my arms around his chest. "Chim, you are like my own son. No matter who comes to claim you, I am your father, even if it means you have two."

Chim looked down at my hands on his chest and clenched his over mine. "He's just a picture I look at. You're the only father I know."

There were pulses on my hands from both within my chest and from Chim's palm, beating a harmonious rhythm that eased into my terrible looming fear. I pulled Chim on my lap and began to speak into his ear. "When your father chose me to take care of you, I thought he was getting me to do him a favor. But now I realize, he was offering me the most precious gift he had."

Chim pulled on my fingers. "Scout, can I call you daddy?"

I pressed my cheek into the side of his forehead. "Anytime you want, Chim, anytime at all."

"And I have two mothers?" He turned halfway around and looked up into my eyes.

I knew Susan would find a way to see Chim even if she never talked to me again. I felt jealous, though I knew that wasn't fair. "That's right. Two mothers who love you very much." My chest ached, a vacuum seeming to grow inside that pushed against my lungs.

"And if they come here?" Chim pointed to the floor.

I glanced at the couch. "Maybe we'll all live together. Won't that be nice?"

Chim leaped up from my lap and began jumping around the room, chanting, "Two mommies, two daddies and Chim," then bounded into the hallway where a piece of paper fell from next to the telephone. He stopped to pick it up then stared at it, moving his lips for a moment before saying, "Wesley? Who's that?"

I jumped to my feet and reached for the paper. "Someone I knew in Vietnam."

Chim's eyes stayed on the paper. "Did I know him?"

I took the paper and crumpled it within my fist. "No, he was in my squad."

Chim stared at my hand. "Aren't you going to call him?"

I squeezed my hand tighter ready to say *no* when the words, "He saved my life," popped out of my mouth.

Chim slid on the floor next to my leg and tried to pry open my fingers. "How?"

I suddenly felt a stab in my shoulder and winced. "He kept Moustafa from killing me, but I don't know why."

Chim pulled harder on my hand. "Because he likes you, Scout. I would save you, too."

I was about to say, *He didn't like me and it's not that simple*, when Chim's stomach gave a loud rumble.

I poked him under the ribs and began to tickle. "I heard that, Mr. Hungry."

Chim giggled and glanced in the kitchen, eyes focused on the freezer. "Can I, Scout?"

I put my hands on my hips. "Ice cream before dinner? You know Susan doesn't...Oh, what the heck. You can even eat it in front of the TV."

Chim squealed and ran for the freezer, already grabbing for the carton of vanilla fudge when I entered. I glimpsed the stack of frozen dinners. "You want turkey and mashed potatoes, or chicken and French fries?"

Chim pulled a spoon out of a drawer. "French fries!"

"Smart choice, my man." I held my hand out for a low five, which he slapped half with the spoon and half with his hand. I slipped two aluminum foil trays in the oven and set it to 450 degrees while Chim scooped ice cream into his favorite plastic cup.

I looked up at the clock. "Thirty minutes. Just enough time to watch *Batman.*"

"Batman!" Chim shrieked, spreading his arms into wings with cup and spoon at opposite ends. He charged out of the kitchen and headed for the living room.

I heard the TV click on and the familiar voices of Batman, Robin and their archenemy, the Riddler. I had political science readings to do for tomorrow's class but was too unsettled to consider it. I started for the TV except five steps out of the kitchen the crumpled paper lay in my path and made my legs stop. I stared at it, unable to kick it out of the way or simply walk past it.

The banter from the screen filled my ears as I stood motionless. "Holy Christmas, Batman, the Riddler has strung the word Riddlerland in lights across the United Nations building."

"It looks like he intends to confuse the peace talks with one of his bad-will-towards-man riddles, Robin. Into the Bat-mobile, we've got no time to lose."

I reached down, grabbed the paper and smoothed it within my palms. Wesley's number seemed to blare at me as if it had a built-in alarm. I rushed to the phone in my bedroom before I lost my nerve and began dialing. My head teemed with explanations of why he helped me against Moustafa. He did it to keep Moustafa out of trouble; he did it to get me off the truck and keep the revolution going; he did it so he could beat me up himself in the beer fight. I steadied my hand on the phone as the first ring went unanswered. I imagined Wesley in a cool bachelor pad with leopard skin blankets on his bed. The second ring felt louder and more urgent than the first as I pictured him in a restaurant with a big chef's hat on and people lined up out the door for his ribs. The phone rang again and I checked my watch, 4:35, thinking if he's doing the dinner shift, he won't be home till late. Another ring, but I decided to hold on. Maybe he did the lunch shift and would walk in any minute. Yet another ring and I imagined the scar on his head as big and round as a baseball. I nearly slammed down the receiver but talked myself into one more ring. This one seemed to blast as loud as a mortar hit, making me hold it back from my ear. I let it ring a few more times, feeling too numb to hang up when the phone was picked up and a woman's throaty voice said, "Who's this lets the phone ring ten damn times?"

A baby's cries wailed in the background and the receiver slid forward on my face. I pushed the earpiece back in place. "I'm looking for Wesley Bates. Does he live here?"

She gave a guttural laugh. "When he's not carousing out and about. You want him, I'll see if he's too busy in front of the TV." The phone clunked down on a table and I heard her call out, "It's for you." A pause, then, "Find out for yourself. I ain't your damn secretary!"

My hand was so sweaty it could no longer hold the phone. I would have hung up, but the lady had already taken the time for me while the baby cried, and it felt too disrespectful to make her effort for nothing. I dried my hand on my shirt and managed a more solid grip.

"Why don't you give her a bottle and soothe the little sugar babe?" It was Wesley's voice, sounding distant but getting louder.

Something like shoes fell on the floor. "Give it to her yourself. You see me getting ready for work. Someone has to earn a paycheck around here!"

I felt like I was intruding where I didn't belong. I nearly hung up again when Wesley's voice bellowed into the phone. "Who's this?"

"Wesley," I began, feeling my throat tighten so it came out as a whisper, "it's me, Scout."

The baby shrieked in the background. "Who? I can't hear you. Speak up."

I took a deep breath and shouted. "Scout, from Vietnam. You know the forty-fourth squad. We served together for a couple of months and we…"

"Yeah, yeah, I know who you are. What do you want Scout from Vietnam, the one who sent me into the thirteenth valley to get my head shot off. It almost worked, too, if the bullet had been another half inch to the left."

I swiped at the sweat on my forehead. "Sorry, man. Billy told me you have shrapnel in your head."

"Those damn pieces of lead gives me headaches so bad, some days I can't hardly get my head off the pillow. Is that what you called to find out?"

I rubbed my eyebrows with my thumb and index fingers. "No, I'm calling about the airlift. Did you see it on TV?"

"Damn sure, only bad thing is they didn't pull out before I got my orders. Would've saved me a whole damned load of trouble. Is that what you wanted to know?"

"No, man, it's this. Billy says the sarge is still in country, MIA, probably POW. He's afraid he's going to be left after everyone's gone, and he wants us to petition to get him out."

"The sarge?" Wesley gave a gruff laugh. "Let him stay and rot for all I care. That racist bastard sent us brothers in the valley knowing it was a trap."

I thought of his threats to me with the *Stars & Stripes* reporter. "I don't want him back either. He had it in for me, too."

Wesley's laugh was higher pitched this time. "Damn, Scout, he gave you a medal!"

I coughed instead of arguing since I wasn't the one sent to the thirteenth valley. Nothing else compared to that. "You know anyone still in there?"

"A few," his voice took on a softer tone. "A cousin and his friend are somewhere around Khe Sanh and my friend's brother is in blasted Cambodia. They's even crazier down there. I hear they got tribesmen that'll eat you alive if they catch you. Don't know whose fool notion it is to defend them, but that's Uncle Sam for you. Any of yours over there?"

I squeezed the top of my nose. "Two. Remember that sniper with the dog? He's still there. Last I heard he's in the jungle, might not even know the war's over."

"Dude like that can't ever come back," said Wesley. "Too used to killing."

I shook my head, not wanting to believe that. "I have his son. He sent him home with me."

"Damn." Wesley gave a long, low whistle. "You must have owed him big time to get roped into that."

I shifted the phone to my other hand. "He saved my life, remember, from Moustafa."

Wesley swallowed like he was taking a long swig of soda. "Yesiree, I'll never forget that day. The brothers was all agitated about not getting desk jobs. We was going to let it be known at the beer fight how it would be if that continued. If any whites started a fight with a brother, we'd all jump 'em and show our strength. That's how it was supposed to go down."

My throat went completely dry. "That would have been me against Moustafa."

Wesley chuckled like he was enjoying this memory. "Right on, my man. You was enemy number one."

I licked my lips and swallowed the tiny drop of spit still in my mouth. "But Moustafa upped the ante."

There was a thud like Wesley hit a table. "That's right. That damned brother thought he was some kind of Stokely Carmichael."

The woman's voice came through. "Here's her bottle, big man. There's another one in the fridge, you know that thing that holds the beer?"

"Don't get smart with me, woman." Wesley's voice was muffled.

"I am smart, smarter than you. And if you don't feed her quick, she's going to cry herself sick. You hear?"

There was what sounded like a sloppy kiss and Wesley was back on the phone. "Look, man, I gotta go; the baby's hungry."

A few minutes before I would have been relieved, but we were so close to what I wanted to know. "One more thing."

"No, man, I gotta go.

I gripped the phone tighter. "I'll call you later."

Wesley chuckled. "Sure, I'll speak to you after the next airlift. Oh, and tell Billy he still owes me ten bucks."

I began, "He'll never pay," but Wesley had already hung up his end. I dropped the receiver in my lap and stared at its tiny holes, feeling a chilly emptiness not only from their quiet, but also from what had been said. It was no laughing matter that they all would have jumped me if the beer fight had gone as planned. Except it didn't all fit. If Wesley was so willing to see me beat up to make their point, why did he try to save me from being killed? I was more confused and upset about it than I had been before.

I slammed my hand on top of his name on the paper. "Don't expect me to care about the lead in your damned head!" The paper stuck to my moist fingers and lifted from the nightstand. I crumpled it into a tight mass and threw it at the wall. I expected it to crash loudly, even to crack the wall, but it hit with a very faint thud. I glared at its spot where it fell on the floor, watching it begin to unravel on its own. I then stormed out of the room.

Batman and Robin's voices resounded as I headed towards the living room.

"Leaping lanterns, Batman, the Riddlerland lights are falling."

"Fortunately, Robin, the Riddler's plan at world domination has failed. His treacherous scheme to send the super powers into nuclear war was seen in time for what it really is, a way for him to take power over the whole world. The truth always wins in the end."

The Batman song began and Chim sang along with the TV. I entered the room in time to see a news reporter say, "Vietnam airlift. Thousands are evacuated while thousands more try to find a way out. Full story in ten seconds. Stay tuned."

I sat down next to Chim who immediately gripped my arm and held it in front of his chest. The reporter appeared with a photo of the American

Embassy behind him and said, "Nearly five thousand troops have already been shuttled by cargo Hueys out of their ground locations to awaiting aircraft carriers in the South China sea. And more than a thousand advisors and personnel stationed in Saigon are being airlifted to Guam from the embassy roof."

The background picture switched to video of inside the embassy, showing crowds of people with bags waiting for their chance to go up to the roof. Chim rushed to the TV for a closer look, pulling me with him. He held the sniper's photo at the edge of the tube, then as the camera scanned the room, Chim ran his finger across the screen.

His finger stopped midway. "That him?"

It looked similar to the gate climber we had seen before, but it was only a partial glimpse of the face. "Could be, but I don't know."

The picture went back to the news anchor. "There's been tremendous reaction to this airlift around the world. And right here in Columbus people are talking about it wherever you go, on the checkout lines in grocery stores, on college campuses, in churches, in elevators. We picked a few places in Columbus to bring you our hometown reaction."

My college campus appeared showing a student holding up a sign that read, *Vietnam for the Vietnamese, bring the troops home!* A crowd in front of it chanted the words directly into the camera, including a boy from my biology class. He'd always sat in the corner and stared out the window. But here he was, front and center, shouting above the rest of the crowd.

I mumbled to the TV, "His student deferment worries are over."

The scene switched to a pub in downtown Columbus where people in a combination of casual and construction clothes leaned on the long bar.

A reporter stood next to a guy in an Army fatigue jacket. "Tell me, sir, what do you think of the airlift out of Vietnam?"

At first the guy smiled right into the camera, then pointed his finger at it and began to scowl. "Our government has no business pulling out. They should stay and finish what they started and stop playing games with the VC."

A guy next to him with a bandana wrapped around his head grabbed the mike and shouted into it, "They should have pulled out years ago before all our guys were killed!"

The reporter put his hand on the mike and leaned into it with a big smile. "That's it from the pub."

The scene switched to a shot of the VA hospital, then inside to a female reporter on the second floor.

Chim pressed his face into the screen. "Scout, look, Susan's floor!" My breathing practically stopped as the reporter stood in the TV room and asked a patient who had been watching this news show, "What do you think of the airlift out of Vietnam?"

He turned his wheelchair around, showing his missing legs from the knees down and talked straight to the camera. "Where's the honor in pulling out? Me and my Marine buddies, we fought for those people 'cause they needed our help. Where's the honor in helping people one day and turning our backs on them the next?"

Chim shrieked and jumped up and down. "Scout, look, Susan!" There was a glimpse of her carrying a tray of medications down the hall. She seemed totally unaware that she was captured on video as she disappeared from the screen's background.

I tried to share his excitement. "Look at that. Isn't it something?" But inside I knew Susan's incognito life had been blown, though I didn't want to alarm Chim to its reason.

Chim kept poking at the spot where she'd been on the screen. "Wait till we tell Susan she's famous! And wait till my class finds out my mom was on TV!" Chim stepped back and pulled on my arm. "Scout, I know we're not supposed to call her unless it's an emergency, but can I call her right now?"

I knew Susan would consider this an emergency. In fact, she'd be furious at me if I didn't let her know. It would also give me a needed chance to apologize. I let Chim pull me towards the phone. "Yes, we'll call. But you have to let me do most of the talking."

Chim ran for the phone and began dialing the number he knew by heart, waiting for each turn of the dial to return before starting the next. Finally he was done and a moment later said into the phone, "Nurse Susan Grayson, please." I watched him tap his fingers on the table until a minute later, he said, "Susan, guess what. You're on TV!"

"What?" I could hear her cry as if it was right into my ear. I feared I made a mistake by letting Chim call. I should have done it myself, but he was so excited I didn't want to say no. *Please, Susan, play along with Chim and then we'll talk. Please understand why I did this.*

"Susan, did you hear? You're famous! The reporter talked to that Marine and you walked by carrying a tray down the hall. Golly, Susan, most people want to be on TV." Chim began nodding. "It's okay....I understand."

I reached for the phone, but he turned away. "I know you don't....I know....Yes, he's here....No, no problems. He wants to talk to you....Okay, I will. Here he is."

I grasped the phone and immediately put it to my mouth. "Don't worry, Susan. It will be all right."

There was a pause that made me fear she'd hung up, but then I heard her gasp, and realized she was crying while holding her hand over the phone.

"Susan, are you all right?"

"I'm scared, Scout. They promised they wouldn't film me. I had no idea they did."

She sounded more scared than she should. "Susan, it was just a glimpse of you for maybe five seconds. And it never showed your full face."

"Was I seen or not?" Her voice had a tremble.

"You were seen," I began, wondering why she wasn't holding herself under more control, even if she was scared. "Susan, tell me, has there been any sign of him, something I should know?"

She began whispering and I had to press the phone harder against my ear. "I didn't want to tell you, Scout, but I thought I saw him last week at the bus terminal when I went to pick up a schedule for Sylvia and Sol. I'm not positive it was him, but if it was, he boarded a bus to Cincinnati."

My chest started heaving like I'd had the wind knocked out of me. I didn't know if it was fear that her husband was so close or alarm that she saw him and chose not to tell me. I clutched the phone with both hands. "What makes you think it was him?"

There was a rustling sound as if she was shifting positions, then a long, slow sigh before she said, "The way he walked from the back. He had that lower bend in his left leg than his right and it was his height and shape, tall and straight at the waist like he was built from a box. That was the giveaway."

Her description sounded conclusive. "Then it was him."

"The problem was," her voice wavered, "his hair was different. It was blond and Kurt had dark hair. And when he turned in my direction, he had mirror sunglasses that covered half his cheeks. It kind of looked like him, but the hair and not being able to see his whole face, then the moustache. Kurt never had a moustache before, so I couldn't be sure. And I was hiding behind a newspaper stand, making sure he didn't see me."

It was close enough and the waver in her voice told of her strong gut instinct. I didn't expect he was stupid enough to display weapons, but guessed he had something hidden. "Do you remember what he wore?"

"Clothes? No, I..." I could hear her hum a long note to herself, then, "Yes, he had on a baseball cap, red I think. And blue jeans with one of those western shirts. You know, the kind with fringes across the chest. And cowboy boots that had those pointy silver tips at the toes."

291

With that much detail, her hesitation confused me. "Sounds like you saw enough to know it was him. Or is there something wrong with me that I can't know the truth?"

"What?" There was a sharp edge to her shriek.

I knew she was still angry with me, but I couldn't hold in my hurt any longer. "Why didn't you tell me?"

There was a tapping on the other end, probably a pen on wood. Finally she spoke. "Because I didn't want to upset you, and he didn't see me, and it might not be him. And what would I tell you, that he boarded a bus for Cincinnati?"

"Yes, that would have been fair."

"Fair for what? That it's on your mind when you had those two big tests this week, and it's probably not even him?"

Was that it? Was she protecting me when I was the one supposed to be protecting her? I stared into the phone wishing I was looking into her eyes. "I would have wanted to know!"

"Scout!" Her tone was that of a scolding teacher. "I told you why. Now drop it!"

My legs felt restless and I began to pace within the constraints of the cord. "Susan, come home. It's not safe. I'll come get you or you can take a cab."

"No, Scout. You know I can't just leave. I'm on alone and there's no one to call to fill in."

My pacing quickened and took on longer steps. "Then I'm coming there, to watch. I'll bring Chim to the McCormack's and I'll be there in forty-five minutes."

"Stop it, Scout. That's ridiculous! No one is going to bother me here. And I told you, it probably wasn't even him. And if it was, he probably watches a Cincinnati station."

I pushed my free arm into the wall and pressed into it with all my force. "The local stations sometimes share programming, and there's no point taking a chance."

I heard a knock through the phone then a man's voice. "Nurse, you're needed in 245."

There was a pause, then, "Scout, I have to go."

"Listen to me, Susan. Be careful. I'll be there soon."

"No, Scout, I'm telling you, don't come. You are not to show up. You hear me?" I felt her glaring at me through the phone like she had before on the steps. She was more afraid of me than her husband. I was about to say, *Susan, trust me, please. I'm sorry about before. It will never happen again.* But before I could start, the phone clicked and she was gone.

I pressed my shoulder into the wall then slid down its smooth edge to the floor. I sat there, rapping the receiver into my knee, when Chim sat in front of me.

"What's the matter with Susan, Scout? Why didn't she want to be on TV?"

I feared Chim had already heard too much and wanted to put him at ease. "She doesn't like having her picture taken, is all. You know how she gets when we try to get her into one of those photo booths."

Chim shrugged then glanced towards the kitchen. Immediately, the smell of chicken and fries struck me, making me realize I had been too upset to notice before. I jumped up, returned the receiver to the phone and patted Chim on the head. "Your dinner smells good, doesn't it, buddy?"

Chim nodded and made chewing noises as he followed me into the kitchen. I put plates for Chim and me on the table, brought out the ketchup from the refrigerator and glimpsed at the clock, 5:22 p.m. One thing I knew: there was no way I was staying home and wait for 12:15 a.m. to see if Susan showed up safe and sound. I put a dinner for each of us on the plates and watched Chim pour himself orange juice and bring it to his seat. He began right in on the French fries and I sat down opposite him.

Chim picked up his first piece of chicken then looked at me. "What's wrong?"

He pointed to my tray, and I realized I hadn't touched the food yet. "Just thinking." I took the ketchup, poured some on my fries and watched it ooze down the pile. "I have a lot of school work to do for tomorrow."

Chim swallowed some juice and nodded. "I have a lot of homework, too," then he looked through the kitchen towards the living room, "but it's hard to think of it tonight. You know what I mean, Scout?"

"I certainly do. Maybe you want to visit Aunt Mary and Uncle Joe tonight. What do you think?"

Chim started shifting around in his seat. "And I don't have to do homework?"

I swallowed a fry, feeling the ketchup glide the small lumps down my throat. "Not tonight. I'll write a note for your teacher."

Chim jumped out of his chair and galloped around the table, yelling, "Yippee!"

I laughed and felt myself begin long, deliberate breaths. Chim would be cared for and I could tend to matters at hand. Susan had to be safeguarded; that was number one. Then I had to find Kurt and make sure he never hurt her again.

It wasn't going to be easy. Susan wouldn't let me close, and Kurt could be anywhere and well disguised. I had no plan and no help. All I had was the mission.

Joe's face flashed in my mind saying, *You're point, Scout. Read the signs and trust your instincts. That's how you save her.*

His vision made me suddenly nervous. *But Joe, I couldn't save you. What if I can't save her?*

I was desperate for Joe's response, but then he vanished and the only sounds were from Chim's chewing and his hums to the tune of "Batman."

I stared out of the window, thinking, *Whatever is out there, I'll be out there, too.*

~ Chapter 17 ~

The Mission

I returned to the empty apartment at 8:30 p.m., anxious to start. The call I had rehearsed in the car had to be placed now.

I dialed Cincinnati information. "Kurt Grayson, please."

An operator responded. "The only listing for a Kurt Grayson is at 15 Grove Street, phone number 513-532-8965."

I quickly wrote it on my pad. "That's the one. Thank you very much."

"You're very welcome, sir." There was a click and the phone went silent.

I pressed the button for a tone and dialed the numbers. It rang, once, twice, three times. Please, Kurt, pick up the damned phone. It rang again, and then again. The phone started to slip within my hold. I squeezed tighter and muttered to myself, "Be home, you bastard. Don't tell me you're already in Columbus!" The next ring was cut short. I held my breath for what had to be a ten-second pause.

Finally a voice, medium-deep male with a nasal edge. "Hello." The word was stated as a fact, not a question.

I swallowed, lubricating my throat so it resonated the way I practiced, warm and smooth as whipped cream melting on apple pie. I spread my hand on my chest and began. "Good evening, sir. I hope you all are enjoying your evening."

A five second pause, then a sharp, "Who's this?"

"Sir, I'm calling from Greyhound bus, and we have some questions we'd like you to answer about your travel habits to help us improve our future service."

There was the clink of a cup placed in a sink. "Where did you get my name?"

My throat tightened, and I stroked it with my fingers. "Sir, your name was right up there on our passenger list. And you have my promise, this will only take a few moments of your precious time."

His response was immediate. "You have one minute. Make it fast."

I had to make the most of my time and went right into the heart of it. "Very well, sir. Can you tell me which bus routes you use and how often you use them?"

There was a momentary rush of water that stopped as fast as it started. "To Columbus about once a week."

Bulls-eye, that's what I wanted to know. He was the one Susan had seen. "And the nature of your trips, are they for personal reasons or for business?"

There was the flick of a lighter and then the blow of smoke. "Business. My boss hands me a round-trip ticket and I go."

I had the urge to yell that he'd better never set foot in Columbus again, but knew I had to keep this going. "And the nature of the business?"

He inhaled deeply and his voice became fainter. "Client meetings. We distribute plumbing supplies to wholesalers." He exhaled hard, then, "One minute, time's up."

There was one more I had to ask and talked fast. "Oh dear, just one more question, I promise. For our statistical graphs we need to know your marital status. Are you single, married, divorced or separated?"

There was a long silence and I feared he'd already gone. "Sir, you still there?"

More silence, but then a heavy breathing, fast like panting. "Sir…"

"Who the hell are you?" His voice exploded, making me unexpectedly lean backward. I pressed against the wall to keep balance.

"I told you, sir, we're…"

His end slammed and I clutched the phone to my chest. If only I'd had the chance to ask the last two questions, specifically, do you ever drive yourself to Columbus instead of using the bus, and, when are you planning your next trip and by which means will you travel? I knew he wouldn't have told me if he was planning to drive in tonight to kidnap Susan, but I would know if he had a car and other information might slip, like the type of car, or a contact's name or a favorite restaurant, something. He had said he was busy at that moment and I feared what that could mean. It would fit with how furious he was at the marriage question.

I slammed my end of the phone down, upset that there was still an important piece missing. I wanted to call back and say I was doing a survey for the local TV stations who wanted to know if he had seen the news segment on citizen reactions to the Vietnam Airlift and which station he had watched. I'd do it myself except if he heard any similarity in the second voice, he'd know I was on to him. I already made him suspicious with my last question.

Maybe Billy could do it? I stared at the phone considering it, but no, he'd start yelling and blow everything. I needed someone cool and collected, like Wesley. My eyes shut and my fingers squeezed the top of my nose. Could I ask him?

I grasped the phone, keeping a finger on the button to stop the dial tone. Would someone who was willing to help the brothers beat me up do this for me? But on the other hand, he did keep Moustafa from killing me, though that meant I owed him; he didn't owe me. I slammed my shoulder into the wall and screamed, "Susan! This is about Susan!"

I began dialing, feeling my shoulder throb where it had hit the wall and continue to throb twice for every ring, as if echoing my impatience.

At last there was a gruff, "Who's this?"

I expected to hear the baby screaming, but it was quiet, only faint music that could have been from a TV. "Wesley, it's me again, Scout."

"Imagine that. Twice in one night." Wesley stopped to let out a long breath. "What's the matter, my man, the airlift got you that homesick for Nam?"

I rubbed at the throb in my shoulder. "No, makes me even more sorry I was ever there."

Wesley chuckled. "You got that right."

An ambulance siren went by and I could see enough of the flash to know it was not going in the direction of the VA hospital. "No, Wesley, the problems I got are right here at home."

"Okay, my man, from the forty-fourth squad," Wesley enunciated each word as if it had a sharp beginning and end, "tell me what's on your mind."

I pressed the phone closer in on my ear. "I need to ask you a favor."

"Favor?" There was a slam at his end, like he hit or kicked something. "Are you calling for money, 'cause I is flat broke!"

"No, not money," I spoke fast, hoping he wouldn't hang up. "It's my girlfriend. Her husband, I mean ex-husband, is out to kill her. That's why she ran off to Nam to be a nurse and get away from him. He hasn't been able to find her since, except now I think he found her. She was shown on the five o'clock news when they interviewed the vets from the VA hospital where she works."

Wesley whistled. "Damn. Talk about bad news bringing on more bad news. You meet her in Nam?"

I flashed back to her first smile. "Yes, the field hospital from when Moustafa stabbed me." This was the wrong time to talk about that, but Wesley's five-second pause let me know it still affected him, too.

"What's her name?"

"Susan." My voice unexpectedly cracked at saying her name. I rubbed my hand down my face before going on. "She healed me, man. Her smile and her care is what did it."

"Ain't that beautiful." Wesley's voice had a musical lilt. "Me, I had Cynthia when I got hit. I'll never forget her smile, sweet enough to make a man jump out of bed and start dancing, no matter what his bandages held."

I nodded, though he couldn't see me. "So you know why I've got to do what I can to protect this nurse?"

There was a cry from the baby then it stopped. "Is that what you called to ask?"

I had to talk fast before the baby cried again. "No, I want you to call her ex-husband and ask him two questions about the news tonight, so I know if he saw her and knows where she works."

"Damn, Scout." There was a slapping sound, like Wesley hit his leg, "You've got to pick easier women. Their only problem is supposed to be pleasing you."

I was uncomfortable with how he said that, like I should trade Susan in for another model. "Listen, Wesley, it didn't sound like your woman was too hot on pleasing you."

"You bad mouthing my woman?" Wesley's voice boomed through the phone. "You got some nerve, calling out of the blue like we was good buddies, which we wasn't, then wanting me to do you a favor, and now giving lip to my lady. I got a notion to slam the phone down right now."

I gripped the phone with both hands and squeezed. "Wesley, no, please. I didn't mean it like that. I'm sure she's the finest lady in Cincinnati."

Wesley cleared his throat with a cough. "You got that right, the finest and the hottest. Something the likes of you couldn't get close enough to handle."

I smiled to myself, thinking no amount of shrapnel in the world could change Wesley. "You're right, man. She's lucky there's you in this world."

Wesley laughed. "Damn lucky. Poor thing almost lost out to the thirteenth valley."

I slid against the wall down to a sitting position. "She's lucky there was a Cynthia."

It went quiet for a moment then I heard a match strike and Wesley inhale. "You know, Scout, there's something about you." He blew out the smoke in one quick rush. "You always end up in the middle of a mess that you ain't no good at cleaning up yourself. So don't think this is for you 'cause it's for your sweet, smiling nurse from Nam. I don't want you messing up her life any more than you already have."

My head leaned back against the wall. "Wesley, you're a sport."

"Just give me the lucky man's name so I can charm him with my down home personality."

I grabbed the piece of paper and jabbed my finger next to the name. "Kurt Grayson, 513-532-8965, address 15 Grove Street, Cincinnati."

"Aha, Sin City. One of us locals, but the bad seed kind." The loud scratches from Wesley's pencil sounded like he was writing on a brown paper bag. "What do you want me to ask?"

"Tell him you're doing a survey for WCPO Channel 9 on which news stations people watch. You want to know which channel he watched tonight at five o'clock."

The scratches on Wesley's paper stopped. "Why don't you call him yourself?"

I shifted the phone to the other ear. "I did, fifteen minutes ago, saying I was from Greyhound because I had to find out if he was the man Susan saw at the bus terminal. Turns out he was. But if I call back, he'll recognize my voice and know he's being watched."

Wesley blew out another rush of air. "Let me get this straight. You called him with questions from Greyhound. Now you want me to call him with questions from WCPO. Don't you think two calls like that on the same night will be suspicious?"

I brushed my hand back through my hair. "Maybe, but I have to know if he saw her."

Another siren went by, this time towards the hospital. "Scout, with you on point, it's amazing any of us came out alive."

I grabbed the back of my neck and squeezed. "I guess once in a while I caught the right sign. Listen, I'll call you back in ten minutes to find out what he said."

"Ten minutes, that's serious! Why so fast?"

I pictured Kurt on his way to the hospital and the moisture under my arms chilled. "Serious is the operative word here. This man could already be on her path. Do it now. The ladies in your bed will have to wait a little longer."

I imagined the grin on Wesley's face, as he said, "Poor things had to wait a full year for me, and now it's ten minutes more. They will never get a break."

I checked my watch, 9:15. "Call you later. And Wesley, good luck."

Wesley tapped on the phone. "Hey, luck I don't need. What I need is cold hard cash in piles of hundreds. You got that Scout from the forty-fourth squad?"

I placed my finger on the button. "Roger and out." I broke the connection and felt several drips of sweat down my sides. I pressed into them with my shirt and the cool dampness spread across my skin. It soothed my overheated body, but at the same time, the wave of nausea returned that I had felt after my incident with Susan. I couldn't lose her, and I absolutely had to keep her safe.

I headed for my closet and pulled out the green duffel that had become buried under a pile of no longer used textbooks. Its camouflage colors seemed to warn that the contents were only benign as long as they remained untouched. I stared at the bag for a moment then pulled impatiently at its zipper. The opening separated slowly, as if trying to remain in darkness. But I didn't have time to give proper homage to the memories it kept enclosed.

I dumped its contents on the floor and stared at the disordered heap, stuffing the snare, waterproof matches, and a small vial of Darvons in my pocket. I paused for a moment to admire the survival knife, then grabbed its handle and slipped it into the back of my pants, with the guard resting on my belt. The one thing I didn't grab immediately, was the 28-caliber revolver. I'd purchased it soon after hearing the details of Kurt's assaults. His brutality warranted a gun in case he ever showed, though if Susan knew I had it in the house, she'd be furious. I grasped the metal handle, a cold reminder of my previous kills which, unfortunately, never go away. I liked to believe that I would never kill again, but once you accept that you can, that realization stays with you. I checked the safety and set it securely in my jacket's inside pocket.

I heaped the rest of the stuff back in the bag, the uniforms, cards, letters, water purification tablets, last can of c-rats and first-aid kit. It didn't fit in the closet the same as it had before, but I left it and rushed back to the phone.

The dial seemed extra slow and I tried to force each number back to position to start to the next number sooner. The rings were also slow, one, two, three, four. Finally it was picked up and I spoke without waiting. "Wesley, you there?"

"I'm still here. Where you think I'd be?"

My hand pulsed into the receiver. "What did you find out?"

"It went down like this," began Wesley, taking his time. "I gave him a whole work up about being from WCPO and how we're double checking the Nielson ratings for tonight because we think they've been inaccurate. I used my executive-type vocabulary, guaranteed to impress even the upper echelons."

I began flexing my arm to the pulse in my hand, wishing he would get to the point. "No one's better with words than you."

"Yes, that is so." Wesley's answer seemed unbearably slow. I began to flex the other arm along with the first. "I asked him what channel news did he watch at five o'clock, and I swear to you, Scout, I asked in my nicest, politest way."

I kept both arms flexed tight. "What happened?"

"The dude attacked me, man!" Wesley's voice boomed. "He began screaming. *'Who are you, and why are you bothering me?'* like I was some sort of deranged maniac. I tried to reassure him that I was totally legitimate and that we were randomly calling three thousand people in the Cincinnati area and his name just happened to be picked. Then I asked him again, keeping myself cool and collected, which news channel he had watched. And he went even crazier this time. He started accusing me of bugging his house and tapping his phone and how he was going to have me arrested for invading his right to privacy and that I should call off the federal pigs that were spying on him. I'm telling you, Scout, I felt like he was in some hidden fox hole, taking pot shots at my head."

My flexed muscles began throbbing. "Sounds like he has a lot to hide."

"Damn." Wesley let the word linger for at least five seconds. "This dude is totally wrong, dodging my charms like they were serrated bullets."

The throbbing in my arms intensified. "He sounds paranoid enough to have an arsenal."

I heard Wesley slap his leg. "Paranoid if you's Dr. Freud. To me he's a one-man war ready for D-Day. This guy is a too tight time bomb. One backfire from a truck and he'll blow away a whole block. He's not the kind you can bust in on alone."

I squeezed my hand into a fist. "You know anyone who would watch my back?"

"Oh, no," Wesley gave a nervous laugh. "I already saved your life once."

I almost asked why, but then switched to, "I meant to thank you for that."

"Thanks is for regular folks. You, Scout, are such a damned fool I didn't have the heart to let you go down. But that's not a habit you can count on, you hear me?"

"I hear you, but…"

"Don't but me, man. This cat is bad—destructo kind of bad, not the kind to mess with, comprendo? Now tell me you've grown some sense in that head of yours since I last saw you and you're not going after him."

I leaned back into the wall, feeling my shoulders hit harder than expected. "Not if I can help it. My guess is he'll come here, to the VA hospital. I know the place and it's public, should be to my advantage."

"Nope, you definitely ain't learned a thing. You still the fool, Scout, takin' on what's too big for you. At least tell me you got help up there."

My shoulder twitched and I rubbed it against the wall. "Only one I know here is Billy and he's in a chair."

There was a pause. "The dude's got an ugly mouth and a mean heart, but he could be useful. Damn, he's probably got a nuclear warhead hidden in that chair."

I slid down the wall to a squatting position. "Don't want that kind of help."

"Scout, you listen up." Wesley drilled like a sergeant. "You call him. You is in over your head and don't even know it. And if you hit trouble down this end, you call me, much as I know I'll regret this."

"Thanks…" I began.

"I told you!" Wesley interrupted. "Thanks is for normal people. You a fool, a lucky one at that."

I bounced up and down on my ankles, letting my back rub along the wall. "I hear you and you can tell your ladies their wait is over."

"They are eminently grateful, my fool." The phone clicked.

It was 9:30 p.m. Wesley had spoken to Kurt at 9:15. It would take Kurt at least an hour to drive to Columbus. His explosive reaction to the question of which news show he watched left no doubt he had seen Susan. And I had to assume the phone calls had made him suspicious. They could also make him more cautious, not go right for her but observe from a distance, learn her schedules and wait till he knew she was alone. My legs charged from one end of the room to the other. But no, he wanted her tonight. I knew it.

I started for the door when the phone rang. I checked the clock, 9:35. What if it was Susan or Wesley or Chim? I had to answer it. "Hello?"

"Scout."

I was immediately sorry I had answered. "What do you want, Billy?"

"You speak to Wesley and Leon about the sarge?"

I turned my wrist and watched the seconds hand tick to each dot. "I spoke to Wesley. He's not interested."

Billy's chair made a sudden squeal against his wooden floor. "Traitor! After the sarge looks out for his ass in that freakin' jungle, he won't do something for him."

"Wesley doesn't see it like that." I wanted to add that I didn't either, but now wasn't the time.

I heard the clunk of his brakes. "What's wrong with that bastard?"

I almost said that Wesley had nicer things to say about him, but didn't want to get into tonight's situation. "He has his reasons. Forget about him."

Billy muttered under his breath, then asked, "When you calling Leon?"

The watch passed the thirty second mark. I had to get off the phone. "Tomorrow. Look, I gotta go."

"Wait a…"

I hung up the receiver and left before he could call back. There was no time to think about Billy. All my thoughts had to go on Susan. I would stop for flowers on my way. That would ease her anger at seeing me. I'd even get a card that said, "I'm sorry."

I pulled into an empty parking space in front of the hospital at 10:34. Lights shown through the glass doors, illuminating a small area of sidewalk. Most of the upper windows were dark, but a few still had light. I checked the second floor, seeing only one lit room. A shadowy movement passed inside that window and I immediately feared it was Susan and someone was watching. I scanned the street, though no one was obvious. I stared back up at that window in time to see its lights dim, blending in with the rest of the building. I hoped Susan was inside at the nurse's station, far from any windows.

No one entered or left the hospital for the next hour, though that wasn't unusual since visiting hours were long past and the next change of shift was midnight. I turned on the radio and heard the Rolling Stones in the middle of "I Can't Get No Satisfaction." I mumbled along with them, worried about the lack of satisfaction by Susan from me. The song ended and the Beatles began singing, "Let It Be." Without planning, I changed the words to, "Yes, I find myself in times of trouble, wishing Susan would come to me, singing that her forgiveness, let it be." I slumped lower in my seat, hid my face in my hands, then realized I wasn't keeping watch and abruptly scanned the street. No one was in sight and I switched the station to an excited voice that proclaimed, "Jackson misses the basket and the Boston Celtics now have possession of the ball!" I left it on the game, letting the chatter fill the empty space in the car, though I didn't care who won.

A man approached from the bus stop on the next block and entered the front doors of the hospital. I checked my watch, 11:45. A few cars pulled into the lot on the side. I strained my neck to see them as they entered a side door. Three out of five were in hospital greens and I recognized the two who weren't. One thing I knew was none had on silver tipped cowboy boots or a red baseball hat.

I watched the door for Susan, grabbed the bouquet of daisies and took a position by the front door. Having her favorite flowers and my plan to say I'm sorry made me hopeful she wouldn't complain about my wanting to pick her up and escort her home. She might even tuck her hand in my arm, lean close and kiss me on the neck as we walked the few steps to the car.

People exited the doors, most nodding to me, having seen me several times before. Susan didn't appear yet and I shifted my weight back and forth from one foot to the other, over and over again. It seemed like an hour had gone by, but my watch read only ten after twelve. I knew Susan didn't leave until she had all the charts filled in and the new shift informed of changing medical conditions. The last car pulled out of the lot, and still no Susan.

I'd had enough waiting. I entered the staircase I knew Susan used instead of the elevator and walked up to the second floor. The only person in sight was a nurse's aide I had met a few times named George.

He smiled at me and then pointed to the staircase door I'd just used. "Didn't she leave? I could swear I saw her…"

My chest began to pound. "Where?"

George rubbed the side of his cheek. "She was beat. I never saw her look that worn out. She had waved to me, like she does, when the light went on in 226. She said she'd see what the old ranger wanted and split. But that was ten minutes ago. I thought…"

I ran towards 226, my chest thumping too loud in my ears to hear anything more from George. The room was dim and I turned on the light. Two of the three patients stared back at me from their fully reclined positions.

I grasped the pole at the foot of the first bed. "Is the nurse here?"

The wounded soldier raised his arm, revealing a ball-shaped bandage where his hand once had been. "She went to fetch Rusty his pain pills, but she sure takin' her time."

A barely audible voice from the corner gasped, "Tell her I still waiting."

I pushed against the pole and darted for the door, muttering, "I'll tell her," though I doubt anyone heard it. All that concerned me was finding Susan. I stared down the empty hallway of closed doors, anxious that Susan could be in trouble behind any one of them. Then a fire exit sign caught my eye and I charged right for it. The slammed door echoed as I listened intently for any other sounds. I heard none but did sense a shrill, silent scream. My fists began pumping in tighter and tighter squeezes and my eyes scrutinized the walls, steps, ceiling, light fixtures, vents and crevices for traces of Susan. I rushed down the stairs, seeing a cracked Styrofoam cup, a broken plastic fork, then a shoe, Susan's shoe, white with a green lace she had left in since Christmas. The lone shoe lay on its side by the bottom step, next to a crumpled rag. I picked up the discarded cloth and put it by my nose, feeling my nostrils hit with the harsh sweetness of chloroform. I immediately threw it down, coughing violently against its traces that entered my throat. It was then that I noticed the dots of red splattered on the shoe's pristine leather.

My head seemed to explode with fear as I screamed, "Susan!" I ran faster down the stairs, feeling a strong pulse behind my eyes and ears, as if they were sending and receiving any signal that could be Susan. My mind raced with images of Kurt overpowering her, dragging her into this staircase with Susan fighting back when he smacked her and made her bleed. She struggled more, tried to kick him and lost her shoe. But by then he had her in a tight hold and slapped the chloroform on her face, knocking her out and carrying her away.

My arms throbbed and a siren seemed to wail inside of me, warning of fierce danger. I pictured trying to rip Kurt apart with my bare hands, though he had a hatchet he kept swinging at my head. I imagined ducking his blows as I rushed out through the door that led to a back area with several big dumpsters. Why hadn't I thought of this spot when I was watching? And why didn't I listen to Wesley about not doing this alone? Billy could have watched this area. It was an inexcusable mistake.

A rectangular fence enclosed this cemented area. The dull light of the street lamps revealed stacks of crates by the dumpsters, and near them, a stack was pushed against the fence.

I ran up those crates, over the fence, and down to the side street of the hospital. The street was deserted as I began screaming, "Susan, where are you? Answer me, Susan!"

There were no signs of her or her clothing or of trash cans knocked over, but then I saw a few drops of blood by an empty space at the curb.

I began breathing hard gulps of air, feeling my insides swell from the pressure. I had to get her back before he hurt her any more, and even worse, before he killed her! I considered contacting the police, but they would delay me with a lot of questions and I had no evidence it was him to offer. This was up to me and I had to do it right.

I pulled at the door to the phone booth next to my car and pressed in Wesley's number.

It rang three times and was picked up abruptly. "Don't y'all look at clocks before you call?" It was the same woman who had answered the first time.

"Sorry, but I must speak to Wesley. It's Scout."

"Who?"

It was clear she wanted more information, but I didn't have time. "Please, he knows who I am. This is an emergency."

I tapped my fingers on the glass as I heard her say, "Some fool in a damned hurry. You want it?"

Finally, Wesley's voice, "Scout, that you?"

"Yes, it's me, man. I need your help." I felt myself panting and tried to slow down. "He nabbed her and got her in his car. He must be taking her back to Cincinnati. I need you to watch for him. Wesley, see what you can till I get there. Can you do that?"

"Damn, man. No problem. Be out of here in ten. I'll get Leon to meet me."

Hearing the name Leon made my panting go faster again. I missed him more than everyone next to Joe, and also felt I wronged him more than everyone next to Joe. He broke rank with the other blacks to help me and I hadn't done anything to try to keep him out of the thirteenth valley. Sweat dripped into my mouth from my upper lip as I said, "Leon?"

"Leon from the forty-fourth squad, remember?"

"Of course I remember." I almost said that I didn't think he'd help me, but didn't want to spend time on that. "Look Wesley, you're right about this guy. He's a definite time bomb. He's already made her bleed and knocked her out with chloroform. My guess is one false move and he'll kill her."

"Don't worry. We'll stay back. Look for us in a yellow Malibu. What you driving?"

I glanced towards my car, seeing the missing rear bumper. "A red Maverick. You can't miss it. And one more thing, what's the quickest way to Grove Street?"

I wrote routes, exits, lefts and rights on my hand and we hung up. I was about to leave the booth when I stared at the phone for a moment and dialed Billy.

"Langdon Residence." Johnny Carson's voice was in the background and then a laugh track.

I squeezed the phone. "Billy, it's Scout. I need your help, man. Susan's been kidnaped by her husband. Can you be ready in five minutes?"

"What?" His scream made me hold out the phone.

I put the mouthpiece back to my lips. "Billy, if you're coming, be downstairs. I'll tell you everything in the car. Oh, and Billy, if you have a gun, bring it."

There was a quick, "I'll be ready," then the phone clicked off.

I rushed into my car, pulled out as fast as I could, and sped down the streets to Billy's, thinking only one thing. This mission was the most important one of my life and I had already screwed up unforgivably. There was no more room for even one mistake!

I reached Billy's house at 12:32 a.m. He was already outside, waiting in his chair with his hand over a jacket pocket. He didn't usually sit that way, so it had to be a gun. I touched my own pocket to make sure I still had mine and left the car to help him into the passenger seat, slipping his chair in the back.

I started towards interstate seventy-one. "It's been a long night and going to get longer," I began, and explained the whole story.

Billy patted his hand on his pocket. "That bastard. I'm going to kill him."

My chest started throbbing. I had to keep Billy from doing anything that could get Susan killed. "No, you're going to watch my back and the places I can't see. We have to work this as a team."

"Teamwork." Billy stretched taller in his seat. "I watch your back, see him, kill him. You carry the fair maiden out in your Prince Charming arms."

I squeezed both hands on the wheel. "Look, Billy, I would like to see him dead as much as you, but this is not about going to jail for murder. This is about getting Susan out safely and only using the gun for self defense and to keep her alive."

Billy's slaps on his stumps made deep thuds. "Jail ain't any worse than a chair."

I shifted into third gear. "The chair has wheels. Your head makes it jail." I changed lanes, annoyed that all the cars were going too slow and floored the gas pedal, accelerating to almost ninety though the shake in the wheel let me know the car wasn't meant for this speed.

Billy pushed against the door, adjusting himself in the seat. "Why's Wesley helping you when he wouldn't help the sarge?"

I saw a flashing light up ahead and eased off the gas. "Says I'm too much of a fool to let die. Maybe he feels sorry for me."

Billy gave a short, curt laugh. "Sorry, my ass. Those brothers always stuck together like they was better than us."

I approached the next car too fast and slipped into the left lane. "They stuck together because they saw others as prejudiced. But he offered to help cause of Susan, not me. He liked his nurse in Nam. Personally, he can do it for any reason he likes. Now listen up. When we get to the scene, you stay in the car and watch who goes in and out of the house."

Billy slapped the dashboard in front of him. "No way. Put me in my chair so I can move."

A green car passed me on the right and I stepped harder on the gas. "If there's time. I'll make that call when we get there."

I turned the radio on, hearing two men argue about who was better, the Celtics or the Knicks. Billy began arguing back and I was glad he was fighting with them instead of me. I concentrated on maintaining ninety and getting around cars in my way. A sign for the exit Wesley mentioned read one-quarter mile ahead. I slowed down and slipped into the right lane, taking the sharp right curve to a stop sign under a bright street lamp. I glanced at my watch, 1:18 a.m. With any luck Kurt had driven slower, but I doubted it.

I flipped the radio off. "Look for a McDonald's on the corner of Mission Street."

I drove for a few minutes when Billy's arm pointed straight ahead. "There it is. See it?"

"Roger, that's it." I made the right, went straight for three blocks, then another right onto Grove Street. It was dimly lit with parked cars lining both sides. I turned off my lights and rolled without touching the gas. "You look for number fifteen. I'll check for the yellow Malibu."

"Thirty-seven," Billy whispered. "Keep going."

My hands tightened on the wheel as I concentrated on sounds beyond the continuous chirping of crickets. Car engines from nearby streets reverberated with distinct depths while distant sirens wailed from police cars. I feared they were coming closer, that maybe Susan had already been found dead, but at closer scrutiny, their sound was getting further away.

I caught sight of the Malibu parked in front of number twenty-three and pulled alongside on my right. Leon was at the wheel and I stared past Billy into the dark shadow that covered his eyes. I wanted to say, *you did right by me in Nam and I've wanted to thank you for nearly three years,* except the situation at hand was more pressing. Instead, I said, "Thanks for coming. You see anything?"

Leon talked like there had not been any time or distance between us. "He's in there, Scout. Drove straight into that garage twelve minutes ago. No sign of him since. We would've looked in the windows, but in a neighborhood this white, we'd have cops on our backs in a second."

I slapped my hands on the wheel. "Understood. I'll block his driveway and look for a way in.

Wesley grasped Leon's open window. "We'll follow. You on point."

I nodded and then tilted my head towards the passenger seat. "Billy watches the exits."

Wesley grinned at Billy. "Never thought I'd see you again, man. Just remember, we still got pending business."

Billy pointed his finger at Wesley. "Don't bring that up, man. You'll lose."

Their argument annoyed me. I pressed the gas, pulled across Kurt's driveway, and bolted out of the car. My instinct was to break right into the house, but I had to orchestrate this just right. I stationed Billy in a shadowed spot by the back door and instructed Leon and Wesley to stay a close four feet behind me as I scanned the house for ways in.

All the windows were shut, but the back door handle turned. I entered, struck by a putrid stench and the sight of several bulging bags of garbage. A dim light beckoned beyond the kitchen. I rushed towards it, kicking a can I didn't realize was in my path. The can clanked against the stove and I froze, waiting for someone to come for me. But no one did and then I heard a shriek. It was Susan, I knew it.

I pulled the gun from my pocket and began running for the dim light that lit a staircase to a basement. I charged down and saw a ten-foot cinder-block square in the middle of a large, unfinished space.

A man's voice yelled, "You'll never get away from me again, you lousy slut. You're mine, Susie, all mine!"

I grabbed the door and yanked it open, pointing my gun inside a bare cement room. Kurt was swinging a baseball bat. It landed on Susan's arm, knocking her to the floor. Susan's cry exploded through me.

I ran towards her screaming, "Susan!"

But before I reached her side, Kurt appeared in front of me and smacked the bat into my right shoulder. My back slammed down on the floor and my gun skidded across the room. I was stunned for a moment but about to get up when Wesley and Leon jumped over me, headed towards Kurt. I cried out to her again, "Susan!"

A soft crying voice uttered, "Scout, help me!"

My shoulder spasmed with pain as I lifted up in time to see Wesley punch the back of Kurt's head. But instead of Kurt going down, he spun around and screamed, "You're dead. You're all dead!" He swung the bat towards Wesley's head, but Leon grabbed it in mid air.

Wesley shouted, "Leon, watch it. This cat's on speed!"

Leon and Kurt struggled for the bat. I jumped up behind Kurt, wrapped my left arm around his neck and screamed, "Drop it or I'll kill you!"

Kurt kicked his heel back into my groin. The pain pierced through me, causing my arm to loosen. He slipped out of my hold and jumped in the air, kicking both feet into Leon's stomach. Leon fell back, his hands released from the bat. Kurt turned fast and swung the bat at Wesley, who ducked just in time. The bat then came at me as I came at him. I lunged for the floor to avoid the hit and turned to see him raise the bat above Susan's head as he screamed, "Stupid bitch!"

There was a loud crashing sound outside of the room, like someone had thrown a garbage can at a window. We all turned to look, including Kurt, giving me the chance to grab his knees. Except Kurt had already begun bringing the bat down towards Susan's head.

"No!" I screamed. But my shout was overpowered by an explosive shot that splintered the air as if it were shattering glass. The walls of the small room shuddered though Kurt still had the bat aimed for Susan. I pulled on his legs, trying to get him to fall when there was another blast and another and another.

My ears were deafened by the reverberating gunshots and my tongue burned from the acrid taste of gun powder. Next thing I knew, Kurt's body came crashing hard on me. My head banged into the floor and my ribs were so badly crushed, it hurt to breathe.

"Get him off, Scout!" It was Wesley's voice and then Kurt was shoved across me till he fell by my side. I took a quick inhale and immediately began crawling to where Susan had been. I reached out to her, desperate for any signs of life. "Susan!"

My hand grasped her leg, but she didn't react in any way to my touch. No! It can't be! I became frantic that she was dead. I pulled myself across the rough cement floor, reaching for her face, her mouth. I had to know if she was breathing. There was a slight warmth from her lips and I pulled myself up to look in her eyes. But her eyes confused me, they kept moving and wouldn't stay still. No, it wasn't her, it was me. I was seeing blurry. I couldn't bring her into clear focus.

"She's in shock, Scout, that's all." Wesley was crouched over her from the other side.

"What if," I began, but couldn't finish saying *she doesn't come out of it?* I began to shake and couldn't stop.

Wesley turned away from me. "We have to get out of here. I'll carry her, you help Scout."

He lifted Susan in his arms and I saw her head falling back and her legs hanging limp. "Susan!" I was desperate for any response at all, but there was none. My head turned down, seeing Kurt lying on the floor. He wasn't moving or moaning or blinking his opened eyes. "Is he dead?"

Wesley looked down at me. "She got him four times. He's either dead or close to it."

She? Susan shot him? Not Susan, it should have been me or Wesley or Leon. Why her?

Leon slipped his hand under my shoulder and began to lift. "Come on, Scout, nice and easy." I tried to push up with my legs, but they were unsteady and I had to lean heavily on him. He guided me out of that fatal room, following Wesley to the street, dimly lit by the moon and a few tall, dull lights.

Wesley turned to us in the driveway and I reached out to Susan, feeling a cool moistness on her cheek. It seemed a mixture of cold sweat and warm tears as I wiped it away and bent down to kiss her, whispering, "Stay with me, Susan, please."

Billy wheeled himself towards us, calling, "I heard shots and told the people next door to call an ambulance." He stopped next to us and stared into Wesley's arms. "No, don't tell me it was Susan!"

"No, man," Wesley turned his head towards the approaching siren. "It's Kurt. He's the one shot. Susan's beat up, but she should come out okay."

Two uniformed policemen followed by three ambulance technicians came at us. Susan was taken from Wesley's arms by a man in white who asked, "Where is she hurt?"

At the same moment, one policeman took me aside and another took Leon. My eyes were on Susan, watching her through fuzzy vision as he asked, "What happened here?"

They strapped Susan to the gurney while one of them placed a stethoscope on her chest. I pointed towards a basement window. "There's a man shot inside, Kurt Grayson. He was beating the girl. We came to get her away from him, but she ended up shooting him with my gun."

He looked at my hands, then at my pockets. "You bring a gun to kill him?"

"No." I shook my head, but it made me dizzy. I leaned my left shoulder into the house, took a deep breath and looked back at Susan. "I brought the gun to protect the girl."

"She a relative?"

I pressed my head back into the house and squeezed my eyes shut. "My girlfriend."

He touched my arm. "You hurt?"

I gave a short nod. "I can't see right."

He peered closer at my eyes then turned to the others. "Hey, Rudy, come take a look at him. And there's a man shot in the basement."

The two policemen entered the house while Rudy began examining me.

He pressed into a sore area on the back of my head then began leading me towards the ambulance. "This has to be checked by a doc."

Leon rushed over to me. "They taking you?"

I touched the back of my head and winced. "Yes. I got a nasty one back there."

Leon's face was out of focus, but then stabilized as he asked, "Want me to drive your car to the hospital?"

I looked at him, wishing I had a way to thank him not only for Nam, but for tonight and now for this offer. I felt inadequate as I reached into my pocket for my keys and put them in his hand, holding them in place for a minute. "This would have gone really bad without you. I don't know how to thank you. And I definitely don't know how to ask you for one more favor."

Leon's eyebrows arched. "No sweat. Name it."

"I have the sniper's boy, Chim. He's staying with Joe McCormack's parents tonight. Can you tell them Susan and I are all right, but we need them to keep Chim till tomorrow night and I'll call when I can?"

Leon pulled out a pen from his pocket. "Can do. What's the number?"

I told him and he wrote it on his hand.

"Done, soon as I see a phone." He returned the pen to his pocket. "You know, Scout, I think of Joe, times I even wonder what that barbecue he promised us would be like."

I looked into his eyes, seeing them blur together but knowing they were sincere. "Maybe someday we'll have it."

Leon shook his head. "I believe that promise is buried. Now you go take care of your head and that girl of yours."

Leon went towards Wesley and I was put in the back of the ambulance, opposite Susan. Rudy came in closing the doors behind him. The siren turned on and we were on our way.

I watched Susan's unchanging expression through my blurry vision, whispering as if I were right next to her, "He'll never hurt you again, Susan. You're free. No more Kurt. This is it. It's over. You hear me?"

Rudy checked her pulse and I said louder, "How bad is she?"

"Not that bad." He let go of Susan's wrist. "Her vitals are stable but they're weak."

I couldn't gauge what that meant. "How long before she'll speak?"

"Hard to say." He wrapped a blood pressure cuff on Susan's arm. "A day, maybe a week."

I watched the cuff expand with air and wondered if Susan felt it. "She will come out of it, right?"

Rudy paused while he let the air escape then looked at me. "The doctors at the hospital will know more. I'm not qualified to answer that. But if you want, you can talk to her. I've heard doctors say it could help."

He moved towards the cab of the ambulance and talked through an intercom to the driver. I reached out for Susan's hand, grasping her drooped fingers within mine. "Susan, don't stay away from me like this. I can't go ahead without you. You have to hear me. Kurt's gone. You don't have to fear him anymore. We can have such a great life together, you, me and Chim. Chim needs you, too. Don't forget that. Please, come out of this and speak to me. I would give anything to hear your voice again, Susan, please!"

At that moment the ambulance came to an abrupt halt and the doors flew open. The ambulance people and a man in hospital greens began pulling on Susan's gurney. My vision was still blurred but my thoughts suddenly cleared. There it was, as if it lifted out of a thick haze. I could see everything Susan would have to go through, not just in the hospital but with the police, the courts, the people at work and with anyone and everyone she knew, but especially with herself. It was then I knew what I should have said to her. I had to get another chance. It could mean the difference between her choosing life or, the unthinkable.

I pushed my way out of the ambulance and held onto her gurney, but Rudy took me by the arm and tried to lead me away.

I shrugged off his hold. "Keep me with her. There's more she must know!"

The man in green spoke directly to Rudy. "Get him into exam three. He's unsteady. He'll get hurt."

Rudy released my hold on the gurney, and it rushed away from us down a hall. "She'll be close by. Don't worry. They'll keep you informed." I watched her get farther and farther away, realizing my vision was clearing. Most of the blurriness were gone except for some haze around the edges. I took note of the no smoking sign and the exit numbers and the directional arrows, making sure I knew her exact path. They pushed her into a room on the left.

I watched for a few moments then turned to Rudy. "Fifteen minutes and I'm going in there."

Rudy led me into room three and sat me on the examination table. "She's in good hands."

"She doesn't understand," I grasped my lower face to steady my gaze. It was clearer, even than a few minutes ago. "She doesn't know what it's doing to her!"

"She's not going anywhere. You'll tell her later." Rudy peered out of the room, looked at me, then left.

I was uncomfortably alone. My shoulder throbbed where the bat had struck. My head ached with a raw tenderness where it had hit the floor, and my body trembled with terror for Susan. They could treat her physical wounds, but they hadn't ever crossed the forbidden line to understand how to treat the rest. I had to get to her soon.

~ Chapter 18 ~

Cincinnati Memorial Hospital

Susan had been sent to surgery to repair her right arm. The doctors treated my fractured skull, admitted me to the hospital and gave instructions to the nurse to keep me still. It was now five a.m., Susan should be in recovery. I had to find her.

Halfway down the hall I stopped to rest. My head had been pounding worse with each step, making it increasingly harder to stay steady on my feet. I couldn't continue and leaned against the wall to wait for a more solid stance. My eyes closed and I saw Susan, her eyes flickering opened and shut as if she wasn't sure which way they belonged. I began to tell her what she needed to know, only we became caught in a spinning tunnel and everything went blank.

The next moment I knew, I was back in my bed with a light shining in my eye. There was a deep cough and then a man's raspy voice, "Order restraints from the main desk."

A nurse left the room and I looked up into the doctor's shifting light. "No, no restraints!"

He turned the beam to the side and peered down at me with dark creases across his forehead. "Next time your brain could sustain permanent lesions. I can't take that chance."

The nurse walked in with two leather wrist straps that made me flash to the village girl, with her hands tightly wrenched behind her back. "No! There won't be a next time. I promise!"

"Nurse, get security."

The nurse left and I pushed myself up a few inches on the mattress with my feet. "Please, doc, this won't happen again. Believe me. You think I want to be brain damaged? And those straps, you have to understand, I can't. It goes back to the war. I'll go nuts, please!"

315

He looked down at me, his forehead creases raised higher on one side. The nurse returned with a large man and I inched higher on the mattress. He turned to the nurse. "Never mind. Mr. Belkin promises to do what he's told."

He left and I lay uncomfortably, shutting my eyes and seeing continual replays of what happened in that basement with Kurt. Poor Susan, I don't even know what happened to her before we arrived. And once there, I didn't even protect her. He could have killed her with me right next to him!

The clock finally read eight, the time the main switchboard opened. I called for patient information and learned Susan had just been placed in room 214. I dialed and let it ring twenty-four times without an answer. My shoulder and whole chest began pulsing with sharp pain. If she was still unconscious, how could they leave her alone like that? She could be slipping farther away, and they wouldn't even know it. I had to get to her. I had to talk to her before it was too late.

I slid out of the bed and went for the door, but found the security guard looking back at me from his chair across the hall. I waved at him and smiled. "Had to hit the head."

He nodded and I returned to bed.

A moment later, Billy wheeled in. "Hey, Scout. They fix that crack in your head or is it the same one you had before?"

I touched my head, feeling it thicker with gauze than I expected, and more sensitive than I wanted to accept. "Listen, Billy, you gotta help me. Susan's still under and I have to talk to her and try to bring her back. The longer she's down the worse it gets. My only way out is in your chair, otherwise that security guard has me stuck in this room."

Billy wheeled a few feet back. "Just 'cause you live with a nurse, don't make you a doctor."

"I know that." I scrutinized the grip bars on his wheels. "I have to tell her things she needs to hear. Some doctors say that helps."

Billy shook his head and slapped his armrest. "Damn, Scout, you don't like being stuck. How do you think I feel? This chair's my only way around. You better be back quick."

"Promise!"

I helped Billy into the seat by my bed, taking his jacket and cap from him. I exited the door fast, keeping the guard from getting a glimpse of my face, and wheeled my way to the elevators. One opened and I pushed myself in, turning to press the button for the second floor. It stopped and I immediately headed for 214.

316

I entered the open door finding the first bed empty. Then, lying near the curtained window in the corner, was Susan attached to an IV and a brainwave monitor. She looked unnaturally still, except for the slight movements of breath in her chest.

I lifted her limp arm to my lips and brushed them gently against her skin. "Susan, it's me, Scout. I have something important to tell you, something I wished I had understood and explained a long time ago so you wouldn't have to do this to yourself." I squeezed her hand tighter. "I know what you're thinking. You're afraid of yourself. You're afraid of what you've done and wondering how you could have killed someone when it goes against everything you believe. You're unable to bear the hatred you feel towards yourself for what you were forced to do. That's why you can't wake up."

A few of my tears dripped onto her cheek and I wiped them away gently. "I have that hatred of myself, too. I didn't know what it was before, but I saw it so clearly from watching it happen to you. It haunts, Susan, but sometimes you have to take away another life to live. At the moment we do it, the choice is very clear. But afterwards it gets muddled by what you know others will say, others who did not have to make that choice to stay alive, others who have taught you what to say to yourself. And then you start to think that they're right and you did wrong, 'cause that's what they taught you. You begin to believe you did wrong and punish yourself for the choice you made. But you had to, Susan. Never doubt that, because the instinct to stay alive is much more powerful than what we're taught our morals should be. It's only afterwards, when the self doubt sets in, that makes the choice to live unbearable. You become haunted by your own unforgiving ghosts, and you even begin to wish you had been the one killed instead of the one left alive."

I gazed into her eyes, hoping for a glimmer of recognition, but they continued staring vacantly. I pressed my cheek directly into hers with my lips right on her ear. "Susan, you have to pull out of this. I know how horrible this is for you. You're a healer and you had to destroy a life. I'm a protector and I couldn't protect those kids that haunt me every night. I couldn't protect them, or the laundry kid from wanting to do what he was told was right, though all this time I hated myself because from everything I'd been taught, I couldn't ever accept that a child might have to be killed. It's the same with you. You're a healer and you've been taught only to heal and that there's never an excuse to kill. This one time you had to kill, and even though you knew you had to, once it was done and you realized it, you couldn't accept that in yourself. No one ever let you consider that this might happen one day.

It wasn't allowed to be part of your thinking. But Susan, it happened and you did what you had to do, and now you have to come back to me. Together we can keep each other strong against our self-hating ghosts."

I embraced her whole body in my arms, pressing my ear on her chest to hear her heartbeat. At least that was still pulsing its life story. If only it could say the words, *I'm here, Scout. I understand that it's against life to let yourself die. I'm coming back to you, real soon. Don't worry. I don't hate myself for killing, or you for not killing for me. I love you, Scout. Thank you for being with me and telling me what you did.*

My eyes started getting her gown wet. I lifted my head and began stroking her hair, smoothing its damp strands against her temples, hoping she'd open her eyes any moment.

The side of her cheek flinched beneath my touch. "Susan, is that you?"

Her neck arched and her head rocked back and forth, then her legs kicked and her arm not in a cast flailed, as she shouted, "I don't want to die!"

Her arm slammed into me and I was so thrilled I didn't want to stop it, but I also didn't want her to get hurt. I grasped her arm and held it to my chest. "Right you are, Susan. You don't want to die."

Her eyes twitched open for a moment, then squeezed tight, as if they couldn't bear what they saw. "It's all right, Susan. I know what you're seeing and you did right."

Her lids separated ever so slightly, and my heart began racing. "Susan, can you see me?"

Her eyes opened farther and there was a soft utter as if from far away, "Scout? Is that you?"

My shoulder and head started throbbing, the soreness blending with my excitement. "Yes, Susan, it's me!"

Her chest started heaving hard and then her lips moved. "I heard you calling me," her voice gasped in faint wisps of air. "And I wanted to go to you, but I couldn't find my way. I was like in a maze and each time I turned a corner, I saw Kurt and had to run as fast as I could, and I'd get lost and didn't know where to find you. Then I heard your voice again and it guided me towards a patch of light, and there you were. You brought me back, Scout. I made it back because of you."

She lifted her hand up towards me and I pressed it to my lips, feeling its trembling within the returning warmth. I caressed each finger, wanting to soothe them to stillness, when she whispered, "You saved my life, Scout. That makes me yours forever."

"Only if he'll take better care of you than he has in the past." Wesley's voice boomed from behind me. "She don't need no more trouble. You hear me, Scout?"

I looked up at him, wishing he'd left us alone, though I knew she could be dead if it weren't for him. "I didn't cause this trouble, Wesley."

Wesley laughed. "I'm only fooling with you, my man from the forty-fourth. But you have to admit, you're the first one to jump in when there's trouble."

I felt unjustly accused. "I had to jump in. You saw what was happening."

"Of course you did." Wesley's wide lips pulled into a pursed circle. "But you didn't have to save us."

I thought he meant I hadn't saved them in the basement, they had saved me. "I tried…"

"Tried, man, you saved us. Remember, against Moustafa's revolt?"

I looked at Wesley's serious face and was confused. "But I got Moustafa killed."

Wesley pointed his finger at me. "No, he got himself killed, but the rest of us got saved. That base was primed for a black against white blood bath, and it wouldn't have stopped till every last brother was dead."

I had never even considered that but now things began to fall into place. "Is that why you helped me?"

Wesley sat on the edge of Susan's bed, keeping focused on me. "Damn straight. At first when you plowed in after Moustafa, I thought you was the biggest fool in the world. But when I saw you wasn't out to kill him, just stop him from getting everyone else killed, I realized you is the kind of freedom fighter this world needs. Someone more concerned with saving lives, 'stead of killing a person cause they treat you bad."

I was stunned. "Is that why you kept him from killing me?"

Wesley dropped his hand on his thighs. "I knew it even then."

I was trying to figure what else I had done. "Knew what?"

His hands slid forward and squeezed his knees. "That I'd need you one day."

I sat up straighter but tilted my head to the side. "Need me for what?"

Wesley began showing more teeth. "I didn't know what it was then, but I know it now."

I leaned towards Wesley. "Know what?"

Wesley shifted in his seat. "I got plans for you, Scout. Not now, now's for you and the lady to heal. But I got plans for when the time is right."

"There y'all is." Leon walked in but stopped five feet away and backed against a wall. "Soon as I seen Billy in your room without his chair, I knew you was out on a mission and had to be the girl." I began to stand, but Leon raised his hands to stop me. "No, man, may as well keep to that seat for all the trouble it's caused."

I sat back down, keeping my sights on Leon's shaking head. "What's he doing?"

Leon raised one hand out to the side. "They gots three nurses in there, a security guard and a man in a suit and what I heard is Billy runnin' on 'bout his rights as a citizen and a veteran and this public hospital better give him a chair."

Wesley chuckled. "I wonder who will win that match?"

I slapped my armrest. "Billy. He'll wear them down. They don't stand a chance."

Leon stuffed his hands in his pockets. "He likes to argue. I remember that." His sight then drifted towards Susan. "How's she doing?"

One of Susan's fingers raised in the air. "Not bad." Wesley and Leon both lowered their jaws at the sound of her voice. Susan coughed, then added, "Thanks to the three of you."

Leon tipped his baseball cap towards her. "A pleasure to help a nurse from Nam."

For the first time I noticed his right hand was covered by a glove with two fingers missing and sewn closed. I stared at that space, feeling unbearably responsible. I turned the chair towards him. "Sorry about your hand. My fault they sent you to the valley."

Leon shrugged and gripped his thumb into his pants pocket. "The sarge was the one sent us in that valley, not you. His ass needed covering from that village, not yours."

I regretted not calling him in the past two years as the word "thanks" rushed out of my mouth, finally getting its chance.

Leon's cheeks spread to the side. "No problem."

"So this is where the party is." Joe McCormack entered the room.

Wesley's eyes shifted between Joe and me. "Damn, Scout, your camouflage days are shot. Everyone's finding you."

I stood and shook his hand, then swept my arm towards Leon and Wesley. "Joe McCormack, Senior, father of our friend Joe, I want you to meet Leon and Wesley from the forty-fourth squad."

Wesley stood with hand extended and gave a firm shake. "Your son was a good soul. It's my honor to meet his father."

Leon grasped Joe's hand as soon as it was released. "I liked listenin' to Joe's plans, how he'd have his own business and house and family and barbecues someday. And was no one better on point than Joe."

Joe blinked a few times and swallowed hard. "He wrote that everyone in his squad was up to the tasks and he admired them all. I can see why. I hope we can talk more soon, but unfortunately," he glanced in my direction, "I had better get Scout upstairs before Billy is arrested for disorderly conduct. The nurses are ready to call the police."

Susan's hand rose a few inches. "Joe?"

Joe rushed to her side. "Susan, sweetheart, you're awake! They told me you were still unconscious."

I leaned in next to him. "Only been five minutes that she came out of it."

Wesley edged over to Leon's side. "You two stay with Susan. We'll put a muzzle on Billy."

They slipped out of the room and Susan's gaze went up to Joe. "Chim, does he know?"

Joe shook his head. "We thought it better coming from you."

Her head turned to the side, facing my chest. "How can he understand?"

I stroked her hair. "He's smart. He will."

She began shaking her head. "I taught him to always choose right over wrong, that right was helping people and wrong was hurting people. How do I explain this?"

Joe sat on the bed and grasped his knees. "When a person's life is threatened, staying alive is the only choice."

Susan's fingers touched his arm. "But this is different."

Joe pressed her hand into his arm. "When Joe came back in a bag, I wanted to put a gun to my head, except no matter how strong the pain, I felt I had to stay alive for Mary, only that wasn't the real reason. Truth was, I had too much fight inside. No matter what I had to live with, the will to live was stronger. You had no choice. You had to stay alive."

Susan shook her head with a force that surprised me. "No, you don't understand. I wanted to kill him! I could have shot lower, but I aimed for his heart!"

I grasped her arm and squeezed. "You had to kill him. It was the only way he'd stop. You knew it at that moment. There was no other choice."

Thin, wet lines slipped down her cheeks. "I wanted to kill him, only I never believed I could. And now what?"

I stroked her arm gently. "You are the same wonderful person as before— nurse to the sick, mother to Chim, girlfriend to me." I paused to see her reaction, but her expression didn't change and I went on, "Only now you realize you can be what you most hated your whole life. But it's instincts did it, not what you assume is you."

Her mouth moved without sounds, then a mere whisper. "Am I a," she paused to swallow, "a killer?"

I would have wanted to immediately shake my head but couldn't and had to help her understand what would haunt her too long if I didn't. "Yes, Susan, 'cause you took a life, but only because you had no choice. Killing in your case was right."

Joe tapped on her hand that was still on his arm. "No, my dear, wasn't killing at all, was self defense. And thank God you're alive and he's not."

Her smile at Joe made me almost regret what I'd said, but I knew it was better to recognize the truth of what you have to live with right from the beginning. As far as the dead person is concerned, they were killed, and that's what their memory in your mind believes.

Susan's head tilted towards Joe. "Thank God you're alive, too."

I wished she had said the same to me, but she didn't.

Joe stood and started pushing my chair away from her. "Susan, this talk is over. What you need is rest. I'll be back later to check if there's anything you need. And don't you worry yourself about anything, you hear me? Chim and Mary have a checkers marathon planned for tonight."

Susan smiled and next thing I knew I was pushed out the door.

* * * * *

Unmistakable voices awoke me, though my eyes fought against leaving the laundry kid before I put that extra bullet into him. It had been a deeper sleep than usual, harder to shake out of. Must have been that shot they gave me last night.

"You think they're in the same room, Sol?"

My chest began throbbing as I feared my mother's questions from, *What kind of girl marries a guy like that?* to *Are you sure she's not going to do the same to you?* I already wished they were leaving.

"No, Sylvia. Susan's on two. And remember, it's better he doesn't know."

"Give me a little credit, Sol. I'm not going to mention it."

Sylvia walked in first, a large shopping bag in each hand, her face pinched together like she was in pain at the sight of me. "Lenny, my poor boy, how's that nasty bang on your head?"

Sol walked in behind her and raised one hand towards me.

Sylvia went on. "Tell me, dear, are they giving you enough pain killers? Are you feverish? Would you like another blanket? Oh, and look at these flat pillows. Should I look for a better one?"

Sol began to slip Sylvia's coat off of her arms. "Give the boy a chance to speak."

The wound in the back of my head began throbbing. "I'm fine, Mom. You didn't have to come all this way."

Sylvia's hand waved in the air. "Nonsense. Turn so I can see where it is." I shifted my head.

"Oh my." Sylvia's touch on the bandage made the throbbing worse. "So swollen! When's the last time the doctor saw this?"

I turned back to face them. "He was here last night. It can't be too bad 'cause he said I can go home in a couple of days."

"No, no, no." Sylvia grabbed her pocketbook and opened the top. "I want to talk to him. What's his name?"

The throbbing increased even more. "I don't know, Mom. He's from the hospital. I never saw him before."

"Ach, a doctor with no name. How do you know he's not a quack?" She raised her hands in the air. "Forget it. I'll ask the nurses for your chart." She leaned down into one of the shopping bags. "Here, so you shouldn't get poisoned by the hospital food, your favorite, chicken salad on a Kaiser roll. Your father had to go all the way to Eighty-Sixth Street for the dry ice to keep it cold on the bus."

I took the sandwich, feeling its chilled wrapper slip within my sweaty palms. I realized I was overly warm and was tempted to put it right on my forehead but knew that would upset my mother.

Sol pointed to the sandwich. "Best chicken salad in the world."

Sylvia's hands went on her hips. "So good he gave one away on the bus."

"I had to," Sol's eyes widened. "That man said it looked almost as good as the chicken salad his wife makes. What could I do? I had to show him what the best was. And you know, Sylvia, he did like yours better."

Sylvia smiled, showing her smooth, broad teeth. "You didn't do his wife any favors, you know." Her focus switched to me. "So what are you waiting for, eat before it goes bad."

The familiar wrapping from long ago felt like a package of memories that was too far away to grasp. I put the waxed paper aside and took a big bite, watching my mother's eyebrows arch up higher with each chew. The taste was wonderfully reminiscent of many lunches made especially for my friends and me, but each chew intensified the pain in my head. I brought my teeth together as gently as possible, mashed it as best I could and then managed to swallow enough to speak. "Delicious, Mom. Better than ever."

Sylvia's forehead relaxed and her cheeks bunched up under her eyes. "My Lenny always had a discerning palate. It's that new seasoning Eve began using, complements the celery. Go ahead. Eat some more."

I raised the sandwich to my lips, the aroma tempting, but all I could do was lick at the filling, getting a small hunk on my tongue.

"What's the matter?" Sylvia glanced at the sandwich then back to me. "I thought you liked it."

"I do. You outdid yourself, Mom. It's just my head hurts real bad when I chew. Wish I could eat more."

"That does it. I want you back in Brooklyn. Maimonides has better doctors than this place. Imagine being told you can go home when your head is so bad you can't eat."

I licked at more of the filling, hoping that would calm her down. "My doctor here is fine, Mom, and I won't leave Susan or Chim."

"That poor boy," Sylvia clucked her tongue, "awful how his mother hasn't come for him."

"It's not that she doesn't want to. It's impossible for the Vietnamese to get out." I watched Sylvia's chest rise and lower with a big sigh and knew my other news about Chim was going to cause even bigger trouble. "Chim understands about Hooang. He also knows he has Susan and me."

Sylvia's arms dropped to her sides. "You mean…"

I had to speak before she said something we'd both regret. "I'm planning to adopt him, Mom. His school called me yesterday. In light of the headlines, the Bureau of Child Welfare had called them, questioning Chim's home situation. I knew at that moment that I'm not taking any chances someone will take him away from me."

Sylvia's palms came together in a prayer position. "But he has a mother and father. What if they come for him?"

I shook my head, trying to release the sudden tightness in my throat. "I could never give him up. He's like my own son. He still would be, even if one of them did come."

Sylvia interlocked her fingers and squeezed. "I know you're attached to him, but don't you think his mother will object? He is her son."

"If she comes, she'll have to live with us anyway. She couldn't afford to live anywhere else. We'll just be a larger family."

324

"But, Lenny," Sylvia's hands shot up to her mouth before she lowered them to her breasts and looked directly at me. "You've done a great thing for Chim, giving him a good life. Most people would have been too selfish. And I have to give you credit. You manage to go to college, which I feared you'd never do. But you only get by because of Susan and that may not last. Susan may end up in jail."

"What?" I couldn't believe she had the nerve to say that. "Susan acted in complete self defense!"

Sylvia crossed her arms over her chest. "Accusations are being made. You must be aware..."

"Sylvia!" Sol came to her side and grasped her arm. "You promised."

Sylvia turned to him. "He's the one mentioned the headlines."

I shifted to the edge of the bed. "I meant about Vietnam. What headlines are you talking about?"

"Of Susan." Sylvia pointed to her shopping bag. "Even the *New York Post*, third page, with a picture no less."

I went straight for the bag when Sol rushed to my side and pulled on its other side. "No, Lenny. It's not necessary."

I managed to pull out the newspaper and turned away from them. The headline stared back at me. "Vietnam Nurse Kills Husband with Vet Boyfriend's Gun." I felt like I was going to fall and gripped the bed. The article went on to say, "Decorated Viet Vet, Lenny Belkin, fought with girlfriend Susan Grayson's husband, Kurt Grayson, before she shot her husband four times in the chest with Belkin's gun." There was more but my eyes shifted to the photo under it, of me with an ominous stare, holding my M-16. It was the same photo that had appeared in *Stars & Stripes*. The caption read, "Marine Lenny Belkin received Bronze Star for bravery under fire, caught in plot with girlfriend to kill her husband."

I slammed my hand into the photo. "It's not that way at all! He would have killed her. She had to save herself. They make it sound like we're murderers!"

Sol put his hand on my shoulder. "Your mother and I know it's not true."

"But you know, Lenny," Sylvia moved to Sol's side, "people believe what they read in the papers. That mother with the do-nothing boy next door, said, '*Sorry, Mrs. Belkin. You must be beside yourself with Lenny.*' And that nosy Mr. Goldberg upstairs, with that daughter who dresses like a tramp, came down and said, '*What a shame. Work hard to raise a child and give them everything, and they end up in jail.*' Can you imagine the nerve of him, thinking a child of mine would end up in jail?"

I pictured my mom slamming the door right on Goldberg's face as I asked, "What did Anna say?"

Suddenly all went silent.

The pain started again in my head. "Don't tell me she believes it?"

Sylvia's mouth opened, but she didn't speak.

"What?" For the first time ever I couldn't wait for her to talk.

Sylvia looked at the floor and fidgeted with her hands. "Anna's turned vicious, like she had lessons from Hitler."

Sol shook his head. "Now Sylvia…"

Her eyes shifted to him and narrowed into thin openings. "It's true. About her own flesh and blood she said that's what trained killers do and that's what we get for sending you out to slaughter innocent people."

My fingers cramped around the newspaper as I screamed, "She's wrong!"

"Of course she's wrong. She doesn't know what she's talking about. We know that." Sylvia pulled on the newspaper, but I wouldn't let go. "Lenny, you saw how she's become."

I thought of how her chin jutted at me when I returned. "I know, but most people are like her. They see me as a criminal just for being in Nam, and now this! And poor Susan, now she's going to be put through that, too."

"And what about the boy?" Sylvia pointed down at the headline I still had in my hand. "Don't you think it will be too difficult to care for him during the trial?"

"Trial?" My heart seemed to explode inside my chest, propelling me into a straight up position. "There's no need for a trial. Susan is innocent and I'm innocent and Chim stays with us!"

"But…"

"No buts, he's my son, he stays with me!" I glared into her eyes, then took in a deep breath and let it out slowly before I said, "And he's your grandson if you want to have one."

Sylvia's hands covered her mouth as she spoke through the gaps in her fingers, "My grandson?"

Her eyes became watery and I feared it was from despair. I wished she could understand how wonderful he was and spoke softly. "Your grandson, and you're lucky to have one as great as Chim."

Sol took hold of Sylvia's shoulders and gazed into her face. "He is a bright boy, Syl. Don't you think?"

Sylvia's hands slid down to her chin revealing quivering lips that began to soften. She looked at me, then back at Sol and raised her head taller before she spoke. "Why shouldn't he be bright? Lenny always read to him and explained things to him. You think it's an accident?"

I was surprised by her compliment and decided it was a good time to give her a surprise I'd been holding back. "And guess what, Mom? Chim's already started your grandmother's poem for Mother's Day."

Sylvia's jaw lowered and her eyes widened. "He has? For me?" Tears streamed down her cheeks finding their way into her quivering smile. "You hear that, Sol? My grandson writes poetry to me, his grandmother."

"And one more thing," I pointed to my mother, "he told Joe and Mary that his grandma is the best cook in the whole world."

Sylvia's lips twitched then spread into a broad smile. "Sol, the boy's got discriminating taste, suitable for a Belkin, don't you think?"

Sol rubbed his hands together. "Sounds like a qualified grandson to me. Maybe while we're out here we can take him to the zoo or the movies."

Sylvia clasped her hands under her chin. "And I can take him shopping for those nice striped shirts with the white collars. They would be so handsome on him. There must be a good department store around, even if it is Ohio."

I leaned back on a pillow. "Yes, Mom, there's a Macy's here and a Lazarus department store you might like.

Sol glanced at the shopping bags, then at me. "Where is he now?"

I caught a whiff of the chicken salad sandwich I'd left on the nightstand and realized my head no longer hurt. "At Mary and Joe's. You were there last year when you visited."

Sylvia looked down at her dress and smoothed the skirt with her hands. "Do you think they would mind if we stopped in?"

"Not only would she not mind," I began, suddenly grateful to the offer yesterday just in case they did show up, "Mary was hoping you'd come and said she wants you to stay in her guest room. Joe's coming to visit this afternoon. He can take you back."

"Oh my," Sylvia's voice suddenly lowered a few notes. "That's very thoughtful of her. But tell me, Lenny, how are they doing? I'm so afraid to say the wrong thing in their presence. I feel terrible because of their son."

My wounded shoulder twinged. "They're managing and I think having Chim helps them. But I'm afraid Chim is entering a rough time of his own, something that might make it more difficult for Mary." I took a deep breath then went on. "He was in a fight yesterday at school. Some kid told him he should go back to Vietnam and live with the rest of the gooks who made Americans lose the war and die for nothing."

Sylvia's hand went up to her chest. "How awful!"

My grip squeezed tighter into the newspaper. "They also told him he was a bastard who no one wanted except a couple of murderers. He punched one of those kids in the mouth, except that got him sent to the principal's office and then sent home. Joe told me after he picked him up, Chim cried for two hours before settling down. They're keeping him home from school for a few days till I figure out what to do."

Sol grabbed the bar on the bed and leaned into it. "Is there any way we can help?"

I glanced from Sol to Sylvia seeing their suddenly wilted cheeks and felt my own despair make it almost impossible for me to speak. I fought against the choked feeling in my voice. "Yes, please, make him feel he does belong here and he had nothing to do with killing anyone." I paused to clear my congested throat. "And let him know people will say things that are not true, and he should not let them confuse him. He needs to understand that Susan had to kill Kurt in self-defense and that I was there to keep her from being hurt by Kurt, not because I wanted to kill him. And most important is to tell Chim that he's not a bastard, but has four parents who love him very much and that right now he gets to live with two of them."

Sylvia's hands went up to her cheeks, and it was Sol who spoke. "We'll do that, son. We've always known that everything you do is on the side of what's right, and we see that again today. And what you did for Susan, and what Susan did, was right and had to be done."

The moment I heard those words I realized he'd been trying to explain his confidence in me when I first came back from Vietnam, but I hadn't understood because all I could feel was hatred and disgust from others since that's what I felt for myself.

I blinked back tears. "I appreciate that, Dad. Now Chim will need to know that, too."

~ Chapter 12 ~

Coming Home

I was home from the hospital after four days and returned to school the following Monday. My classmates kept farther away than usual, and I had to assume they'd all seen my photo either on the TV news or in the newspapers. They portrayed Susan and me as accomplices in a murder for insurance scheme. Susan, as it turned out, was beneficiary to ten thousand dollars. She wanted no part of it and donated every cent to the Veteran's Hospital, but that information was not in the news. The report on our acquittals was five minutes after the major stories had played and on return from a commercial break. It was fair to assume most people missed it. The newspapers were similar. We were front page when they sensationalized our guilt and only a small headline on the ninth page to state our innocence.

There was one student in my class who asked how I was doing and offered me copies of his notes from the past week. I told him I was much better and gratefully accepted his offer, then was told his brother died in Vietnam and he felt sorry for all vets and what they had to go through. I thanked him, though didn't want his pity. I just wanted to be considered a normal person who had been involved in an incident for which the police determined the killing was self-defense.

The reactions I received from the department store where I worked security were a bit different. The saleswomen couldn't take their eyes off me, though the moment I returned their gaze, they looked away. The other guards patted me on the back, saying, *"That creep deserved to get blasted,"* and, *"Can't let no one mess with your girl,"* and, *"Acquittal, lucky break."* They didn't grasp the desperateness of the situation, but I couldn't expect them to. That part was never mentioned in the news.

That Tuesday I brought Chim back to his school and entered his classroom behind him.

His teacher approached. "Welcome back, Chim." She then looked at me. "And you are?"

I noticed her eyebrows lift. "His father. I would like to speak to the class for a few minutes."

She slipped her smooth hair behind her right ear. "It would be better if we spoke after school…"

"No." I cut her off. "It would be better to speak to the class now."

Her arms crossed in front of her chest. "It's against policy to have unauthorized speakers. The principal…"

I held up my hand. "This will only take five minutes and I'll be done."

Her eyes flashed to the door, then back at me. "Sorry, Mr. Tell, but…"

This time she was interrupted by Chim's shriek. We both turned to see him surrounded by four boys with one saying, "Your people are all murderers and even your white father is a murderer. My dad says if you come near me I should blast you away!"

I wanted to grab that kid and throw him on the floor. Instead, I inhaled deeply, faced the class, and let out a very long, loud whistle. The buzzing voices stopped as I looked as many students in the eyes as possible, then raised my arms and began. "All of you, sit down and look at me. I have something very important to tell you."

The teacher took a few steps towards the door. I feared she was going to go for the principal, but then didn't mind if she did.

I dropped my arms to my sides and looked into the mass of faces focused on me. "Hello, class. As many of you know, I'm Chim's father."

A voice from the back yelled, "We figured that. What we don't know is why you're not in jail."

I stared back at the boy and pointed to my chest. "Because I didn't do anything wrong. And if you listen to what I have to say, you'll find out what's true and what's not true."

The room became absolutely silent, and even Chim looked up at me with his mouth wide opened.

I began rubbing one hand with the other. "All right then, let's begin. I want to tell you about some people you've heard mentioned in the news. Susan, who is Chim's mother, was once married to Kurt, who used to beat her up because he liked to do that. She ran away from him to keep from getting beat up. That worked for a while, but then he found her, knocked her out and brought her home with him to beat her up again. This time he was even madder because she had run away from him, and he told her he wanted to kill her."

A few gasps filled the room.

"Would you want someone to kidnap you, beat you up and try to kill you?"

A strong, unified, "No," came back at me.

I continued. "I went to find her, to keep him from hurting her. Do you think that was a good idea?"

A strong unified, "Yes," came back this time.

"I had a gun with me because I knew how mean Kurt was and he was too strong to stop with a punch. I was going to threaten him with the gun and bring him to the police if I could, but then the gun fell out of my hand. Kurt had a baseball bat in his hands and had started to swing it right for Susan's head. That's when she picked up the gun. Do you think she should have stopped him from smacking her head with a baseball bat?"

Another unified, "Yes."

"The judge also thought she did right to stop him and called it self-defense. Are there any questions about that?"

Hands went up and the teacher took a step towards the class. I motioned to her that I would keep in charge myself.

A child shouted, "What did the police do to stop Kurt?"

I shook my head. "Nothing. Susan told the police about Kurt, but all they did was write on a piece of paper that Kurt is not allowed near her. Kurt didn't care about the piece of paper."

A girl's voice shouted from the corner. "Why did the TV say you killed him for money?"

I smiled, surprised at how much they knew. "The TV reporters didn't wait to find out the whole truth. The money Susan received from Kurt was donated to the Veteran's Hospital. She didn't want any of it for herself."

A boy in the front raised his hand, and I nodded to him. "If you were a gook, you could have murdered him before Kurt swung the bat."

I felt my left knee give way for a moment, then glanced at Chim, whose head had retreated within hunched shoulders. I wanted to wrap my arms around him but knew more importantly, I had to answer that question right. I scrutinized the kid who asked it.

"Did your mother ever tell you that your round eyes make you a good cook?"

The kid shook his head.

I glared at one of the boys who had surrounded Chim. "Did your father ever tell you that your round chin made you a garbage man?

The kid leaned his chest over his desk and yelled, "No, of course not!"

I pointed to the kid who had been Chim's tormentor. "What makes you think that a person's looks makes them a murderer?"

The kid jumped out of his seat. "It's in the news. My father said so."

This time I jabbed my finger in the air towards him. "Does that mean all American-looking people are good? Or are there any bad Americans like Kurt?"

The kid began swinging his arms, like he was at a punching bag.

I pointed to the girl next to him. "Does your mom tell you to be careful of strangers, even if they are American?"

The girl looked down at her hands, then up at me. "My mom says I shouldn't trust any strangers 'cause you can never tell by looks who's good and who's bad."

I looked across the room. "Does anyone else's mother say that?"

Several hands jumped up in the air.

"Does anyone's mother say something different?"

A girl on the side shouted, "My mom says you can't judge a book by its cover."

"Does anyone else agree with that?"

There was a united shout of, "Yes!"

I pointed both hands to my face. "If I looked like a gook, would you say I was a murderer?"

The whole class except the kid swinging his arms shouted, "No!"

"Is there anything else you can say about this?"

The third boy who had surrounded Chim suddenly stood and shook both hands high in the air. I nodded towards him. "Yes, you have something to say?"

The kid fidgeted with his hands as his focus shifted from me to Chim. "I want to apologize to you, Chim, for saying your father should be put in jail. He's a nice man."

There was sudden buzz in the room when the fourth boy stood, and everyone went silent again. "Chim, I shouldn't have called your mom a murderer. I don't mean it anymore."

Six more kids stood to take back what they had said to Chim till finally the kid swinging his arms got up and pointed at him. "Some of you gooks are murderers, but not every one of you."

Chim gave him a quick nod, then raised from his seat and turned to face the whole class. "I have two mothers, one here and one in Vietnam. They both told me not to hurt people and I think they're right, that hurting people and killing is wrong." He glanced towards me, lingering his gaze for a moment, then looked back to the class and added, "Except if someone is trying to kill you."

I walked behind him and squeezed my hands into his shoulders. "Are there any questions on what we talked about today?"

No one spoke. "In that case, it's time for me to leave." I raised a hand to wave. "Goodbye everybody, peace."

There were shouts after me of "Peace" and "Goodbye" and "Come again" as I started for the door, then a few started to clap. I turned to give one more wave when Chim ran to me and threw his arms around my waist. The clapping intensified and one kid began chanting, "Chim, Chim, Chim, Chim." A few others started, then more and more till it was louder than the claps. Chim buried his face in my arm and I could feel him laugh into its muscle. "They understand now," I whispered down to him. "People need help to understand."

* * * * *

Susan's reentry to her usual life brought trouble that wasn't as easy to resolve. She returned home after ten days in the hospital, and at first seemed in relatively good spirits. She was happy to be back in her own home, and I was ecstatic to have her caring presence back in my days and her tender warmth near me through the nights. Mary McCormack came for the first three days, cooking for all of us, doing the shopping, and helping Susan with chores hard to do with one arm in a sling, such as washing dishes, opening canned food and folding laundry.

The fourth day, I had to be home immediately following my morning class to take Susan to see Dr. Barrows, an appointment that had been set at the Veteran's Hospital doctor's insistence. Susan had balked at the idea of seeing a psychiatrist, claiming, "There's no reason for this." But the physician said it was required before he could recommend she return to work.

I held the car door open, extending my hand for her to grasp, though she didn't. Susan settled herself onto the car seat and stared through the window. "I don't know what all the fuss is about. I'm fine. Anyone can see that."

Susan turned on the radio and began singing along to Don McLean's "Bye Bye, Miss American Pie," adding her own harmony to the song's simple tune. I was enjoying her sweet voice when she began to shriek, "Stop the car! Don't get any closer! He's in there. I can feel it!"

I had just turned a corner and there before us was the hospital. It was the first time she'd seen it since that night. I reached across to her and grasped her arm. "It's okay, Susan. Kurt's dead. He can't hurt you."

She screamed even louder, "Stop taking me to him. He'll kill me!"

I was confused by her lack of reason. "Susan, he's dead, remember? You never have to worry about him, again."

"No!" Susan ducked behind the dashboard. "He's there, waiting for me. Can't you feel it!"

I didn't know what to do and turned left at the corner to get the hospital out of sight. "It's all right now, Susan. I'm turning back. We won't go there."

Her whole body was trembling. "It's not all right. He'll stay there, waiting for me, forever if he has to!"

I began to stroke her arm. "He's gone, never to come back. I promise. And don't worry. I'll keep you safe. I'll never let anyone hurt you again."

She yanked her arm away from under my touch. "You can't! You promised before, but it didn't work!"

Sharp pain shot through my shoulder where it had been struck. I wanted to scream but fought hard to keep my voice soft. "You wouldn't let me come to the hospital, remember?"

Susan slammed her hand into the seat. "You were at the hospital!"

My shoulder pulsed, feeling like bullets were trying to burst through the skin. "I was outside in my car, not inside where I should have been."

Susan grasped the top of her hair and squeezed. "You were still there. You should have seen him!"

I slammed on the brakes, forcing an abrupt stop and turned to face her. "I saved you, or don't you remember that?"

A car honked behind us, but her only reaction was to point at me. "You came, but you didn't stop him!"

People screamed at us as they drove by, but Susan's accusations were already sirens in my ears. "You're alive because I was there and I tracked him down!"

Susan turned and glared out of the back windshield. "If you tracked him down, how did he get back in there?"

I thought she was kidding at first, but then she began to shake and I didn't know whether to be hurt by her blame or to pity her irrational state. Several cars behind me began honking their horns. I lifted my foot from the brakes and began going forward. "I'm taking you home. No one's going to force you into that hospital. Lean back. We'll be home in a minute."

Susan continued to sob, her trembling adding to the already rough vibrations of the car.

I drove the last few blocks and was grateful to find a parking spot right in front of our house. I immediately opened my door, wanting to help her out as quickly as possible. But before I reached her side, Susan had already burst out of the car and began running up the steps. She reached the apartment a few moments before me, and when I unlocked the door, she bolted in like she was desperate to breathe its air.

She threw herself onto the couch and began crying into a pillow. I started towards her, hoping we could forget the angry words said in the car and feel the affection we had before we started for the hospital. But as I neared, the phone rang and Susan peered up at it, then at me. I turned back to the phone and picked up the receiver. "Hello?"

"This is Dr. Barrows' office." I cradled the phone into my neck not wanting Susan to hear. "We had a ten-thirty scheduled appointment for Susan Grayson."

"Yes." I covered my mouth with my hand. "She won't be coming. Sorry. She's not feeling well."

"I see. Would she like to reschedule for tomorrow?"

I glanced back at Susan who had one eye focused on me. "No, she won't be coming at all. It's the hospital, she's afraid to go back in."

"Oh, my." There was a pause and a rustling of paper. "Would she prefer to see Dr. Barrows at his office on Chestnut Street? I have a one o'clock today if that's convenient."

I didn't have to be a work till three, but didn't know what to do and glanced in Susan's direction. She now had both eyes on me, glaring like she didn't trust me. I placed my hand over the receiver and spoke across the room. "You want to see Dr. Barrows at his Chestnut Street office?"

She shrugged with one shoulder, letting it remain higher than before.

I uncovered the phone. "Yes, that will be fine. Can you give me the address?"

I wrote it down, hung up and went towards Susan. She raised her sling towards me. "What did they say?"

I stuffed my hands in my pockets. "Another appointment, today at one.

Susan turned and gazed into the blank television screen. I sat next to her and placed my hand on her back, feeling it tense under my touch. She began sobbing into the pillow again and I wondered if she was thinking of what Kurt did to her. My throat tightened and I mumbled, "I'm sorry. I'm so sorry."

Susan's trembling increased. I stroked her back, feeling it stiffen beneath the quivers and wished I could make all her anger at me go away. She sat up, sliding away from my hand, then went to the bathroom. Her sobs through the door hurt me more than Kurt's strike, making me feel helpless and unbearably empty. But it was useless to go to her, she wouldn't let me in.

I turned on the TV and watched *The Price Is Right* for a while, trying to guess what each item cost. The washing machine was five hundred, though I guessed four. And the stereo was three hundred, though I guessed five. It was two commercial breaks later when Susan returned and sat on the couch. She leaned her head straight back onto the overstuffed cushion and turned partially to me. "Scout, would you make me some tea?"

I reached out and tapped her knee, which she didn't move out of my way. "Sure."

I went to the kitchen and made tea and sandwiches for each of us, then set them on the floor in front of the couch. We ate them quietly, watching *I Love Lucy*, laughing out loud at the funny lines, then resuming silence during the rest. Susan dozed off for a while and I covered her with a blanket, letting her rest till it was time to leave for the doctor's office. The car ride itself had a calm stillness. There was no talking, but more importantly, there was no crying or screaming.

I pulled into a parking space and Susan turned to me as she grabbed the door latch. "You mind waiting out here? I should be done in an hour."

My first thought was she wanted to talk about me without my hearing it. I almost protested but then realized the doctor could make her see how much I did help her and raised my economics textbook from the back seat. "I'm two weeks behind in the readings. Doesn't matter where I read it."

Susan went inside a yellow house with small shrubs in front, and I ran my fingers over the book cover, thinking about how much school work I had to do. But instead of opening the book, I found myself staring at a few children across the street. They were maneuvering a large cardboard box with a picture of a refrigerator on the front. I watched them lay it on its side across the sidewalk. All three went in the side opening, with one peeking out every few minutes. If anyone was spotted, they retreated quickly as if the box was a fortress that would protect them from any kind of enemy in the outside world. I found myself wishing I could join them in that box and stay within that fortress for a while.

Susan emerged from the yellow house and settled herself into the car.

I turned to her before starting the engine. "How did it go?"

She crossed her arms in front of her chest and slumped down in her seat. "I need time to think."

I grabbed the keys hanging from the ignition and squeezed. "Think about what?"

Susan raised her shoulders up towards her ears. "I don't want to talk about it."

I felt hurt at being shut out and couldn't bear a trip back in silence. I reached for the radio. "Mind if I listen?"

Susan shook her head then rested her chin on her chest.

I started the engine and turned on the music, hearing Marvin Gaye sing "What's Going On?" and wishing I could get an answer to that question from Susan. I hummed along for a moment then remembered what happened that morning when Susan hummed to the radio. After that, I listened without adding my own voice. The song changed to James Taylor's "You've Got a Friend." It was a song I usually liked, though this time it made me feel uncomfortably alone.

We arrived home and Susan went directly into the bedroom to lie down. I followed her in, watching her head fall back on her pillow, and became disturbed by the strained lines that formed around her mouth. "Susan, I don't feel right leaving you alone. I'm calling in sick."

Susan's hand went right to her forehead. "No, we can't afford any more lost pay. It's been a tiring day is all. Don't worry. Chim will be home soon and he'll help me if I need it."

"But..."

Susan shook her head. "No, I'm fine. Go. Don't miss work, please!"

I left, feeling wrong about it, but knew if I stayed Susan would be annoyed. I called home two hours later at five. Chim answered and said he was doing homework and that Susan was making macaroni and cheese for dinner, that it was his favorite dish and he couldn't wait till it was ready, though he wished she would let him eat ice cream before dinner the way I did. It sounded normal and I relaxed enough to let myself believe all was fine. I went back to work, feeling the day's tension dissipate the way a nightmare's anxiety vanished from being awake for a while.

I returned home at ten-thirty surprised to see Chim still awake and in his school clothes, watching TV alone in the living room. "My, young man, isn't your bedtime nine o'clock?"

Chim didn't move his head from the couch pillow and kept his eyes on the screen. "I'm not tired, and I wanted to stay awake in case Susan starts crying again."

There was a sudden rush of sweat from under my arms. "She was crying?"

Chim nodded, his head rubbing against the pillow. "She's sad because her Aunt Bessie in Virginia is very sick. She might have to go there to take care of her."

I knew her aunt had died several years ago and squeezed my hand tightly inside my jacket pocket. "She told you about Aunt Bessie?"

Commercials started and Chim turned to look at me. "She told me after she received the phone call."

I sat down next to him and placed my hand on his arm. "What phone call?"

Chim's eyes were only half opened. "The one when we were eating dinner. Scout, can I go to Virginia with Susan?"

"What?" I felt like running into Susan and asking what the hell was going on, but needed to stay calm and hear what else Chim had to say. "Why do you want to go to Virginia?"

"You know," Chim paused to yawn, "to take care of Susan. She's still nervous from what happened with Kurt."

It felt like he meant he could take better care of her than I could. Was that what he said or was that my own imagination? I touched his arm and left my fingers there. "Did she ask you to go with her?"

Chim shook his head then rubbed a knuckle into his ear. "But I thought I should, you know, keep her safe."

I dropped to one knee wondering if he saw my failure as so blatant he thought he could do better. "What are you going to do, walk around with a loaded M-16?"

Chim's nose wrinkled. "No, not that! I'll just be with her so she doesn't end up alone, like last time."

Was he blaming me for not being with her when Kurt appeared? Or did he see it as Susan's fault since she insisted I not come? Or was he accusing me of hurting her and making her not want me there? My brain felt like it was being pounded with nails.

Chim pulled on my arm. "Scout, you're not answering. Can I go with Susan?"

I grasped his hand and pressed it hard into my arm. "No! No one's going anywhere. We're all staying here, together!"

Chim glanced at the phone, then back at me. "But Aunt Bessie?"

"If Aunt Bessie needs help, she can come live with us."

Chim filled his cheeks with air then gave a quick release. "You think she'll die?"

I squeezed his arm. "Don't worry about Aunt Bessie. We'll do whatever we have to and make everything fine." I really wished I could say that for Susan and me.

Chim nodded and then yawned, his mouth opening so wide it covered most of his face.

I shook his arm. "Time for bed, big boy. Tomorrow's school." Chim sat up and stretched his arms before starting for his room. I was torn between helping him settle into bed and going straight to Susan to ask what was going on. Chim pulled his pajamas from his drawer and I continued past his door to my own room, entering to see Susan lying on the bed with her eyes closed. I pushed the door against the wall to make noise. She opened her eyes, saw me, then covered her face with her arm.

I stood at the foot of the bed looking down at her angular position. "Who called tonight?"

Susan's lips tightened. "No one."

I sat down to the side of her feet and leaned my hand into the bed. "Chim said it was Aunt Bessie."

Susan brushed her hand through her hair, holding it still on the top of her head. "That's what I told him. I didn't know how else to tell him I have to get away."

"Away?" I grasped both her feet and stroked my thumbs down her soles. "Susan, why?"

She glanced at the window then shifted her gaze to her sling. "I can't face it, Scout. It's too painful."

I placed my chin gently on top of her toes. "You mean you can't face me?"

"Don't think it's just about you. It's everything." She shifted on the bed, her feet moving upwards a few inches, though I continued to hold on. "It's too hard to stay here in Columbus after what happened."

I stared up into her face, but her eyes didn't look back at me. "And you were planning to take Chim and leave me to face it alone?"

She placed her hand on her upper chest and glared at me. "I was not going to take Chim and, for your information, there are things going on that you don't know!"

My back stiffened. "Like what?"

She drew her lips in tight and began shaking her head.

Sweat rushed down my neck. "What things are you talking about?"

Her lips trembled as she tried to speak, and it took an extra moment before she began. "There's a reporter I haven't mentioned to you. He keeps calling and won't drop the story."

My thumbs slid down the sides of her feet. "The story's over. What else is there to write?"

A rush of tears ran down her cheeks. "I wish it was that simple." She wiped her face with her sleeve and went on. "He called the day after I came home from the hospital, asking how I felt, saying that news readers wanted to know. I told him to please not call again, that I didn't want to be in the news anymore." She dropped her hand on the bed and continued. "But he did, three days ago, asking if I had any intentions of marrying soon, now that my husband was killed and out of the way. I was furious and told him not to call again." Her fingers scratched the blanket, then grabbed it and squeezed. "He called back this afternoon," her voice now at a hoarse whisper, "after you left for work, asking how I felt about being let go so easily from all charges. I told him to go to hell and hung up."

My hands throbbed wanting to wrap around this guy's neck. "What paper is he from?"

She raised her hand. "Wait, Scout. There's more." She cleared her throat and wiped her mouth with a tissue before going on. "He called back while Chim and I were having dinner, wanting to know how long ago I had planned this murder and if that's the only reason I went to Vietnam, to find a murderer to do it for me."

"What?" I jolted upright, wishing the reporter was next to me to punch in the face. "Did you get his name?"

Susan's feet jerked and I realized I'd begun to squeeze too hard. "Scout, you want to hear the rest?"

I nodded, then loosened my hands and began massaging her soles, trying to keep calm enough to hear what she had to say.

Susan clutched her hand loosely around her neck and continued. "He then asked me three horrible questions." Her lips sucked into her mouth for a moment before she went on. "First he wanted to know if I was sorry I hadn't picked someone else for the murder."

My gaze jolted straight to her face, expecting to see her tilt her head in a way that would show she wasn't sorry. But her eyes stayed on my hands at her feet and she continued on fast.

"Next he asked if I would dump you since you let me down." She glanced at me for a moment and I hoped for a smile of reassurance, but she quickly turned away to her hands and started fidgeting.

"And the worst one was when he asked how did it feel to have to do it myself?" Her hands squeezed and I could see the whites of her knuckles protruding larger, and then her feet pulled away from under my touch. I felt like I was kicked in the face and jumped up from the bed, desperate for her to look up at me and tell me his questions were all absurd.

She did look back at me, her cheeks puffed close to her nose, but said, "I was crying, Scout. I couldn't control it, and when I put down the phone, Chim asked what was wrong. All I could think to say was Aunt Bessie was sick and needed me to come right away."

I was too hurt to respond to the Aunt Bessie part and turned away to the window, hoping for a clearheaded view of what I was to Susan. But instead, I felt stares coming back at me from the reporter and Anna and all the rest of them out there, looking in and seeing me for what I really am, a killer. I had been trained and used as a killer, attacked and responded as a killer, and planned to protect as a killer. It was expected of me, forever forward. It was mine to do if it was needed. I had no business letting Susan cross into that realm. I had let her down, and I didn't know if I could ever face her again.

I turned to the door, unable to let my eyes meet hers, then ran from the room straight out of the apartment and down the steps. I burst into the night's darkness, rushing onto the street, confused by what was around me, like I was in the midst of a murky, misted jungle. I wanted Joe on point so I could follow and I'd watch his back. I'd watch his back right this time if only I could see him. I reached out ahead of me. "Joe, where are you? Stop moving so I can find you? You there, Joe? Is this where I place my next step, Joe?"

There was a voice that startled me. "You all right, buddy?"

I reached for my rifle only it wasn't there and screamed, "No!"

I watched the tall figure run away and yelled after it, "I need Joe, but Joe's dead. I let him die. It was all my fault. I wasn't a good enough killer. I should have killed them all—the VC, the ARVANs, the laundry kid and Kurt, I shouldn't have let them breathe with life for one second after I saw them, then Joe and Susan would be all right!"

I saw a long strip of darkness to my side and thrust myself into it, collapsing next to two metal cans. I huddled in their shadows, not able to bear being seen. This is where I belonged, hunched in a dim gloom in the midst of unwanted garbage. I grabbed my legs and pulled them tight into my chest and felt uncontrollable tears gush onto my knees. My jaw suddenly dropped down for a scream that wouldn't come and I felt like I was gagging on my own fist, only it wasn't really in there. I began to gasp for inaccessible air when a wail came out like a howl into the night, "Joe, Susan, I'm sorry! Unforgivably sorrrrrrrrrrryyyyyy!"

* * * * *

I returned to the apartment at three a.m., shivering from the chilly air outside. Susan was tightly wound in the blanket with her arm over her face. I lay down in my clothes and shut my eyes, feeling like I'd just come back from hell, or actually that I was still there. I felt myself falling through a tunnel of fire and looked to the bottom seeing a big cauldron of boiling red liquid. The three Vietnamese kids were in it and raised their hands to me, shouting, "Save us, Scout. Get us out of here!" I was falling closer, but if I reached for their hands, I'd go in with them instead of being able to pull them out. I was just about to hit the cauldron when my hand latched onto a hook that was holding the boiling pot in place and I began screaming, "I'm not going in there. You're not going to do this to me!" A siren sounded and I thought it was the cauldron ready to explode when I realized it was my alarm. I reached for the clock, slapped the off button and dropped my head back on the pillow, breathing frantically.

I reached for Susan, longing for the soothing feel of her warmth, but all I felt were cool wrinkles of the sheet. I bolted up from the bed, screaming, "Susan!" I was ready to run to the bus terminal to find her before she left for Virginia when I noticed her by the window. She was like a silhouette of black velvet, staring out into the dark air. I started for her, wanting to wrap my arms around her shoulders.

But as I approached, she abruptly turned to the side. "You can get ready for school. I'll be all right by myself."

I grasped my own shoulders instead of hers. "You leaving?"

She looked back out of the window. "Not today."

I walked up behind her and peered outside through strands of her hair. "Don't leave me, Susan. Anyone ever threatens your life again, I'll kill them immediately. I promise."

She crossed her arms and leaned forward, her lips practically touching the window as she spoke. "I had thought that's what I wanted. I had hoped for that with Kurt."

I watched a patch of fog appear on the window from her breath and longed to touch its warmth. "Susan, I swear to you, I would have done it if he hadn't knocked the gun from my hand. I wish it had been me."

"I know." Her voice was barely audible, like it was meant only for the glass. "That's what I told Dr. Barrows, that we had that understanding, but now I can't rely on you anymore to protect me."

"Susan," my fingertips fell on her back, but she cringed from under their touch.

"And I'm so awfully afraid," her head shook and her hand covered her mouth for a moment. "So afraid I'll be attacked again and left on my own to stop it."

I rubbed my arms as if they were cold. "Susan, I promise, it won't ever happen again, never. Even if you insist I stay away, I won't. Please, trust me."

Her good hand grasped the side of her face, half covering her eye. "It's too late. I can't trust anyone. Dr. Barrows said that all the protection I used to rely on is gone, and my primal instincts have taken control. He said now that they're in charge, I'm going to see everyone as a threat for a long time to come."

I dug my fingers into my arm. "Even me?"

She covered her wounded arm with her good one and leaned the side of her forehead against the window. "Even you. If you get mad enough, you could hurt me. I know that."

The healed wound in my chest seemed to suddenly receive a thousand stabs. "That will never happen again, Susan. I promise!"

Her hand gripped the window then slid down the glass. "Promises are no more than honorable intentions. I once wanted to believe they were a guarantee, but they're not."

The inside of my shoulder throbbed with unbearable pain. "I mean it. I'll be different. Give me another chance."

Her hand fell on her knee and seemed to go limp. "Not everything can be controlled. Not even in yourself."

I stepped closer and leaned into her hair, feeling it graze against my lips. "I would do anything for you, Susan. I love you." I kissed into her soft strands and let it linger for a moment. "Please, don't leave me."

She didn't move or speak and I stared over her head, feeling drawn in by a dark alley across the street. I had the sense that someone was hiding within the blackness, someone like me. A figure emerged, looking like Kurt. I wanted to run for a gun and shoot him when he suddenly switched into me. I slammed my hand into the window frame and shouted, "No, we're nothing alike!"

Susan looked at my hand then peered out of the window. "Nothing like who?"

I looked again seeing no one was there as I spit the name out of my mouth, "Kurt."

"Kurt." Her whisper was emphasized by her hand slapping against the window, her palm remaining flattened on the glass. "I'm a little like him. I wanted him killed all along, and that makes me as bad as him."

"No!" I lightly touched her hand still on the window. "It's not the same. You had cause. He's purposely evil. You're not."

Her hand twitched under mine, like it had a sudden shiver. "Part of me is. Dr. Barrows said most people don't get to meet their killer side, but because I did, if I admit that I have it in me to intentionally hurt others, it will help me stop hating myself. But," she paused, leaning closer into the window, staring down at the sill, "I don't know if I can ever forgive myself for being that way."

I rubbed my fingers on her hand, only she pulled it away and dropped it in her lap. She then turned to look directly up in my eyes and I thought she was going to tell me to never touch her again when she said, "How long did it take you to stop hating yourself after you returned?"

I stepped back as if hit and had no idea how to answer. But her widening eyes made me open my mouth and suddenly words came. "I haven't stopped."

She touched my arm, pressing my hair ever so gently into my skin. "You feel evil?"

A sudden rancid taste made me wish I could spit, but instead I looked back at Susan, swallowing it before speaking. "Yes, I feel evil, but I sure as hell never said it out loud. Who would I tell who could understand?"

Her hand gripped around my once unfeeling arm. "Me?" I stared back at her, watching her eyebrows arch higher as she went on, "I think if you could accept your evil side, then maybe I could accept mine."

My gaze shifted to the floor and my hand clasped over my mouth. But she began stroking my arm and I wanted to keep talking to her. I dropped my hand to my side and looked back at the tight crease above her nose. "I can't ever accept that I was part of killing kids. And every time I look at Chim, I can accept it even less."

She gripped my arm and held tight. "You had no choice. It was life or death, like for me. But in my case it was worse because I hoped for his murder. I prayed for it for years."

My arm pulsed under her touch. "I hoped for his murder, too, but I wish I could change who did it."

Susan looked down at her hand and loosened its grip. "Me, too."

I was suddenly terrified her next words would be she was leaving. I raised my arm to her chin and tilted her face till she was looking straight in my eyes. "Susan, I have something to tell you and I hope you can understand and forgive me." A siren went off in my head, though I knew I was the only one to hear it. "The dead kids were screaming that I was a cold-blooded killer when I pushed you into the wall. I know that's no excuse, but that's what happened. They can never forgive me, I know that. Maybe one day I will be able to forgive myself, especially if we can learn to do that together. But all I can say is, no matter who is screaming in my head, I will never hurt you again, I promise."

A thin stream slipped from the side of one of her eyes. "Is that an honorable intention?"

The sight of her tears dampened the siren in my head to a wavering hum as I tried to keep my voice steady and firm. "No, it's a sealed fact."

Her eyes shut and she grabbed my hand from her face and held it at a distance. I thought that meant we were through and she was about to tell me which day she was leaving. She pulled my hand close to her mouth and began whispering into my fingers. "I hurt you, too. I blamed you for what I had to do myself. That was wrong, but I also want you to know..."

She paused and the siren in my head became loud again. I almost screamed over it, but instead forced my voice into a calm and asked a tender, "What?"

Her thumb began rubbing up and down the center of my palm. "I want you to know I didn't choose you to kill for me. What I wanted was for you to be my protector."

The siren became a deafening wail, but I swallowed hard and forced it to silence as I asked, "Did I do that?"

She pressed my opened hand against her cheek and rubbed her soft skin into my tender palm, "Yes, and with the most honorable of intentions." My hand throbbed as she whispered into it the letters, "L – O – V – E."

~ Chapter 20 ~

May, 1973
Back in the World

I was startled awake by my alarm, but for the first time, I wasn't frantic. The other times it's wakened me I was in the midst of a horrifying nightmare. It was that or else I'd been awake all night and was watching the coral light filter in around the sides of the shades. I slammed my hand on the off button and heard my American history textbook thump on the floor.

"Are you ready for today's test?" Susan's arm draped across my chest and I grasped it, having missed its comfort the past five weeks when it was confined to a sling.

I tried to remember the section I'd reached before falling asleep, but it was vague. "I could still use a couple of hours. Lucky they don't start the finals till nine."

Her body slid closer to mine, momentarily soothing my constant fear she might leave. "Scout, no one studies more than you. I'm sure you'll do fine."

I patted my hands on her arm. "Thanks for the vote of confidence, but how about you? Sure you're ready to return to work today?"

Susan turned on her side, pulling her arm halfway back from my chest. "I can do it, and I told you, Dr. Barrows said my anxiety levels are back to normal. Besides, I can't stand staying home another day. I'm going."

Her crying spells loomed in my mind along with the unshakable guilt that they were my fault. I stroked the back of her hand. "You're very brave, and the vets will be lucky to have your smile again."

Her head closed in on my shoulder and her warm breath was like an embrace on my neck. My face turned to her hair, feeling the satiny strands caress my cheek. I made a mental note to call her exactly ten minutes after she arrived at work and squeezed her hand into my chest. Her lips grazed my neck, easing my fear of her one day disappearing when she pushed herself out of bed and headed for the shower. There was an unsettling coolness where she had been and I sat up, trying to minimize its loss.

I noticed my American history textbook on the floor and reached for it, grabbing the opened binding that was still where I had last been reading, on the first page of the last chapter. The bold heading read "The Presidency of John Fitzgerald Kennedy." A sidebar extolled ten highlights of his years in office, giving the dates 1961–1963. The list was numbered as follows.

1. Established the Peace Corps.
2. First man sent into space.
3. Signed the atomic test ban treaty with Russia.

My eyes glanced the rest quickly then winced at the last one.

10. Ordered military advisors to South Vietnam.

My thumbs pressed hard into the page as I pictured Anna living on a commune in Oregon and my cousin Steve a junior manager for AT&T. Would I have been like either of them? Whatever would have happened to me, I knew I'd still have believed I could never kill. But it was all too impossible now even to imagine. It also would have meant I'd never met Susan, Chim, Joe, Mary, Wesley, Leon, Billy, the sniper, Hooang, and the terribly missed Joe. Damn, I couldn't even fathom life without Moustafa, his coarse words challenging and goading me even today.

The paper I'd begun to write stuck out from fifteen pages back. Its title, "The Morality of the Vietnam War," pulled me and repelled me at the same time. The teacher wanted me to write it from the perspectives of torture in the prison camps, the killing of women and children in My Lai, and the destruction of food crops and forests by Agent Orange. It wasn't that I didn't consider these moral issues, it was that every time I sat down to write, all I could think of was Moustafa's desire for a desk job, the great injustices that exposed, then the ensuing war on base with its inhumane results. To me, that's what symbolized the underlying morality of this war, any war. Groups inbred with hate towards each other, proving their superiority by conquering everything the others have and finally believing they are entitled to that supreme power.

Susan's voice boomed through running water, clearly enunciating the words to Stevie Wonder's new song, "You Are the Sunshine of My Life". The gloom of the paper began to drift into the distance as I imagined she might be thinking of me. I stuck the paper back into the book and began mumbling the words along with Susan, though I was concerned the paper might not be done in two days when it was due. I glanced back at the textbook and began to read: *Kennedy called his dynamic programs at home, abroad and in outer space, the New Frontier.*

The door to the bathroom opened and Susan emerged in a robe. She glanced at the clock then rushed out of the room. I heard her ask Chim what he wanted for breakfast, then a frying pan rattled on the stove and I went back to my reading. The humanitarian goals of the Peace Corps impressed me, though I wondered if they succeeded in practice when I was startled by the phone's ring. I glanced at the clock, 5:56. Who called at 5:56 unless it was about Grandma? She was in the hospital. I grabbed the phone on the second ring. "Hello?"

"Scout, it's Billy. I had to catch you before you left for school."

I flopped back against my pillow, feeling the tenderness in the back of my head tell me I had let it hit too hard. "What is it, Billy?"

"There are still miracles on this God-forsaken planet. Guess who I heard from?" He let out a heavy breath but didn't wait for my response. "The sarge, can you believe it? Part of the Kissinger prisoner exchange. Touched back on U.S. soil two weeks ago."

I glanced back at my book, the next heading stating, "Mercury's Mission." "That's great, Billy. Give him a slap on the back for me. But right now I'm in the middle of…"

"Damn you, Scout. Stop thinking of yourself once in a while. This was hard on him, man. Says he's never going to leave American soil again, staying stateside for the rest of his life no matter what happens in the world. I told him about you, Scout, about you and Susan and the boy and the squad pulling together to help you."

I wanted to tell Billy *he's the one should learn to care about others*, but was more interested in a military reaction to our squad's rescue. "What did he say?"

Billy coughed and started to speak with his voice still hoarse. "Said he wasn't surprised everyone helped you after the way you deactivated Moustafa. Said you saved all of them a heap of bloodshed, even though what you did was sheer idiocy. Made you sound so heroic, Scout. I wished I'd been there to see it."

My fingers pressed into the center of my forehead. "You didn't miss much. Moustafa got killed and I came too close for comfort. You saw what I looked like after."

Billy gave a half laugh. "You were whacked out is what I remember, screaming about a shot taking too long and a snake eating your eyes. But I didn't know then that Moustafa was the snake."

A sharp pierce seemed to strike behind each eye, only the picture of who was holding the knife stunned me. I opened my mouth feeling my voice involuntarily tremble. "The snake wasn't Moustafa. It was me. It was that I couldn't bear to see what I'd done."

"Damn, Scout. Don't go crying on me. It was just a post-op hallucination. But thanks for the birthday tip."

My fingers pushed back into my hair, leaving my palm pressed into my forehead. "What birthday tip?"

Billy chuckled. "A snake skin belt. Every time you open it to piss, you can recall the high points of your life."

My hand rubbed across my eye and fell next to me on the bed. "Save your money, Billy. I'm not scared of them anymore."

I heard the familiar slap on his stump. "Then I'll do one better. I'll bring live snakes to the barbecue to roast, like we did in Nam."

My stomach lurched, but more from not wanting to eat snakes again than from fear when I realized what he'd said. "What barbecue?"

Billy huffed into the phone. "Don't play dumb, even if it does come natural. You know what barbecue. The one Joe promised and you said in the hospital you would do. I called Joe's dad last night to tell him about the sarge and he was real anxious to meet the man who gave his son a medal. Said let's have him come to the barbecue and do it on Memorial Day since it would be a fitting way to honor him for his POW ordeal. And said it would be a surprise treat for the squad."

"What?" I was furious that my intended barbecue of thanks to Leon and Wesley would have to include the man who sent them into the thirteenth valley, who forced me to lie, and had okayed Billy's killing the kids. "Call Joe and tell him it's a bad idea and that I'll explain."

"What's with you, Scout, sleep on rocks or something?" Billy's voice was like sandpaper in my ear. "Listen, it's too late. Joe called Leon and Wesley last night and it's all set. You weren't home so I'm telling you now."

"I was at Chim's play!" My voice squeaked and I swallowed against the tightness. "Couldn't you wait half a day? And what did Leon and Wesley say about seeing the sarge?"

Billy gave out a long whistle. "Slow down, boy. You're going to have a stroke. It's like this. Joe said you had too much to do to plan a barbecue. He was doing you a favor. And I told you, the sarge is a surprise. Leon and Wesley don't know, and don't you spill the beans."

I banged my head back on the wall, hearing it reverberate in my ears. "I told you how we feel about the sarge. Why couldn't you leave it alone?"

"Man, you are one unforgiving son of a rodent." There was a pause, then a rush of released breath. "I was at the VA checking on his status, like I do every week, only this time I got positive news and wanted to spread it. You weren't home so I called Joe. The rest is history. And I even got more news. Remember Richard?"

His good natured smile immediately came to mind. "Richard, sure, volunteered for paratrooping."

Billy's chair squeaked from pushing and pulling the wheels with fast jerks. "More like he got stuck on one of them kamikaze missions and was listed as KIA in January '71. Bought it in An Xuyen, a half mile from the Cambodian border."

I felt a clog swell within throat when I heard Chim skip into the kitchen for breakfast. "Hear about anyone else?" Chim laughed in the background and I gripped my leg.

"Not hard to guess who you do care about." Billy sighed. "Sorry, man, but the lieutenant's location is still unknown. They took my message of the barbecue in case he surfaces. There's three weeks, you never know."

I slid my fingers over my eyebrows then cupped my hand around the phone. "Promise you won't say anything to Chim until we hear something for sure."

"Hey," Billy started, "I know better than that. Trust me. Won't even mention the barbecue if you think that will upset him."

I glanced at Chim's school photo on the dresser, seeing a long, thin streak of sunlight across his eyes. I kicked at the air as if that would force the shadow to move. "Just don't tell him about the sarge. It could make him worry more about the sniper. And what day did you say it was?"

I sat up straighter trying to see Chim's face without the shadow as Billy spoke. "Write it down this time. Memorial Day, May 31."

I slapped my hand over my eyes. "No, that's Chim's birthday. He'll want a party!"

Billy tapped on the phone with sharp hits. "What do you think this will be, a funeral?"

I squeezed my eyes shut and saw Wesley walking out at the sight of the sarge. "Maybe not far from one."

"Look, man," Billy began, "I know you carry hard feelings towards the sarge, but the war's over, remember?"

I glanced up, seeing the cracked paint in the ceiling. "Evacuated, but not over."

Clicking noises sounded as if Billy were tapping a pen on his wheel. "Look, Scout, I don't know what's bothering you, but you're acting like a whole heap of sour grapes."

I heard Grandma echo those same words about Anna and shot back, "Listen, Billy, I've got four finals this week and a term paper. What do you want from me, singing telegrams?"

There was a cough from the other end, though it seemed too shallow to be real. "All right, school boy, enough. I'll leave you alone. Wouldn't want you to fail because of me."

There was a sudden click and I dropped the phone to my thigh for a moment before placing it back in its cradle. My hand stayed wrapped around the receiver as I considered calling Joe to have him cancel the barbecue. But then I'd have to give the explanation, tell him what really happened in that village, and tell him things about Billy that he didn't need to know. No, I didn't want to hurt him with that sort of information. I'd have to go along with it, no matter what. This had mushroomed beyond my simple mission of thanks. It was now for Joe, in his mind honoring his son, and hopefully somehow, a not too painful birthday for Chim.

I looked back at the textbook, my hand still pointing to the "Peace Corp" heading and shoved it towards my feet. The term paper flew out, its heading, "The Morality of the Vietnam War" staring up at me from the bed. I grabbed it. Tests or no tests today, this paper could not wait. There was a history of hatred that needed to be immediately unveiled.

I began with Vietnam's past four hundred years of division between north and south and which rulers were from which side, mainly the Trinh family of the north and the Nguyen family of the south. In the early 1900s the French colonized Vietnam and divided it into north, south and central. During World War II, the Japanese conquered and afterwards it went back again to the French. Finally a unifying election was set for 1956, but it never happened because neither side would take the chance the other would win. By the time the U.S. tried in the 1960s, they were dealing with one people divided by four hundred years of hate, resentment and fear. The bloody war had no chance of fixing that.

Moustafa jumped into my mind, saying, *How do you think it was for me? The masters and the slaves, you and me divided by four hundred years of the same thing. When was it ever going to stop so I could get my desk job?*

I squeezed the pen, feeling my palm pulse into the faceted plastic. "I'm sorry, Moustafa," I whispered at the paper. "Fighting each other was not only the wrong war, but it made it worse."

I began a new paragraph starting with the question, *How can atrocities be avoided when hate, resentment and fear of a people designated as your enemy are encouraged for hundreds of years?*

~ CHAPTER 21 ~

Memorial Day

The Memorial Day parade played on the news as I gathered the items for Wesley, Leon and Billy. The presents were mere tokens of thanks but I still wanted to give them, even if the sarge's presence ruined the rest of the day. Susan said I had to take into account other people's viewpoints, that to Billy the sarge was a hero, and to Joe he was the man who chose his son to put on point and then honored him with a medal. I tried to put my uncomfortable feelings aside as I placed the wrapped gifts in my duffel and left the old items that had been in it, in a heap on the floor.

Sylvia and Sol's bus was due in at 11:15, which meant I had five minutes to get out of the house. Sylvia had insisted on being here not only for Chim's eighth birthday, but as she also called it, Chim's first birthday as her grandson.

I peered in at Susan preparing salad in the kitchen. "Anything you need before I go?"

Susan pursed her lips towards me.

Her gesture made my hands throb, anxious to hold her close to me. I wrapped my arm around her waist then pressed my lips firmly on hers. She leaned back and I felt her lips spread to the sides and then heard her giggling voice. "Oh, no. You're not going to blame me for being late."

I lifted my head and winked. "You know I never want to leave you." She smiled and it gave me the encouragement I so badly wanted. She hadn't mentioned leaving in almost five weeks. I glanced at my watch. "Oh well, my darling, must depart. The clock is ticking."

Susan winked. "I'll be here waiting."

A warmth spread in my chest as I faced out of the kitchen and called, "Chim, let's go."

* * * * *

We set foot in the Greyhound arrivals area a few moments after the passengers began to descend. I scanned the area on the side of the bus when Chim pulled on my arm and pointed to the front steps. There they were, Sylvia in a pink flowered dress with a matching tennis visor and Sol in plaid pants with a green knit shirt. They stepped off the bus towards the opened luggage bins.

Chim ran up to Sylvia, throwing his arms around her waist. "Grandma!"

Her teeth shone brightly in two neat rows as she leaned over him, wrapping her arms around his back. "How's my grandson? Excited about your birthday?"

Sol came to me and gripped my hand. "Lenny, good to see you."

Sylvia peered up at me. "You have a kiss for your mother?"

I went to her side and kissed her cheek, then watched her turn back to Chim and hold him at arm's length. "My, my, don't you look wonderful." Her head tilted halfway towards Sol. "See, I told you that shirt would look handsome on him."

Sol's gaze shifted from the luggage coming out of the bus to Chim. "Nice shirt, Sylvia."

I tapped my father on the arm. "I see she bought you a nice shirt, too."

He looked down and shrugged. "She knows a good bargain when she sees one."

I smiled, recalling the times Sylvia used to have him drive us from one discount store to the next for my back-to-school clothes and whispered in his ear, "She's got the eye."

Sol grinned at the expression we used to use when she was out of range then turned for his luggage that was coming off the bus.

Sylvia had already grabbed a shopping bag and placed it in Chim's hand. "Hold this for me like a good boy."

Chim looked down at the red box with gold ribbon sticking up between the handles and gave it a shake.

Sylvia gripped his wrist. "Careful. It could break."

Chim turned away from her and she patted his hand. "Now don't pout at your grandma. It's okay. It's time to call on Mr. Patience. That's what big boys do. Helps them to wait for later. Can you do that?"

Chim's lower lip started to push forward, but then Sylvia gave him a playful shake and his cheeks spread into a wide grin. "Yes, Grandma."

Sylvia looked up at Sol. "You hear how sweetly he said grandma?"

Sol turned to her with their two valises in his hands and smiled. "The boy knows a good grandma when he sees one."

I reached for one of the suitcases, having to pry it out of my father's hand and glanced at Chim, seeing him peer into the shopping bag with one eyebrow much higher than the other. "Everybody ready?"

Sylvia stretched herself as tall as she could and took Chim's hand. "Yes, we'll follow you."

We were practically at the outside door when I noticed a flower stand and reminded myself of what I had meant to do. I turned to Sylvia and pointed to the standing bouquets. "For you, Mom, for Mother's Day. Which ones do you like best?"

Sylvia's hand pressed against her chest. "My heavens, I just don't know. They're all so beautiful." Her chest moved up and down with heavy breaths and then she pointed to a mixture of red and white roses. I picked up the bouquet, noticing her give a side glance to Sol who gave a quick nod in return and placed it in her hands. Sylvia placed her nose into the roses then held them out for Chim to sniff. I slipped ten dollars to the saleswoman as Chim's nose crinkled and he pulled back. "Tickles my face, Grandma."

We all began to laugh when Sylvia gave me a hug. "I could always count on you, Lenny."

Sol gave her a wink, like there was something between them they had discussed before. I wrapped my arms around her and gave a squeeze, realizing I should have sent a Mother's Day card.

Sylvia stepped back, and inhaled the flowers with her eyes half closed. "Mmmm, these are sweeter than the wilted ones she got next door from her son."

Sol leaned in for a quick sniff and touched her arm. "Good grandmas get lucky."

Chim stamped his feet while turning in a circle, chanting, "Grandmas are lucky; grandmas are lucky."

Sylvia hugged the flowers to her chest. "Yes, grandmas are lucky."

I was glad the stand had been there and turned towards Sol. "How's Grandma doing?"

His left shoulder raised then lowered. "She wouldn't eat the nursing home chicken broth, said it tasted of the foil it came in. And she wouldn't eat the toast, said it was too soggy to chew. Finally your mother taught the cook how to make tapioca pudding and she'll eat that."

Sylvia waved the flowers out to her side. "Such a shame. Independent her whole life, and now never to go home again."

The high stool in her kitchen suddenly flashed in my mind. It would never be there again, and neither would Grandma, making me feel important. I looked at Chim, then at my mom and dad. They nodded without speaking and the words *sour grapes* rang in my ears like an unsettling alarm. I shifted the suitcase to my other hand. "Any news from Anna?"

Sol and Sylvia kept glancing at each other till finally Sol turned to me. "After six months with no word, we received a postcard that she's leaving the commune in Oregon because the people there are too selfish and don't know the true meaning of communal living. She's looking for a farm collective in California."

My empty hand slipped in my pocket. "Guess I'm not the only one she disapproves of."

Sol's suitcase clattered onto the vinyl floor, and he picked it up with the other hand. "She'll appreciate you when she's older."

I began walking towards the exit. "If I'm willing to talk to her."

I pushed the door open and held it for the others, feeling a warm breeze give some relief to the sweat that covered my face. The two-block walk outside cooled my cheeks to a more comfortable temperature and we all settled into the car. Sylvia sat with Chim in the back, asking him questions about school. Sol sat next to me, tapping his hand on his knee as I told him about the three A's and a B on my exams and the term paper than earned me an A minus in the Global Issues class.

"You're a hard worker, Lenny. That's the best lesson you learned." Sol's hand had stopped moving and remained still. "I remember a time that wasn't true."

I glanced at him, seeing his lips tighten into a straight line. My hand touched down on his. "I know it could have been different for me, easier for sure. But I'm not sorry how things turned out. You understand?"

His eyes glanced towards the back seat then returned to me. "You pulled through a rough time and made a good life for yourself. That's what any father hopes for his son."

My hand pulsed against the steering wheel and I stretched my fingers, leaving my palm to keep our direction straight. "Dad, I'm glad that's what you see."

His other hand slapped on top of mine and I was sandwiched in his warmth for a block till it was time to make the last turn. I pulled my hand from his hold and brought the car into a parking space right in front of our house.

Chim bounded out of the car with the shopping bag clutched in front of him and ran up the steps. "Susan, Susan, we're home. Come see."

Sylvia followed right behind and then came Sol and me, carrying the suitcases.

Susan peered down at us from the third floor landing. "Welcome! How was the trip?"

"Just fine, dear." Sylvia held up her flowers. "And see what my Lenny bought for me?"

Susan's hand reached over the banister. "How lovely. I'll put them in water for you."

Sylvia pulled them back towards her chest. "Not yet, dear. I'd rather hold them for a while longer."

Chim jumped onto the top step and pushed the shopping bag against Susan's leg. "Look what Grandma gave me for my birthday."

Susan's hand clasped the front of her shirt. "So big! What do you think it is?"

Chim looked back at Sylvia who waved the flowers over the bag. "Go ahead. Open it. I see Mr. Patience has stopped doing his job."

Chim began pulling the box from the bag, blocking our way up the rest of the steps. Susan took it from him and marched into the apartment with Chim's hands reaching for the paper and ribbon. Sol and I entered behind Sylvia in time to see Chim rip the wrapping to reveal a tan wooden box with black Asian writing on it. Chim lifted the lid and I stared in from above, watching him unlatch the hinges in the corners and ease the sides down. The box flattened into a village scene of huts along one edge, grass and a stream in the middle and rice paddies on the other side.

Chim's mouth opened wide as his eyes shifted back and forth on the village. He touched the grass roof of the hut then picked up a woman statue with a baby in her arms and brought it right in front of his eyes. His finger slid down the Asian features of her face, then touched the baby and lingered. "Hooang and me." His whisper hung in the air as he brought it to his lips and gave it a gentle kiss.

Susan gripped my arm as Sylvia leaned over, her face next to his. "You like it?"

Chim pressed the statue into his cheek and nodded. "Hooang and baby Chim. She send it for me?"

Susan crouched down quickly. "Grandma saw it and knew Hooang would want you to have it."

Chim's arms flew around Sylvia in a tight hug. "It's beautiful, Grandma, same as I remember and the pictures in the book."

Sol bent down, touching Chim's back. "That's what your Grandma said the second she saw it in Chinatown, *'That beautiful village is for my Chim.'*"

Chim turned back to the board and stared at the rest of the pieces, the farmer holding a scythe, the boy and girl, the chicken, the water buffalo, and the outside hearth. I couldn't take my eyes off the boy and girl, then finally reached down and placed them by the stream. I wanted them to begin to play and I would protect them right this time and have them for a brother and sister to Chim. But Chim moved them to the rice paddies and I was distracted by Susan's voice.

"Is this another piece for the village?" Susan pulled a smaller box, wrapped in gold and white paper, from the shopping bag.

Sylvia straightened up and smoothed the sides of her skirt. "No, dear, this one's for you and Lenny for the new apartment."

I came to Susan's side. "But, Mom, we've been here two years."

Sol slid his suitcase flat against the wall and came towards us. "To your mother that's new."

Susan handed the box towards me, but I stepped back. "You open it. You're the woman of the house."

Susan glanced at Sylvia, who smiled and pointed to the box. "Go ahead, dear. It won't bite."

There was a pause, then Susan carefully slipped off the paper and lifted the top. "Oh, my." Her fingers grazed the inside. "It's beautiful. Did you embroider this yourself?"

I began to peek in the box when Sylvia reached in and pulled out a rectangular gold frame bordering colorful letters. I stared at the words and read out loud, "Home sweet home."

Sylvia held it against the wall and stepped aside. "May you be happy and healthy with no more troubles."

Susan's hands covered her cheeks as she stood directly in front of the frame. "That's so thoughtful of you." She then wrapped her arms around Sylvia and gave her a close hug. "I can't ever thank you enough."

"No need, dear." Sylvia patted Susan's back while glancing at me.

"Thanks, Mom." I came next to her and kissed her on the cheek. "And also thanks for your encouragement these past months and your long calls to Chim."

Sylvia raised the frame higher. "What? A mother isn't expected to help when her child's in trouble? Your happiness is my happiness. Your pain is my pain."

Susan reached for the frame and held it in front of herself and me. "It will be perfect in the kitchen, don't you think?"

Sylvia nodded. "And should you get married, I'll make another one for your bedroom like Grandma made for us."

Sol came up behind her and grasped her shoulders. "Now don't push."

Sylvia waved her arms to her sides. "A mother's entitled to speak her piece."

I glanced at Susan, hoping for a nod that didn't come. "When it does happen, Mom, you'll be the first to know."

"You hear that, Sol?" Sylvia gripped her hands on his. "They could be legal yet. Maybe even all use the name Belkin."

My hand raised. "All right, Mom, I hear you, and it's time we get going. Mary's expecting us early to help." I then glanced at the floor. "You ready, Chim?"

I noticed he put the mother statue with the baby in his pocket as he said, "Ready."

I leaned in close to him. "Maybe you should leave that at home."

Sylvia grabbed his arm and held it next to her stomach. "Nonsense. It's his and he does what he wants with it." She focused on Chim. "Ready, Grandson?"

Chim looked up at her, smiling. "Ready, Grandma." They started for the door, hand in hand.

I followed with Sol, who whispered near my ear. "The grandmother hath spoken."

I nodded as we walked, watching my mother and Chim swing their clasped hands in unison and wondered if Chim felt like a king on a high stool throne.

* * * * *

Joe pulled his car into the driveway just ahead of us, having Billy in the front and Billy's mom in the back. She stepped out of the car and began opening her son's door.

"You ever see such tight pants and that makeup..." But Sylvia's voice came to a sudden halt. She gripped the back of my seat as we watched Joe and Mrs. Langdon help Billy into his wheelchair. "Vietnam?"

I nodded. "That's Billy and…"

Sol leaned forward into the dash. "The one you saved?"

I yanked the emergency brake tight. "The one I kept alive, but no need to mention that."

"No, of course not." Sol shifted towards his side window as Billy began to approach.

I opened my door and waved. "Hi, folks."

Billy held up a forward fist. "Where's the birthday boy?"

"Uncle Billy!" I opened the back door and Chim ran out, pulling the statue from his pocket. "Look, see what I got!"

Joe came right for Sol who was exiting the car. They shook hands and everyone was introduced as I opened my hatchback for Susan's two bowls of salads and my duffel. I put the duffel strap on my shoulder, arranged the bowls in my arms and started for the kitchen. There was a wonderful aroma of chocolate as I entered. "Mmmm, sure smells good."

Mary looked up from smoothing frosting on a cake, her lips trembling and the tops of her cheeks reddened. "Devil's food, his favorite. And everyone will be here but Joe!"

Tears rushed from her eyes and she tried to wipe them with her shoulders, but they just smeared on her face. I placed the bowls on the counter and the duffel on the floor and rushed to put my arms around her. "He's always here, embedded in our hearts. You know that."

Her face rubbed into my shoulder. "But he would want to see everyone today."

I pressed softly on her back. "We're all here because of him and for him. He is here and you should be feeling his smiling self."

A few tears dampened my shoulder. "I couldn't make it without you, Scout. You and Susan and Chim are the only reason I can go on."

I patted her back and began to sway her gently from side to side. "Everyone else was uncomfortable around me when I came back except you and Joe. You welcomed me from that first moment we met at the grave. It's you that made it possible for me to go on."

She gripped my arms and squeezed. "Thank you for coming to us, Scout."

I stepped back, looking down directly into her face. "No, I'm the one that thanks you."

She smiled as she lifted the spatula, spread one last section with frosting, then held it out to me. "Go ahead, you like it as much as Joe did."

I took the handle and began licking the fudgy chocolate, watching her write across the top of the cake with a tube of white icing, *Happy Birthday Chim.*

I pointed the spatula at the cake. "Wait till he sees that."

She opened a box of candles and started placing them around the edges. "And these, they don't blow out!"

We both began to laugh when Sylvia's voice seemed to burst into the room. "A hundred calories just to breathe the air in here, but worth every one."

Mary turned to the door, wiping her hands on her apron. "Sylvia, how wonderful to see you. Come sit down and keep me company."

"Sit down nothing." Sylvia gripped the back of a chair and leaned all her weight on one foot. "I've been sitting on a bus for ten hours so tell me what to do—slice vegetables, wash dishes, set the table. You name it, I'll do it."

Mary placed her right hand on her hip. "The first thing you can do is give me your opinion on my onion dip.

Sylvia's hand flew out in front of her. "I have to warn you." Mary started for the dining room and Sylvia followed. "I have my Aunt Esther's taste buds, never enough salt and must be fresh ground pepper."

I grabbed my duffel and went out the back door to the backyard. Billy was under a tree with a beer in his hand and Chim was standing in front of him. I approached, hearing Chim ask, "But if you had two legs, what would you have done to him?"

I took three fast strides to Chim, grasped his shoulders and pulled him back against my stomach. "You talking about Kurt?"

Billy extended his arm with the beer towards us. "I was telling Chim that you can't show mercy when someone's out to kill you. You have to get them first, like Susan did."

My hands pressed harder into Chim. "Susan defended herself."

Billy clanked his beer on the arm of his chair. "That's what I was saying. Only if you're sure they want to kill you, no need to wait for the beating. If I'd had Kurt in my sights from second one, Susan would never have been hurt at all."

I thought of the village kids and felt my fingers tighten into Chim when Wesley's voice boomed from behind. "That only works in war, my man."

Wesley had a baby in his arms and a woman in a snug yellow dress beside him. Behind them were Leon and a lady in green chiffon. Wesley's hand extended towards Billy. "Now don't go contaminating these fine virgin ears with your murderous talk. You got that?"

Billy grasped Wesley's hand and looked straight in his eyes. "Only because of the baby, but nothing around you will stay innocent for long."

Wesley chuckled. "I'll let that slide, Private Langdon." He shook my hand, ruffled Chim's hair then turned to the side brushing the hair from the sleeping baby's face. "Now I'd like you all to meet the divine Benita," he paused and raised his wife's hand, "and the most elegant Yolanda."

Billy pointed to Yolanda. "So you got hitched to that big mouth?"

Wesley's head shook as clicking sounds emerged from his mouth. "My man, you is still thinking with your missing legs. Time to start using your heart. Then you could find love, man, love like these sweet things I have around me and Leon has with his enchanting Dolores."

I smiled at Leon and Dolores and began to extend my arm, but Billy's slap on his chest interrupted. "There ain't no heart in this stump."

Leon stepped one foot forward, gripping Dolores' hand in front of him. "You had heart in the car to the hospital, remember? You was worried if anything happened to Susan it would be awful for the boy and Scout. That's heart, man, caring heart."

Billy raised his front wheels and slammed them down hard. "That's different. That's for Susan. There aren't any others like her."

"Bullshit!" All eyes turned to Wesley who whispered, "Sorry, darling," in Benita's ear as he placed her in Yolanda's already outstretched arms and watched them walk towards the house with Dolores at their side. He turned back to Billy and glared. "Face it, Billy. You're too quick on the trigger 'cause you don't want anyone you know getting hurt. That's heart. I'll take you watching my back any day."

Billy zig-zagged his chair and raised a thick puff of dust. "Who says I care about you?"

Wesley slapped his hands on the front of his shirt. "I do. You care about people you know. You don't fool me. You got your soft side, even though you don't come close to Scout here. He's something else."

I stepped back, tripping on my own foot, when I grabbed hold of the tree and looked up at Wesley. "What do you mean something else?"

"Because," Wesley's hand pointed to me but his eyes stayed focused on Billy, "his heart extends to those he doesn't like and even to those about to do him in. I don't know anyone else with heart that big. That's why I need him."

My hand scraped against the bark at the same statement he'd made at the hospital. "Need me for what?"

Wesley began to turn to me when Billy shouted, "Not true. We all know he didn't want to save me."

Chim's gaze snapped to me, his stare feeling like it was piercing right through my eyes. I shifted my attention to the ground, wishing I was hidden in its protective depths, when I felt pricks on my arms and looked up to see unmoving mouths seeming to shoot out the question, *"Why?"*

I glanced from Leon to Wesley, then to Billy and shouted, "You tormented me from the first day and then you slit the throats of those poor kids for no reason and you expected me to want to save you?"

Billy's shoulders rolled back and his hands gripped his wheels. "My only regret is that you listened to Joe and came back. You should have done what you wanted and let me fry."

I almost screamed *I wish I had, too,* but an approaching scratchy voice seemed to cut the air. "Find legs and stand on them!"

I turned towards this hoarser, weaker version of the once commanding voice and stared into a face I wouldn't have recognized if I'd seen him on the street. He looked thin and frail and his eyes seemed deeper in their sockets.

"Sarge!" Billy's voice called into the otherwise stunned silence. "You made it!"

The sarge glimpsed the group as he went straight for the only extended hand, Billy's. "I wanted to see the condition of my old squad."

Wesley stepped forward and rapped the sarge on the arm. "Condition? I got you to thank for the shrapnel in my head. I hang your picture on every headache that makes me miss work."

The sarge stepped back and looked Wesley up and down slowly. "Sorry, I didn't come here to fight. I was pulled from that privilege a long time ago by the Viet Cong."

Leon fidgeted with his diminished hand, taking one step closer to the sarge. "How long did they have you?"

The sarge made lines in the dirt with the toe of his shoe. "Twenty-three months, or more accurately, six hundred and ninety-nine days." He glanced from me to Leon to Wesley and kept his gaze on Wesley's white collar, as if it had a message he wanted to read. "Everything you think I did to you is nothing compared to what was done to me. You may still hate me, but I've been worked over too much to feel anything anymore." He then lingered his gaze on Leon. "I want you to know this. Everything I did was because it was best for the war. Hell, I would have gladly stayed another six hundred and ninety-nine days in a dirt hole if it meant we would have won. I'd still do it."

I looked at the deep set creases down his cheeks, trying to summon the anger I had towards him these past few years, but it wouldn't come. Instead what came was his concern for me on the field before the beer fight and when I went after Moustafa. I watched him press his heel into the dirt and extended my hand towards him. "The hard feelings were for another place in another time zone. Welcome back, Sarge."

He gripped my hand with both of his. "I feared you'd never survive your one-man offensive and was relieved when the lieutenant announced you'd made it through surgery." He stared into my face then scanned down to my feet. "And no apparent damage. You lead a charmed life, my one-time scout."

Wesley approached, hand out to the sarge. "Man, you had enough pay backs for your life time. Ain't no sense all of us making it back if we can't celebrate we's alive and here."

The sarge's head bowed towards Wesley then he took his hand. "Mighty gracious of you." He glanced up to Wesley's forehead and settled on his face. "And sorry for your headaches. That's a damned shame."

Leon came next to him and rapped the sarge on the arm. "His head's too hard for headaches and I'd give up my two fingers 'stead of two years in a VC hole. Glad you made it back."

The sarge grasped Leon's hand and began to shake when Billy's voice blared. "Hell, I'm about to cry. And to think if Scout had left me to die, I would have missed this soap opera. Anyone got some tissues?"

Wesley kicked his heel back into the chair's wheel. "Shut up, Billy. The sarge is right. Go get some legs and get a stand-up job so you can pay me that ten bucks you still owe me. Not that I came here to bring back old grudges. I can let bygones be bygones. Real reason I came is to eat good grub and talk business with my man, Scout."

I hunched my shoulder towards Wesley. "You said that before, but I don't know what you're talking about."

Wesley glanced sideways at Leon then focused on me. "We need you, Scout. It's important and getting worse." He began walking towards the other side of the tree and I followed. "Black kids' big problem today is they scared of white folks. Don't know what to say or how to act when they see one, so they don't go for jobs. You the one that could teach them."

I slapped my chest to loosen a sudden tightness in my throat. "Me? Why me?"

Wesley turned to face me straight on and placed both hands on his hips. "It wasn't till I saw you go after Moustafa that I knew for sure. You fool enough to jump in after a person out to ride your ass and stop them from setting off a bloodbath, then you could do that for these kids."

364

I was about to protest when Leon's hand grasped my arm and he began to speak. "There's boys we's coaching in the neighborhood basketball league. We heard them talking how they'd just as soon kill a white man as talk to one. And it could happen, Scout, same as it almost did on base."

Wesley gripped my other arm. "That's not the world I want for my Benita, bloody war right on her own street. And you're the only one I know would do this."

My arms pulsed under their grips and I shook them free. "And you expect me to change the world?"

"Not the whole world!" Wesley's hands dropped to his sides. "Fifteen kids, man. They's headed for trouble down the road and someone's gotta show them they have a chance. You're the only one I know with the foolhardy nerve to try."

I turned away, staring at the chest-high fence, not sure if I'd tell these kids to shoot first if someone's out to get them or to play by the rules 'cause it might come out fair in the end when I realized a figure was approaching from only ten feet away, staring back at me with intense, blue eyes.

"I chose you, too," his voice riveted into my ears, "as the one who would protect my son as your own." His gaze lowered to the back of Chim's head. "Seems I chose right."

I reached for Chim's shoulders and spun him around. "Look, Chim. Your father's here!"

Chim leaned against me instead of running up to him, like I'd expected. "Lieutenant?" Chim's voice was soft, almost a whisper. "Was that you on TV climbing the rope?"

The lieutenant looked directly in Chim's eyes and began rubbing his chin. "Didn't know that was on TV. I went in because I feared it could be my last chance to check on you, but all phones were out. I needed to know if you grew the way Hooang hoped, with a warm heart like Scout, and not with a hard heart like mine."

Chim shrieked, then I realized he'd said Hooang's name. "You see her?"

The lieutenant held out his khaki-covered arms towards Chim, who walked towards them slowly. The newly appeared father cupped his hands around the sides of Chim's head and looked directly in his face. "You have kind eyes. She will be very happy."

Chim's legs began bouncing up and down. "I want to see her!"

The lieutenant hugged Chim into his chest and began stroking his hair. "I found her but still can not get her out. I will go back with good news and try again."

Chim grasped at his shirt. "I'll help you get Hooang!"

The lieutenant's lips brushed on top of Chim's head. "No, my boy. It's too dangerous. I can't chance it."

Chim began hitting his arms. "No, I want to go!"

The lieutenant hugged him tighter. "The only way is if I bring her to you. But if Scout has space, I can stay for two weeks and you can help me plan her rescue."

Chim burst out of his arms and grabbed at my shirt. "Can he, Scout? Can he?"

I stared straight into the eyes I had once searched in to find out why he stayed in the war and realized his response for me had been Chim, the one family member he had left in the world who could be saved. I squeezed Chim's hands within my own as I looked back into those intense eyes. "We share the same son which makes us family. You're welcome in our home whenever you want and for as long as you choose. Forever if you will."

He saluted me with his right hand. "Thank you. Two weeks and I go back in. But I would appreciate time with Chim."

I turned Chim around feeling the fast beat of his heart through my grip on his shoulders. The lieutenant held out his arms and Chim ran into them. My own chest started pounding, as if trying to fill a sudden empty space inside.

I watched the father and son hug and talk in quiet voices and felt like an intruder. I turned away, catching Billy, Leon, Wesley and the sarge all staring at me. It made me uncomfortable and I looked down, seeing my duffel by my feet.

"Two fathers was two too many for me." Billy's voice shattered the near silence.

Wesley gripped the steering handle behind Billy's chair and gave it a shake. "One father for me would have been a gift. Don't be ungrateful."

I glanced back at Chim and the lieutenant, then at those around me, and reached into my duffel, pulling out a flat item covered in green paper. "I have some gifts myself." I held it in front of Billy.

"What's this?" Billy pushed himself farther back in his chair. "A run-over grenade?"

I pushed it into his hand. "It's the poison you've been asking for. Open it."

Billy pulled off the paper, revealing a bronze medal hanging from a red, white and blue ribbon. He thrust his arm forward, trying to reach my hand. "That's yours you got for saving me."

I stepped back out of his reach. "Now it's yours for saving Susan. If you hadn't thrown that rock at the window at the exact moment you did, Kurt's bat would have slammed down on her head. You saved her life. It's lucky you're alive."

Billy held the ribbon, letting the medal fall centered in his palm when with an abrupt turn, he faced the house, raised the medal high in the air and shouted, "You hear that, Mom? It's lucky I'm alive!"

Wesley slapped him on the back. "Of course it's lucky you're alive. You're the best human diversion machine ever existed. Came in real handy in the hospital and who knows where we'll need you next."

Billy shook the medal in front of him. "I can create so much fuss you could get into Fort Knox."

Wesley pointed at Billy. "Save your mouth for guys who might ever mistreat my Benita. We'll disrupt their lives so bad, they'll run from the state and never come back."

Wesley and Billy laughed and slapped high fives as I placed a round gift in Leon's hand. Leon tried to return it, but I slipped my hands behind my back. Leon then shook his head. "There's no reason for a gift."

I leaned into the tree. "It's already yours. May as well see what it is."

He looked at each person, received nods in return, then ripped off the paper and held up a leather strap with a tarnished metal cylinder dangling from it. "Why you giving me your compass?"

"It's from what Joe once told me." I spread my arms straight out to the sides, letting them balance into a settled position before going on. "A compass is more than direction. It's a direct signal from deep within the earth that always points the right way and never has to stop and question what is right. It just knows." I paused and tapped my hands to my chest. "Joe told me if I learned to get my signals from deep within me, they will always point me the right way." I pointed towards the compass with my chin. "And that's for you because you never hesitate to do what's right. In Vietnam you were always helping me even though it could get you in trouble. And you went right to Kurt's house when your color put you in danger and you didn't know what to expect inside. You and that compass are operating on the right, unhesitating signals. I want you to have it."

Leon rolled the compass within his hands, staring at the quivering needle. "It must have started with my ancestors having to point themselves north to get free."

Wesley laughed and slapped Leon on the arm. "Good one, but more likely it's your magnetic personality from those pennies you swallowed as a kid 'cause you didn't have a piggy bank."

Leon grinned, showing smooth white teeth except for one that jutted outward on the left. "No more pennies in there and my mama gave me hell for that. Besides, I like Scout's reason better." He slipped the compass in his pocket, keeping his hand in there with it, and I placed a wrapped rectangle in Wesley's hand.

Wesley stretched his arm out, holding it as far away from his body as he could. "What's this, some damned land mine?"

I took a few steps away and put up my hands. "More like a time bomb."

Wesley raised his eyebrows at me, then ripped off the paper and held up a watch. "You trying to tell me my time is up?"

"No," I clasped my hands in front of my stomach, "but if it weren't for you, my time and Susan's time would have been up in March." I stretched my clenched hands forward towards the watch. "What that's for is offering to watch my back."

Wesley shook his head and held out the watch toward me. "You want to show your gratitude, keep this watch that probably don't work anyway, and meet with our basketball team. Get to know them and let them get to know you, that's all."

I pulled on my lips for a moment, then let my hand drop. "You'll make me those Tabasco eggs you promised?"

Wesley's thumbs slid into his belt loops. "Hell, yes. You on?"

I kicked a rock out from in front of me. "I'll be down next Sunday."

Wesley's hands slapped together and he pointed them as one at me. "You are in for a treat, my man. I'm the Sunday chef at Soulful Joe's. You can count on all my specialties, grits smothered with pepperjack cheese, bacon-grease biscuits, and my down-home, hot-as-blazes eggs."

I pressed my hands into my stomach. "Easy on the grease and don't give me an ulcer on the first bite."

"No chance." Wesley's hands pointed towards the sky, making what seemed like a steeple around his head. "My food's straight from heaven. People come in and say, *'Give me Wesley's holy trinity.'* That's a fact. Come from uptown, downtown and the country, just for my grub." He paused and directed his fingers at me. "Be there at noon. I'll introduce you to the team at two."

I glanced at Chim, seeing him walk with the lieutenant towards the fence. "I'll bring Chim. He can shoot hoops with the other boys."

"And this is for those unfortunate kids." Billy held up a ten-dollar bill. "Don't think it's from the bet 'cause it's not. Get that team of yours some pizza and spare them getting sick from your grits."

Wesley snatched the bill from his hand. "You know I won that bet. It's your guilty conscience buying pizza for the boys. But pizza they get along with a lecture to be thankful the man is still alive to buy it for them."

Billy raised his medal but then there was a scream from Chim. Everyone turned to see him in the lieutenant's hands, held high in the air, then placed feet first on the fence. The lieutenant stepped back and Chim jumped to the ground, falling back on his rear when he landed. But his laughter let us know he wasn't hurt and the lieutenant helped pull him up and they started back together. I couldn't help but hear Chim ask, "When can I jump with a parachute?"

The answer was blocked by the intrusion of several high pitched voices as Susan, Sylvia, Mary, Yolanda with Benita, Dolores, Mrs. Langdon, Sol and Joe all came into the backyard at once. Chim ran to Susan and pointed to the lieutenant. She rushed over to him and gave him a hug, while the others set bowls on the picnic table and platters of hot dogs and hamburgers by the grill.

Joe handed Chim a pogo stick with a bow on top and Chim began bouncing all around the yard. Mary came along with a tray of ice teas and beers and for a moment we all gathered as a group selecting our drinks.

The lieutenant raised his glass and spoke into the momentary silence. "I want to thank you all for giving my son a life of hope, something I could never provide."

Susan grasped his arm. "But you can. We're all just people trying to live through our battles. You can do it, too."

The lieutenant tapped his hand on hers. "I've been at war too long to turn back, but when I return with Hooang, I may stay for a while."

I raised my glass. "Do that. I'd like your take on who the real enemies are on this side of the world." Would he choose the disconnected Annas and the sensationalizing reporters, both of whom continually distorted facts, though I guessed he'd be for freedom of speech. It was possible he'd focus on corrupt politicians and hate groups who terrorize the lives of innocent people. I knew that would make him angry from his own experience in Texas. It was definite he'd see drug dealers who turn neighborhoods into war zones as the enemy. He would never put up with it where he lived. Without straight out killing them, I saw him setting physical traps or else plotting legal entrapment. I wished I could get him to go with me to the street where Diego's sister lived and looked into his face that was further hardened by recent scars, feeling that together we could be a force to defeat true enemies. But in a civilized society it would take the warrior and the protector to make an impact that would last. I hoped someday our forces could merge.

His eyes scrutinized mine in return. "You already know who your enemies are and you have your squad to help you."

Just then Joe called out, "Hot dogs are ready!"

The lieutenant started with the crowd for the grill, stopping to give me a firm rap on the back. "You have done more than I hoped for with Chim. He is strong in body and mind and also knows love and kindness. Hooang and I are honored."

I could feel his admiration in his lingering touch. I rapped my hand on his back, feeling the warmth where our arms crossed. "The honor is mine. I cannot imagine my life without him."

We started together towards the grill, though separated soon after. He went to sit by Chim and Susan and I stopped to spend a few minutes alone and observe. I watched the lieutenant, who it no longer seemed right to call sniper, chewing on a hot dog, his gaze alternating between Chim and the fence as if distracted by what was not within obvious sight.

Sol and Joe approached with Sol handing me one of two full plates in his grasp.

I pointed the plate in the direction of the lieutenant. "He changed my life."

Sol swallowed the potato salad he had in his mouth. "Of course he did. He gave you Chim."

I noticed the lieutenant's gaze encompass a full circle as he ate. "It's more than that. He showed me that the enemy can't defeat you, no matter how rough the odds, if you don't let them."

Sol nodded as he finished chewing a piece of hot dog. "That's the sign of a true hero."

I turned to Joe. "My truest hero was your Joe." He squeezed his eyes shut for a moment, then opened them and stared into my face. "If he hadn't shown me how to trust the signals from my own instincts and look for the unusual in the foliage, we'd have fallen in the snake pit my first day in."

Joe looked at Sol. "Sounds like our sons have a lot to teach us."

I felt a twitch behind my ear and scratched. "It could be better not to know this stuff. The most important lessons came in ways I didn't want."

Joe gripped the back of his neck. "Unfortunately, tragedy is the great teacher."

I mashed my fork into the coleslaw. "It's the inexcusable teacher, I think, but it has helped me understand the two sides of the human that I am."

Sol stopped himself from biting into his hunk of corn bread and looked at me. "How's that?"

I put my plate down on a chair and held up both hands. There's the human animal and the human being. The human animal," I shook my left hand, "will do whatever it takes to survive." I jiggled my right hand. "But the human being works together with others to survive in a more humane way."

Joe pulled at the bottom of his chin. "You mean like in small tribes?"

I waved my arm in a big sweep towards where everyone was eating. "I was thinking more of family, friends and a squad."

Joe slapped me on the back. "Amen, Scout. We all need each other."

A smoky haze blew in my face and I looked in its direction to see Wesley in front of the grill dropping patties on the grate. "Any way you like it, well done or rare, spicy hot or with cheese, or drowned in barbecue sauce with my own secret kick tossed in. Speak up and tell Chef Wesley what's your burger-eating pleasure."

I watched everyone shout their choices, astounded that we were really all here having a barbecue, just like we talked about that night in the jungle. The sarge, Billy and Leon were laughing with Wesley by the grill. Chim, Susan and the lieutenant were examining the bottom springs of the pogo stick. Mary, Sylvia and Dolores were smiling and talking to Benita on Yolanda's lap. I was with Sol and Joe, sharing learned wisdom from my life. We were together, an extended squad-family of people, cherishing each other and the gift of life we were lucky enough to keep.

I raised the hot dog to my lips, suddenly feeling it like a toast to Joe, but not only Joe, also Diego, Richard, Moustafa, the village kids, and even the laundry boy. I held it in the air, and gasped into the humid breeze, "Peace."

Printed in the United States
35362LVS00004B/43-153

9 781413 760712